Borne in Blood

BORNE IN BLOOD

A NOVEL OF THE COUNT SAINT-GERMAIN

Chelsea Quinn Yarbro

TOR®

A TOM DOHERTY ASSOCIATES BOOK

NEW YORK

BORNE IN BLOOD: A NOVEL OF THE COUNT SAINT-GERMAIN

Copyright © 2007 by Chelsea Quinn Yarbro

A Tor Book
Published by Tom Doherty Associates, LLC
175 Fifth Avenue
New York, NY 10010

www.tor.com

Tor® is a registered trademark of Tom Doherty Associates, LLC.

Library of Congress Cataloging-in-Publication Data

Yarbro, Chelsea Quinn, 1942-
    Borne in blood : a novel of the Count Saint-Germain / Chelsea Quinn Yarbro.—1st ed.
        p. cm.
    "A Tor Book."
    ISBN-13: 978-0-7653-1713-1
    ISBN-10: 0-7653-1713-3
    1. Saint-Germain, comte de, d. 1784—Fiction. 2. Vampires—Fiction. 3. Paramours—Fiction.
4. Switzerland—History—1815-1830—Fiction. 5. Nobility—Austria—Fiction. 6. Blood—
Examination—Fiction. 7. Guardian and ward—Fiction. I. Title.
    PS3575.A7B67 2007
    813'.54—dc22
                                                                        2007026070

First Edition: December 2007

Printed in the United States of America

0 9 8 7 6 5 4 3 2 1

For

Brian Leerhuber

bel canto

Author's Notes

The first part of the nineteenth century in Europe was dominated by one figure: Napoleon Bonaparte, whose military campaigns took him, and his long-suffering armies, from Egypt to Moscow to Spain before he was brought to heel. The semi-exile of Napoleon to the island of Elba in 1814 ended in 1815, when he returned to France to lead a popular uprising against the Bourbon rulers. His defeat in the summer of 1815 at the Battle of Waterloo in Belgium was final, both militarily and politically; he was sent to the island of St. Helena in the south Atlantic Ocean to live out the remaining six years of his life.

His departure left scars on Europe that required more than a generation to heal, and thousands of former soldiers without jobs or prospects. There were also record numbers of refugees, widows, and orphans cast adrift in the tumultuous societal confusion that marked the end of Napoleon's ambitions, and their presence made a significant impact on every level of European communities, few of which discovered an equitable way to deal with the ruined families. To make this more difficult, women had no legal recourse to raise their own children unless specifically provided in the terms of the marriage and reiterated in the husband's will, so many families were shattered as male relatives claimed or abandoned children as suited their purposes. Almost no women owned property or controlled their own money; without male relatives to support them, widows often found themselves without means of survival, caught between penury and prostitution in one form or another.

In 1816, just as the magnitude of the European disaster was beginning to be assessed, a year of severe weather took hold of most of the world as a result of the volcanic eruption in Indonesia the year before. Poor harvests, freezing conditions well into June, and outbreaks of typhus and cholera throughout Europe as well as one of ergotism in France oppressed the population as war had not been able to do. Although 1817 saw a lessening of the crisis, the winter was still colder and longer than usual, and harvests were significantly reduced throughout the temperate zones on the planet.

Yet all was not defeat and gloom: the early years of the nineteenth century saw the (re)invention of the steam engine and its immediate offspring, the steam locomotive and the paddle wheeler. The velocipede, and the Celeripede, the immediate ancestors of the bicycle, were invented to help ease the traffic congestion in the burgeoning cities. The first tentative steps toward what would become mass transit systems appeared in European and British commercial centers. Scientific experimentation was also on the rise, as were new studies in linguistics, mathematics, astronomy, antiquarian studies (called archeology after 1890), and biology. Experiments in electricity were becoming more acceptable to the scientific community. In 1817, cadmium, lithium, and selenium were all identified as elements. In 1816, Krupp steel began producing low-grade files in Essen, and by 1836 was leading the industry in high-grade cast steel. Although many universities were growing in size and influence, a significant percentage of the most active scholars were not directly associated with universities, but were involved in independent studies sponsored by wealthy patrons on subjects that were the areas of interest for the wealthy men themselves. Beethoven, Schubert, and Rossini were among those composing for a growing audience, and Walter Scott, Byron, Shelley, and Keats were all writing: 1818 saw the publication of both Mary Shelley's *Frankenstein: or the Modern Prometheus* and John Polidori's *The Vampyr.* After a very long moribund period, education and literacy for the middle class and yeomanry was on the rise; even education for women was possible for a fortunate few, with schools established especially for girls of upper-class and upper-middle-class backgrounds. In America, Harper and Brothers Publishers and the Harvard Law School were both founded in 1817.

Medicine, although not as haphazard as it had been in previous centuries, was still fairly primitive: surgical instruments were not washed for procedures, let alone sterilized; "bleeding" was common practice and used fairly indiscriminately; epidemics were often regarded as supernatural in origins. But the climate of scientific inquiry was making inroads in many disciplines, including the practice of medicine; vaccination had been around since 1796, and its benefits were largely accepted. Studies into the workings of the body were increasing, as were related experiments that contributed to new theories of human origins.

The map of Europe was quartered somewhat differently then than now: Germany was not yet united, nor was Italy; Prussia held several territories in Germany, which operated under a taxation union but were held together by little more than convenience. Part of what is now France south of Lake Geneva was then nominally Swiss. By 1816, between the pressure of national aggression and scarcity due to bad weather, long-running regional rivalries started up again, and only the loss of Napoleon left a military vacuum that was sufficient to slow any sudden renewal of ancient hostilities.

By current standards, travel was slow: a four-horse coach could expect to travel an average of ten leagues (thirty miles) a day in good weather on good roads. Well-sprung coaches could sometimes manage eleven to twelve leagues (thirty-three to thirty-six miles) in optimal conditions. A man on horseback, with regular remounts, could double that. Private courier services were used by merchants, scholars, and lawyers with increasing regularity, and generally moved at about fifteen leagues (forty-five miles) on good roads in good weather. A few men and companies maintained their own messengers, which also meant maintaining a system of remounts. As the ravages of war diminished, commerce and the notion of progress rushed in to take up the slack left by the military, leading to improved communications and the promotion of railroads within a decade of this story. Commerce with the Americas was expanding steadily, with the result that many East Coast port cities such as Baltimore and Savannah doubled their European trade in less than ten years. Explorations of the Pacific Islands continued to produce increased trade from Tahiti to Japan, which fed a rediscovered European hunger for the exotic. Trade in Chinese ceramics became a major industry for the European markets, as did Indian brasses and textiles, screens and wood-block prints from Japan, and precious woods and gems from southeast Asia. The first, tentative steps toward genuine world trade had been taken.

Fashion had abandoned the wedding-cake excesses of the Louis XVI court, along with aristocratic decadence supposedly stamped out during the French Revolution, in favor of a more classical line, based on Greek and Roman statuary bought or pilfered by ambitious travelers. It worked rather better in women's clothes than men's; the high-waisted, gauzy ensembles of the Empire (French), Regency (English), and Jacksonian (American) periods were a significant departure from the elaborate, broad-skirted costumes of the Louis XVI period. By the end of the 1700s men's coats were narrow, the unmentionables (trousers) ankle-length instead of britches gartered at the knee, and the lower leg booted or silk-stockinged. Elegant austerity rather than gaudy superfluity was fashionable, except for those going to the extremes of fashion: this group of men, called Macaronis in England and America, were known for their colorful and exaggerated clothing and effete manners.

Most prosperous households required a fair number of servants to man them, but the conditions of service were changing. In Europe, slavery was being made illegal in most countries, and bonded-servitude was on the way out. Experiments in electricity would lead to the end of domestic service as it had existed; however, the scientists exploring electricity in this time did not anticipate the vacuum cleaner and air conditioner when they undertook their studies in galvanism. What the social revolutions of the end of the eighteenth century could not accomplish, the technological developments during the nineteenth century did, and set the stage for the vast transitions of the twentieth century—transitions that continue to this day.

✧　　✧　　✧

Many thanks are due to six friends of Swiss descent who allowed me to borrow family names for many of my secondary characters: Gina, Harry, Loren, Matthew, Serena, and Willis, your generosity is much appreciated; any error I have made in the names you have provided is on my head, not yours. Thanks—in no particular order—are also due to Edward Milner for information on European roads and travel in the early nineteenth century; to Susan Altermaat for information on publishing in Amsterdam during this period; to Emily Burge for her references on the fate of Napoleonic soldiers after their defeat; to J. P. Keel for providing maps and charts on the Napoleonic aftermath, as well as for passing on a number of links to related Web sites; to Doroteo Tordellos for access to her collection of early-nineteenth-century travel guide-books; to Howard Leibermann for information on clothing and textiles in Europe from 1810 to 1825; to Nathan M. Parriser for his material on the state of early-nineteenth-century science and medicine; to Melinda Tapuy for references on Swiss and Austrian law of the period; and to Philippa Veuier for some insights on language-drift present in Switzerland at that time.

At the other end of the process, thanks are due to Irene Kraas, my agent; to Wiley Saichek, who does so much to get my work out on the Internet; to Paula Guran, Web master and designer of my Web site www.ChelseaQuinnYarbro.net; to Lindig Harris for her *Yclept Yarbro* newsletter available at www.Lindig@charter.net; to Samuella Gonsalves, Pat Derringer, and Doris Seikama, who read the manuscript for clarity; to Libba Campbell, who read it for accuracy; to the www.Yahoo.com group; to Peggy, Charlie, Megan, Gaye, Steve, Lori, Marc, Bill, Brian, and Patrick just because; to Maureen Kelly, Sharon Russell, Stephanie Moss, and Alice Horst; and to Paolo deCrescenzo and his Gargoyle Books for the grand time in Italy on Saint-Germain's behalf; to the Lord Ruthven Assembly and the International Conference for Fantasy in the Arts; to the Canadian chapter of the Transylvanian Society of Dracula and Elizabeth Miller; to the International Horror Guild, for the honor, which surely belongs as much to the Count as to me; to Melissa Singer at Tor, and to Tor itself; to the bookstores and readers who have kept this series going for twenty books so far, and counting.

CHELSEA QUINN YARBRO
Berkeley, California
July 2007

PART I

HERO IOCASTA ARIADNE CORVOSAGGIO VON SCHARFFENSEE

*T*ext of a letter from Helmut Frederich Lambert Ahrent Ritterslandt, Graf von Scharffensee at Scharffensee in Austria, to his daughter-in-law Hero Iocasta Ariadne Corvosaggio von Scharffensee at Château Ragoczy near Lake Geneva, Yvoire, Switzerland.

Graf von Scharffensee sends his greetings of the season to his daughter-in-law, and hopes that the new year of 1817 will bring her good health and better weather than we have seen this last year.

Let me assure you that your children are doing well. My son would be proud of their progress, were he still alive to see it. You will be pleased to know that Annamaria has begun her study of French and is already able to say a great many words correctly. Her tutor, Frau Linderlein, has said that by the time she is nine, she will be fluent in that tongue. Bertram and Berend have acquired a second tutor for mathematics and geography: Herr Wilhelm Klebber has been engaged to instruct them in these things; he has a gift for dealing with their high spirits, and claims he can tell them apart, which Herr Gunther Drossler still cannot do, much as he may know of letters and humanities. Siegfried has celebrated his eleventh birthday on the 2nd day of this month, as you no doubt recall, and I am pleased to tell you that he is finally applying himself to something more than hunting and shooting. He, too, is receiving instruction from Herr Drossler, and may soon begin his military training, if such can be arranged. He saw the 8th Hungarian Hussars on parade and is now most keen for a career in a fine regiment, although he decries the lack of a foe to fight now that Bonaparte is no longer rampaging about Europe.

I will take the children to Vienna at Easter, to purchase their annual wardrobe and to let them enjoy some of the luxuries and elegance of that splendid city. I am not yet prepared to have you join us, and for that reason, I recommend that you not ask that I include you. There will be time enough when they are a little older for you to become acquainted with them again, when their characters are fixed and they no longer answer to every turn in the wind. For now, it is fitting that they continue with me. As their grandfather, I can provide them the guidance and maturity that men must naturally impart, and which will engender the respect for their father's memory that they will need in later life. Rest assured, they are receiving the best care and instruction that I can provide them, and that I will continue to do so as long as you continue to agree not to interfere in my guardianship. We are agreed, are we not, that you have neither the position, the money, the standing, nor the ability to care for them yourself. In any contest of law, the courts must uphold my claim over yours.

Should you remarry, as much as I would dislike that to happen, I will, of course, return my grandchildren to you, provided I am satisfied that your new husband is sufficiently comfortable in funds and standing to care for them in the manner to which they are now accustomed. Your present arrangement can hardly be deemed appropriate for the company of your children, but I will not oppose it so long as you and the Comte remain discreet. If you bring scandal upon my name, I will have to take measures to constrain you, for your children's sake as well as for the preservation of my family's good name. You must still agree that as things are, you cannot offer them either education or material opportunities for the future, nor can you establish them in the world when they are older. My son ought to have provided both, but as we are aware, he did not, and his political alliances have proven to be inadequate to the changing conditions around us. The law, in its wisdom, has entrusted his estates and his children to my care. I hope to instill a distrust of radical notions in the children so that they will not commit the same order of folly that their father did. Fridhold did not expect to die in the full flower of his manhood, but still he did, and his children, without my help, are left with little or nothing to sustain them.

You may repose complete confidence in my devotion to my

grandchildren, and to their welfare in life. At this time of year, it be-
hooves us both to renew our pledges of agreement, and to make every
effort to ensure as pleasant a surround for them as is possible. That
they should have had to spend eight years traipsing after Napoleon so
that my son could embarrass us all with his enthusiasm for that Cor-
sican fool is more than enough hardship for them to endure in their
young lives. You cannot escape the taint of revolutionism, and that
must affect your children so long as they remain under your care.
With me, they have regularity in all things, and responsible instruc-
tion, and the firm and affectionate hand of a man to secure the edu-
cations and the futures you and I must want for them. As the
daughter of so famous a scholar as Attilio Corvosaggio, you should
appreciate the value of learning, especially in these erratic times.

I write this to you from my Schloss, and send it by regular post;
I extend my good wishes to you, on this, the Eve of Christmas, 1816,

Your father-in-law,
Helmut Frederich Lambert Arhent Ritterslandt
Graf von Scharffensee

1

"Ah! Excellent! Excellent!" exclaimed Wallache Gerhard Winifrith Sieffert, Graf von Ravensberg, as he continued to draw blood into the glass syringe. "So glossy." He lifted the syringe, pulling on the tubing connecting it to the subject so that the afternoon sunlight struck it with full brilliance, making brass fittings, glass, and blood shine. A complicated apparatus stood on the low table at his side, a device of his own invention, one of a dozen littering this third-floor room that von Ravensberg called his laboratory. He took care not to brush his Turkish dressing-gown with the syringe, more to protect the blood than the fine damask silk.

Heinrich Thorbern was lying on a cot between von Ravensberg and the apparatus, his long, boiled-wool coat draped over the single chair and his shirt-sleeve rolled up to above his elbow; he gasped as the needle in his arm pulled. "Is that good?" he asked, becoming a bit worried as he watched von Ravensberg marvel at the blood in the glass syringe. He was a pleasant enough man in his late twenties, regular-featured and healthy, a successful independent farmer, able to read and write—all in all, an ideal subject for von Ravensberg: exactly the fine example of German yeomanry he sought.

"It is most . . . encouraging," said von Ravensberg, scowling at Thorbern. "Do lie still, Herr Thorbern."

"But it hurts when you pull."

"Lie still," von Ravensberg repeated. "You must not move about in that way."

"But Baron—" Thorbern protested.

"I will not take much longer," said von Ravensberg, annoyed that his exuberance was not shared. "I need to complete getting the sample, you understand. Then I will subject the blood to tests, and you may be on your way. With my gratitude." This last was an afterthought.

Thorbern sighed and did his best to be comfortable. He was feeling a bit cold, attributing the chill to the coolness of the room; there was snow on the roof of the Schloss as befitted this January morning, and although a fire burned on the grate, the heat did not spread much past the hearth. "So long as it is useful, Baron."

"All inquiry is useful, young man; you should appreciate that," said von Ravensberg with finality. He made a point of putting his full attention on the man's blood. "This rich, fine color and shine is an indication, I believe, of superior composition. You may be confident that I will examine it closely."

"Because of its color?" Thorbern had slaughtered enough cattle, hogs, and sheep to have seen great quantities of blood: never had he noticed much difference in the color or characteristic of any of it.

"The color, the luminosity, the texture and composition of it, the characteristics present in its nature," said von Ravensberg, mildly distracted. He indicated his fine microscope, its brass gleaming, with a wooden box filled with glass slides beside it. "Thanks to this wonderful device, we know there are many components to blood, and it is my belief that when we truly understand the whole nature of blood, we will have a definitive measure of all men." He tapped the syringe, now almost full. "This will help me to uncover what the blood has hidden."

Although this made little sense to Thorbern, he was too well-mannered to say so. "It sounds very complex."

"That it is, that it is, far more complex than anyone would have thought, and possibly possessing many more mysteries than what is currently surmised," said von Ravensberg, He tapped the syringe, watching the movement of the blood. "It is a daunting task, to discover all that blood has within it. Many other scholars would recoil at the demands of so ambitious an undertaking, but not I; no, I am determined to—" He broke off as he heard a rap on his door. "Who is it?" he demanded gruffly.

"It's Hyacinthie, Uncle," she called through the door. "A messenger has arrived. He brings you word from—"

"I'm almost done here. Have him wait in the library. Give him something to eat and a tankard of our beer. And see you don't make a pest of yourself." He resumed his work with the syringe.

"Do you wish to stop?" Thorbern asked.

"No. Not yet." There was still a little room left in the syringe. "A minute more, or two, and it should be done." He tried to offer an appreciative smile but without success. "You must know that I value your cooperation and your participation highly. Very highly. Many of the people in this region are ignorant, superstitious, and out-right fools. But not all countrymen are louts. You have enough education"—five years in the local school—"to grasp the implications of this study, why it must be done, how much it will change our—" He stopped. "The syringe is full. If you will lie still for a moment longer, I'll remove the needle and you can sit up."

Thorbern could not conceal his relief; his mouth quirked, but no smile emerged. He winced as von Ravensberg reached over and carefully drew the needle from the vein on the inside of his elbow. Taking his pocket kerchief, he pressed it to the welling of blood that followed; after a minute he lifted the corner of the handkerchief and scowled as his blood continued to run. "Will this be all, Graf?"

"For now," he said, his attention focused on the blood in the syringe. "You are fortunate to have such fine blood, Herr Thorbern. Not many specimens look as fine as this one, or show such promise."

"Pleased to be of service," said Thorbern automatically. He sat up, feeling a bit queasy as he did; his head ached dully and he felt thirsty. "How much blood did you take, Graf, if I may ask?"

"Hum?" He turned, the syringe still in his hands. "Oh. You can see for yourself."

The sight of his own blood in that shiny glass tube with the brass plunger and needle-casing made Thorbern's stomach churn. "It would fill a cowmaid's ladle," he said in mild surprise, for it was more than von Ravensberg had taken in the past: it was less than would fill a beer-stein, but more than a cup. He nodded and turned away, doing his best to regain his composure. "Thank you, Graf. I—"

"You are advancing the cause of science; do not doubt it, Herr Thorbern."

"I am pleased to be of service," said Thorbern. He started to rise but thought better of it; he tucked his handkerchief back into his pocket and busied himself with rolling down his sleeve, although he noticed the blood had not completely stopped.

"And I thank you for it," said von Ravensberg without any attempt at sincerity. "If you know any others like you—strong, healthy, young, German or Austrian—ask them if they would be willing to participate in my studies, would you? I would welcome all such specimens to my Schloss, rest assured. That would be most useful for my researches. No Czechs or Bohemians or Poles, mind: Germans and Austrians only." He put the syringe into an aperture in his device, and slowly depressed the plunger. "If you're feeling a bit unsteady, go down to the morning room and have my niece bring you a restorative dish for you to eat. Hyacinthie needs something to do. A tankard of beer should set you up, and some bread and sausage."

Thorbern made another attempt at getting to his feet. This time he succeeded, though he lurched a little and his vision swayed. He reached for his coat as much to steady himself as to don the garment. His thoughts wandered and he blinked several times. "Would they have to be relatives, or would comrades do?"

Von Ravensberg gave this his serious consideration. "Both would be welcome," he decided aloud. "Yes. Send me word if you find appropriate subjects."

"Jawol, Graf. I will." He struggled into his coat and took an unsteady step toward the door.

"Will you be able to let me take more blood next month?" Von Ravensberg knew he had asked this too quickly, but he could not hold himself in check. "The same arrangement as we have had before? So I may determine what impact the weather may have upon your blood."

"Do you think it does?" Thorbern asked.

"I think it might," said von Ravensberg carefully. "And for that reason, comparisons are necessary to make a full and accurate analysis. One set of analyses is not enough to demonstrate anything useful. It is the comparisons that matter. I will subject this sample to an electrical current. Surely you can see the value in that. I will do the same with the rest." He finished shunting the contents of the syringe and turned to face his subject. "Think about it, Thorbern. You could be among the first men to have the mystery of his blood at last understood. It is a great honor."

"A very great honor," Thorbern echoed dubiously.

"You will come then?" von Ravensberg pursued.

"I suppose so, God willing, and there are no more avalanches." He looked toward the window. "There will be more snow tonight, and if the storm lasts, it will be several days before the roads are safe to travel."

"Even from four leagues away? Surely one of your strengthy cart horses could make the journey?" He was losing patience and was no longer willing to conceal it. "Without another four or five donations, I will not have sufficient information to—"

"I will try, Graf. I will try. It is the best I can promise you," said Thorbern, making his teetery way toward the door. Just as he was about to lift the latch, he asked, "Will you be wanting more animals to test, Baron?"

"Animals?" He considered it. "No, I think not. At least not for the present. Later they may be useful."

"Very good," said Thorbern, as if agreeing to a difficult undertaking. "I may not have any to spare this year. After two hard winters, my livestock are doing poorly, as are everyone else's. I have sows and ewes who may not manage to produce more than a few young this spring."

"Lamentable," said von Ravensberg flatly.

"Well, if you change your mind, Graf, send me word; I'll try to find the best of the lambs and shoats for you." Three years ago von Ravensberg had purchased nine animals from him: two shoats, two lambs, two kids, two calves, and a colt-foal; he had paid top prices for all of them: three of them were still alive.

"I will do. Danke." He paid no more attention to Thorbern, his concentration fixed on the glass-and-metal box through which the blood was moving along a complex of tubes toward various vials.

Thorbern stepped out into the corridor. "Many thanks, Graf." He said this without thought, more out of custom than intent; he received no answer, and after nearly a minute, he closed the door and went down the stairs, buttoning his jacket as he went. He had reached the landing between the first and second floors when he heard a merry shriek of delight.

"Herr Thorbern!" Hyacinthie Theresa Katerina Sieffert von Ravensberg cried out, clapping her hands together as she came tripping across the inlaid-marble floor in the entry-hall. "You are through for the day?"

"Yes, Fraulein von Ravensberg, I am," he said, flattered and uncomfortable; the Baron's niece was almost beautiful, and, awkward as it was for Thorbern, at seventeen she was becoming flirtatious; Thorbern suspected she had yet to realize the impact her prettiness had on men, thinking their attentions were games, not a prelude to something more. "Thank you for asking."

"And you're hungry and thirsty after everything my uncle has done to you?" She smiled winsomely, her face rosy from the morning's chill, and gave her head a toss. She was as fashionably dressed as she could be in so cold a house as the Schloss was, in a high-waisted dress of iris-colored wool, long-sleeved and high-necked in concession to the winter weather. Around her shoulders she wore an Indian shawl of heavy silk twill; its gray-green color almost matched her eyes. Her dark-blond hair was done in a knot on her head, a few tendrils artlessly escaping around her face. She knew that Thorbern found her attractive, and that pleased her tremendously. "The morning room still has a fire lit, and you may be comfortable there."

"Thank you, Fraulein," he said, disturbingly aware of her intense femininity. He wondered if her uncle had noticed how much his ward had changed in the last year, and decided that the Graf would not notice such things.

"You know the way by now, don't you, Herr Thorbern?" She lifted her chin and looked at him over her shoulder, her lower lip caught in her teeth as if trying to suppress a smile. "I would take you, but I am looking after the messenger, just come for my uncle, and must attend to him first."

"Yes, danke, I do know the way." He gave her a nod that was almost a bow, and hastened down the back half-flight that led to the rear of the Schloss, the east side of the building where the morning room was. Little as he wanted to admit it, he was glad to be away from Hyacinthie; the Graf had made him sufficiently uncomfortable for one day, and a round of Hyacinthie's precocious coquettish attentions was more than he could endure in patience.

Untroubled by Thorbern's distress and humming softly to herself, Hyacinthie hurried along toward the library where the messenger was waiting. He was, she thought, a strapping fellow, big-chested and heavy-armed, with a broad forehead and upswept eyebrows that hinted at Hungarian blood as well as Austrian. His four-caped coat was hung on a hook near the door, and she touched it as she entered the library. "Herr Haller?" she called, and saw him half-reclining on the old-fashioned divan in front of the fire.

"Fraulein?" There was a shine in his eyes that revealed his appreciation for the Graf's niece.

"Has Werther brought you your refreshments yet?" She approached him demurely. "Not even a mug of hot brandy?"

"No, Fraulein. Not yet." He stretched out, as if he might accidentally brush the skirt of her morning-dress.

"I will see why he has delayed," she offered. "You will want to be warm."

"Your company warms me very well," said Haller boldly.

"You will be better for food and drink," she said, and turned away to leave the room.

Haller sighed loudly, and leaned nearer to the fire.

On her way to the kitchen, Hyacinthie came upon Herr Arndt Lowengard, her uncle's man-of-business, just emerging from the estate office. She offered him a pert good morning and a quick bob of a curtsy, then continued on, certain he was watching her as she went, for all men watched her. In the outer kitchen she found the under-cook, Werther, busy preparing trays for the guests of the house; he blushed as Hyacinthie came up to him. "The messenger still doesn't have any food," she said.

"I know."

"And Herr Thorbern is in the morning room. My uncle has finished with him, so he is hungry and thirsty." She leaned across the wide cutting-table, and twirling one pale tendril around her finger said, "Can I help with anything?"

"No, Fraulein. I am almost done." He stared down intently at the sausage he was slicing. "I have beer and warm brandy for them both."

"I'll put them on the tray, shall I," she suggested.

"It isn't fitting," said Werther, feeling dreadfully inadequate; he was so flustered he almost nicked his thumb with the heavy carving-knife.

Hyacinthie tittered. "You must be more careful, Werther." She stopped playing with her hair and leaned toward Werther again. "But you better hurry, or my uncle will be angry."

"Of course, Fraulein. And I'll be quicker," he added with the temerity of desperation, "if I may attend to it on my own."

"If you like," Hyacinthie said, a dangerous gleam in her eyes as she flounced to the door. "I won't dis*turb* you any longer." It took her a few seconds to compose herself; when she was certain she had steadied her temper, she sauntered down the hall, her pace steady, her expression benign; she had managed to discomfit Werther, which she had intended to do, and her satisfaction increased. She knew what it was that men wanted. Her uncle had taught her all about it when she was seven, coming to her bedroom at night to show her how much he cared for her; he had been utterly entranced by her until she turned fourteen: in the last three years he had all but ignored her. Had she not seen the look in other men's eyes she would have despaired. As it was, she knew how to find solace in the attention of those who desired her. With this reflection to guide her, she returned to Herr Haller, assuming a demureness that she suspected would intrigue him.

The messenger was still on the divan facing the fire, his big body almost dwarfing the furniture. He swung around to look at her. "No refreshments?"

"They are coming directly; things are a bit slow in the kitchen," she said, making her way slowly over the fine Belgian carpet toward the crocodile-footed chair near the window; it was colder there than near the fire, but the light was particularly flattering, falling on her with the clear luminosity of a northern winter. "The cook is busy with baking, I think, and the under-cook doesn't work with dispatch yet. He'll have a tray ready shortly. I'm sorry to keep you waiting."

"Well, I don't mind, to tell the truth. This room is very pleasant and warm. I'm in no hurry to be out in that cold, not with the wind picking up. You should see the drifts—and they'll only get deeper. I'll be lucky to make Bludenz tonight."

"Is that where you are bound?" she asked.

"Eventually I will reach Zurich, and will carry private messages back to Salzburg. That's my region: Zurich to Salzburg."

"It must be very arduous," she said, licking her lip delicately.

What a minx she is! he thought, but said, "Not so bad as you might think. I used to be a military courier—rode dispatches starting at Austerlitz my first time out. That was a baptism, I can tell you."

"Were you in danger?" She sounded a bit breathless to encourage him.

"We were all in danger." He made a shrug of dismissal. "After that—"

"Were you injured?"

"Nothing to speak of. A ball through the outside of my thigh." He chuckled now, but at the time he had gasped and wept with the pain of it. "Not the kind of things for a well-bred young lady like yourself to be bothered with." He fell silent, uncertain how to proceed.

"The winter is very hard," she said wistfully.

"It was worse last year. Not that winter's over." He grinned at her, sure of himself once more. "A man likes to be all warm and cozy when there is so much snow."

"So does your horse, no doubt," she said with an exaggerated air of innocence.

"He's a Holsteiner. He can take the cold. I put a sheepskin wrap on him, and he can get through a blizzard, if he has something worth reaching." His boasting was more for effect than to convey any facts, an obvious ploy to encourage her coquetry; his gaze lingered on the rise of her bosom, although he knew if he were caught by the Graf in such a flagrant intrusion, he would be thrown out of the house with a blow to his shoulder for his outrageous behavior.

"A warm stall, perhaps?" She moved a little so that the clear winter sun could make a halo of her dark-blond hair.

"And a good brushing down," Haller said, with unvarnished sexual implication; he was rarely so blatant with the women of the posting-inns he frequented—to be so forward with the niece of a man like Graf von Ravensberg was nearly as seductively gratifying as the girl herself. He was about to say something more when a discreet scratch at the door stopped him.

With a petulant little sigh, Hyacinthie called out, "Come in, Werther."

The door opened and the young under-cook came in, his face rigidly expressionless, a tray with a stein, a cup, a plate of sliced sausage, a basket of bread, and a small tub of butter carried before him like a horizontal shield. "Sorry for the delay, Herr Haller."

"No harm done," said Haller, sitting up properly and pulling the end-table around to the side of the divan. "This is as good a place as any."

Werther blinked as he set down the tray; he did his best not to look at Hyacinthie. "Will you require anything more, Herr Haller?"

"Not at the moment," said Haller, preparing to eat. "I'm hungry. This will do me very well."

"Then I will leave you to your repast," said Werther, who ducked his head and all but bolted from the room.

Amused and annoyed at once, Hyacinthie moved her chair a

little closer to the divan, smiling as she did. "The sausage has venison in it, as well as pork."

"Fine," said Haller, smearing butter on a thick slice of bread. "If you'll excuse me, Fraulein?"

She glared at him, then rose and left the room, her eyes shining with anger. How dare he dismiss her! Her cheeks flamed as she hastened toward the morning room. Herr Thorbern would provide more sport, or he would answer for it! She had almost reached the door when Herr Lowengard appeared as if from out of the wood paneling, saying in his quiet, self-deprecatory way, "Frau Schale is looking for you, Fraulein." He nodded his head. "She is in the—"

"—schoolroom, no doubt," snapped Hyacinthie, her chin jutting out. The last thing she wanted just now was to do lessons—any lessons—with her impossible tutor. Her mouth turned into a thin, hard line.

"Your uncle wouldn't approve of your tardiness," said Herr Lowengard, and turned into the narrow stairway leading to the second floor.

Hyancinthie bit back a loud retort and did her best to bring her temper under control. She counted each step as she went to the kitchen, saying to Werther, "I will be in the schoolroom. Please send up some hot wine." It was galling to have to admit that she was still a student, but so her uncle insisted; Hyacinthie would rather have spent the year in the city, acquiring beaux. "Frau Schale will probably want some, too." Her expression dared him to say anything beyond acquiescence.

"I will. And perhaps a morning pastry?"

"That would be welcome," said Hyacinthie, swallowing hard, trying not to give way to the outburst that welled within her. She waited the better part of a minute to compose herself before she left the kitchen and made her way to the schoolroom on the second floor, directly over the morning-room, where she much preferred to be; for the next two hours, she translated *The Corsair* into German and ten pages of Fichte's *Grundlage der gesammten Wissenschaftslehre* into French, all the while longing for the opportunity to be revenged on her uncle for this latest humiliation. How dare he ignore me, she repeated silently as she attended to her schoolwork. *How dare he.*

Text of a letter from Reinhart Olivier Kreuzbach, attorney at law and factor, at Speicher near the Kyll River, Rhenish Prussia, to Saint-Germain Ragoczy, Comte Franciscus at Château Ragoczy near Lake Geneva, Yvoire, Switzerland; carried by private courier and delivered ten days after being dispatched.

To the Honorable Comte Franciscus, Saint-Germain Ragoczy, my sincerest greetings on this, the 4th day of February, 1817;

> *My dear Comte,*
>
> *I write to inform you that your castle above Zemmer has, as you feared, suffered damage thanks to all the years of fighting this region has sustained. It is not yet a ruin, but it is not truly habitable, except for rats and owls, and will not be until massive repairs are carried out. My information comes from Pasch Gruenerwald of Zemmer, who has visited the castle recently, and drafted an account of all he observed. I have consulted builders regarding the restoration of the castle, and when the winter is over, I will submit the reports they will provide. I have been told that it may be more prudent to tear down what remains and begin anew. If that is your decision, I will supervise the project, or I will, should you prefer, recommend someone to attend to that part of the enterprise. Whatever you choose to do, I am instructed to tell you that the building, as it stands now, cannot weather another hard winter without sustaining significant damage in addition to what has already occurred, and the longer repairs are delayed, the more catastrophic the damage becomes. If you wish to see the building made truly habitable, let me urge you to authorize the expenditure and the work at once.*
>
> *I have already contracted for a timber-road to be installed once the snows have melted, and that will enable the wagons to climb the hill to the castle without being bogged in mud or risking broken axles. No matter what else is or is not done to the castle, such a road*

is a necessity, if only to remove the stones and the furnishings if you abandon the place in the end, and I will order the tree-cutting for the road to begin as soon as it is possible to do so. I have talked to three wood-cutters, and they are all certain they cannot begin until April, which would suggest that the earliest work could begin on the castle would be June. To have sufficient repairs completed in time for next winter, it may be necessary to pay for double work-crews, which can become very expensive. At least we will soon be part of the Zollverein, so the work will not have to be taxed beyond all reason, assuming that the plan is adopted throughout all German territory. Luxembourg may not support the act, but the Dutch will probably agree to the terms, as well. Until then, I will make every effort to secure as many of the items and services from our taxation region, to prevent any unnecessary additional costs.

I will conduct a full inspection once I can reach the castle without undue risks, and at that time, I will amend my report to something that is more truly comprehensive regarding the present state of the castle. I have no doubt you know for yourself how remote it is, though you have not visited for many years. I feel it my duty to tell you that I would not recommend selling the land at this time. Prices are low, and given the location and the condition of the castle, I believe you would not realize anything approaching its worth. In another two or three years the market should improve, and if the castle is in good condition, you could profit from it quite satisfactorily. If you can afford to restore it, then it might command a reasonable sum, but as it is, unless you must make such a sacrifice, I would be remiss in my duty if I did not inform you of the risks you would take if you decided to try to find a buyer at this time. Having said that, I will, naturally, carry out whatever instructions you give me to the full extent of my capabilities and the ethics of my profession.

Most truly at your service,
Reinhart Olivier Kreuzbach
Attorney-at-law and factor
Speicher, Rhenish Prussia

2

A howling storm had kept them inside for two days, hovering near fireplaces, reading by wavering candlelight. Just now they were in the smaller of the two withdrawing rooms—the one on the sheltered south side of the château—the draperies over the six tall windows drawn to keep in the warmth. Hero huddled in front of the hearth on a large ottoman, a wolf-skin rug wrapped around her; Ragoczy sat on a low stool at her feet, his black coachman's cloak worn negligently over his shoulders, more as a concession to Hero than to keep out the chill, which hardly bothered him. There was a book in his hands, lit by the unsteady flames from a standing candelabra set behind his shoulder, and he turned the pages slowly, looking for another story to read. Although it was just past noon, the room was dark as twilight, with shadows clinging to the corners or the apartment augmenting the gloom.

"Do you really like ghost stories? or are you just indulging me?" Hero asked; she spoke in Italian, her pronunciation northern. Under the wolf-skin rug, she wore sensible clothes—a woollen round dress with a high waist and a swallow-tail riding jacket; her hair was braided and done in a coronet, all covered in a small cap edged in black, an indication of her widowhood; her hair and eyes were the same sunny shade of brown. She was thirty-two, the only surviving child of the great antiquarian scholar, Attilio Corvosaggio, and at present, alone in the world but for Saint-Germain Ragoczy, Comte Franciscus.

"I find them . . . intriguing," said Ragoczy, his tone thoughtful. "And just at present, they are in vogue."

"Yes, they are," she agreed, shivering in spite of the heavy fur cocoon she had made for herself. She pulled the wolf-skin rug higher so that her face was framed in the silvery fur; shifting her place on the ottoman, she leaned onto her elbow, offering him a smile that was achingly sad. "Do you think it is because I still miss Fridhold? that I like ghost stories?" Her question was wistful.

"I think you will miss your husband all your life, no matter what you choose to read," said Ragoczy gently. "I believe you still grieve for him."

"But he has been dead nearly six years," she protested. "Surely I should not mourn any longer. We were married not quite seven years."

Ragoczy studied her for a long moment, then said, "You mourn as long as you mourn. There is no set time on it."

"But it is a year of mourning, and then it is over," said Hero. "I am well-beyond that time."

"There is no blame," said Ragoczy. "And if ghost stories ease your grief and give you solace, who am I to deny them to you?"

She motioned to the book he held. "What more would you like to read? Or would you prefer to stop for now?"

"There is a story here by Hoffmann. You like Hoffmann, do you not?" He knew the answer, but waited for her to decide.

"Yes," she said. "But not the one about the Devil's Elixir, if you please. You read that to me last week, and it's too soon to hear it again."

He rose and went to the small bookcase across from the hearth. "Would you like something entirely new? I have a book of Spanish tales, if you would enjoy them? They're not quite like the ones we have been reading." He had collected half of them himself, not quite a century ago. "The Catalonian stories are the most interesting of the lot, not the same flavor as most Spanish tales."

"Are they in Spanish?" She stared into the fire, her expression astonishingly blank. "I don't know Spanish."

"I will translate them for you, if you like," he offered, taking the book from the shelf. "As you have translated Turkish for me." He spoke Turkish quite well, but found her skill engaging, and more in the modern style than the version he knew.

She said nothing for a short while; the ticking of the grandmother clock by the door to the parlor provided an orderly counterpoint to the snap and rush of the flames. "If you think I would like them, why not?"

He pulled the book from the shelf and began to thumb through the pages. "Here's one: *How Pedro Defeated the Night-Hag.*" He had a brief, intense recollection of Csimenae and her vampire clan, and wondered if she still haunted the eastern peaks of the Pyrenees; he had lost all but the most fleeting sense of her since she had disavowed their Blood Bond over five hundred years ago.

"Try it," said Hero, and leaned toward him as he returned to the stool and made himself comfortable. Before he began to read, she said, "Do you think the roads will be passable next week?"

"It depends on how long this storm lasts, and how much snow it drops. It is possible, but just now, not very promising." He took her hand without pulling her arm from the protection of the wolf-skin rug. "You need not fret. There is food and firewood enough to last us three months, assuming a little hunting can be done between blizzards. Rogier often goes out for small game when the weather is clear, and Uchtred likes to fish."

"It is venison today, isn't it?"

"Yes; unless you would prefer something else," he said, aware of her discontent. "Order what you like."

She shook her head. "It's not that. It's nothing to do with food," she said. "I haven't had a letter from my father-in-law since the one in September, and I worry."

He kissed her hand. "As soon as he can, Rogier will go into Geneva and get the post. No doubt you will have news waiting. You remember how long it took for his winter letter to reach you last year, when the weather was worse." He prepared to open the book once more, when something struck him: "I will say this for the Graf, much as I deplore his keeping you away from your children, he writes to you every quarter."

"It is very responsible of him. But I miss them. I haven't seen them in four years." She said this last quietly, as if expressing it more loudly would add to her loneliness. "Do you think they are much changed?"

"I think they are growing up, and that must change them," said Ragoczy as kindly as he could. "But I suspect you would know them anywhere."

"I hope so," she said, touching his shoulder before pulling her hand back into the folds of the wolf-skin rug. "Go on. You've caught my interest, I confess it. How did Pedro defeat the Night-Hag?"

Ragoczy opened the book and commenced to read: the tale was a dark one, with the Night-Hag pursuing Pedro as he attempted to sleep; she sat on his chest, she rattled bones around his head, she summoned monsters to gibber and howl at him. He tried prayer, but his saints were indifferent to his plight. He summoned the priest, but the exorcism was ineffective. He tried sleeping by day and ploughing his fields by night, but the Night-Hag still bedeviled his attempts at rest. Finally, in desperation, he set fire to his cottage and nearly burned it to the ground, but the Night-Hag would not be routed. At his wits' end, Pedro begged the local prostitute to help him, and she agreed—for a price—to join with him in doing battle with the Night-Hag. And what a battle it was! The prostitute mounted Pedro's loins and leaned over his body so that the Night-Hag could find no purchase upon him, then Pedro and the prostitute bounced so heartily that the Night-Hag was dislodged from the bed, and when she keened, the prostitute shrieked more loudly. After a night of harrowing feats, the Night-Hag was beaten; she retreated and never tormented Pedro again. For the first time in months, Pedro slept soundly and awoke without dread. The prostitute continued to visit him, and to earn her pay, but never again would Pedro allow her to be on top of him, for he feared that would tempt the Night-Hag to another attack.

For a minute or so after Ragoczy finished the story, Hero said nothing. Then she gave a shaky laugh and said, "Not precisely a children's story, is it?" Without waiting for him to respond, she went on, "Still, the Greek legends of long ago are as carnal as this one, and everyone believes they are improving myths."

"It is a way to explain what is not understood," said Ragoczy, and set the book aside.

"It is a strange thing to me, that so often folktale explanations are much worse than the actual reasons are." She sighed. "What is it in us that longs so for large disasters instead of small accidents and happenstance?"

"Importance," said Ragoczy. "Or so I have come to think—many men would prefer to be the object of malign destiny than one unfortunate enough to have ended up in harm's way for no more reason than that of inauspicious coincidence. An angry god after you lends you importance that accidents do not." He thought of the monks on Dhenoussa and the storm that brought him into their hands; his Egyptian steersman had believed that Poseidon had been the source of their ordeal, which was an act of vengeance for slighting his power, but Ragoczy had concluded at the time that contrary winds and high seas were the forces responsible.

She shook her head. "I can't imagine that anyone would seek to magnify misfortune in such a way," she said, then went on in a brisker tone, "No, I don't mean that. I can understand, and I have seen it happen. But losses are hard enough to bear without burdening them with greater significance than they possess for themselves."

He reached out and touched her cheek. "As you have cause enough to know."

"I don't intend to dwell on the past: it is fixed and cannot be changed." She shook her head twice.

"You may change your understanding of the past," he suggested gently.

"As you have done?" she suggested remotely. "But I haven't your centuries to provide perspective."

"Ah," he said, a bit ruefully.

She contemplated the middle distance. "The fire in my room is still burning. We will be warm there."

"Are you sure you want to retire so early in the day? It is barely one o'clock." He glanced toward the clock. "Dinner will be ready in an hour. It would be unkind to Uchtred not to eat it while it is hot."

"Surely we will be done in an hour? An hour?" she ventured,

rising and moving her wolf-skin rug so it was around her shoulders more securely. "Not that I want to hurry you."

"It is you who should not be hurried," he reminded her.

"It is lovely of you to be so thoughtful," she said, going toward the double doors that would give the nearest access to stairs. "For all you say you benefit from it."

"I assure you that I do," Ragoczy said, following her without haste yet with obvious pleasant anticipation.

"Think of how we might make the most out of the time we have together," she encouraged him as she opened the door and beckoned him to follow her.

He closed the door and called out for Rogier. "We will be upstairs for an hour or so. If you will keep the fires lit in the private dining room and the withdrawing room, I would appreciate it."

Rogier, who stood in the doorway leading back to the kitchen, said, "Very well, my master."

"If you have any questions, perhaps they could wait for an hour or so?" Ragoczy suggested.

"An hour or so? Certainly. I doubt there is anything so pressing that it cannot wait until tomorrow, if necessary."

"Very good," said Ragoczy, and prepared to follow Hero up the curving stairs toward the narrow gallery above; at a signal from Rogier, he swung his cloak off his shoulders and handed it to his manservant as he began his ascent.

Hero took the corridor on the west side of the gallery, following it along to the large bedchamber at its end. Like the rest of the nineteen-room château, its draperies and curtains were drawn and the metal fire-screen protected the fine Turkish carpet from stray sparks. A single candle protected by a glass chimney stood on the bedside table, providing enough illumination to make the room into a grotto, full of promise and secrets. As she threw the wolf-skin rug onto the foot of the bed, Hero shivered, and swung around to face Ragoczy. "Tell me what you want."

"I ought to ask that of you," he said, as he went up to her and took her into his arms. "You should not be cold." He glanced at the nearest window where the blizzard drummed icy fingers and whimpered.

"How could I be?" She leaned her head on his shoulder. "Outside is cold. In here, there is heat."

"Then we must make sure it stays that way." He touched her hair, loosening the three long ivory pins that held the coronet in place; the single, thick plait swung down her back. Slowly he kissed her forehead and closed eyelids, then put his attention on her shoulders, caressing them through the fabric of her jacket and shirt before unfastening the first of the three military-style frogs that kept it closed. He put a dozen little kisses along her brow and cheek; all the while, he listened to her breathing, to the sound of her pulse, matching his pace to her arousal. He reached over and pulled back the goose-down comforter, revealing the pristine linen sheets. "Where is your robe?"

"Inside the door of my closet," she whispered.

He gently assisted her to be seated on the bed, gave her a long, soft, searching kiss, then went to fetch her robe. "I would not wish you to be cold," he said, as he brought the long, heavy, quilted-silk garment to her. "Let me help you with your jacket and your dress." He unfastened the stud holding her jabot and set it aside.

She held out her arms to the sides, her palms turned up, her eyes slightly averted. "Thank you," she said softly.

Skillfully, unhurriedly, he eased her out of the jacket, setting it on the dresser between the closet and the bed; next he unfastened the lacing at the back of the high bodice of her round-dress; he worked the shoulders down her arms and was left with the camisole to unbutton. "If you will stand, I'll remove the dress and shirt now."

Before she did, she touched his face, still not looking directly at him. She quivered at his touch as he unfastened the buttons. Clad only in her undergarments she accepted her robe without any hesitation, snuggling into its deep folds with every sign of relief. "I don't want you to be cold," she said, leaning back onto the exposed sheets. "Come lie next to me. Here. You'll be warm."

"I will, but not for fear of cold," he said, kneeling beside the bed in order to slide the robe open so that he could reach her garters and lower her stockings before removing her kid-skin house-shoes.

"You have the most wonderful touch," she murmured as his hands moved deliciously over her legs. Although it was cold, she didn't mind it; his attentions more than made up for the momentary chill.

"And you have the most wonderful skin," he countered, as he dropped her shoes to the floor, and then finished sliding off her stockings. He bent and kissed the arches of her feet, then moved up onto the bed and resumed his task of loosening her stays, allowing himself to be enveloped in the folds of her robe as he did.

She sighed, contentment and regret in the sound. "I wish I could . . ." Words faded as she felt his small hands on her breasts. She reached languorously to embrace him, her eyes dreamy, her breathing slow and deep. This was what she needed, she realized, and returned his kisses with her own, feeling her ardor stir and commence to unfurl within her flesh. "Oh, yes. Do that again."

He complied, taking longer than usual in order to intensify her sensations. When her nipples swelled against his palms, he leaned down and used his lips instead of his fingers to excite her. "Tell me what you like," he said softly.

"You know what I like," she said, holding him less tightly in order to give him more access to her body. "Don't make me choose, just do what you know I like."

He hesitated a brief moment, then whispered, "If anything displeases you, tell me."

"You have never displeased me, not in bed." She ran her fingers through the short, loose waves of his dark hair. "Not once."

He fingered the top of her hip, tracing the line of her body along her abdomen toward the deep folds between her legs. He parted the delicate tissues and sought out the small, hidden bud that responded to every nuance of passion. Many of the women he had known over the centuries had taken great pleasure in having that knot worked with his tongue, but Hero did not; she preferred what his fingers could do, so he continued to nuzzle her breasts while his hand awakened her desire to a state of rapture. She hovered on the brink of release while he moved to her neck. Now her breath quickened and shivers of ecstasy ran through her; she sank her fingers into his hair. As the first paroxysm surged through her, she let out three soft cries, gathering him close to her and rocking him through the throes of her fulfillment. She continued to enfold him as her excitement waned, as if their embrace would prolong and enhance her gratification.

The bracket-clock sounded the three-quarter hour as they finally rolled apart. Hero looked over at the clock and scowled. "We probably shouldn't linger. I can smell the venison already."

He uttered a single chuckle. "The meal will be on the table in another fifteen minutes," he said as he started to sit up.

She poked him in his side. "You don't have to get dressed. I depend on you to help me."

"Certainly," he said promptly. "You have only to tell me what you require," he said as he rose to his feet and held out his hand to assist her.

She slipped her hand into his. "I'll want my Polish velvet walking-dress for this afternoon, the raspberry-colored one, with the standing collar."

"Very good," said Ragoczy, opening her closet door and selecting the garment in question; this he laid on the bed, close at hand. "For a chamise?"

"The Italian silk," she said. "It's ivory, with lace on the neck-bands." She held her robe closed while she bent over to retrieve her stockings and shoes. "It's warmer than what I was wearing this morning."

"Then by all means," he said, "choose something that will keep you warm." He waited while she pulled on her stockings and garters, and stepped into her shoes, then found her corset where he had dropped it; he came back to her, reached under her robe and prepared to lace up the back of the corset. "Will you want to wear an under-shift as well, or is this satisfactory?"

"You do make an admirable ladies' maid," said Hero, enjoying the last flicker of her fading tantalization conveyed in his touch. "Not that I expect a ladies' maid to attend to me so completely."

He kissed her as he aligned her corset, then began to tighten the lacings, working them carefully so the corset would not bind. "Just as well, given Wendela's temperament. It pleases me to serve you," he said with a slow smile before he kissed her, still continuing his efforts on her corset.

When their kiss broke, she was a little breathless. "If only dinner wasn't ready," she said with a trace of regret. "Although you have already—"

"Been nourished?" he suggested when she stopped speaking.

"I suppose you could say that," she told him quietly. "Yes, I want an under-shift. I should have put one on this morning; I wouldn't have needed the wolf-skin rug if I had."

"But the wolf-skin rug becomes you," said Ragoczy gently.

"Do you think so?" She reached out and laid her finger against his lips. "Don't talk about this, will you?"

"No; I never would." He finished tying her laces and stepped back. "In which drawer to you keep your under-shifts?"

"The second from the top, on the left." She closed her robe. "The one with the blue embroidery, if you please."

"It will be my pleasure." He slid the drawer open and removed the under-shift she sought; it was soft, made of fine knitted goat-hair yarn and silken decoration. He held it out to her. "If you want to slip into it?"

She nodded again, and pulled off her robe, flinging it onto the bed before she could change her mind. She tugged the under-shift down from her shoulders and looked for her chamise. "The fire isn't making much headway," she said as her teeth chattered.

"I will make sure it is built up for tonight, from the furnace next to the kitchen, not on this hearth." He handed her the chamise.

"Doesn't that worry you? Mightn't the chimney catch fire?" She shivered again, this time from fear.

"The flues are constructed along Roman lines, and they do double duty, as chimneys and as comprehensive heaters. They are better ventilated, and have six shielded channels up through the walls that meet at two chimneys on the roof, as the old Roman household holocaust did in the floors, and the hotter-burning hypocausts did in the walls and floors in the baths. These channels are more like a hypocaust than a holocaust." Over the centuries he had tried many variations on the Roman design when he had the opportunity to adapt his dwellings to his standards. This château had been no exception, being partially ruined when he bought it, and providing him with an opportunity to include Roman engineering as part of his own uses.

"I suppose you got your idea from them?" She reached for her shirt and pulled it on, fastening its eighteen pearl buttons with unseemly haste; she felt something beyond cold now—a loneliness that touched her to the marrow.

"To a large degree, yes. Some I learned from the Russians, more than two hundred years ago." He offered the body of the gown to her.

Hero pulled the garment over her head, wriggling to get it settled in place. "If you will tend to my laces?"

"Of course," said Ragoczy, and moved around behind her. "Stand still and I'll finish this in a minute."

Hero lifted her heavy plait of hair and said, "Why is fashion so complicated? Not that the Parisians or Romans would call this fashion."

"It is complicated so that you can show that you can afford a chambermaid or a 'tire woman to dress you. And neither Rome nor Paris has the winters Yvoire does, even in mild years." He slipped the knots into the back of her gown, then reached for the long, broad-skirted jacket with the standing collar and eased this onto her arms and settled it on her shoulders. "There. I hope I've done the task correctly. So long as Wendela is recovering from her putrid lungs, I am willing to do my poor best for you."

"Your poor best is more than satisfactory," said Hero and turned to kiss his cheek. "It is inconvenient that she should be ill, and it is most kind of you to offer to treat her."

"Her family did not think so," he said with a wry smile.

"Then her family should—"

"It is their decision and we do well to honor it," he said. "And it is not as if you haven't managed without a maid before. I know your father did not provide you one when you went with him to Anatolia."

"No, but there was Madama Chiaro, and we traded maid duties with one another." She chuckled. "It meant more than tying laces— it meant looking for scorpions in our shoes and cases, and trying to keep the sand from ruining our clothes. I must have destroyed four muslin dresses before I learned how to care for them properly. You know Anatolia. You know what it's like. And you know Egypt."

He had a short, sharp recollection of his long centuries at the Temple of Imhotep; he said, "Not from the point of view of modern women's clothing."

"You must tell me about it, one day," she said, carefully putting hooks through eyes in the front of her jacket. "I hate to think what would have become of me if Madame de Montalia had not sent her recommendation to you."

"And entrusted her manuscript to you for delivery," added Ragoczy. "I, too, am thankful to her."

"Sometimes I fear I have done her an ill turn."

"You have not," he said.

"I hope that's so," she said, then made a final adjustment to her collar. "There. I believe I am ready."

"And so, I presume, is your dinner," he said, offering her his arm. "Before Uchtred becomes annoyed, permit me to take you down to the smaller dining room."

"And wish me bon appetite?" she ventured with a lift of her brows.

He opened the bedroom door and bowed her out. "Of course, dear lady: bon appetite."

Text of a letter from Klasse van der Boom in Amsterdam, to Saint-Germain Ragoczy, Comte Franciscus at Château Ragoczy near Lake

Geneva, Yvoire, Switzerland; delivery delayed five weeks on account of severe weather.

To the most Excellent Saint-Germain Ragoczy, Comte Franciscus, the greeting of Klasse van der Boom, printer and publisher, Eclipse Press, in Amsterdam, on this, the eleventh day of March, 1817.

My dear Comte,

As you no doubt realize, I am sending you copies of our latest editions, as per the terms of our agreement of nine years ago.

I think you will find that the diCaponieve has the best illustrations, and may prove the most rewarding of the six books in this package. Certainly for those traveling through the Alps, diCaponieve's guide to roads, villages and towns, monasteries, inns, spas, hotels, and hostelries should prove invaluable. I have taken the step of ordering two thousand copies in Italian for the initial printing, and an additional eight hundred in French—an unusually high number, I realize, but one I believe will prove to be well-founded. I have approached many hoteliers along the routes diCaponieve describes, in the hope that the work will find readers with an immediate need of it.

Kreutzerlinder's book on the history of the Crusades through the exploration of ruins in the Ottoman Empire may not find as wide an audience, but anticipating an interest from universities, I have ordered twelve hundred copies of it. The illustrations in the volume are not as well-done as those in diCaponieve's book, lacking in the fine detail and artistic presentation of the guide-book. But the text is informative and presented with concision, and will doubtless provoke lively discussion, given Kreutzerlinder's theories on the role of the Byzantines in the conflict. I will be certain to approach German booksellers, to take advantage of the language in which it is written.

Juencleu's book on the French in Canada is not likely to find as broad a readership as either the Kreutzerlinder or the diCaponieve, and so I have ordered nine hundred copies of it, and will send letters to booksellers in Montreal in the hope that they will want to supply the work of one of their own to their clientele. I must confess I still have doubts about it, but I will, of course, abide by your instructions regarding its publication. It may be as you say, that the New World may eventually become as important as the Old.

Donsky's book on game- and song-birds of Russia is handsome, but I agree it is not a subject of avid interest here in western Europe. Fortunately there are many illustrations and all but two turned out well, a feature that could interest more readers than the topic can be expected to attract. At least it is in French and not Russian, for which I am grateful.

The deMontalia text on Rhodes and Cyprus will also have a first edition of twelve hundred copies, with nine pages of illustrations to increase its attractions. I have come to think that you are correct in your assumption that because of Napoleon's expedition to Egypt almost twenty years ago, many in Europe have become fascinated with antiquities, and works of this kind may find a continuing intellectual appetite for such works, especially as it is in French and should enjoy a vogue in Paris.

I trust I will not offend you when I say that I have only ordered one thousand copies of your Legends and Folk-Tales from the Carpathians. I have put the name of G. Tsarogy on it, as you have stipulated. I will see that it is offered in Vienna as well as Paris and Rome, for all it is in French; the Austrians have good reason to familiarize themselves with the traditions in the Carpathians. This should complement the book by G. Tsarogy on the Byzantine Empire that sold so many copies in the last three years; at least that is the way in which I will present it to booksellers.

Now as to those solicitations for publication that you may wish to consider as part of the program for next year: Captain Rupert Burchell of the Royal Navy has submitted a work on improved navigational devices; his style is pedantic but his concepts are intriguing; he writes in English. Ermingard Frement of Trier has sent a guide to the Roman ruins in that city; her work is in French. Casimir Skolodi offered a manuscript in Polish on farming techniques to reduce crop losses due to harsh weather; I have translated a sizable portion of the work into German and asked my Friesian cousin to evaluate what Skolodi recommends and will relay his evaluation to you. Wallache Sieffert, Graf von Ravensberg, an Austrian, has submitted a work in German on the properties of the blood based on his experiments; it is a thorough work, with a great deal of information. Morgan Belclair has submitted a long manuscript in English on weather variations in western Europe and England for the past century; it is more informative than the Skolodi book, but less practical in its application. Professore Bonaldo Certi has submitted a work in Italian on the trade-routes of the Romans and the role they played in establishing ports still actively trading; I have shown this to Jules Forcier for his analysis, which is included in this parcel. I should mention that submissions are up by twenty percent over last year, and we are having to reject six for every one we actually consider.

I remined you we have five books already scheduled for next year and to include more than one or two of these would require an expansion of the program. I am more than willing to undertake a more comprehensive program, providing certain adjustments are made in the actual press and bindery here in Amsterdam. Such improvements would increase our production, but would require a further investment in equipment and materiel, which figures I include for your consideration. If you decide on expansion, I will need to employ another pressman and at least two more typesetters; the sooner I have your determination, the sooner I can begin our work.

With my assurances of my continued dedication to our shared endeavors

> I remain
> Yours to command,
> Klasse van der Boom
> printer and publisher
> Eclipse Press
> Amsterdam

3

Otto Gutesohnes was muddy to his knees and his face was ruddy from the effort of his ride, and although he was only twenty-three, his long, cold journey had left his bones aching like an old man's; he stood on the top step at the door of Château Ragoczy clutching a dispatch-case while he waited for his knock to be answered. Around him the late-arriving spring showed boughs wreathed in the shining snow of apple-blossoms in the shattery brightness of noon, but he was too tired to pay any attention to this extravagant display.

The door was opened by Balduin, the steward, who took one look at the state of Gutesohnes' clothing and indicated the path around to the rear of the château. He spoke in the German-tinged French of the region. "Please use the rear door, and remove your boots before you enter. While you make your way there, I'll fetch Comte Franciscus." He nodded toward the stable. "I trust your horse is in the grooms' hands?"

"My mule, actually; yes. They manage the mud better than horses," said Gutesohnes, his French heavily accented with his native German. He backed down the steps and did as the steward had bade him, calling out as he went, "Otto Gutesohnes of Waldenstadt Messenger Service, with a delivery for Comte Franciscus. I am supposed to hand him the item in person." He cleared his throat. "You're over a league back from the lake, and the directions I was given were very poor, or I should have arrived an hour ago."

"No matter; you are here now." Closing the door, Balduin went along the corridor to the study, and knocked on the door. "There is a messenger here for the Comte; an Otto Gutesohnes. He has brought something in a case for personal delivery. He didn't say what it is."

"Merci. The Comte is in his laboratory," answered Rogier from within; he came to the door and opened it, addressing Balduin directly. "I will inform the Comte of this arrival at once. See the messenger is fed and given an opportunity to rest. He must have had a hard ride coming here, with the roads so wet. Tell him the Comte will join him in about twenty minutes."

"Very good," said Balduin, and continued on to the rear door immediately next to the pantry when he called out, "Uchtred, a messenger has arrived."

"I heard," said the chef, coming into the kitchen corridor. "There is a fire in the rear parlor. Let him rest there. I'll put together a small meal for him, and give him something hot to drink. The Comte will not object."

"I will attend to it," said Balduin, opening the outer door and waiting for Gutesohnes to appear. He noticed the midden was already steaming, an excellent sign in this laggardly April, and May less than a week off.

Gutesohnes appeared, breathing a little hard, his dispatch-case held tightly to his chest. "If you'll hold this for me"—he proffered the case—"I'll take off my boots. And my coat."

"Very good," said Balduin automatically, accepting the dispatch-case.

"I've come from Zurich," Gutesohnes said as he steadied himself against the door frame with one hand and worked his boot off his foot with the other. "Shall I leave these outside?"

"For the moment; I'll have the under-footman clean them." Balduin's mouth pursed with distaste at the thought of the chore.

"Danke," said Gutesohnes as he set down one boot and went to work on the other.

"How long ago did you leave Zurich?" Balduin asked, truly curious. "The weather has not been good."

"I left eleven days ago; between the mud and that last snowstorm, I was fortunate it didn't take longer to get here. This is my third stop along Lake Geneva." He put his second boot down, peeled off his coat, and stepped into the small entry-way. "Where shall I hang this?"

Balduin indicated pegs on the wall, then swung the door closed. "The sun is warm, but the shadows are still cold."

"That they are," said Gutesohnes with feeling. "And this house must hold the damp."

"So if you will follow me?" Balduin said, handing the dispatch-case back to Gutesohnes; he led the way to the rear parlor, opening the door to the cozy chamber for the messenger. "If you will sit, re-freshments will be brought to you directly. Do not hesitate to ask for more if you are hungry. The Comte will join you shortly." He was about to close the door when Gutesohnes stopped him.

"May I have a basin of warm water to wash my hands?"

"Certainly," said Balduin, a bit nonplussed. "At once. Dietbold will bring it."

"Thank you," said Gutesohnes said as he pulled off his heavy gloves and set them on the table in front of the fireplace. "My hands feel like marble, and they smell of wet mule and old leather."

"Dietbold will bring you the basin." On that assurance, he with-drew from the room and sought out Dietbold, who was busy in the main dining room, applying beeswax to the table. He passed along his orders before returning to the kitchen to assist with preparing a tray for the messenger.

A few minutes later Dietbold appeared carrying a good-sized metal basin; he went to the cauldron in front of the massive cast-iron stove where water was kept hot, ladling out a generous amount. "Shall I take a towel from the linen chest?"

"One of the older ones," Balduin recommended. "The man is very muddy, and there's no reason to ruin a good towel on his ac-count."

"Of course," said Dietbold, and made his way to the linen chest in the supply room between the pantry and the laundry. He selected a towel with worn spots and a few minor stains, then went to the back parlor. He knocked and entered the room, remarking as he did, "I trust you are getting warm."

Gutesohnes half-rose. "I am. Danke."

"I'll take the basin and towel when you are finished with them," said Dietbold, handing them over to Gutesohnes, who had seated himself on the broad, upholstered bench behind the low table in front of the fireplace. "Your knuckles are chapped; they must be sore."

"They're more stiff than sore." Gutesohnes set the basin on the table and sank his hands in the warm water. "Much better," he said as he rubbed them together vigorously.

"Do you require anything more?' Dietbold asked.

"Not for the moment," said Gutesohnes, drying his hands.

"Then I will leave you. The Comte will be down directly." He inclined his head, picked up the basin and towel, and left the room.

Rogier encountered him in the corridor. "How is he?"

"The messenger? Well enough." He was about to continue on when Rogier stopped him.

"What has he said?"

"About what he carries? Nothing." Dietbold prepared to depart.

"All right," Rogier said, moving aside. He stood still as Dietbold went to the side-door and tossed out the water in the basin, then continued on to the kitchen. When he was sure he was unobserved, he let himself into the parlor. "Good day to you."

"Comte?" Gutesohnes stood up.

"No; his manservant. He asks you to take your ease for a little while longer."

"Manservant." He studied Rogier. "Treats you well, does he?"

"I have served him many years," Rogier answered, deliberately oblique.

"Then he must be a good master, or a rich one."

Ignoring that remark Rogier took in the man's general appearance, and said, "Carrying messages: is it easier than driving a coach?"

Gutesohnes blinked in surprise—how had this man discerned his former occupation?—but responded readily enough: "Most of the time it is. I was worn to the bone driving coaches. But in hard weather it is more dangerous to be a messenger; you must set out long before coaches are expected to." He saw Rogier gesture to him, and sat down again.

"Do you often come to Geneva?"

"Three times a year, on our current rounds; we serve over fifty subscribers," said Gutesohnes. "It may be four times this year, with the demand for our service increasing." When Rogier said nothing more, he went on. "I wanted the Italian routes—milder weather, better hostels, wonderful food, and only two circuits a year—but I was assigned to the Geneva, Bern, Basel, Zurich, Bern again."

"Has that been so disagreeable?" Rogier asked.

"Given the weather, it hasn't been easy, but still better than driving a coach." He studied Rogier. "Why do you ask?"

"My master is considering employing his own courier, a private one, not a service. He has tasked me to find suitable candidates for the job." He said it calmly enough so as not to create expectations in the young man.

"And you think he might consider employing me?" Gutesohnes brightened at the notion. "Why should he make such an offer to me? Or do you make this offer to every messenger who calls here, in the hope one will suit the requirements?"

"I think it will depend on what the Comte decides, but it is not impossible, if such a position interests you." Rogier was calm, his polite manner unfazed by Gutesohnes' effrontery.

"Of course," said Gutesohnes. "I do understand."

Anything more they might have said was lost in the gentle knock on the door, and Dietbold's return with a tray of broiled eel in herb sauce, fresh bread and butter, a selection of pickles, and a large cup filled with hot cognac with a thick float of cream. He put the tray on the table, nodded, and left.

"I'll leave you to your repast," said Rogier, letting himself out of the parlor; he was thinking over what Gutesohnes had said when he saw Ragoczy coming toward him. "My master."

Ragoczy paused to adjust his black-silk waistcoat and the black super-fine claw-tail coat over it. "Have I got it right?"

"Yes," said Rogier, adding with a suggestion of amusement, "You couldn't have done better with a reflection to guide you." He adjusted the silver watch-chain so that it lay more discreetly across his waistcoat, and then nodded his satisfaction. "There. That should do the trick."

"Always the final detail," Ragoczy approved.

"If Hero were here, she would attend to such matters," said Rogier. "She has a better eye than mine for the current vagaries of fashion: fobs and seals and watch-chains!"

"Yes: she knows the fashion of the present day," Ragoczy said. "Well, she should return in two weeks if the weather holds."

"And her uncle's widow is no worse, and the road from Vevey is open to travel; that late storm last week surely delayed her journey," Rogier said, and tweaked the elaborate silken bow of Ragoczy's neck-cloth. "There. What do the English call it—a rose of good taste?"

"A tulip of the ton, I believe," said Ragoczy in that language.

"A flower, in all events," said Rogier in French. "No one could quibble with your appearance."

"Thank you, old friend," said Ragoczy. "It is always important to observe the niceties."

Rogier did not quite laugh, but his lips quirked and his faded-blue eyes shone with amusement. "As you say."

"How much longer should I let him eat?" Ragoczy asked.

"Five more minutes; he won't mind the interruption then."

"What do you think of him?" Ragoczy inquired.

"Young, strong, sensible. He likes his comforts but not to the point of laziness, or so it appears—after all, he came here as soon as the road was clear enough of snow to allow him passage. You can tell by his shoulders that his days as a coachman were demanding." Rogier coughed once. "He will probably not want to carry messages or drive coaches for all his life, at least not as an occupation. But he does appear to be willing to do the work for now, and he would seem to have an aptitude for it."

"A sensible position," said Ragoczy. "If he is willing to work for five years, I will consider myself fortunate, assuming he is capable and honest. I must hire someone in the next four to five months, and if this man seems qualified . . ."

"You must determine that for yourself," said Rogier. "But he is the second messenger to arrive here since winter broke, and he came farther than Conrade did. I think he is able to do the work, and he would be accepted by the household."

"I will keep that in mind." Ragoczy laid his small, elegant hand on the door-latch, but said to Rogier, "I suspect there is more to it, this endorsement of yours, and I am curious to know what that may be. You are usually reluctant to give such a sanction to an unknown fellow as you have for this man. Why is that? What about him is so different that you are inclined in his favor?"

Rogier took a long slow breath. "I don't quite know. It may be that something about him reminds me of Hercule," he admitted at last.

"Truly." Ragoczy regarded Rogier contemplatively. "In what way?"

"It is a question of manner." He said, choosing his words carefully. "He doesn't look like Hercule, he isn't injured, he is not so old nor so burly as Hercule was, but you know how Hercule was willing to drive through fire? Well, this young man has some of the same quality about him."

"Does he. Most interesting. I will bear that in mind." Slowly Ragoczy opened the door, saying nothing as he took stock of Otto Gutesohnes, who was cutting into the broiled eel with gusto. He stood still, a figure in dignified black but for his dove-gray silken shirt and the shine of his watch-chain; the austerity of his clothing served to display their richness. Finally he allowed the door to close behind him, its sharp click announcing his arrival to the messenger.

Gutesohnes looked up, nearly dropped his utensils as he shoved himself to his feet. "Comte. You must be he." He stared at the man, taking in everything about him; Gutesohnes was struck by the self-possessed presence of the man, his quiet air of elegance and position, and how, although he was a bit less than average height, he had the manner and comportment of a tall man.

Ragoczy bowed slightly. "I have that honor." He indicated Gute-sohnes' food. "Do not let me stop you enjoying your meal."

Somewhat awkwardly Gutesohnes sat down. "If you permit, then I thank you."

"I know what it is to be hungry. Please." He moved a few steps farther into the room and studied Gutesohnes in silence while the messenger continued to eat. "I understand you have something for me?"

"I do. It is in a sealed box, which I have in my dispatch-case, along with the other items I am delivering in Geneva. If you want, I can get it out for you now." He began to reach for the leather bag at the side of the bench. "This might be a good time to . . . I am or-dered to hand you the box myself, so I can vouch for its delivery."

"It can wait until you've finished your meal," said Ragoczy with an unconcerned wave of dismissal.

"You are not eating?" Gutesohnes said, indicating his tray.

"Not just at present. But do not let my abstaining stop you from completing your meal." Ragoczy gave a single, slow nod.

"Danke schoen." Gutesohnes thrust his fork into another sec-tion of broiled eel and applied his knife to the meat; the piece he stuffed into his mouth was fairly large. "This is very good," he said around his chewing.

"I'll tell my cook," said Ragoczy without a trace of sarcasm.

Gutesohnes colored to the roots of his hair. "I did not mean to over-step . . . It's not my place to . . . to—"

"It is a compliment and I will deliver it to Uchtred. He deserves to know his work is appreciated." Ragoczy pulled one of the four straight-backed chairs away from the wall and sat down.

"Would you prefer . . . ?" Gutesohnes asked, meaning the up-holstered bench upon which he sat.

"No, thank you anyway. I am comfortable where I am, and you have been in the saddle since dawn, unless I am mistaken, and there-fore that bench must be very welcome." Ragoczy offered a swift, easy smile.

"Yes. I was off at sunrise from the Leaping Trout. Do you know it?" He picked up the cognac and sipped the hot liquid through the cream.

"More than three leagues from here, on the main road, about two hundred years old, with a tavern and an inn." He considered the distance. "You must have kept your mount at a steady walk to arrive here at this hour."

"Um. That's why I ride a mule—a big one, to handle whatever we may have to contend with." He broke a section of bread and wiped it through the herb-sauce on the broiled eel. "This one can walk for hours through mud and snow and rain, never mind how mired the roads are. He gets tired but will not halt until I prepare to dismount. I've had him sink to his knees in mud and continue on— annoyed but not halted. Same with snow." He bit into the sauced bread.

"A good animal, then," said Ragoczy.

"An excellent animal. The messenger service has a dozen such animals. We buy from the same breeder for all our mules." He had more eel, his eating slowing down a bit.

"A fine arrangement, no doubt," said Ragoczy, beginning to see what Rogier had perceived in this young man.

"Herr Waldenstadt has established high standards for his messengers, and a regular schedule to which we must adhere; that way we can give superior service. He insists that we account for all our time while traveling, to justify his charges." He said it dutifully enough, but with real purpose. "If we cannot prove more reliable than the post, why should anyone spend the money to subscribe?"

"Why indeed," said Ragoczy. He watched Gutesohnes drink more of the cognac, then said, "How long have you worked for Herr . . . Waldenstadt?"

"Two years. I was a coachman out of the Frederich in Basel before that." He began on the pickles. "Herr Waldenstadt brought me to Bern."

"And how long did you drive a coach for the Frederich?" Ragoczy inquired calmly.

"Three years. I had learned from my aunt's husband, who took me in after my father died." He picked up the napkin and wiped his mouth.

"I suppose you read and write?" Ragoczy pursued.

His German accent grew stronger. "I was taught for five years in the local school. I know French, a little Italian, a few words in Polish, and some Czech. I can write in French as well as German, but the others, no, not really. I know Russian and Greek when I see them but I cannot read them." He dropped the napkin back in his lap and screwed up his courage enough to say, "Your manservant said you might want a private courier of your own: is that true?"

"It is," said Ragoczy, remembering Yrjo Saari, who had said the same thing over a century ago.

"And that is why you're asking me these questions?" He looked at Ragoczy directly, making no apology for doing this.

"That," said Ragoczy, "and curiosity."

Gutesohnes flushed again, feeling increasingly awkward. "Comte . . ."

"Would such a position interest you?"

"It might," said Gutesohnes, doing his best to regain his composure. "What do you offer, and what duties would it entail?"

"I have businesses in many cities throughout Europe, and it is important that I be able to send various contracts and similar instruments to those businesses promptly and with a modicum of privacy, which inclines me not to use the post. Confidentiality is necessary in the conduct of honorable business—would you agree?" Ragoczy put his hand to the silver watch-chain swagged across the front of his waistcoat. "I would like to have my messenger be willing to travel on short notice, to keep what he carries secret, and to return promptly with whatever responses are entrusted to him. In exchange for this service, I will provide housing, meals, horses and mules, three new suits of clothes each year, and a salary double what you receive now—assuming you and I decide that this would be acceptable to us both."

"I admit I am interested, providing you don't expect me to ride into Russia, or set sail for the New World." He had another pickle and finished his cognac.

"At present, I would have no such requirements to make of you," said Ragoczy.

"At present?" Gutesohnes repeated skeptically.

"Who can say what the future may bring?" Ragoczy suggested gently.

Gutesohnes thought this over. "All right."

"Think of the two hard winters we have had," Ragoczy went on, his thoughts casting back more than twelve centuries to the dreadful Year of Yellow Snow, when all the world seemed to be locked in perpetual winter. "Had the weather taken such a turn in 1812, the losses Napoleon suffered in Russia might have been utterly complete rather than devastating; he might have fallen in the snow as so many of his men did. But it did not strike until Napoleon had done his worst. Who could have anticipated it? Yet now it is here, we must, perforce, accommodate it."

"I take your point, Comte," said Gutesohnes.

Ragoczy coughed discreetly. "All things being equal, I will not expect you to go any farther than Poland, or England, or Spain or Greece. If circumstances should arise that required your services beyond those places, a special price would be negotiated for such a journey, and paid in advance of your travel. If you require a bond to that end, I will establish one. Would that satisfy you?"

"I suppose it must." He buttered a wedge of bread, taking time to do it properly, all the while saying, "If you wish me to work for you, I cannot begin until I have completed the current deliveries I have to make. Once I return to Bern, I may end my employment, but not before then."

"What would be the earliest you could return here?" Ragoczy asked; he did not mention that this display of responsibility had inclined him to want to employ Gutesohnes.

"Probably the end of June, weather permitting. I would need to purchase a horse or a mule for the return. Herr Waldenstadt will not give me one." He thought a moment. "He might not even sell me one."

"I can arrange for you to purchase the mount of your choice, if you decide you want this position. You have only to choose what you want to ride, and from whom you would like to purchase it." He got to his feet; Gutesohnes almost tipped over his tray in his haste to rise. "I will return in half an hour to answer any questions you may have, and to let you know my decision. If you would like something more—some cheese, some nuts—tell Dietbold and he will bring it to you."

"Half an hour." He glanced down at his dispatch-case. "Do you want your parcel now, or would you prefer to wait?"

"If you would give it to me?" Ragoczy said, holding out his hand to receive it.

Gutesohnes opened the case and pulled out a chicken-sized package—a wax-sealed wooden box with the impression of a signet-ring showing three sheaves of wheat sunk in the heaviest pooling of wax. "There. I will report to Professor Weissbord that you have received the box."

"Thank you," said Ragoczy, a bit startled. "Professor Weissbord, do you say?" He glanced at the signet-impression. "I see: Weissbord."

"Is something wrong, Comte?" Gutesohnes asked.

"No; nothing," said Ragoczy. "I had assumed the parcel was from someone else."

"Is this an inconvenience?"

"No, of course not." Ragoczy motioned to the tray. "Finish your meal and think over what I have offered." He went to the door and lifted the latch.

"Comte?" Gutesohnes had managed to gather the courage to speak.

"Yes?" He waited politely for Gutesohnes to go on.

"Is it that you wish to employ me, or would any messenger do? And are you offering me employment?"

Ragoczy stood still while he considered his answer. "Yes, I need a messenger, but no, I would not engage just anyone to do the tasks I will require." He held up the box in his hand. "In any event, thank you for bringing this to me."

"Oh." He nodded twice. "Danke, Comte."

"Bitte," said Ragoczy, and left the parlor. He found Rogier waiting ten steps away.

"So: do you, too, see the resemblance to Hercule?" he asked as Ragoczy approached him.

"I do," said Ragoczy. "And I agree about his demeanor. This is a cleverer man—not that Hercule was not clever, but this man thinks about many more things than Hercule did, with a broader sense of the world than Hercule had."

"No doubt you are right," said Rogier. "I believe he is someone who will perform to your expectations."

"Oh, yes. I have no doubt of that." Ragoczy glanced over his shoulder. "Not for money alone, but to give himself a leg up in the world."

"You: cynical?" Rogier regarded Ragoczy with skepticism.

"Not cynical, old friend—appreciative. This man's self-interests match with my intentions, which should stand us both in good stead." He paused. "That is, if he agrees to work for me."

"He would be a fool not to," said Rogier.

"Ah," said Ragoczy, "but how many men are fools?" Without waiting for an answer he turned away toward the front of the château.

Text of a crossed letter from Hero Iocasta Ariadne Corvosaggio von Scharffensee at Vevey, in Switzerland, to her father, Attilio Aurelio Augusto Corvosaggio in Padova; carried by regular post.

To my very dear father on this, the 6th day of May, 1817, the affectionate greeting of your daughter, presently in Vevey with your brother Dario's widow;

I was saddened to learn of your illness this last winter, and I hope your recovery is now under way. From what Ortrude told me before she became incapacitated by her affliction, you have had much to burden you since October. I am pleased to hear that you are receiving such excellent care, and I am grateful to the good Widow

Caglia for all she has done for you—far in excess of what you might expect from a housekeeper. I agree it was wise to send your wife out of danger. There was no cause for both of you to be at risk. I must suppose that you will return to Anatolia and the ruins you found there last year as soon as your health is restored; I wish you every success in your expedition, and ask only that you inform me when you decide upon your departure.

Yet, heartened as I am by your tidings, I am duty-bound to inform you that your brother's widow is not long for this world. It may be that by the time you receive this, she will have passed beyond this earthly abode. I have consulted the local physician and he has said that her lethargy is a sign of approaching demise, that there is nothing more that can be done for her. I have sent for my protector, who has a vast knowledge of medicaments and treatments not always known to the general run of healers, and he has promised to come here in two days. He will do what he can for Ortrude, but his note has warned me it may be nothing more than easing her dying.

I have heard from my father-in-law, who informs me that my children are well, that their studies are going on properly, and that they are growing as one would expect them to grow. I devour his words as if I were starving and they were meat and bread, and at the same time, I resent him for all he has done to keep us apart. Hard as it was to lose my husband, it was a single blow—having my children growing up away from me is a new anguish every day. I miss them with more vivid emotions than I have words to convey; their grandfather has asked that I not visit them for this summer, a request that falls like a lash on all my hopes for being with them soon. How I wish my husband had left his affairs in a more ordered state, but, as he had no Will as such, I cannot challenge the Graf's authority. What court would support my claim while the Graf provides for them so handsomely, and I have only the support of the Comte to preserve body and soul?

Enough of such gloomy reflections. There is nothing you or I can do to change how matters stand, and although the Comte has offered to sponsor my court actions for the housing and care of my children, I have discussed the matter with an experienced advocate, who has assured me that any such action would fail. Had I a fortune of my own, I might be able to put forth an argument a justice might consider, but lacking fortune, a house of my own, or any other unencumbered security, I am unlikely to present a convincing case. It would mean that I would add needlessly to my children's suffering, and my own. So I have decided that when the Comte travels this summer, I will go with him. It will be nothing so exciting as what you will undertake in Anatolia, but it will provide a change of scene and a chance to stop brooding, which I confess I have done for most of the winter. I will content myself with Amsterdam and Bruxelles, and hope that one day I may again venture beyond Europe.

It has been quite warm and pleasant this last week, and I believe that spring may finally have arrived in earnest. The trees have budded and unfurled their leaves, the ice is gone from the pond behind the château, and the first lambs have been born. I have seen farmers in their fields, and every day, the cowherds take their animals up into the mountains to graze, and shepherds are now away from their winter quarters, going with their flocks into the high meadows, where they will remain for most of the summer. Yet in spite of the hard weather we have endured, it is wonderful not to have the threat of war hanging over us as it did for so long. All those fine men, lost to life and home, or forced into beggary! It is shameful that the soldiers who were cheered a decade ago are daily spat upon in the street, useless flotsam now that their fighting has ruined them for other work.

In addition to the travel I have already described, the Comte has promised me a journey to Italy next year, and he will take me to hear whatever new work Signore Rossini has composed at that time. I have received some piano transcriptions of airs from his work Il Barbiere di Siviglia *and enjoyed playing them; so amusing and witty. The instrument in the music room at his château—a forte-piano—is a bit old-fashioned but in excellent condition, and so it is always a pleasure to spend an hour or two at the keyboard. It is something I will enjoy as soon as I return to his château. He has penned a few melodies of his own for me to play, and a duet for us to play together. His musicianship is superior and it puts me on my mettle to play with him. Stickler that you are for accurate performance, I am persuaded you would find his playing to your satisfaction; he certainly performs beyond my capacity. The Comte also plays violin, viola, and guitar: he has one of each in his music room as well as some regional instruments, in particular, a Hungarian cimbalom, a kind of large, hammered zither. I am not overly fond of its sound, but I allow that he plays it well. If you should ever have occasion to visit here, I hope you will give him the opportunity to play for you on any or all of his instruments.*

When your new book is published, I ask you will send me a copy so I may see how your discoveries are progressing. I often think of those days when we journeyed together, and all the places we saw: Rhodes, Cyprus, Egypt! While I realize it is impractical for me to accompany you as I did when I was a child, I cannot help but yearn for those days, and tell you how it saddens me that you are not able to give my children the same opportunities as I had from you; I fear they will be the worse for the lack of them. Perhaps when they are a bit older something may be arranged, for little as the Graf likes the Turks, he is an avid admirer of the ancient heros; in time he may see the advantage to permitting at least Siegfried, Bertram, and Berend to visit you at your excavation; I doubt he would permit Annamaria to travel into Ottoman territory, for fear she might be the victim of an outrage.

With every assurance of my continued affection and devotion,
    Your most allegiant daughter,
       Hero Iocasta Ariadne Corvosaggio von Scharffensee

4

There was mud on the hem of Hero's walking-dress, and her kid shoes were all but ruined; still, she was laughing as Ragoczy helped her over the stile that connected his outer fields with those of his neighbor; her activity had excited her so that her cheeks were flushed and her eyes sparkled. Her high-brimmed bonnet *à la Hussar* set off her face and the curls that clustered at the edge of this confection. She gathered the frilled front of her walking-coat more tightly and released his steadying hand. "What a beautiful day! I thought we wouldn't get any spring again this year. Last year was so dreadful, it was troubling to think what might lie ahead. Yet here it is, sunshine and warmth, and not quite the end of May."

"Two hard winters in a row have burdened everyone, from farmer to housewife. It will be some months before the land can be restored, assuming the improvement continues." Ragoczy indicated the fallow field beyond where they stood. "I hope Herr Kleinerhoff is able to bring in all his crops this year; I hope all the farmers of Sacre-Sang do." The last year had been almost a total loss for Augustus Kleinerhoff, and this year promised little improvement with the late arrival of spring and the poor display of developing fruit in the trees. "He will have to plant soon, and trust that the autumn is not an early one."

"All men with fields must share that trust, not just those of Sacre-Sang," said Hero. "You must have some concerns yourself, Comte."

He shook his head, his dark eyes fixed on a distance only he could see. "Not so many as those whose fields are their livelihoods. I have shipping companies and other businesses that can sustain me through times of hard weather. Although shipping also suffers in hard years."

"You also have forcing houses—nine of them," she said with a tight little nod. "You can bring in cabbages and chard, at least."

"Remember that two of my forcing houses were damaged by ice," said Ragoczy. "They will need to be repaired shortly, or be useless this year."

"Climate dictates all," Hero said fatalistically. "When my father visited Egypt, he said that the people there suffered for the harshness of the climate: heat instead of cold, dry instead of wet. I remember many flies, and, because we were the only Europeans in the town, my step-mother and I had to wear veils whenever we went about."

"It is the custom," said Ragoczy.

"Yes; my father said so, as well. I wish it had been otherwise." She glanced toward the mountains rising around them. "There have been avalanches this year, more than in most years."

"There is a build-up of snow on the slopes; with more snow there comes more avalanches." He started along the fence, helping her to pick her way over the uneven ground.

"No doubt you're right," she said, concentrating on where she stepped.

"If you would prefer to seek out the road?" Ragoczy offered.

"No. It is just as muddy as this field, if not more so." She smiled at him once more, but there was more sadness than merriment in her expression. "Since Fridhold died, I keep thinking of how many perils are around us, and all the time. A beam becomes a bludgeon, a carriage becomes a death-trap, an open fire becomes a conflagration. I know it is foolish, but anything can distress me, from an unguarded fire in the grate to a sagging branch on a tree. I see danger in the field, and I see danger on the road." For more than a minute she neither moved nor spoke, but then she said, "If you had not taken me in, I have no notion what would have happened to me."

"Your father would have provided for you," said Ragoczy, resuming their progress across the field.

"His second wife would not want me in their household, and he is not rich enough to provide for two households and his expeditions as well. Men of his profession spend their money, such as it is, on their expeditions, not on their comforts and families. He would have had to arrange a marriage for me, or a position as a governess, or a teacher at a girls' school. At worst I would have had to become the nurse for some ancient relative, one whose body or mind was gone; I know from my days with Ortrude that I lack the patience for such continual employment; the few months I cared for her were sufficient to show me that. I try not to dwell upon it, but sometimes—" She sighed. "And the Graf—well, he might pay me to keep away from my children, but not one pfennig more than absolutely necessary to sustain me as little above poverty as his reputation could endure."

"All because your husband left no Will to provide for you," said Ragoczy.

"He didn't think he would die so young," she said, as she had said many times before. "And neither did I."

"There is always a risk of dying." Ragoczy paused by a narrow rill running through the center of the field; the amount of water, although small, caused him discomfort.

"Even for you?" She was almost teasing him.

"Even for me," he said somberly; he glanced down at the sparking surface of the rill. "I'll lift you over," he offered.

"Just let me take your arm and that will suffice," said Hero, testing the narrow bank of the rivulet to determine how slippery it was. She laid her hand on the arm he held out to her and stepped across the water. "There; you see?"

He crossed to her side of the little stream. "There should be a stone path along on your right."

"I think I see it," she said, trying to hold her skirts above the worst of the mud.

"Then proceed," he said, still providing a steadying hand. "It is tricky underfoot, I fear."

She made her way to the path and looked down at her shoes. "Quite ruined," she said with a hint of a giggle. "Doubtless my own fault."

"You *will* walk with your feet on the ground," said Ragoczy, matching his tone with hers.

"So I will," she said, continuing down the road. "At least the other fields are almost planted."

"This one will lie fallow another year, I must suppose," said Ragoczy. "The orchards are finally in full bloom—that arguers well."

"Herr Kleinerhoff has always taken pride in the fruit his orchards produce, or so his son told me last autumn." She waited while her wistfulness washed through her. "Siegfried loves apples."

"I thought most boys liked apples," said Ragoczy with steady kindness.

"Yes, but Siegfried is especially fond of them. So was Fridhold."

He rested his hand on her shoulder for several seconds. "You miss him."

"I keep thinking I should stop," she said by way of apology. "Missing him does no good."

"Why do you say that? He was dear to you, he was the father of your children, you shared his life and his bed for nearly eight years, and he was not yet thirty when he died." Ragoczy turned her to face him. "How can I fault you for your affection?"

"But you aren't jealous, are you?" she asked tentatively as she resumed her progress along the stone path.

"Why should I be?" he countered. "Your love for him does not diminish your affection for me."

"No," she conceded. "At least, I don't believe it does."

He regarded her thoughtfully a short while as they reached the gate leading to the road to the small Trappist monastery farther up the mountain. "Every love is different, Hero," he said as he drew back the bar that held the gate closed. "You may compare them all you try, yet no two loves are alike."

"This is something you have learned in your life?" She regarded him curiously, her eyes fixed on him with steady purpose.

"Yes: long since."

"You still miss Madelaine de Montalia; I know you do," she said, not quite accusing him.

"Certainly; and many others, as well," he said in his unflustered way, aware that his attachment to Madelaine was unlike most of his connections to those with whom the Blood Bond still pertained.

"But not the way you miss her," Hero insisted.

"No, not the way I miss her, nor anyone else. Everyone I have known is unique in my experience and holds a singular place in my memory." He had almost said *my heart,* but memories of Csimenae stopped the words before he spoke them. "You need not fear I will forget you, Hero." As she walked through, he closed the gate behind her. "Those of my blood learn not to be distracted by one love from another. When you live as long as we do, any other understanding is folly."

She considered this, her face somber. "What was it that drew you to me? I can't imagine it was my beauty or my manner."

He took almost a minute to frame his answer. "It was your honesty that led me to seek you out. Manner and beauty change from year to year, and what is handsome at one time is brutish at another; honesty is a constant, and rarer than pleasing faces." He touched her chin lightly, smiling briefly. "You did not try to flatter me, or to deny your grief. You did not batten on me, or on any man, although the law and custom would encourage you to do so. You have made your own way in difficult circumstances." He took a step away from her. "Such force of character commands respect."

"And Madelaine de Montalia?" As soon as she said the name, she bit her lower lip and averted her eyes.

Ragoczy took her chin in his hand and turned her face toward him. "Madelaine knew me for what I am—for all that I am—from the very beginning, and had no fear of me. For such as I, that encompassing is beyond reckoning." He kissed the side of her mouth. "Do not fret: you have nothing to worry about on her account."

"I'm not worried," she said staunchly. Then she swallowed hard. "Not too much."

"You need not worry at all," said Ragoczy. "Neither she nor I can provide what the other seeks."

"But I feel so . . . haunted."

"Haunted?" He paused. "Not by Madelaine, surely?"

"By Madelaine, by Fridhold, even by my children, although they are alive." She reached for her handkerchief, tucked into the breast-pocket of her walking-coat. "I didn't intend to . . . Comte, pardon me." She dabbed at her eyes, embarrassment overtaking her with other emotions.

"Everyone is haunted," Ragoczy assured her gently. "By the loss of friends and relations, the fading of youth, the opportunities lost—all haunt us. It is one of the prices of living."

"That may be so," she said, doing her best to regain her self-possession.

Five hundred years before he might have told her that in time she would understand, but he knew now that such assertions meant little to the living, particularly to the young, who felt the weight of time more sharply than those who reached old age; he took her mittened hand and kissed it. "You have been given hard choices, and you have made them without flinching. That is a true accomplishment."

"I have flinched often," she said by way of confession.

"And mastered it," said Ragoczy.

"Have I? Sometimes I wonder." She turned her head sharply as a large dog began to bark, running toward them from out of a lane ahead of them.

"Stay still," Ragoczy told her as he stepped forward to intercept the dog.

The animal was chestnut-colored with black smudges around his eyes and muzzle; his coat was shaggy from winter and mottled from shedding, and his paws were caked in mud. He bounded up to Ragoczy, barking enthusiastically. He leaped up and struck out with his paws, half in challenge, half in play. His barking became higher, turning almost to puppylike yips.

"Be careful," Hero called.

"Oh, Behemoth will not hurt me, not intentionally," said Ragoczy. "He is just expressing his delight at being out for the day. A dog his size frets in confinement, and this winter he had more than his fill of it." He held the dog's front paws in his hands with seeming lack of effort even while the big dog bounced energetically on his hind legs, tongue lolling. "This is all very well, Behemoth, but it is fitting that you should get down now." Firmly but without overt force, he settled the big dog on the ground. "You can come now, Hero. He won't fly at you."

"I hope that's true," she said dubiously.

"It is. Unless he's badly startled." He stood back from the dog and held his hand out for Hero.

She allowed him to guide her past the dog, who lay on the matted weeds at the side of the road, his head resting on his paws, ears slightly perked. "I shouldn't fear him, I know, but he is so large."

"And he is trained to protect Herr Kleinerhoff's property," Ragoczy added. "A task for which he is truly apt."

As if in agreement, Behemoth let out a rumble deep in his chest, although he did not move from where he lay.

They reached the walk-way to Herr Kleinerhoff's house. "It is just beyond that copse of trees," said Ragoczy.

"I've seen it from your laboratory window," she reminded him. "Or the western half of it, at any case." She walked a bit more quickly, her face showing no emotion at all. Finally, as they passed into the shadow of the yews and larches, she said, "This is just the sort of place I always imagine my boys playing."

"Herr Kleinerhoff's children sometimes play here," said Ragoczy kindly.

"I know," she said. "I've watched them."

"From my laboratory," said Ragoczy.

"Yes." Her head came up sharply as if in anticipation of a reprimand. "I didn't think you'd mind."

"Nor do I," he said as they emerged from the cluster of trees onto a broad swath of flagstones that fronted on a large, hundred-year-old farmhouse slightly in need of repair. Halfway along the front of the house the midden steamed ripely in the morning sun.

"Will Herr Kleinerhoff be here?" Hero asked.

"He and his wife and mother, and his children. Today only his hired hands work in the fields, clearing weeds and preparing for plowing." He approached the front door, made of thick planks of pine painted blue and banded-and-hinged in iron. An old bell hung on a rusted rocker with a frayed cord attached to the clapper; Ragoczy pulled this and set off an unmelodious clang. "One of the privileges of being head-man in Sacre-Sang."

"I hope they won't be offended by my presence," said Hero in a sudden wash of uncertainty.

"Why should they be?" Ragoczy asked, expecting no answer, which was just as well, for before Hero could speak, the inner bolt was drawn back and Herr Kleinerhoff himself threw open his door, bowing respectfully and beaming with painful determination as he welcomed Ragoczy and Hero to his home.

His wife, a substantial woman with a sagging face that spoke of many hungry days, hovered in the arch between parlor and kitchen, flapping the ends of her long, embroidered apron, flushed with excitement. When her husband barked an order for wine, she hastened away, glad to have something to do.

"I know you foreigners like wine more than our beer," said Herr Kleinerhoff.

"A glass for my companion would be welcome," said Ragoczy, "but I, myself, do not drink wine."

Herr Kleinerhoff's expression showed that he did not believe Ragoczy, but he said, "If you would prefer beer? I'm afraid what we have isn't the best—the harvest being so . . ." He gestured to show his disappointment.

"Neither is needed. Just the wine for Madame von Scharffensee." Ragoczy looked around the parlor with the kind of tranquil curiosity that banished Herr Kleinerhoff's embarrassment, so that when his wife appeared with two squat glasses of butter-colored wine, he gave one to Hero and kept one for himself without apology.

"Let me welcome you to my home, Comte." Herr Kleinerhoff lifted his glass, but hesitated to include Hero in his toast.

"Thank you, Herr Kleinerhoff," said Ragoczy. "Madame," he went on to Hero, "I rely on you to express our gratitude for this hospitality."

Hero smiled and lifted her glass to Herr Kleinerhoff. "Thank you," she said, and took a sip; the wine was from late-harvest grapes, its flavor intense and sweet, its texture syrupy. She managed not to cough at its overwhelming sapidness, nodding to Herr Kleinerhoff to show her approval.

Herr Kleinerhoff was not so rude as to stare at her, but watched her out of the tail of his eye. "How kind of you to—"

Ragoczy held up his small, elegant hand. "Let us consider the politesse fulfilled, Herr Kleinerhoff, and get on to our discussion."

"Of course, of course," said Herr Kleinerhoff, bowing Ragoczy to the best chair in the room. "If you will?"

Ragoczy sighed as he sat, thinking that to refuse would offend his host, but also aware that the chair was Herr Kleinerhoff's own. "This is quite comfortable," he declared in cordial mendacity.

"I will take a stroll in the sunlight," Hero announced as she set down her half-finished wine. "When you men have finished your business, call me and I will return." So saying, she went to the door and waited for Herr Kleinerhoff to open it for her.

As soon as he had closed the door behind Hero, Herr Kleinerhoff bustled back into the parlor, his small, blue eyes shining with intent. "I had your note, Comte, and I must tell you, I was hopeful for the first time in well over a year. But reflection taught me that perhaps I had been too hopeful, and that your offer was other than you laid out in your note." He sat on an upholstered stool, leaning forward, his elbows on his spread legs. "So I would be less than forthcoming if I said my hope was untrammeled. Your offer is so generous, so . . . reasonable, that I fear there may be more to it than I comprehend from what you wrote. Before I agree to accept your apparently most magnanimous offer, I would like to be certain of the terms. And I would like to know how far you would extend them within this district. Am I the sole recipient of your boon?" He stopped abruptly, as if his breath and courage had failed him at once.

"Very prudent," said Ragoczy when it was clear that Herr Kleinerhoff would not go on. "I meant what I said. I know how bad the past two winters have been for you and your neighbors, and I know you have few reserves to carry you through another lean year. I am proposing to provide seed for planting and grain for feed for the next year, until we might all be certain that this spate of cold is over or at least lessening. I have stores of my own upon which I can draw for some time if necessary; I will use these for our mutual benefit. I am willing to extend this offer to all the landholders in the parish."

"There," said Herr Kleinerhoff, rocking back so that he nearly tipped himself over. "That is what most concerns me. How do you envision this mutual benefit for me or for my fellow-landholders?"

Ragoczy gave a single, sad chuckle. "Nothing to your disservice, Herr Kleinerhoff," he said. "I will ask for ten percent of your first full harvest, that to be stored against another such hard time, the same provision to be made for five years from all those who accept assistance from me, assuming there is improvement in the weather." He thought back again to the unrelenting hardships of the Year of Yellow Snow.

"But why should you do this? How can it benefit you?" Herr Kleinerhoff gulped the rest of his wine and stared at Ragoczy as he waited for an answer.

"Herr Kleinerhoff," Ragoczy said distantly, in a tone that chilled the portly farmer to the bone, "I have traveled a good deal in my life, and I have seen what famine does. It is not starvation alone that kills in famine, it is disease and violence born of desperation. I do not wish to see these things come to this parish. Europe is just emerging from Napoleon's devastation, and to have the weather add to his burden bodes ill unless something is done, and quickly, to prevent the depredation of famine and its handmaidens."

Herr Kleinerhoff swallowed hard. "My own great-grandparents came here in a time of famine," he said.

"Famine always brings refugees," said Ragoczy. "As does pestilence, and war."

"As we have seen," said Herr Kleinerhoff. He sat upright. "Then, if it is your intention to spare us the suffering so many others endure, I will accept your offer, with the understanding that you require I store a tenth of my first full harvest and those of the next four years as provision against a return of famine. I will speak to my neighbors in this parish and see if any among them would want to join with me."

"Thank you," said Ragoczy.

"Some of them may be wary. A few still regard foreigners as enemies of this region." He coughed apologetically.

"War and famine are relentless enemies of humankind, not I," Ragoczy said, and saw Herr Kleinerhoff nod.

"They are the tools of the Antichrist. Our minister has told us that the End Days are coming, and we must prepare for travail. Your kindness will help us be ready."

Ragoczy shook his head. "The End Days are always coming, Herr Kleinerhoff." A series of images of men proclaiming the End Days, from the second Christian century to the present day flashed through his mind; he recalled their thundering dread and determined penitence with a touch of chagrin. "From the day the world began, the End Days were coming."

"Amen," said Herr Kleinerhoff.

"Of course." Ragoczy suppressed a sigh. "Amen."

Text of a letter from Cados Gaspard Adrien Rivage, business factor in Le Havre, France, to Saint-Germain Ragoczy, Comte Franciscus at Château Ragoczy near Lake Geneva, Yvoire, Switzerland; carried by hired courier and delivered in twelve days.

To my most highly regarded employer, Comte Franciscus, Cados G. A. Rivage sends his greetings on the 9th day of June, 1817.

Four of your ships have returned from their voyages, three of them many months delayed but safe for all that. I must tell you that the Aeolus *has lost part of her mizzenmast and will need substantial repairs before she can set to sea again, and the* Petrel *had half of her cargo of silks seized in Alexandria, and four of the men taken by the city on a charge that has not yet been made clear. The balance of her cargo is in very good condition. It is my intention to write to the customs officials in Alexandria to demand an explanation of their actions, but I doubt this will result in any return of men or of silks. On the other hand, I have received confirmation that the* Odysseus *is in Boston and will set out for Baltimore before returning to European waters later this summer. The* Epheginea *has sent back word from Australia that all is well, and she will be bound for India when the winter there is past.*

The Sagittarius *is now the only ship unaccounted for. I have reports on all nineteen of the rest in hand, most of their information current as of four months ago, and I hope to provide you with more information as the month wears on. Now that winter is finally over, I begin to hope that shipping may once again become more regular.*

Captain Clairmont has asked to be relieved of his command for a year. His wife and three children are missing from his parents' home in Charleroi and he is determined to find them. I have given him provisional leave with the understanding that he must maintain regular correspondence with me so that his whereabouts may be known. I realize he is one of your best captains, but he is distraught about his family, and will not be able to carry out his duties while their fate is unknown to him. His parents have said that they were taken by French officers last November, but who they were and what their true purpose was, they cannot say. His father was beaten by these men, and has lost the sight in one eye on its account, so you can understand why it is that Captain Clairmont might fear for the worst. If you are willing, I will forward true copies of his letters to you as they arrive.

I have received a payment from Darius Spiridion at last, brought by the Hypolita *three weeks ago. Captain Rosenwald carried it in a sealed strongbox, so there is no question as to the total amount paid. It is not the full amount he owes, but a reasonable portion of it, and I will do as you recommend and continue to allow him to deal with Eclipse Trading Company for as long as he makes bi-annual payments on the debt. It is hardly his fault that his four warehouses burned with your cargos still in them, but he was responsible for it while it was in his care, and the amount you settled on for the value of what was lost is reasonable for both parties.*

Some of the sailors have been spreading rumors that Napoleon plans to escape once again and summon his soldiers for a last attempt at reclaiming his title and conquests. I, myself, do not think this is likely, but I believe it is a good precaution to know what is being whispered in the taverns. I cannot imagine that France would allow more tragedy to claim her people again, but there will always be those who see this man as their deliverer, and who care nothing for the damage he may bring with his deliverance.

I await your orders in regard to the Flying Cloud. I would recommend scrapping her, since there is so much damage to the keel and the rudder has been badly damaged. She has lain in port now for ten months, and the shipwrights here are disinclined to spend any more time in attempting to make her seaworthy. I will, of course, do as you command, but in this instance, I hope you will let the shipwrights prevail.

Submitted in the honest performance of my duties and in accordance with the instructions issued to me on the day our contract was signed,

Most truly at your service,
Cados Gaspard Adrien Rivage
business factor
Eclipse Trading Company
Le Havre, France

5

Hyacinthie's laughter quickly gave way to tears as she held up the package her uncle had given her: the small box contained an exquisite portrait cameo of her dead mother, certainly valuable as jewelry as well as a memento, but it seemed nothing more than a trivial thing, given the manner in which he had presented it—leaving it on her breakfast plate with only a length of embroidery floss to secure it. She flung herself down on her bed and let herself give way to her roiling emotions. "How *could* he?" she demanded of the thick goose-down comforter that lay folded at the foot. Pressing her face against the glossy satin, she pretended to muffle her sobs. The presentation note that accompanied the brooch dropped from her fingers and seemed to mock her from where it lay on the carpet.

My dear niece,
   On the occasion of your entering the age of marriage.

Your uncle and guardian
von Ravensberg

It was bad enough to be eighteen, but to be reminded so callously that she was single was intolerable. This rebuke—for it could be nothing less than a rebuke—was the harshest he had given her in four years of increasing rejection. How dare he slight her? Had he not pledged his devotion to her a decade ago? Had she been a fool to believe him; he had changed so much in the last four years that she felt she no longer knew him, nor he her. Now she sighed and put her hands together, her face stinging from her concentration and tears, and rolled onto her side, as guileless as a child. She wanted to strike back at him for this dreadful insult. Studying the patterns painted on the ceiling beams, she let herself contemplate how she might best be revenged on Uncle Wallache. One notion took her fancy and she smiled ferociously, certain she had hit upon the very thing that might wound him as deeply as he had wounded her: she should ask him to find her a suitor, someone rich and powerful, someone who would care for her as her uncle had when she was younger, someone who would devote himself to her pleasure and contentment. Then let him try to be indifferent to her. She let this happy notion carry her thoughts to far more pleasant realms than she had been dealing with. Her face softened again, and the hint of a smile that touched her mouth was no longer predatory, but tantalizing. Yes, she would have a suitor, and she would lead him a merry dance; Uncle Wallache would ache with jealousy and need, and she would not feel anything but amusement at his plight.

She sat up and looked at the brooch again. Had her mother really looked like that? Her memory was uncertain: there was a resemblance, she was almost sure of it. On impulse she rose and took a fichu from her chest-of-drawers, pulled it around her shoulders, and secured it with the brooch. For a minute or two, she regarded herself in the mirror over her wash-basin, then nodded her approval. To complete her toilette, she took her bottle of violet cologne and daubed her temples and wrists with the fragrant liquid. With a deliberate little giggle, she flounced out of her room and went in search of her uncle.

A quick search of the Schloss brought her to Herr Arndt Lowengard's office behind the library, where she found her uncle and his man-of-business deep in conversation. She stood in the half-open door, waiting to be noticed.

"—should arrive tomorrow or the next day: two sisters, Lowengard, six and eight. Rosalie and Hedda. They are cousins of my late wife, their parents are dead, and I know it is my duty to take them in." He chuckled, a dry sound, like pebbles underfoot. "I can't very well let the nuns have them, can I?"

"The provisions here are most generous for indigent relatives," Lowengard remarked as he looked at the page in his hand.

"It is expected of me. Girls need protection that boys do not require. Their brother will manage for himself." He rubbed the lapel of his Italian robe. "Rosalie and Hedda. We must make them welcome."

From her place in the door, Hyacinthie curled her hands into fists, nails digging into her palms like claws. Two girls coming? Indigent cousins? She wanted to scream but forced a smile onto her face and giggled.

Both men looked up. "Hyacinthie," said her uncle. "I didn't know you were there."

She broadened her smile painfully. "I wanted to thank you for this brooch. It is so beautiful."

"Good of you," he said, losing interest.

She decided to take a chance. "You said something about two cousins?"

"You wouldn't know them. My late wife's cousins, once removed—their father was my wife's cousin germane, so you and they are not related at all," von Ravensberg corrected, losing patience with his ward. "They will arrive in a day or two. I expect you to welcome them as your sisters. Keep in mind that they are in mourning."

"Of course," she said, bobbing a curtsy, because she knew it was expected of her.

"You need something more to occupy your time than what Frau Schale gives you to study. These two girls will be just what's wanted, filling your hours and preparing you for the married state and motherhood."

Hyacinthie stared. "What do you mean?"

Von Ravensberg sighed and explained. "You have to think about your future, dear niece. What is going to become of you when you are twenty if you have no skills at those many offices that an intelligent man demands of his wife? I am in no position to continue to house you as a dependent, and your other relatives have daughters of their own to see established in the world. So it is fitting that you take advantage of the presence of these girls in order to show your aptitude for woman's most sacred role: motherhood."

This was too much for Hyacinthie to take in, but she continued to smile. "Then you will find me a suitor?"

"And a husband, I should hope," said von Ravensberg, his voice filled with purpose. "I won't have you dwindling into a spinster."

A dozen retorts filled Hyacinthie's thoughts, but she said none of them. "I want to be married, Uncle Wallache."

"Good; good," said von Ravensberg, motioning her away from him.

Lowengard's neck and ears had turned deep red as he listened; now he coughed as if to remind the two of his presence.

Von Ravensberg took the hint. "So run away now, Hyacinthie, and let my man-of-business and me deal with the details of taking on the two girls. Take a turn about the garden, if you like. It is a fine day. I will see you at dinner." Saying that, he put his hand on Lowengard's shoulder. "We must be sure all is in order by the time the two arrive."

Lowengard ducked his head. "As you say, von Ravensberg."

"Ah, good. You remembered this time. Titles were what got so many high-born Frenchmen killed, a generation since. You may call me Professor, if you prefer, but von Ravensberg truly suffices. I cannot have all of us lost in the past."

"No," said Lowengard as the sycophant he was; he drew out another sheet of paper and handed it to von Ravensberg. "If you will review this? It is the same, but for Hedda, not Rosalie."

Hyacinthie let herself out of the room as silently as possible. Her thoughts were in tumult, and she could not hold any one of them clearly for long. She hurried to the side door and let herself out into the walled garden, where flowers and herbs grew in profusion. It was warm in the sunlight but still a bit cool in the shadows, as if winter were touching summer, and the wind off the distant snowy peaks carried the promise of an early return to cold. Below the white, cloudy crests the mountains loomed around them, purple-blue in the hazy light. A large stand of rosemary stopped her, its small purple blossoms adding to the strong fragrance of the needle-like leaves. Ordinarily she would have enjoyed the odor, but now she slapped at the stalks with her fist, trying to break them. June twenty-third was supposed to be a happy day—*her* day. Now this. "Cousins!" she cried. "Rosalie and Hedda. Six and eight. And he takes them in for charity!" She felt an insect on her hand and angrily flung it away. "He took *me* in for charity, and he has discarded me!" Making her way down the flagged path, she stopped at the fountain—not yet spouting water due to damage on its mechanism during the winter—and scooped the shriveled brown leaves out of it stone embrace. "He told me to run away," she mused as she sniffed at this ugly mélange. "I wonder if I should?" Surely, she thought, he would have to come and find me, and the two girls would be left to fend for themselves. Surely he wouldn't put them before her. But she could not forget how he had ceased to visit her, and had been more and more occupied with his work. Would he be glad she was gone, and give all his attention to Rosalie and Hedda? Would he even notice she was missing? He'd probably be relieved not to have to care for her anymore, especially not with two children to hold his attention.

The sound of the kitchen bell caught her attention: dinner would be ready in half an hour. She let herself pout, thinking this would be the last day she would have to herself. It bothered her to contemplate her future, girls and all. She realized she had to find a suitor, and one who would command Uncle Wallache's respect, and it had to be done before the cousins were too deeply sunk in her uncle's affections. Hyacinthie's face felt taut, as if her skin had been shrunken tightly over her bones. "He must take care of me!" she declared. "He must!"

The banging of doors on the far side of the garden announced that the servants were leaving the cow-barn for the Schloss; the sound of their voices drifted over the wall. She recognized Adelinde, the oldest of the three milkmaids, who was recounting some village scandal to her to companions. They seemed so contented, Hyacinthie thought, as though they had not a care in the world but to titter over a rumor. What must it be like, to have nothing to worry you? She contemplated that happy state as she wandered back through the garden, letting the dessicated leaves from the fountain dribble through her fingers.

The small dining room seemed uncomfortably warm; the fireplace was filled with pine logs that spat and filled the air with the scent of burning sap. Von Ravensberg sat at the head of the table, a large glass of white wine by his plate, his elegant jacket protected by the spread of his napkin from his neck to his lap. He nodded to Hyacinthie.

"Good afternoon, Uncle Wallache," she said at her meekest.

"And to you, my girl. Sit down." He beamed at her. "I trust you're pleased to have company coming?"

She swallowed her indignation and said, "I should think so, Uncle.

I have had you and my governess for tutors for so many years, I hardly know what to do."

"Frau Schale will help you, if you have questions." He looked up as a platter of buttered turnips with sliced cabbage was carried in. "Ah. Excellent." After he helped himself to a generous portion, he offered the serving spoon to Hyacinthie. "Good German food, my girl. Make the most of it."

"Of course, Uncle," she said as she chose a small amount of the dish and set the spoon back on the platter with care.

"Later this summer, I plan to take you on a journey westward. There is someone in Trier I want you to meet—not that he is entirely a stranger—and then we must call upon my publisher in Amsterdam." He beamed with self-satisfaction.

Hyacinthie let out a little shriek. "Amsterdam!"

"Why, yes. Eclipse Press has accepted my manuscript on blood. It is a great day for me—a great day."

She wanted to scream *it's my day, too!* but the words stuck in her chest and she only touched her cameo brooch as she brought forth a little sigh. "Congratulations, Uncle. When did you find out?"

"The messenger who came two days ago brought me an offer. Yesterday I penned an acceptance of terms, so in two weeks or so I may expect a formal contract." He began to consume his turnips-and-cabbage, still talking as he chewed. "This is a most encouraging development. I have no doubt it will lead to wide acceptance of my findings."

"How . . . how splendid," she said, her head buzzing with hidden fury.

"It is, it is." He continued to eat with gusto. "I have to tell you, my girl, that this is the very opportunity I have sought for years. I am beside myself with enthusiasm."

"That's wonderful, Uncle Wallache," she said listlessly.

"And coming at just such a time! It is as if my life has emerged from obscurity into renown and delight." He reached over and patted her hand. "Now, if only I can get you properly established in the world, at least one obligation will be behind me."

"But you will have two more obligations," she said, so sweetly that none of her malice showed in her voice or on her face.

"True, true. It befits a man of my position to assume these responsibilities." He took a long draught of wine. "If the weather improves, I may soon restock the wine-cellar. It is time we had some decent vintages laid down again. I anticipate the need to entertain once my work is read in the academic community."

"Yes, Uncle," she said softly and tried to choke down her food.

Werther brought in a tureen of soup, this one made of sausage and chicken meat with herbs and onions. He set this down and got the wide bowls from the cupboard, removed the first-course dishes from the chargers, and set down the bowls, then fetched the spoons. He left the first course in case either von Ravensberg or his ward should want more of it. With a little bow, he left them alone.

"The soup seems especially good today," von Ravensberg announced as he reached for the handsome Baroque ladle. "Let me have your bowl, Hyacinthie."

Obediently she handed it to him, and watched as he all but filled it with the soup. "There. Hold it carefully; it's hot." He had issued the same warning every day for the last eleven years, but she nodded as if she had heard it for the first time; he continued as he always had: "Mind you have bread with it. The strength is in the bread with the meat, not the meat alone."

"Yes, Uncle Wallache," she said, and dutifully took a slice of bread from the basket at arm's-length down the table. She knew it would taste of straw as she spread a little fresh-churned butter on it.

"These two girls—they're going to need a lot of attention from you. They have lost much. You know what it's like, becoming an orphan suddenly." He smacked his lips as he poured out soup for himself. "I depend upon you. Yes, I depend upon you, to shepherd them through their first months here. Let them benefit from your experience, if you will."

"I suppose I can," she said, imagining her uncle in the girls' beds already.

"Calm their little fears, keep them from . . . from making fools of themselves. They may be disconcerted for a time, and you may spare them difficulties." He took the largest slice of bread and slathered it well. "You know how it is."

"Yes," she said tonelessly; when she had told the minister's wife what her uncle did to her at night, when she was nine, the minister had beaten her for lying and ingratitude. Perhaps she could spare the girls that humiliation. Much as she did not want them here, she did not want them exposed to such degradation even more.

"Good; good." He consumed a good portion of soup, finally saying, "This journey to Amsterdam—you will need a few new gowns for it. I will arrange for you to visit Frau Amergau for a fitting some day next week, so she will have them ready in time for your travels. You'll want a walking-dress, a morning-dress, a calling-dress, and something for fancy occasions. I can't have my ward presenting a shabby appearance, not if I intend to marry her well. I might even provide for a dancing-master, so you may participate in the balls in Trier and Amsterdam."

"Thank you, Uncle," she said, despising herself for feeling grateful to him.

"Accept Constanz Medoc and I will consider it money well-spent." He drank more wine, apparently unaware of her widen eyes.

"Constanz Medoc?" she burst out, her eyes filling with tears. "The one who came here two years ago?" She didn't add *the old man,* for he was more than forty.

"Yes; yes." Von Ravensberg nodded. "A very good man, my girl."

"But he's *bald!*" Hyacinthie sobbed, trying to express her repugnance without exposing herself to her uncle's disdain. "And he smells of snuff."

"He's bald because he thinks so much. He is a most upstanding man, with an excellent reputation, one he has worked hard to establish and maintain. He is a very well-respected scholar, one whose work is known throughout Europe. He has been searching for a wife, a woman to ornament his life and tend to his pleasure. He is of an age when he wants children to carry on his name. His expectations are reasonable; the wildness of his youth is gone." He stopped, staring at her. "But you seem distressed."

"Because *I am!*" She pushed back from the table and lurched to her feet. "I don't like him, Uncle Wallache."

"You don't know him, my child. No doubt you have dreamed of a handsome young man who will carry you away to the city. Cities are dangerous places, and handsome young men have poor judgment in such matters. You are trying to suit your dreams to your life, and that is most unwise." He patted the table next to her place. "Sit down; sit down. You're overwrought. I oughtn't to have told you all this so suddenly." He waited while she complied. "You won't have to marry him if you truly dislike him. But you will have to marry someone, and you may decide, after you have a look at the world, that there are many worse men than Herr Medoc, for all his father was a Frenchman. I am in no position to keep you around here forever, and I will not have my niece working as a governess or a tutor. You know how that would reflect upon me, to have you earn your living. That would abash the family. So. A year from now at most, if you have not made another choice, I will accept Herr Medoc's very gracious offer for your hand."

"But how can I find anyone else?" she wailed. "Ravensberg is *leagues* away from *anything*!"

"Perhaps in Amsterdam, or in one of the cities during our travels, you will find a man who suits you, and who is willing to marry you; I will do my utmost to see you have the opportunities you seek," he said without any suggestion of confidence.

She tried to stop the tears from falling, and very nearly succeeded. "Thank you, Uncle Wallache," she told him demurely.

"You must be realistic, my girl," he said sympathetically.

"I have no fortune and you are my only real connection," she recited, repeating the phrase he had told her regularly since she was seven.

"That's right." He glowered at her as he spooned up the soup, then broke off sections of bread and began to sop up the broth.

"You don't want to end up on the shelf. I have nothing to leave you, and I cannot continue to support you—"

"Not with Rosalie and Hedda coming," she interjected.

"Exactly." He popped a bit of soaked bread into this mouth. "You mustn't think that I mean you any harm, of course," he went on as he chewed. "But there are limits. Perhaps, if my work is well-received, I will be able to provide a stipend for the youngsters, but I doubt I can afford to do it for you."

"I see," she said, very coolly now that she had mastered her outrage.

He nodded to her. "You sit down and finish your dinner. You don't have to decide everything right now."

"Not with the girls coming," she said, too brightly.

"Yes. I have set two of the maids to preparing rooms for them, down the hall from mine." He dropped his spoon into the small puddle of soup at the bottom of his bowl. "I'm going to have to assign one of the maids to them permanently, so you will have to share Idune with them."

"As you wish." She moved her soup-bowl aside, its contents largely untouched.

Von Ravensberg persevered. "I know you'll be courteous with them. These accommodations need not be an occasion for distress."

"Certainly not," she said, planning to discover how to reclaim her one privilege—her maid—from the cousins.

He reached for the bell, ringing it emphatically. "They say they have trout today for our fish, with potatoes in a Dutch sauce." He studied her for several seconds, as if truly seeing her for the first time. "Your appetite is lacking, my girl. You should eat something more than those nibbles you've had."

She blinked. "I suppose you're right," she said. "I'll have a good portion of fish," she assured him, wishing she could vanish from the room.

Werther appeared in the door. "Are you ready for the fish?" he asked. "It is ready to be served."

"That and another glass of wine," said von Ravensberg. "And

bring a small glass for my niece. It *is* her Natal Day, and she is now a woman. She should have wine when I do. But no beer. Gentle-women should not drink beer."

"Nein, von Ravensberg," said Werther.

He smiled his approval. "Is it truly trout we're having?"

"So I am told. With potatoes, bacon, and Dutch sauce." He picked up the platter of turnips-and-cabbage. "You'll want more bread, too, I see."

"Soon, lad, soon."

"Yes, Graf—" He stopped himself. "Von Ravensberg," he corrected himself.

"Exactly," said von Ravensberg as the under-chef let himself out of the smaller dining room.

"Thank you for ordering wine for me, Uncle Wallache," Hyacinthie said, suspicious of his sudden magnanimity.

"It is time you learned how to behave as a woman. A sensible man expects to have a sensible wife." Von Ravensberg coughed once. "You must not cause disgrace to me and our family by your conduct, which means you must establish how much wine you may safely drink."

"Oh," she said, lethargy coming over her again like a pall.

"You owe me that much, my girl—not to bring a poor opinion upon me through your carelessness. I have housed and clothed and fed you since you were seven when no other relative would do so." He rapped his knuckles on the table. "You don't realize how the world is. Every aspect of your behavior reflects upon me as your guardian. Never forget that."

"I won't," she promised, and looked toward the door where Werther was returning with a basket of bread, a bottle of pale-yellow wine, and a tulip-shaped glass along with a large covered platter of what smelled like fish. "I will never forget you, Uncle Wallache," she vowed.

Text of a letter from Klasse van der Boom, printer and publisher, Eclipse Press, in Amsterdam, to Saint-Germain Ragoczy, Comte

Franciscus at Château Ragoczy near Lake Geneva, Yvoire, Switzerland; carried by private messenger.

*To the most excellent Comte Franciscus, the greetings of Klasse van
der Boom in Amsterdam on this, the 21st day of July, 1817:*

My very dear Comte,

*Herewith find my account of sales from January to the end of
June. As you can see, sales are up and averaging eight percent per
title, which is a most encouraging sign. I am hoping you will agree to
another expansion of our publication list, and a larger initial print-
run for the three titles I have indicated have enjoyed the greatest
sales of the last year, for I believe we may rely upon those titles to
continue to sell and to attract more readers to these books. I have
broken down the reported sales by month, as much as that can be
determined, and by country, so that you may better appreciate
where the interests of our readers lie.*

*I must also inform you that the new presses of your own design
will be delivered next month, and I remind you that you have expressed the desire to be here to supervise their installation. This
would please me not only for the opportunity it will provide for us to
speak again, but to make certain that the presses are working to
your specifications and satisfaction.*

*The summer has been fairly cool thus far, and I would think you
need not worry that you will encounter oppressive heat in your
travels, but I urge you to discuss with your coachman the requirements you may have for travel in a day. This may be summer, and
the days may be long, but it is also the time when footpads and
highwaymen are most active. Be sure you do not find yourself on
the road at sundown, or be prepared to fight all manner of thieves
for your possessions. Since Napoleon is no longer a menace, many
of his men, left portionless in the world, have taken to outlawry as
a means of preserving body and soul. This, above the usual criminals who prey on travelers. I would not like to see your profits lost
to paying your ransom.*

As soon as the time of your arrival is generally known, I will bespeak rooms for you at whichever hotel suits your purposes most completely. Your courier will also be received with hospitality, and I will take it upon myself to ensure his entertainment. You have only to inform me what concerts and balls you would like to attend and I will see you have the proper invitations. If there is any event you would like to sponsor, I will be honored to put it in motion, if you will let me know what you seek.

Let me address one other point to you: Graf von Ravensberg has declared he will come to Amsterdam to review the pages of his book prior to publication, as he has been afforded the opportunity to do. If you have any desire to meet him, I will find out what his plans are in this regard, and make arrangements for such an engagement. If you would rather not meet this man, then tell me, and I will see that no such encounter occurs.

Believe me to be ever at your service,
Klasse van der Boom
printer and publisher
Eclipse Press
Amsterdam

enclosures: accounts as described above

6

Ragoczy studied his coachman's twisted leg in silence, not looking at the man's contorted face as he inspected the damage done to his body; the heavy dust smirching his black swallow-tail coat and his superfine black unmentionables did not bother him, nor did the smear of blood on his discreetly ruffled white-silk shirt-cuff. Finally he rose from beside the cot on which Ulf Hochvall had been laid; the coachman was dazed by pain but he did his utmost to concentrate on what

Ragoczy told him. "I will set the leg, of course," he said. "It should heal straight if no further damage is done, and he stays off it while the bone mends."

"The coach . . . will need repair," Hochvall confessed.

"It will need replacement," said Ragoczy, unperturbed. "Your repair is more important. I will see you have it, and the time you will need to recuperate. You need not fear that I will not employ you because of this, but I will need to find an alternate for you through the rest of the summer." He wiped his hands and glanced at his two field-hands. "If you will add to your kindness and bear Hochvall into the château, I would be most appreciative."

Jiac Relout nodded to his companion. "I suppose we can do this." He looked up at the sky. "No rain coming yet."

"Certainly not for a day or two," said Ragoczy, indicating the way to the kitchen door into the château. "You should have him within doors before then. I will have bread and drink of your choice ordered for you in thanks for your service." He was already moving toward the door, compelling them to come after him.

"Food and drink. Why not?" said Loys Begen, shrugging before he picked up his end of the cot.

"Careful," warned Relout. "We don't want him to fall."

"No," said Hochvall, his voice suddenly loud and panicky.

Ragoczy paused near the garden-gate. "Yes. You have no need to hurry. Think of how his injuries would feel on you and be gentle with him."

Relout ducked his head and signaled Begen to lift his end of the cot and move on.

It took almost ten minutes to get the cot into the château and to set it down in the antechamber to the pantry. The two field-hands were panting with exertion when they were done, and Begen looked down at Hochvall. "If you must be moved again, someone in the household will have to do it."

"C'est vrai," said Hochvall with emotion; his face was pale and sheened with sweat, and his skin was clammy to the touch, as Ragoczy discovered when he took the coachman's hand.

"Fetch a blanket," he said to the two field-hands. "One of the household staff will find one for you."

"It is a warm day, Comte," said Begen.

"It may be, but this man is cold, and in his condition, such cold is dangerous." He turned as he heard a discreet knock on the door. "Who is it?"

"Rogier," said his manservant from the hallway.

"Ah. Very good," said Ragoczy. "Will you bring me a blanket—one of the light-weight woollen ones, if you would?"

"Of course," said Rogier.

"There. Now you need not be put to the trouble of doing it," said Ragoczy to Relout and Begen. He reached into his waistcoat pocket and drew out two gold coins. "For your trouble. They are English guineas. Any reputable bank will honor them."

The field-hands, who had never set foot in any bank, took the money and ducked their heads; they would keep their treasure in their hidden strong-boxes. "Many thanks, Comte," they said almost in unison.

"And mine to you," said Ragoczy. "Now, let me tend to Hochvall before his condition grows worse."

"What about the coach?" Relout asked.

"I suppose it should be levered out of the ditch, at the very least," said Ragoczy, "and the road shored up so that it will not happen again. The three sound horses should be stabled and groomed, then turned out in the paddock until sundown, and observed for signs of tie-ups or bruises. I will examine the fourth animal in an hour or two, and dress his cuts. If you and four men will tend to the horses and the road after you have had your refreshments, I will pay for your efforts." He was bending over Hochvall, his manner slightly preoccupied as he took stock of the coachman's worsening condition. "Post a lad on either side of the damage to warn others of the danger. I will pay for their service, as well."

"Yes, Comte," said Relout.

Rogier came into the room without knocking. "I have the blanket you asked for, my master, one of good size," he said in the Venetian dialect, and handed over a large, dense, satin-edged blanket of Ankara goats-wool. "This should keep him warm without being heavy."

"An excellent choice, old friend," said Ragoczy, taking the blanket and spreading it carefully over Hochvall. "Next a tisane, a soothing one, and the vial of syrup of poppies. He should sleep through a cavalry assault then. And if you will show these two good men to the kitchen for their bread and drink. When they are finished, please accompany them to the site of the wreck."

"Certainly. This way," said Rogier to Begen and Relout; the two men were glad to leave the room, and made for the kitchen with alacrity. Rogier led them to the workers' room and summoned Uchtred. "These men have borne Hochvall home, and they deserve something more than a glass of beer and a slice of bread."

"Hochvall is hurt?" Uchtred asked, his large eyes seeming to grow even larger.

"There was an accident. A portion of the road gave way and the coach was damaged. One of the horses was cut up; Hochvall was thrown off the driving-box into the ditch. He was injured; how badly I do not yet know. The Comte is attending to him now." He motioned to Begen and Relout to sit at the long plank table. "Is there a sausage and pickles you might be willing to spare?"

"And cheese," said Uchtred. "Poor Hochvall." He paused for a moment, then said, "I have beer. Jervois will bring these things to you."

The field-hands exchanged uneasy glances. "We can get food for ourselves," said Relout.

"The Comte prefers that his guests be served, as a sign of respect," said Uchtred.

Once more Begen and Relout faltered, unused to such courtesy from a man of the Comte's position. Finally Relout took a seat and reached for a trencher. "If it pleases the Comte, we are his to command."

Rogier excused himself, promising to return shortly.

Uchtred smiled as he left the two alone for a short while, returning with a pitcher of beer and two tankards. As he poured for the men, he said, "You may want coffee, in addition to the beer."

"The day is too warm for coffee," said Relout, taking the brimming tankard in hand and lifting it to his lips. "This is most welcome."

Begen said nothing, but drank deeply before setting down his tankard and nodding his approval.

"Then I'll go prepare your tray. It will not take me long, so you needn't fret," said Uchtred, and left the men alone. In the kitchen, he summoned Jervois. "Bring the cheese—the pale round, if you will, a board and a knife to slice it. There are two working-men to feed."

Jervois, who was fifteen and in his second year of service, gave a small, disapproving shake of his head even as he obeyed. "Why so much courtesy? These men are laborers, already paid for their services. Field-hands should be happy to be useful to the Comte; they should not take advantage of his liberality."

"Would you say that if you were a field-hand? They have done work beyond their hiring, and that deserves distinction, or so the Comte says. It is his way, and so we must honor it." He went into the pantry to choose a sausage, and emerged with a long, dense tube of spiced boar and venison cured with pepper, coriander, and smoke. Using a heavy kitchen knife, he cut a good portion of the sausage and sliced the portion onto a wooden trencher. "Butter, too, Jervois."

The youngster nodded after a minute hesitation. "I will," he said, and made his way out of the château, returning from the creamery with a tub of butter. "Yesterday's. Enough for dinner and those men. Today's isn't done yet. Therese said she won't get to it until after dinner. The day is too hot for the butter to catch, so she is cooling the milk in the creamery."

"Yesterday's should be sweet still, even in this weather. No doubt the men will be satisfied with it," said Uchtred, pulling a lipped platter toward him, setting a jar of mustard sauce in the middle of it, and beginning to select pickles to array around it. When he had achieved a presentation that satisfied him, he stood back. "There." His expression changed, darkening with his recollections. "You may not remember how many times we were raided for food during the wars; you were still a child, not aware of how things went on around you. War meant more than guns; it meant raids and confiscation. After the wars came hard winters. If the Comte were not a man of foresight, we could not maintain the expectations of guests in the château as we are doing. There is still food in the larder, enough to see us beyond the harvest. To have this bounty to give to working-men is an achievement. It has been some time since we could offer proper hospitality to those who came here, and many still cannot. Let us not lose track of our duty."

"Napoleon was greedy," declared Jervois, repeating his parents' complaints. "My two brothers followed him, and died for it."

"Many men followed him and died for it," said Uchtred preparing to take the food in to the two field-hands. "Don't linger with them—they'll assume we don't trust them," he warned. "It is unseemly to distrust guests."

"But we *don't,* do we," said Jervois. "Field-hands have taken as much as soldiers. And abandoned as many children."

"The same reason for all—they were hungry," said Uchtred. "The merchants had raised their prices and turned away apprentices."

"All the more cause to be careful of these men," said Jervois as if he were decades older and experienced in the ways of the commercial world. "Better to be circumspect now than to be sorry later."

"You will not hover over them, nor will you spy upon them. The Comte has invited them to his table. They have the right to our reservation of judgment. See you treat them well." He motioned Jervois away and resumed his preparation of the mid-day meal for the household. At least, he thought, they were not going to have to eat rabbit. He had cooked nothing but rabbits and scrawny birds for three full years during the height of Napoleon's belligerence, and had sworn never to do so again: it was lamb and pork and venison, fish, and occasionally veal from now on, with fresh eggs and butter, and new, wheaten bread. He looked around the kitchen in satisfaction, and smiled as he considered all the provisions in the smokehouse and storerooms in the cellars of the château. He was turning two fat game-birds on a spit in the main kitchen hearth for the widow's dinner when he heard someone come into the kitchen behind him.

"The Comte has set Hochvall's leg and given him a sleeping draught; he should not wake until tomorrow; sleep will ease him through his first hard hours of recovery," Rogier told the chef, thinking back to the many times that Ragoczy had taken charge of the care of injured men in the past. "The Comte knows what will be best for Hochvall: he will remain in the pantry antechamber for tonight. Tomorrow he will be moved to his own quarters. I will have one of the household servants watch him for tonight and tomorrow, and longer if it seems a good precaution, to be sure no greater ills develop."

"No doubt that will please Hochvall," said Uchtred. "Which servant are you going to appoint to watch him?"

"Either Hildebrand or Ulisse. Neither should impinge upon you very directly."

"Footmen," said Uchtred in a tone of unconcern. "Ulisse is accompanying the widow on her daily walk, but Hildebrand is in the side-garden, airing out the withdrawing-room cushions. Dietbold is cleaning the silver in the Grand Hall." He felt smug that he—the chef—should have such information to offer; he hoped he was showing himself to be the equal of Balduin. He often took advantage of the steward's absence to demonstrate his comprehensive grasp of the household.

"I will inform Hildebrand of his new work at once; I may assign Dietbold to sit with Hochvall tonight; it will be Dietbold or Silvain, depending upon which of them is better-rested," said Rogier. "I suppose Balduin is still in the village?"

"So I assume; he has not returned to the château, in any case. I have held dinner back an hour so he could plan to eat with the rest of us, as is fitting for one in his position. It is observations like this that keep the household functioning properly." Uchtred managed a superior smile. "The widow should be back from her walk shortly. I will order the dining room readied for the meal."

"And we are still expecting Otto Gutesohnes tomorrow or the next day?" Rogier asked, although he knew the answer.

"That is my understanding," said Uchtred primly. "You have had no news to the contrary, have you?"

"No, nor have you," said Rogier.

"Then he should be here. He has been reliable on his first errand—why not on his second?"

"I will be relieved to see him, and so will the Comte," said Rogier, going to the cauldron hanging over the hearth and preparing to take a measure of soup from it. "In case Hochvall wants something to eat. He will do better with soup than with bread. Be certain it is hot."

"If that is what the Comte wants," said Uchtred.

"It is what will suit Hochvall best," said Rogier.

"As you say," Uchtred conceded, and basted the plump fowl with butter mixed with lemon-rind and minced scallions; he watched the stones sizzle as the run-off splashed. "An hour and I'll summon the household."

Rogier nodded. "You are an ornament to your profession, Uchtred." With that compliment, he left the kitchen and sought out Ragoczy, who was in his study, poring over a number of letters that had been delivered from Yvoire that morning. "Dinner will be ready in an hour, Uchtred says." He spoke in the Latin of the first century, in the dialect of Roman merchants.

"The household will be pleased," said Ragoczy in the same tongue, breaking the seal on a letter from Rome, which he scanned quickly, reporting as he read. "I fear the villa needs a new roof," he said. "The vinyards are flourishing, and the fields are much recovered from the winters. Lambing has gone well, and calving. Piero is certain that a good harvest this year and the next and all should be satisfactory again."

"Piero is always careful," said Rogier, his tone showing his approval more than his demeanor. "Is the news as good from Lago Como?"

"I have not yet heard from Stanislao." He put the letter down. "I'll send Piero authorization for the roof as soon as possible."

"By Gutesohnes?" Rogier suggested, anticipating the answer.

"I fear I have need of him in his capacity of coachman, so I must engage another courier. With Hochvall unavailable until autumn, I must either hire a coachman, or ask Otto Gutesohnes to do this for me." He shrugged. "If he refuses, then I will have to seek out another coachman for the summer."

"Gutesohnes is a sensible man; he will be willing to drive your coaches for you," said Rogier. "How badly is Hochvall hurt?"

"Two breaks in the leg, one in the femur, one in the fibulae. The second was trickier to set but the more apt to heal cleanly now that the alignment is made. It is difficult to feel the bone under the calf-muscles, but—"

"—you have some experience in these matters," said Rogier with an expression that bordered on a smile.

"Precisely," said Ragoczy.

Rogier took the letters Ragoczy had set aside and began to separate them in anticipation of filing them later. "There is news from Persia?"

"Yes." Ragoczy frowned. "I will need to make up my mind what to do about my holdings there, and sooner rather than later."

"Will you need a second courier for that?" Rogier inquired.

"Very likely. Perhaps that Greek messenger, the one who has carried letters from Turkey. He has been reliable and quick, and Kypris vouches for him. No doubt more couriers will be needed in a year or so, as science increases our desire for rapid information." He thought for more than a minute, then said with a touch of amusement, "In many ways it was easier, three centuries ago. Messages moved slowly, and not always reliably, but it was understood that such things took time, and nothing could be done to hurry a fast horse, especially in bad weather. Now, with ships plying the oceans and more roads than

ever the Romans made, speed has become a factor no one can ignore. Decisions must be made in days, not months, and information
must travel as swiftly as time and tide will allow."

"For a thousand years, you lamented how slow such communications had become once Rome no longer controlled Europe and
the roads were neglected," said Rogier with a trace of dry humor.

"So I did, and now I have my comeuppance." He studied the
next letter. "I think it would be prudent to open offices for Eclipse
Shipping in Baltimore as well as New York. From what Mannerling
says, there is less graft in Baltimore, and industry is expanding there.
It is not so closed as Boston, according to Mannerling."

"Graft is everywhere," said Rogier, preparing to leave the study.
"You cannot hope to escape it."

"Certainly that is so; but some cases are less egregious than
others, which is what I would prefer to find," said Ragoczy, opening another sealed envelope. "Ah. This is about the damage to my
country estate in Poland. It appears that the main house is a ruin,
and only one barn is sound enough for reconstruction. All the rest
will have to be built afresh." He tapped the letter against his
palm. "This will take some negotiating to keep it from becoming a
debacle."

"Anything from Kreuzbach about the castle above Zemmer?
You are planning to visit it on your way to Amsterdam, are you not?"

"Just the report of ten days ago," said Ragoczy. "And, no, I will
not be deterred from pursuing the restoration of my Polish estate.
Too much of the region was damaged, and too many farmers and
craftsmen are in need of work and protection. Rebuilding the estate
will provide wages and shelter, and that is—" He set the letter
down. "I believe Hero has returned."

"It does sound that way," said Rogier.

There was a wry lift to Ragoczy's fine brows as he met Rogier's
steady gaze. "No, she is not the companion of my heart that Madelaine is, but she is a woman of integrity and passion, which suits me
very well. And I do not intrude on the enshrined memory of her
husband, which suits her."

"I said nothing," Rogier reminded him.

"But you are worried that I have withheld some portion of intimacy from Hero—which I have. Just as she has kept a part of herself inviolate." He went and opened the door. "I am satisfied, and so is she."

"Perhaps too satisfied?" Rogier suggested. "You long for Madelaine."

"Yes, but it is an impossible yearning, since neither of us has life to give the other." He continued on in slightly old-fashioned French. "I do not think you have any reason to be concerned, old friend."

"If you tell me so, what can I be but satisfied?" said Rogier, and pulled the door closed behind them.

Hero stood in the corridor, two envelopes clasped in her hands. "My father-in-law has written again," she said. She had removed her bonnet and her lace gloves; her face was slightly flushed from the heat of the day.

"So I see," Ragoczy said as he came up to her. "Whoelse has written to you? You have two letters."

"My oldest son. Siegfried. He's eleven, and will soon go to school—in the autumn." She looked over the ends of the envelopes to Ragoczy. "Comte, I am afraid to open them."

"Small wonder," said Ragoczy, "given how strictly the Graf has controlled your communication with your children."

"He is careful with them, and knows his responsibilities," said Hero automatically.

"And uses them as a Hussar uses a saber," said Ragoczy, his voice light and cutting at once.

"You make him seem a monster." She took the letter from the Graf and broke its seal.

"Because I think he is. It is not his intention—most monsters have no notion of their enormities—but it is a great unkindness to you and your children. Done for the best of worst of reasons, his actions cause you pain." His dark eyes looked steadily into hers. "You go in fear of him because you do not wish to lose all contact with your sons and daughter. For a family to be sundered as yours has been is cruelty."

"No, Comte. Don't say that." She spread the letter within and scanned it quickly. "He is encouraging Siegfried to tell me himself of the school he will attend."

"The same one his father attended?" Ragoczy guessed. "Your husband?"

"Yes," said Hero. "How did you know?"

"It seems the sort of thing your father-in-law would do," said Ragoczy.

Hero read the rest of the Graf's letter. "The twins are well, and Annamaria has recovered from the putrid sore throat she had in April." She smiled a bit too brightly, refolded the letter, and opened the one from Siegfried. "Oh! His grandfather has chosen a horse for him to take with him to school."

"A considerable gift for such a young child," said Ragoczy.

"That it is, and Siegfried is most grateful to his grandfather," said Hero. "I could never have provided so well for him." The sadness in her voice ended on a quiver; she pressed her lips together and hoped her eyes would not fill with tears. "He says it is seven years old, trained for hunting, and that his summer is being devoted to improving his riding skills so that he may ride to school with his tutor in the autumn."

"He will be the envy of his classmates, no doubt." Ragoczy saw Rogier motion to him from the end of the corridor. "Yes?"

"Dinner will be served in half an hour," Rogier announced. "I am putting Ulisse to watch over Hochvall."

"Hochvall?" Hero asked, startled. "What is the matter with Hochvall?"

"He had an accident earlier today and broke his leg," said Ragoczy. "He is recovering from having it set."

"An accident?" She paled. "How serious an accident?"

"A portion of the road gave way, or so I have been told, and the coach fell sideways into the ditch," he said calmly. "Three of the horses fared well enough, but one has been injured, and I will have to attend to him this afternoon. Hochvall had the worst of it: he was thrown from the box. He sustained a lump on his head, a broken right leg, and a bruised shoulder."

"And the coach? Is it badly damaged?" She stared at him as if trying to read his expression.

"It is best left for firewood," said Ragoczy, and held up his small hand to stop her volley of questions. "I know little more than what I have told you, and will not know more until I have seen what is left of the coach."

"But if it is so . . . so damaged, we cannot travel in it, can we?" Hero stared at him, trying to read what was in his mind.

"Not in the old one, no: I will order a new one in a day or two, once I know what our traveling needs will be, and once I have determined whether or not Gutesohnes will drive for me until Hochvall recovers."

She blinked. "You appear to have considered the whole; there is nothing I can do now, is there?" she said, adding playfully, "I suppose it is too much to hope you might dine with me?"

His smile lasted a little longer this time. "Later," he promised her as he offered his arm to her and started toward the dining room.

Text of a letter from Madelaine de Montalia in Varna on the Black Sea, to Saint-Germain Ragoczy, Comte Franciscus at Château Ragoczy near Lake Geneva, Yvoire, Switzerland; carried by academic courier and delivered two months after it was written., while Ragoczy was returning from Amsterdam.

To my most dear Saint-Germain, the greetings of your Madelaine de Montalia, just as present—the 4th of August—in Varna

As you can see, I have not yet reached Egypt, but I am determined to do so, and as soon as possible. In the meantime I am occupying myself with various ancient buildings and ruins about this port, some of which are most fascinating. I do not yet know how much longer I will stay here before returning to Constantinople, or as the Turks pronounce it, Istanbul. I was kept dancing at the doors of various officials for almost nine months before I set out to find places of interest while I struggle to get from this place to the Nile. I begin to think I will have to purchase my way into an authorized expedition or languish here for a decade.

You have said that the horses in this part of the world are superb, and I am sure you're right, although they look a little small to me. If I were more amused with riding, I might spend a week or two investigating the regional breeds. But I am not as fond of high-couraged mounts as the Ottomans are, and I am not tempted to careen across hard-baked ground or dry riverbeds to see how willing the horse is to submit to my will, although I long for a good gallop, now and again. I did have a fine afternoon on a large ass, one that rarely moved above a trot and preferred a steady pace to anything more dramatic. He carried me from a ruined monastery on a hill behind the harbor to the old Greek ruins near to what the local people call the Spring of the Virgins. I have yet to find out much about these Virgins, although I have asked. The Orthodox priests who will deign to talk to me—a Catholic and an unmarried woman!—tell me it was once the site of the manifestation of the Virgin Mary, but the fallen pillars are very old and Greek, so I suspect there is another, much older, source of the legend. The guide who accompanied me on this excursion is a fellow called Eteocles Hadad, and a fascinating rogue he is, more full of tales than the local story-teller, and curious as a hungry cat. He speaks a smattering of Arabic, Albanian, Russian, Hungarian, Greek, Slovak, Croatian, Albanian, Italian, French, and who-knows-how-many other odd dialects from off the ships that call here.

How I have wandered through that last paragraph! It is as peripatetic as I have been, and as disoriented, in every sense. I will blame it on the heat, which is thick in the air and sodden as an old sail. Even I am affected by it, and not simply because of the sunlight. I have spent the last four nights sitting out on the inner balcony of this hostelry so that I can take in enough of the little breeze and the night to help me make it through the day. I have enough of my native earth to last for another six months, but I am beginning to think that I should send for it now, in case this heat should continue. I will ask your shipping office in Athens to get Montalia earth for me, if you are willing to permit me to do this. Your suggestion that I purchase more holdings in Europe is probably a good one, and I intend to act upon your recommendation as soon as I return. Since I am as yet unsure when that will be, I cannot select a time by which this will be accomplished, yet be sure it will not be more than a decade. To think I will be a century old in another seven years! I am astonished to add up the decades, but there they are. You were right when you warned me that it is difficult to see your contemporaries fall away until only you remain, and that it is distressing to realize that all of youth is gone, no matter what appearance may remain. I am more ancient than any woman I have met save one—a nun who was ninety-six—but she was as wrinkled as a raisin and as bent as a willow. Yet we were almost the same age, although I still seem to be no more than nineteen or twenty. It is a luxury to know time as an ally, not an opponent, but time also creates a gulf no one but those of your blood, or of your restoration, like Roger, can cross.

There is so much to learn, and I know I will not have to limit myself for the demands of years. Still, learning creates a trail that may prove too easily followed, especially if I take my lovers among my colleagues. You were right to warn me about choosing my knowing partners with care. I have kept your admonitions in mind with every new encounter, and so far have revealed myself only twice. You, of course, understand my predicament, and I feel you can comprehend my ambivalence without jealousy or a desire to approve my decisions. I know that you and I seek life before all else, since it is the one thing we lack, and that neither of us would deny the other the fulfillment that is the very core of existence for us. I am pleased to hear that you have made a friend of Hero von Scharffensee, for she truly needs friends. As the daughter of Attilio Corvosaggio, I know she is a woman of good education and well-trained mind, but I also know that her father is not of a temperament that would incline him to take her in, and her four children. All his purpose is set upon scholarship and the discovery of antiquities. On those occasions when I have met him, I have been struck afresh with the singularity of his devotion.

So you have the comfortable life and companion you seek, and I have my explorations, and we are able to live with the knowledge that all of our undead lives will make this demand of us—that we must sustain ourselves on the passions of the living, not our Blood Bond with each other. You have much more experience of this than I, yet I can sense your feelings for me are as enduring as you yourself, no matter what your feelings for others may be.

I astonish myself at how reasonable I am; I realize this may be my own inclination to avoid any hint of animosity from you, which would be unbearable, or it may be acceptance of our natures, but whichever it is—or something else entirely—I am relieved to know that no matter what may come, the love and the Bond we share will remain unbroken from now until time loses all hold upon us. And before I become maudlin, I will end this by wishing you a pleasant good-night from the city of Varna, a place that stinks of low tide and fish.

*Now and forever
Your Madelaine*

7

Herr Perzeval Einlass stood aside so that Ragoczy could examine his new coach, a modified Berlin but with elements of a Parisian landau, an attractive, modern carriage that would command attention for its elegance anywhere in Europe. It occupied the sunniest part of Herr Einlass' courtyard, immediately adjacent to his warehouse; half a dozen craftsmen lingered in the warehouse door, waiting to hear what the Comte would say. "All the modifications you requested are complete: eight elliptical springs, just as you required, Herr Comte," said Einlass. "The box has its own set of springs as well, so that the driver need not fear that he will be thrown from his place. As you see, the box is placed deeper in the body of the coach, as you requested, and there are braces on either side of the driving-box. The wheels are lip-rimmed and the spokes are reinforced, as are the axles."

"Yes," said Ragoczy, squinting a little in the bright morning. "And the interior done with padded arms for the passengers to use? Long hand-straps as well?"

"Of course. And in your servants' coach, as you stipulated. My men will fit it out as soon as you have the coach brought down to my warehouse: all the modifications we made to your coach but the device that turns the seats into a bed. It will take less than a day to make the changes." He paused. "Most men wouldn't do so much for servants. You are catering to their comfort as much as you are accommodating your own." His expression showed that he considered this to be a bit too much indulgence for servants. He strode the length of the shiny new vehicle. Heavily burled Alpine fir was set-off by panels glossily black with lacquer, and the windows had black-leather curtains. "I could still arrange for your device to be painted on the door-panel, Comte," he suggested. "It would be a handsome addition to a handsome vehicle."

"Very generous, but I think not," said Ragoczy. "In these republican days I think it is prudent to keep titles unannounced. No matter how nations are led, their people are now deciding their course, and it may not always include recognizing nobles." He had a brief, intense recollection of the crowds in Lyon, and the narrow escape he and Madelaine had had, thanks to the de Montalia device on her traveling trunks. The howls of the mob seemed to sound in his ears again, and he said more firmly, "The coach is elegant as it is, and suits my purposes."

Hero, who was standing a few steps away, her parasol raised against the August sun, now came up to Ragoczy, saying, "I think Gutesohnes will like it."

"The balance should please him," said Ragoczy, once more inspecting the tiered springs. "We should have less sway and more comfort over rough roads."

"I have made the changes you wanted in the seats," said Einlass. "The device you have contrived is a clever one, and I would imagine many another traveler would be glad of such improvements in his coach. Many would pay well for these improvements. It could make travel more pleasant for those who wanted your modifications, Comte." His implication was plain—that Ragoczy could make a profit if he would license Herr Einlass to provide these modifications for others.

"Let me test them out on my journey to Amsterdam," said Ragoczy firmly but without loss of geniality. "If they perform as I anticipate, then perhaps we should have a discussion." He regarded the coach-maker for a long moment, seeing something crafty in his demeanor. "You, of course, would not provide my modification to any others without securing proper contracts first, would you?"

Einlass' eyes flickered. "No, Comte. Of course not."

Ragoczy shook his head. "Tell whomever you have offered my modifications to that you will not be able to provide them for yet a while. They have not yet been rigorously tested, and until they are, it would be premature to offer them to others." His voice was cordial but there could be no mistaking his purpose.

"Yes. I will. Of course," said Einlass, all deference. "It is just that your innovations are so . . . so . . ."

"Practical?" Ragoczy suggested; in the two centuries he had been adding such modifications to his coaches, he had been able to refine them to a state of utmost utility. "Advantageous?"

"Exactly!" Einlass enthused. "Those clips you have for the curtains, top and bottom, they are also a most pragmatic addition for the traveler. Do they need to be tested?"

"Another thing we can discuss later," said Ragoczy as he held out his hand to Hero. "Would you like to inspect the interior?"

"Yes, please," she said; she closed her parasol and allowed him to assist her into the new coach.

"The upholstery is just as you required, Comte," Einlass assured him. "The colors are the colors you chose."

"Because this is the cloth I supplied. You would be hard-pressed to find it anywhere in Europe." He stood in the open door. "Are you comfortable, Madame?"

"I am," she said. "So many windows, and such well-padded seats." She ran her hand over the rich damask silk that covered the seats, walls, and ceiling of the interior. "You've thought of everything."

"Probably not, but I have anticipated most problems, or so I hope." Ragoczy moved out of the doorway and gave his attention to Einlass. "I will send my coachman tomorrow morning with the team and the harness."

"Grays?" Einlass asked, knowing the Comte's penchant for gray horses.

"No: matched liver sorrels," he answered. "Very elegant animals, all four of them, from the same sire; sixteen hands with strong forward action. I had them from a breeder near Verona." Although it was more than two hundred years since Olivia had died the True Death, he never missed her more than when he was buying horses.

"They are at the château; they arrived just eight days ago," said Hero in a carrying voice as she prepared to emerge from the vehicle. "Very fine animals. Their coats are so dense a brown they are almost purple, and their manes and tails are pure flaxen. They will set off this coach admirably."

"Will you take them all the way to Amsterdam?" Einlass asked. "You keep teams at inns along the road, I know."

"It will depend on how we do. If we go straight through, then we will need to change teams on the way, possibly at Liège and Saarbrücken, or Zemmer. If, however, we spend a day or two along the road to allow the team to rest, then I may not change them until Amsterdam." Ragoczy helped Hero to come down from the coach. "Do you think you will enjoy the journey?"

She nodded. "Oh, yes. This will be much easier than traipsing about after my father."

"Very likely," said Ragoczy with a nod to Einlass. "Be ready for my coachman—Otto Gutesohnes is his name."

"Your courier?" Einlass was a bit surprised.

"Hochvall is recovering from an injury; Gutesohnes is driving for me while he does," said Ragoczy.

"I had heard something of the sort," Einlass admitted as if he rarely listened to gossip. "Very well. Everything will be ready after eight o'clock."

"I assume the payment I provided was sufficient to your supplies and labor?" Ragoczy asked, well-aware that the sum he had advanced Einlass was more than sufficient for the work he and his men had done.

"You have a credit with me, one that I will provide in my accounting at month's end." Einlass bowed, then wiped the sweat from his forehead, doing his best to keep a determined smile on his face and reminding himself that all patrons should be as forthcoming and generous as Comte Franciscus.

"Thank you," said Ragoczy, and started across the courtyard to where his calash was waiting, two striking gray horses harnessed to it. The top was down, so as Ragoczy lowered the steps he gave Hero his arm to assist her into the carriage, lending her his stability as she mounted the narrow steps. When she was settled Ragoczy climbed into the driving-box, took the reins and the whip, loosened the brake, and put his pair in motion. As he tooled the calash out into the street, he said over his shoulder, "Would you like to stop for dinner, or would you prefer to return directly to the château?"

"How long will it take to reach the château?" she asked, her parasol open and her face in its shadow.

"Just over two hours, I should think," said Ragoczy.

"Two hours," she repeated. "The horses are not too tired in this heat? They would not be worn down?"

"Not too exhausted, no. And they have been watered and walked while we saw the coach." He could feel the pair pull on their bits as he kept them to a strict walk along the cobbled streets; they were ready to return home.

"I think I would prefer to go back to the château, then," she said after a brief silence. "I wouldn't like to be on the road in the late afternoon. They say that robbers are attacking travelers, and there are more abroad after sundown."

Ragoczy, who carried a primed pistol in the deep pocket of his four-caped driving-coat, said only, "Robbers can rob at any time of the day or night."

"But they more often prowl at night," said Hero, frowning a little. "Darkness aids them, light works against them."

"Probably so," said Ragoczy, expertly threading his pair through the confusion of wagons, carriages, carts, buggies, traps, and coaches that filled the streets of Yvoire. At the market-square where potters displayed their wares, Ragoczy pulled his horses in to a slow walk, saying to Hero, "These wares are fragile. I would not like to damage any in a rush to leave the town."

"No doubt the potters know what they can afford to lose," said Hero, then sat up, chagrined by what she realized sounded like callousness. "I didn't mean that, not entirely. I meant that they know not to put their most valuable work where it could be broken."

"I should hope so," he said, and edged the calash past a large wagon laden with haunches of smoked meat.

As they went along the edge of the market where fruits and flowers were sold, Hero said, "It looks as if there will be more fruit this year again."

"Wise housewives will still make preserves and comfits, and put up berries in brandy, in case the cold returns," said Ragoczy.

"Or there is another war," added Hero as she heard a distant roll of thunder from the clouds piled up against the mountains. "We will be late for dinner, won't we?" Without waiting for an answer, she settled back, and said nothing more until the town was behind them and the horses were moving at a steady trot down the dusty road. As they passed over a narrow stone bridge, she said, "There seems so much to do before we depart. Do you truly plan that we should leave for Amsterdam at the end of this week? That is only three more days."

"Yes. I can see no reason for more delay, and after the first full day of travel, we will be glad to have a day to rest." He noticed movement at the side of the road and saw a fox sitting in the bushes, calmly unimpressed by the calash.

"There is so much to do." She stretched out one hand as if to try to gather in everything that had to be dealt with.

"Inform Rogier of your needs, and he will make sure the maids have all your things ready. Take what you would like—the coach can carry a fair amount of luggage." He checked the grays as they came to the turn-off for the château. "This won't be like following your father into the desert, or preparing for an expedition to distant ruins, you know. Amsterdam is a proper city, and you need not fret—anything that you may wish to replace, you will be able to find without trouble."

She laughed. "I know that. The habits of my youth stay with me; I never travel but I believe I must take provisions of all sorts for a year, and everything that I might need in any circumstances, no matter how unlikely." She leaned back on the squabs once more, then asked, "Do any habits of your youth linger, after so long?"

"Other than my nature?" he inquired. "There may be a few, faint echoes. I always remember that I was born at the dark of the year, during the five days of the Solstice. It was the time of my birth that selected me to join the priests of my people, and to be one with them upon my death."

"The Solstice is a single day," she said, a bit startled that he should make such an error.

"In these enlightened times, yes, but I was born almost four thousand years ago; the priests who protected my people had to measure the long nights by the burning of measured amounts of oil; this could not be precise to the exact day, but it could show the five days that were dark the longest." His dark eyes were distant. "For some reason, I cannot, even now, fail to count the years."

"Does that sadden you?" she could not keep from asking.

"Occasionally. There was a time—many centuries ago—when such reckoning only served to bring me pain, for it reminded me of what I had lost, and I could not yet comprehend how much I had gained. I had only loathing and dread around me, and no means of learning, since I knew only a few words of the languages of my various captors. I found a barbaric justification in my ferocity then. That was before I understood that the blood is touching, and that touching nourishes more than this un-dead body, which is beyond nourishment of that kind: intimacy restored my humanity and brought me to value all life for its uniqueness and its brevity. If you decide to rise at your death, you will learn these things for yourself. Unless you plan to die the True Death at the end of this life, you will have my life, and will have to learn what I have learned. You needn't decide now, but before you die, you will need to choose what you will do." In the silence that followed this warning, he reached the gate to his château, reined in the pair, set the brake, and jumped down from the driving-box to unlatch the gate and swing it open. He secured the gate, returned to the calash, drove through the gate, halted the horses, got down to close the gate, then climbed back onto the box and drove the last tenth part of a league to the stable. "Clement!"

The head groom was already emerging from the stable, half-running toward Ragoczy's carriage, two other grooms following in his wake. "Comte," he said, not quite bowing as he came to a halt.

"The wheeler has a loose on-side front shoe. Other than that, they'll need to be walked for a quarter hour, then brushed. Have Joachim tend to the shoe after they're fed, and he has had his supper."

"He's in the smithy. I'll tell him," said Clement.

"And do you know if Gutesohnes is in his quarters?"

"He is tooling the spider around the orchard, working in the young English bay," said Clement. "He said he was getting ready for the journey to Amsterdam, loosening up his arms."

"Will you tell him I would like to see him in my study when he returns?" Ragoczy asked.

"Of course, Comte," said Clement.

"Thank you." He got down from the box, assisted Hero out of

the carriage, and watched while Clement attached a lead-rope to the chin-strap of the lead gray's bridle. "There may be a thunder-storm this afternoon, so keep this pair in the exercise arena in the stable; turn out any horse who gets restless into the arena with them until the storm passes. I do not want them to kick their stalls to flinders."

"We'll attend to it." Clement, who was half-a-head taller than Ragoczy, deferred to him automatically, whistling to the grays as he led them away, the calash rattling along the flag-stones that marked the front of the château.

"What shall we do now?" Hero asked, putting her hand through the crook of his arm.

"You will want to compile your list for Rogier; I will make sure the household prepares for our absence. Decide whether Wendela or Serilde will accompany you, and have her choose a portmanteau for her clothes. I will join you after you have supper, and we can spend a private evening in the bath, if you like."

Her smile broadened. "That would please me very much, espe-cially the bath," she said, as she furled her parasol and allowed him to open the door and usher her into the château. "I will attend to the lists and other matters of travel before supper, do not fear. And while I dine, I will decide which of my maids will accompany me. I will look for you in the antechamber of the bath after sundown." She leaned over to kiss his cheek. "And I promise I will think about what you said just now."

"I will be at your service, after sundown," he promised her, and went off to his study, where he received Otto Gutesohnes some ninety minutes later, just as the sky began to darken and the clouds took on a lurid, bruised light.

Gutesohnes was covered in dust and his brow shone with grimy sweat, but he was smiling as he accepted Ragoczy's offer to sit down. "That English bay works well between the shafts. I wouldn't have thought he'd do well as a single horse, but I've changed my mind. Keep him for the lighter carriages and the lanes, and he'll give real satisfaction."

"Very good to know," said Ragoczy. "I had hoped he might prove good for solo harness."

"He should. It would be wise to have a horse for these hilly roads; you can't take the calash everywhere." He clapped his hands and a small cloud of dust erupted from his gloves. "I wanted to thank you for those hearty Spanish horses you provided me on my last ride to Praha. I was doubtful about them at first, but after my third remount, I realized I would save a day on each side of the journey. They're strengthy and they've got excellent wind, and light mouths, all of them."

"Very good. I will continue my orders for the Andalusians for my courier. You will find them at posting inns from Calais to Roma, and from Praha to Barcelona, all in my name," said Ragoczy, reflecting that ten years ago most of his courier's horses had been confiscated by Napoleon's armies for his cavalry and aides-de-camp; Ragoczy continued in the same tone, as if the loss meant little to him. "Tomorrow I am sending you riding postilion into Yvoire with the liver sorrels to fetch the new traveling coach. We will leave at first light on Saturday morning, and at the end of the day, we will find an inn where we can spend Sunday as well, so the horses will be fresh on Monday. I want to use them all the way to Amsterdam if it is possible."

Gutesohnes considered this. "I imagine I can keep up a good pace without exhausting them. Where the roads are flat and in good repair, we will go at a trot, and otherwise at a walk. That should keep from wearing them out." He grinned suddenly. "After this journey, I should know the way to Amsterdam in my sleep."

"So long as you are awake when you drive," said Ragoczy. "We will break the journey at Zemmer, to inspect the work being done on my holdings there, and we will have a full day in Liège so I may consult with my trading company there. I will stay in Amsterdam for about ten days. I will give you four days' liberty while there, and I will provide you spending money, so that you may make the most of the liberty. I depend upon you to be sure the horses are properly cared for during our stay. I have decided that Osbert Nadel will drive the servant's carriage, and that they will have the four Nonius geldings in harness. They should be able to keep up with us without trouble."

"From the horses, no, but Nadel is lazy," Gutesohnes warned.

"He will not learn to be less so unless he is given work more demanding than driving the hay-wagon and the buggy. He must begin to expand his knowledge or he will stay on this mountain for all of his life, which he claims not to want to do." Ragoczy folded his arms and said, "Give him a trial, if you like: have him ride postilion with you tomorrow when you go to get the coach."

"If you think it best," said Gutesohnes in a tone that barely escaped insolence.

Ragoczy ignored his manner. "You will have the opportunity to correct his faults while you are with him. Try not to demoralize him completely. He is only seventeen, and a youngest son."

"Seventeen is old enough to have some purpose in life," said Gutesohnes. "But I will do as you instruct, Comte."

"I thank you for that," said Ragoczy, just a tinge of sardonic humor in his dark eyes. "I will expect you to tell me how the coach handles when you return tomorrow, and to make note of any problems you may have with it so they may be addressed before we are on the road. It is easier to fix an anticipated problem than a realized one." He considered for a few seconds, then added, "I think it best if the servants travel in the Bohemia; it may not be completely fashionable, but it is sturdy and it can carry a heavy load without being much slowed by the weight. Also, it drives well." He had driven it before on two occasions, and both times the Bohemia had performed better than he had hoped.

"Does Nadel know which coach he is to drive?" asked Gutesohnes.

"No; I will inform him before supper," said Ragoczy, giving Gutesohnes another long, measuring stare. After a minute or so, he asked, "Would you like to return to coaching, or do you want to remain my courier when this journey is over? Have you a preference? You may be candid in your answer."

"I do like driving a coach now and then—especially well-made vehicles with fine teams—but I much prefer being a courier. The work is more varied, fewer things can go wrong, and I have a greater aptitude for it." He pulled off his gloves. "I must go wash. I'll be cased in dried mud if I don't."

'The bath-house has been heated, if you want to use it," said Ragoczy.

"On such a warm day? No, I'll wash down behind the stable with the others. When it turns cold again, I'd welcome the bath-house. For now, the washrack will do as well for me as it does for the horses. Two buckets of cool water and a good scrub with a brush and I'll be fit for company." He rose from his chair and nodded to Ragoczy. "About tomorrow: I'll be off to Yvoire shortly after dawn, and should be back in time for dinner."

"Very good. I will look for you then." As he spoke, a flick of brightness came and went. "The storm is gathering. You'd best hurry if you want to get washed before the"—he stopped as thunder trundled overhead—"storm begins."

Gutesohnes touched his forehead and left the study, whistling as he went as if defying the elements to overwhelm him.

It was another hour before the rain began, accompanied by dramatic crashes of thunder and sudden eruptions of lightning, often so close together that they seemed to be in the same instant. The windows of the château rattled, the heavens let down their bounty in profusion, and half the household kept to their quarters, waiting for the tempest to pass; Ragoczy sat in his study, unperturbed by the display the storm provided, although the abundance of running water made him a bit uncomfortable. As the light dimmed, he did not bother to light the lamps but continued to make entries in his notebook, his dark-seeing eyes unhampered by the fading day. After a while the aroma of roasting boar filled the château, and while the sunset began to delineate the break-up of the clouds, the household of Château Ragoczy gathered in the servants' dining room for their supper, and Hero ate in solitary state in the smaller withdrawing room above-stairs.

As night came on Ragoczy left his study and went out to the

bath-house; the air was clear, the ground was wet, and the sky was luminous with the last vibrant glow of sunset. He stood at the bath-house door for a minute or so, taking in the end of the day, then he stepped into the vestibule and began to remove his clothes, hanging them on pegs before retrieving a large, square Turkish towel, which he wrapped around himself before he stepped into the steamy room where the three large, water-filled wooden tubs waited. The room smelled of damp and witch hazel, and was lit by six lanterns set in glass-fronted wall-niches. Ragoczy went to the bench at the foot of the largest tub, dropped his towel, and went to climb up the steps and into the oblong tub. Quite warm water rose to the middle of his chest, made pleasant by his native earth under the tub, and the advantage of advancing night. He lay back, letting the water support him while he waited for Hero to arrive.

It was twenty minutes later that she came into the room, her towel in one hand, her dressing-gown wrapped around her. "I'm sorry," she said. "I couldn't get away until just now."

"No matter. The holocaust keeps the water warm." He held out his hand to her. "Come in."

She folded her towel and took off her dressing-gown; she laid this on top of the towel, then removed her slippers before climbing into the tub to join him. "I wish I knew how you managed to keep hot water flowing through these tubs—probably another Roman technique," she said, adding, "but don't explain it to me now. Tell me later." She slid into his arms and his embrace with ease, delighting in their kiss. "I have been waiting for this all evening."

"How kind you are to my vanity," he said lightly, his hands trailing over her with the movement of the water.

Her laughter was low and delicious. "You have less vanity than any man I have ever known. All your centuries of life have burned it out of you, I think." She pressed up against him and with one hand loosened the knot of her hair, so that it cascaded around her shoulders and fanned out around her in the water. As she tossed the two ivory pins out of the tub, she murmured, *"Such locks will then/Ensnare the hearts of men."*

"Petrarch was right," Ragoczy whispered as he stroked her hair, following down the wonderful curves of her flesh beyond it.

She kissed him again, taking his hand and moving it to her breast. "Start here, if you would."

He cradled her breast in his palm. "And go where?"

She let his arm hold her up as she stretched out in the water. "I leave that up to you," she said, and gave herself over to the passion he ignited in her, and the gentle embrace of the water.

Text of a letter from Wallache Gerhard Winifrith Seifert von Ravensberg at Munchen, Bavaria, to his banking factor, Herr Luitpold Oskar Sporn, in Salzburg, Austria, carried by private courier and delivered three days after dispatching.

To Herr Luitpold O. Sporn, the greetings of Graf von Ravensberg on this, the 10th day of August, 1817, from the city Munchen,

This is to inform you that my journey has begun well. We have made good time on the roads and have been able to put up at superior inns. I commend you for all the care you devoted to my travel, for there have been no difficulties encountered through any failing of yours.

My ward Hyacinthie has found travel tiring, but has not complained overmuch, and although we have endured the heat as best we can, she is troubled because she is not in her best looks at present, and it is important that she present a very good appearance.

We will spend some days at Trier and then proceed on to Amsterdam. My publisher there is expecting me, and I have said I will make a stay of at least a week. If I receive attractive invitations either for myself or for my ward, I may extend my stay for up to a second week; I shall inform you of any changes in plans.

During my absence I rely upon you to keep yourself informed on the conditions at Ravensberg, most specifically on the health and condition of my two young wards, Rosalie and Hedda. I have authorized my man-of-business, Herr Arndt Lowengard, to serve as their guardian in my absence, but I task you, as well, with concern for their well-being. Having become orphans, they are at the mercy of charitable relatives, and in that capacity I have undertaken their care. I would not like to think that anyone working on my behalf would not do his utmost for those two unfortunate girls.

I have the letters of credit you furnished, and so far have not needed to produce them to secure the elegancies of travel. I am carrying a fair amount of money with me, but as I leave Austrian and German territories, I am sure that these letters of credit will be more efficacious than coins or bank-notes. Upon my return, we will regularize all the sums involved.

Tell my wards that my thoughts are always with them, and inform my household of my progress. I look to see you again in October.

> *Wallache Gerhard Winifrith Sieffert*
> *Graf von Ravensberg*

8

It was mid-afternoon on the twelfth day after leaving Château Ragoczy that Otto Gutesohnes, as dusty and sweating as his team, drew the fine new traveling carriage up in front of Ragoczy's house in Amsterdam; it was a warm, windy day, smelling of saltwater, tar, wet stone, vegetation, and humanity; the narrow streets fronting the canals were filled with traffic and the sound of busy citizens hastening about their business, for Amsterdam was a commercial center and its purpose filled it as a palpable presence, imbuing everyone in it with determined energy.

The house had been built in 1662 by a successful merchant; situated at the intersection of two canals the front was boastfully and expensively wide and there were four steps leading up to the front door. Ragoczy had acquired the building in 1729 from the merchant's grandson, and had added his own improvements. The house had recently been refaced and a third floor added to expand his laboratory; new draperies hung in the windows and the shutters were bright with fresh paint. On the narrow, canal-side street, the house stood out for its restrained elegance and advantageous location.

"The stable is behind the house, reached by the alley opposite the canal from the side of the Oude Kerk," said Ragoczy to Gutesohnes as he got out of the carriage and held out his hand to help Hero get down. "The stable-master will tell you where to put the horses and the coach. When the team has been groomed and fed, and the trunks unloaded, you may have a late dinner and the rest of the evening to yourself."

"Thank you, Comte," said Gutesohnes, rolling his shoulders to relieve them of the long strain of driving.

"Unless there is an emergency, present your report on the team and the coach to me in the morning." Ragoczy nodded to him, allowing him to pass on.

"I will. The horses have done well." He tapped his driving whip as he put it back in its holder, then lifted the reins and kissed the team to move on. "Almost done, my lads, almost done," he reassured them.

"This is a very impressive house," Hero approved when the coach was out of earshot. "Is it the first you have owned here?"

"No," said Ragoczy. "I have had others before this one." He did not add that this house had not yet been built when he first visited the island village that had become Amsterdam.

"The location is fortuitous: two stone bridges and a small square in front. It conveys a sense of prosperity," she said.

"It does, does it not?" Ragoczy asked, amusement glinting in his eyes. He escorted her up the steps and lifted the heavy brass ring-knocker. "Welcome to Amsterdam, Hero von Scharffensee," he said with a slight bow just as the door was opened.

"Comte Ragoczy!" the steward exclaimed. "We did not expect you until tomorrow."

"You may thank my coachman for our swift journey," said Ragoczy. "How do I find you, Kuyskill?"

"You find me quite well, Comte, thank you for asking," said the middle-aged steward; he stepped back to allow Hero to enter the house. "And so is the rest of the household, except for Ursula, whose eyes trouble her now and again. I shall present that in my report to Rogier when he arrives."

"Is her work making her eyes worse? Seamstresses often suffer from eye problems," said Ragoczy as if he had not noticed Kuyskill's last remark.

"She has spectacles and they help, but there is some sign of veiling, and that causes difficulty," said Kuyskill.

"I will have a look at her eyes myself, later today. Ask her if she will permit me to assess her vision before supper." He indicated Hero with a gallant half-bow to show the respect he required his household demonstrate toward her. "Madame von Scharffensee is my guest. She will want the large room overlooking the hot-house for her use: I asked the chamber be made ready in my note in July, as you recall. Her maid is traveling with Rogier, and should be here to supervise unpacking her bags in an hour or so." He favored Kuyskill with a penetrating look. "There will be no rumors spread about my guest, of course."

"Of course," said Kuyskill in a tone of such neutrality that it was obvious he suspected the worst.

"My guest and I will observe all the proprieties due a widow," said Ragoczy. "You may assure the household that any scandal attaching to her presence will begin with them, and I will know it."

"No one will talk," said Kuyskill. "I am confident of that."

"Tell me," Ragoczy went on as if he was convinced by Kuyskill's assurances; he moved down the corridor toward the stairs to the upper floors, "can you spare a footman to carry a note around to Klasse van der Boom? I want to speak with him about the press as soon as possible."

"I'll send Koenraad. Let me know when the note is ready." He swung around as a bell sounded at the rear of the house. "Your coachman will need help in moving your trunks and bags into the house."

"I should think he would," said Ragoczy. "Go supervise. I will write my note." He offered his arm to Hero. "You will want to rest from the journey."

"I am a little stiff," she said, and stretched just enough to demonstrate the truth of her assertion. "And a bit tired."

"Then you will be restored after an hour of quiet. I ask you to be punctilious until the household is accustomed to your presence, especially this afternoon, when you will be under close observation," he said. "By evening, Serilde will be here, and the luggage and baggage will be ready to carry to your room; the household will have found out about you to their satisfaction. There will be a supper laid by seven in the evening, but if you want something before then, you have only to ask Kuyskill to bespeak it for you."

"I thank you," said Hero, stifling a yawn. "You know me too well, Comte."

"If I had not known you before, I would surely do so now: I have been sharing a carriage with you for a dozen days—I can see when you are tired." He bent to kiss her hand, then indicated a door at the top of the stairs. "That is the entrance to your chamber."

"You are very kind," she said, partly as a show of good manners, partly as the truth.

"I will join you before supper, if you would like. After I tend to Ursula."

"For conversation," she said, with the hint of a question in her words.

"Yes, and to review whatever plans you may wish to make for our stay here."

"And later?" she asked, lifting her brows provocatively. "Will you join me later?"

"Not tonight. But in a day or two," he said, giving her room enough to open the door. "When the servants are less curious."

"I suppose you know best; servants are always wondering what their masters do," she said, and slipped through the door into a room filled with cool, limpid, northern light from four tall windows that overlooked a greenhouse that took up half the cobbled courtyard below. The walls were papered in a pattern of pale forget-me-nots and the shutters were wonderfully white. The bedspread was of a soft lilac satin, and the hangings were a very pale blue-green. "Oh! This is lovely, Comte."

"Thank you for saying so," said Ragoczy, taking care not to go beyond the limits of the door, and aware of the covert attention of the household staff. He bent his head. "I hope you will have reason to remember your days here with happiness."

"I'm sure I shall," she said, and tossed her reticule onto the bed, watching it fall. As she turned back, she discovered that Ragoczy had closed the door. She shook her head a little sadly, then began to unfasten the frogs on the front of her traveling coat; like it or not, she was weary and glad of a chance to recuperate from the long journey.

Descending the stairs, Ragoczy encountered Kuyskill struggling with the first of his chests. "Madame von Scharffensee is resting. I am going out."

"But your note?" Kuyskill asked.

"I will go along to see Heer van der Boom on my own; please inform Rogier where I have gone when he arrives. There is no need for you to delay the meal upon my account, although I should be back before suppertime." He moved aside, allowing Kuyskill to position the chest to be carried up two floors.

"Suppertime. Will you be dining?"

"I hardly know," said Ragoczy. "Do not wait for me, and do not save food for me. I will attend to my hunger in my own way." With a curt nod he was off into the brilliant afternoon, moving along the canals, feeling the disconcerting vertigo from the running water and the anodyne pull of his native earth in the soles of his shoes. His stride was long and clean, and in less than five minutes he had reached the square building that housed the Eclipse Press.

Klasse van der Boom himself, a square-faced man with a square body, opened the door to Eclipse Press; his leather apron was heavily stained with ink and his hands were permanently grimed with it. "Comte!" he exclaimed as he flung the door wide. "Come in, come in."

"Thank you," said Ragoczy, stepping into the front office of the press.

"It is most fortuitous that you should arrive today," van der Boom went on with emphatic exuberance. "Just two hours ago, Graf van Ravensberg arrived; he came from Austria to see the preparations for his book on the nature of blood. No doubt he will be pleased to meet the patron of Eclipse Press." He said *patron* with such heavy emphasis that Ragoczy had to resist the impulse to wince.

"Is there some difficulty?" Ragoczy inquired levelly.

"Not precisely that," van der Boom hedged. "But he will prefer to talk to another man with a title, if you don't mind?"

"Whatever suits your purpose, Heer van der Boom," he said, and smoothed the front of his black, fine-wool traveling coat.

"For which I must thank you," said van der Boom under his breath. "This Austrian is filled with self-importance."

"I will keep that in mind," said Ragoczy, and followed van der Boom back into the noise and heat of the press-room.

Amid the bustle and industry of the press-room, a tall, angular man in a high-crowned beaver hat, an elegant dark-blue claw-tail coat, white silk shirt, tapestry waist-coat over buff-colored unmentionables stood with five uncut sheets of printed paper in his hands. He was frowning, muttering in German as he peered at the sheet, paying no attention to the activity around him. As van der Boom approached him, he said in awkward Dutch, "I have corrections."

"No doubt you do," said van der Boom. "And we will attend to them directly, Graf. But for now, allow me to present Saint-Germain Ragoczy, Comte Franciscus, who is patron of Eclipse Press." He bowed between the two men and took a step back. "This is Graf von Ravensberg."

"A great pleasure," said Ragoczy with an urbane smile in impeccable German. He held out his ungloved hand as he looked up at the Austrian.

Von Ravensberg set the sheets of paper aside on a rack, clicked his heels, bowed sharply, then took Ragoczy's proffered hand, speaking German as if his wits had been restored. "Ragoczy. A name of some reputation—in Hungary."

"That it is," said Ragoczy calmly, extricating his hand from von Ravensberg's talonlike grip without visible effort.

"You are of that House?" von Ravensberg pursued.

"Another branch than the part of the family that gained such notoriety a century ago," he said.

"Very old blood, then," said von Ravensberg.

This time there was an ironic twist to his mouth as Ragoczy said, "Very."

"You could be a fascinating study," said von Ravensberg. "Most of my studies have been conducted with Austrians and Germans, but the descendant of so illustrious a line as Ragoczy must provide valuable information."

"In what regard?" Ragoczy asked politely, although inwardly taken aback.

"In regard to blood, of course," said von Ravensberg, pointing to the pages hanging on the rack. "It is the subject of my book, as I assumed you must know." His face was set in accusatory lines.

"To be candid, Graf, I have just arrived in Amsterdam and have not yet had the opportunity to review the progress of our present projects," said Ragoczy, and nodded toward van der Boom. "I came here to discuss the publishing schedule. It is an unexpected pleasure to meet you while I am on this most pedestrian task."

Von Ravensberg relented a little. "Just arrived?"

"Not two hours ago," said Ragoczy. "My trunks are not yet in my rooms."

"Then you are most punctilious, Comte; an admirable trait, no doubt one that is the legacy of your breeding."

"I would like to think so," said Ragoczy, his face revealing nothing of his long memories.

"It is important for us—the high-born—to preserve the virtues inherent in our kind. There are so many who care nothing for breeding, who are willing to disregard centuries of alliances and unity for the sake of the exotic. I hope you aren't one of those modern men who see mixed blood as a token of the times." Before Ragoczy could speak von Ravensberg took one of the sheets off the rack. "You must examine my thesis, Comte, and discuss your thoughts with me."

"I will try to do so, but I cannot give your work my full attention until the day after tomorrow. On Friday I will read your book, and, if you are still in the city, I will—"

"Friday evening I am having a reception," said von Ravensberg.

"Then, perhaps, Saturday?" Ragoczy proposed.

"Oh, no, no. You must come to the reception. A little dancing for the youngsters, cards and conversation for their seniors. Supper at midnight, and wine throughout the evening—mostly Italian wine, since many of the French vineyards have had poor harvests these last two years. No matter. Many of the Dutch prefer beer in any case, though it isn't suitable for such a reception; champagne will be offered at midnight, of course. The hotel has managed all for me. My ward and I will be receiving fifty guests, all from families of stature and merit; I insist you must be among their number." He waved one arm as if to banish the press-room. "It is a chance to step out in society, to make new acquaintances and renew old friendships. I suspect you may have the same problem I do: I have so little time to spend here that I am determined to make the most of the occasion, as you must be. So you have to come, or I will not have the opportunity to entertain you in a manner appropriate to your rank for the remainder of my visit. Let me have your direction and I will have an invitation carried around to you tomorrow morning."

"I thank you for your offer," said Ragoczy, taking a half-step back from the Graf. "I do not yet know what my guest will want to undertake, but if you will permit me to wait until tomorrow, no doubt I will be able to tell you if I will be able to attend."

"Bring your guest. Of course, you must bring him." Von Ravensberg gestured emphatically.

"My guest is a widow, Graf." Ragoczy could see the surprise von Ravensberg felt before he was able to conceal it. "She is the daughter of a distinguished Italian scholar, whose husband died during the wars."

"Such is the fate of women who marry soldiers," said von Ravensberg.

"Her husband was an engineer," said Ragoczy.

Van der Boom came up to Ragoczy, his posture self-deprecatory and his tone uncharacteristically subservient. "If I may have a word with you, Comte?"

"Certainly, Heer van der Boom," he said, and looked up at von Ravensberg. "If you will excuse us?"

With an expression that showed his disdain for van der Boom, von Ravensberg picked up another sheet of paper. "I have my work to do."

Ragoczy and van der Boom moved away from the tall Austrian to the corner of the room where the bindery was set up, about as far from von Ravensberg as it was possible to be and remain in the same room. "I don't know how you want to deal with his changes. I fear he intends to make a great many of them."

"A problem, to be sure, but a reasonable expectation for a man in his position." Ragoczy considered this briefly. "I will do what I can to discourage too many alterations. Perhaps I should attend his reception; it would be a useful place to encourage him not to rewrite his book at this stage. But you may want to be very observant of any corrections, as opposed to interpolations."

"I will do my best to keep that in mind," said van der Boom. "And I will try to accommodate the man when his demands are not too outrageous."

"Most sensible of you," said Ragoczy, and then waited while van der Boom brought the business ledgers for him to inspect. "I will take this to the front office, if you do not mind."

"Away from the Graf?" van der Boom said with a knowing wink.

"And the noise, and the heat," said Ragoczy, aware that in such an environment, his inability to sweat might draw unwanted attention.

"I'm used to both," said van der Boom. "I'll come in an hour to see how you are faring."

Ragoczy took the ledger and slipped it under his arm. "You keep excellent records, Heer van der Boom, for which I am most grateful."

"May you say the same thing when you are through perusing them," said van der Boom.

Von Ravensberg was glaring at the page in his hand as Ragoczy passed by him on his way to the outer office; noticing the ledger Ragoczy carried, von Ravensberg transferred his disapproval to that volume. "The demands of tradesmen! Do you not have factors to do that for you?" He waited for a suitable answer.

"I have been cheated by factors before, Graf, so I am now inclined to trust myself in such matters." He patted the side of the ledger.

"You assume that the figures entered are correct," said von Ravensberg.

"Yes. That much I do expect, and if they are incorrect, I should see the pattern of it in the pages." He had caught more than one factor shifting the sums in the records in years past, and had learned how to recognize such manipulations. He kept on walking until he reached the front office and found a work-table with two tall stools set in front of it. He perched on the stool, laid out the ledger, and began to read.

More than an hour later, van der Boom joined him, saying, "The Graf has corrected ten sheets of four pages, each side."

"That must be a relief for you," said Ragoczy, slipping a sheet of paper into the ledger to mark his progress; he closed the book, saying, "It all appears correct thus far."

"It should be. I try to keep full records of everything. No matter what von Ravensberg may suspect, I conduct my trade honestly."

"I have never thought otherwise," said Ragoczy quietly.

Van der Boom was quiet for a short while, then asked, "Will you go to his reception?"

"Probably," said Ragoczy. "It would seem odd that I, a participant publisher, did not accept his hospitality."

"That's plausible," said van der Boom as he thought about the possibilities.

"For the sake of Eclipse Press, I will make an appearance," said Ragoczy, making up his mind.

"On behalf of Eclipse Press, I thank you." He chuckled. "Strange, what business may demand of us."

"Strange, indeed," said Ragoczy.

"He'll be back tomorrow, to find more errors."

"No doubt," said Ragoczy.

Van der Boom leaned on the table. "It is good that he takes so much care, given that his text is so . . . technical, and the topic is such a daring one. The work is bound to generate discussion, which should mean good sales. But he is also going to be criticized, and not just by the Church, but by physicians and students of anatomy." He looked toward the hazy window. "It's getting on to evening. He will have to wait until morning if he wants to read carefully."

"You will be closing the press-room shortly," said Ragoczy.

"And you may want to be gone before the Graf can offer to take you to your house. You will have him with you all evening if you permit him that courtesy." Van der Boom righted himself. "I'll tell him that you have departed, if you like."

Ragoczy rose from the stool. "Very well. I will call again at midday tomorrow, if that suits you."

"It should do," said van der Boom. He tapped his nose. "The Graf has a ward. You heard him say it."

"A ward is a child," said Ragoczy.

"Child or no, he may be looking to find her a husband," van der Boom cautioned Ragoczy. "You have a fortune and a title. He may hope you will be something more than a dance partner for her."

"Since I never dance, I think I will be safe," said Ragoczy. "But your timely reminder is appreciated," he said as he made for the front door and went out into the long, angular shadows that spread along the narrow streets, under a sky that lit the canals with sunset fires.

Text of a letter from Helmut Frederich Lambert Ahrent Ritterslandt, Graf von Scharffensee at Scharffensee in Austria, to Hero Iocasta Ariadne Corvosaggio von Scharffensee at Château Ragoczy near Lake Geneva, Yvoire, Switzerland; carried by private messenger and delivered in four days, but was not read until Hero's return on September 9th.

Graf von Scharffensee sends his greetings and condolences to his daughter-in-law, on this, the 16th day of August, 1817, with the assurance that her daughter received the finest medical care possible.

It is my sad duty to inform you that your daughter, Annamaria, took a fever in late July. At first it seemed nothing more than the usual summer fevers that one endures, but in your daughter's case, the fever spread to her lungs and they became putrid. When the usual remedies failed, a physician from Salzburg was called, Herr Doktor Schalter, whose reputation is of the highest order. He prescribed purging and a course of poultices to draw out the putrescence, but in spite of all that was done, she could not rally, and last night passed into that deadly lethargy that indicated the end was near. The priest from Scharffensee was sent for to administer Last Rites, and she died at two in the morning. I have arranged for her to be interred in the family chapel at Scharffensee, and will place an appropriate plaque on her tomb.

Her brothers are much shocked by her death, and so I have promised them a special entertainment at Christmas, which must, perforce, delay your visit until next summer. I am sure you can see the wisdom in this, and will not embarrass them, or me, or yourself in emotional protests at this most difficult time. I have no doubt that you will want your sons to put their grief behind them as quickly as possible, and you must see that your presence, with the loss of their sister so new in their lives, can only aggravate their sorrow. Better to give them time before visiting them.

With Annamaria dead, I will discharge her teacher, Frau Linderlein, with three months' pay and a letter of commendation. She, I must tell you, is most distressed by the loss of her pupil, and has spent the morning in weeping. This unseemly display of copious tears has caused Berend great anguish, and I feel the sooner Frau Linderlein is gone from Scharffensee, the better for all of us.

Know that my sympathies are with you, and that your daughter is in the care of God's Angels. It is no easy thing to part with a child—as I have cause to know—but it is what has been sent for us to endure. I pray you have fortitude enough to weather this sorrow.

> *Your father-in-law,*
> *Helmut Frederich Lambert Ahrent Ritterslandt*
> *Graf von Scharffensee*

PART II

SAINT-GERMAIN RAGOCZY, COMTE FRANCISCUS

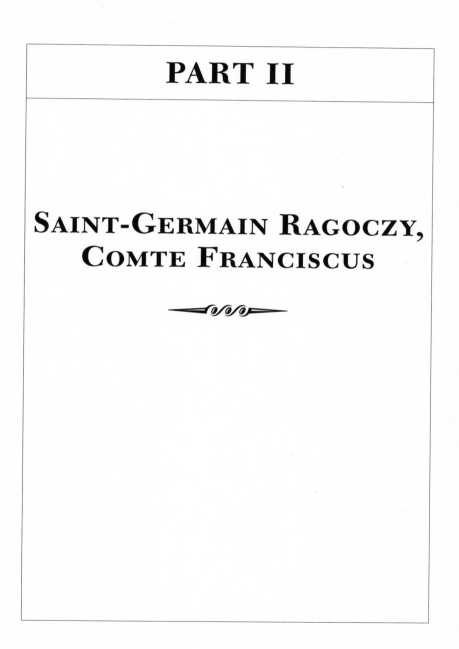

*T*ext of a letter from Edgar St. Andrews, Scottish merchant resident in Amsterdam, to Wallache Gerhard Winifrith Sieffert Graf von Ravensberg at his Amsterdam hotel, written in Dutch and delivered by messenger.

To the most excellent Graf von Ravensberg the greetings of Edgar St. Andrews on this, the 18th day of August, 1817

My dear Graf,

I have to thank you for the many displays of hospitality you have shown me and my wife in your stay in this city which is foreign to us both, as it is to you. In the two years I have resided here, I have not, until now, been so graciously and magnanimously entertained by anyone, Dutch or foreign, so your kindness to me and my wife is welcomed for its novelty as well as its benignancy. I am sincerely obliged to you for your courtesy.

This being the case, I am deeply sorry that I cannot recommend anyone known to me as a potential suitor for the hand of your ward, lovely young woman though she is, and worthy as she must be of finding a suitable spouse, a man of rank and character who will maintain her consequence—and yours—in the polite world. Even so charming a girl as your ward is at a disadvantage in these difficult times, and I am all sympathy to you in your plight; her future happiness is in your hands, and the fate of your House. So many matters to consider, and you with your own work to do.

Since the wars and the many upheavals that have convulsed the Continent, it must be doubly difficult to launch a young woman of noble birth into a union that is acceptable not only to you, but to the family of the apposite men. My employers make it a policy only to employ married men, and therefore all my colleagues are constituted as I am. But I will keep your request in mind, and if any appropriate fellow should make himself known to me, I will at the first opportunity inform you of it.

Having two daughters of my own, I understand how you are concerned with establishing your niece well in the world. With the loss of so many men in the Great Army in Napoleon's dreadful Russian Campaign, it is astonishing that there are not more unmarried women in the world. As it is, there are far too many widows. I have been considering sending my daughters to their aunt in London for their coming-out, for just the same reasons as you have discussed with me.

I look forward to the publication of your book, and wish you every success with it. I cannot, myself, imagine what work it must be to undertake such an enterprise; I am in awe of your attainment, sir, and I cannot tell you what a privilege it is to know a man who has done as much as you have.

I wish you a safe journey back to Austria. I am pleased to hear that the roads are supposed to be clear most of the way: I trust they will remain so. Let me reiterate again my thanks for your kind invitation to call at Ravensberg if ever I reach Austria. Rest assured that I will do so when I have the good fortune to visit that land.

> *With cordial personal regards,*
>   *I am,*
>   *Edgar St. Andrews*
>   *Campbell & Ochie, Importers*
>   *Amsterdam*

1

"That child is back," said Hero as she looked out the window of the reception room at the front of Ragoczy's Amsterdam house. "Walking unattended, at the height of the morning when half of Amsterdam is abroad, and without a carriage to accompany her." She frowned. "No—wait; she's not alone. Gutesohnes is with her."

Ragoczy, at the secretary on the far side of this sunny chamber, continued to review the pages in his hands. "Is he."

"I don't know if his being with her is better or worse than if she were walking alone. Silly, isn't it? Her own coachman would be more than acceptable, but I don't think Gutesohnes is. The Dutch aren't as strict as the Austrians, but this is still beyond the acceptable bounds of what young single ladies may do," said Hero. "Not that I am for all the limitations imposed on women: I am not. Yet it is folly to flout them, or to fly in the face of convention. For girls like her, some allowance may be made for high spirits. Still, if she wants to be careful of her reputation . . ."

"That seems to be a concern of her guardian, and one for which he is strangely lax," said Ragoczy, thinking back to the way Hyacinthie had behaved two nights ago, making a display of herself while her uncle entertained four booksellers and Ragoczy in anticipation of the publication of his book.

"Her uncle, if I may say so, pays little heed to Hyacinthie. He is far more concerned for his book than for her."

"Without doubt," said Ragoczy.

"It must be difficult for her," said Hero musingly. "To be attractive and yet to live in the shadow of her uncle's study."

"And to live in the isolation of Ravensberg—no wonder she flaunts herself here, while she has the opportunity."

"She is a flirt," Hero declared, watching Hyacinthie twirl her parasol as she looked up at Gutesohnes.

"Hardly surprising: she is young and her uncle is determined to sell her to the highest bidder or most high-born—to that extent he is concerned for her at all." Ragoczy frowned as he said this, his sympathy going out to the young woman even as he considered her predicament. "She is attempting to secure herself."

"If that is the case, she would do better not to flirt with the coachman." Hero laughed, a little sadly. "But I understand you—she is practicing, isn't she?"

Ragoczy put the pages aside and came to the divan where Hero was sitting. He lifted the curtain. "Ah. I see what you mean," he agreed. "Practicing, indeed."

"Such a pretty child," said Hero. "But so determined to ensnare every man she sees. That may yet bring her to grief." She rounded on Ragoczy. "She will probably try to engage your attention."

"She already has, upon two occasions at least," said Ragoczy with a single shake of his head.

"She has?" Hero said, not entirely surprised.

"Yes," he responded. "I was certain you had noticed: once at the reception we attended, and once when she came with her uncle to Eclipse Press. I would not be astonished to learn that her uncle encourages her."

Hero pulled the curtain out of his hand and settled back on the divan. "She's coming this way."

"Paying a visit?" he ventured, and went on in a singularly neutral tone, "How . . . how charming."

She gave him a short, uncertain look. "You're displeased."

"I am uneasy," he said as he heard the knocker sound, and Kuyskill go down the hall to open the door.

"Do you suppose she will—" Hero began, then fell silent as she heard Hyacinthie ask for Comte Franciscus.

Ragoczy held up his hand in caution, and moved back to the small secretary where the pages he had been examining were stacked.

"—from my uncle, Graf von Ravensberg," Hyacinthie's raised voice sounded from the entryway; she spoke in French.

"I do not know that the Comte is home to visitors. I will inquire." Kuyskill's tone made it clear he disapproved of young ladies paying visits without escorts. "If you will wait?" Giving her no time to answer, he left her standing on the front steps and came into the reception room. "Comte," he said apologetically, "there is a caller, who claims she brings a letter from the Graf von Ravensberg. Shall I admit her or send her—"

"Admit her, by all means," said Ragoczy. "And bring a glass of lemonade to her. On a warm day like this, she must be thirsty."

Kuyskill pokered up, but nodded. "Of course, Comte." He turned to leave the room.

"You see what I mean; the servants will call her a hoyden," said Hero quietly.

"All but Gutesohnes," said Ragoczy, equally softly.

"That will only make it worse," said Hero, and rose to welcome Hyacinthie to the house.

Hyacinthie, her flower-patterned parasol furled, stood in the doorway, resplendent in a fashionable walking dress of sprigged muslin in a pale shade of lavender accented with knots of blue-green floss at the neck and cuffs. Her bonnet was abbreviated, showing more of her dark-blond hair than was thought fitting for her age and position in society. She bobbed a polite curtsy to Ragoczy, then to Hero as Kuyskill announced her in disapproving accents. "Good morning," she said when the steward had withdrawn from the reception room.

"And to you, Fraulein Sieffert," said Ragoczy, using French for everything but her title and name. "To what do we owe this pleasure?"

"I have a note from my uncle that he charged me to bring to you." She held out her lace-mittened hand, proffering a small envelope of cream-laid paper on which Ragoczy's name had been written with a flourish. "He instructed me to wait for an answer."

"It is urgent, then?" Ragoczy inquired as he took the envelope and broke the seal.

"Yes. We are leaving the day after tomorrow, you see," she said with a blinding smile. "We return to Ravensberg."

"A considerable journey," said Hero. "You must be busy, making preparations."

"The hotel is doing everything for us. My uncle and his valet are supervising. I was in the way until I was given this task to perform." She looked a bit forlorn. "I will miss Amsterdam."

"I should think so," said Hero. "It is exciting to see new places and meet new people."

"Especially when I do not often get to receive guests or travel." Hyacinthie sighed. "Visitors come rarely to Ravensberg. Except for the people who call in so my uncle may study their blood, we go from year to year seeing the same twenty faces. And the servants, of course."

"Not an easy thing for a young woman," Hero sympathized.

"Not what I would prefer," said Hyacinthie in a rush. "It would be *so* much nicer to go to parties and balls in Vienna, or even Salzburg. But my uncle cannot spare the time or the money from his research."

Hero had sat down again, and now indicated the chair at the end of the divan; she did her best to make the girl feel welcome. "Do have a seat, Hyacinthie, and tell me more about yourself. We haven't had much of an opportunity to become acquainted. The Comte will finish reading your uncle's note and he will prepare an answer for you to take back to him." She smiled encouragement even as she noticed Hyacinthie's ill-concealed disappointment at not acquiring all of Ragoczy's attention. "For how long have you lived with your uncle?"

"There is little to tell about my life," said Hyacinthie. "My parents died when I was seven and my uncle took me in. He has cared for me ever since." Under her gentle words there was an implacable note, something hard that turned her remark bitter. "Now he will find me a husband. He says he has to do so. He has two other wards, younger than I am, to care for."

Hero was spared the necessity of responding to Hyacinthie's revelations by Kuyskill coming into the reception room with a glass of lemonade and a plate of sweet biscuits on a tray. He bowed as he put this on the occasional table between the divan and the chair, then withdrew, radiating disapproval.

When the steward was gone, Ragoczy said, "The Graf has kindly invited me to attend a celebration for the publication of his book in November. I am going to request that he send an invitation when he has set the time of the festivities, and if it is possible, to do my utmost to attend, weather and business permitting." He drew a sheet of fine rag paper out of a shelf in the secretary and moved the stacks of paper aside so he could write a response to von Ravensberg.

"Have your refreshments," Hero recommended to Hyacinthie. "I don't care for sweet biscuits, and the lemonade was requested for you."

Hyacinthie picked up the glass, saying, "I am of an age that I prefer wine," before she took a sip. "I'm sure you prefer wine, Comte." This last was accompanied by a sidelong glance at her host.

Ragoczy was busy selecting a trimmed quill for his pen, so it took him a short while to answer. "I am afraid I do not drink wine."

Hyacinthie blinked. "Never?"

"Not since I was a very young man," he said, his memories of his long-ago breathing life flitting through his recollections; he retrieved the ink-well from its drawer, setting it in the rack provided for it.

"Oh." She picked up one of the sweet biscuits, broke it in half, and chose the larger of the two to set down again. "Your cook makes these?"

"Yes, he does," said Ragoczy, continuing to write.

"Wine doesn't agree with him," Hero explained.

"Oh," said Hyacinthie again, and took a bite of her biscuit.

"We will be leaving shortly, as well," Hero went on. "I share your aversion to long hours in a coach, but I prefer it to the same hours on a horse or on foot."

Hyacinthie nodded. When she had swallowed, she said, "It is so hot in the coach. But it is probably just as hot riding or walking."

"Hotter, I fear," said Hero. "When I traveled with my father, I often longed for a coach. We were lucky to have open wagons to transport us and our things."

Hyacinthie stared at her. "Your father was with the army?"

"No, my father is a professor of antiquities. He has been on many expeditions into Ottoman lands; I have accompanied him when I was younger." In spite of herself, Hero found Hyacinthie's fascination flattering. "Before I was married, I sometimes traveled with him."

"Into Ottoman lands?" Hyacinthie's voice rose four notes. "Truly? What was it like? Did handsome Turks seek to woo you? Did you walk in perfumed gardens surrounded by beautiful birds and pet tigers?"

"It was dusty," said Hero, feeling she owed it to the child to divest her experiences of any tinge of romance. "Often hot, sometimes windy. When we were among Muslims, we were forced to go swathed and veiled as their women do, and the people most often avoided us because we were from Europe. Many times we had poor food and brackish water, and no means of gaining other supplies. The local villagers would not sell food to us, and there were no hostelries for us, so we lived in tents. My father could find no tobacco for his pipe. The Muslims do not drink wine, just as the Comte doesn't, so no wine was to be had."

"How exciting!" Hyacinthie gulped down half of the lemonade. "How grand! Not the lack of wine, of course, or the other problems," she added, "but everything else. How wonderful!"

"How hot and inconvenient," said Hero, correcting her. "You wouldn't enjoy it at all. I didn't."

"But you *must* have," said Hyacinthie in astonished reproach. "You must have known that what you were doing was extraordinary. Didn't you?"

Hero thought a moment. "Well, yes, from a certain point of view, it was. But in terms of how we lived, it was far from pleasant or remarkable, except for the discommodation. I would have traded half of the wonders for a reliable bath, a chance to wear my own clothes, and freedom from flies."

"But . . . you must have liked some of it," Hyacinthie protested, then added, "Well, flies, yes. No one likes flies."

"And we lived in tents that were stifling in the day and cold at night, and filled with dust." Hero smiled briefly. "I am glad to have seen as much of the world as I have, but I do not claim that the experience was delightful.

Again Hyacinthie nodded. "It may be that you didn't appreciate all he had done for you."

"I believe I did," said Hero. "At least sufficiently to know it wasn't the way I wanted to live all my days."

Hyacinthie drank the last of her lemonade and said with determination. "*I* would never slight such a splendid adventure. *I* would thank my father for providing so much for me, even if I were sometimes uncomfortable. *I* would not be ungrateful. *I* wouldn't ignore my obligation to my father; *I* would make myself useful to him at every opportunity." She almost got to her feet while she struggled with her growing indignation.

"My dear Fraulein Sieffert," said Hero quickly, holding out her hand to her guest. "I had no intention of distressing you." She sat a bit straighter. "I am deeply grateful to my father for including me in his expedition. I don't think I could have endured having to stay in the care of relatives or the nuns. But that doesn't mean that all was unalloyed delight and wonders, or that it was an experience that I am eager to repeat, for that would not be the case. I am content to remain in Europe for the rest of my days rather than face the demands of an expedition in Ottoman lands. Most of what we did was drudgery, as daily life is for almost all of humanity."

"You must not speak against your father, you know," Hyacinthie said forcefully. "He has done you a great honor by permitting you to go with him on his travels."

"My father is a remarkable man, very learned. He has lectured in France and England—he gave me an English name because he liked it better than the Italian version—and he has published eight books, three in Italian, one in English, three in French, one in German." She made no attempt to disguise her pride in him. "I am a fortunate woman to be his daughter."

"Very fortunate," said Hyacinthie darkly.

"And I was mindful of all the opportunities he provided me, before I was married."

"Yes. My uncle told me you were a widow. That's sad." Hyacinthie regarded her in sudden concentration, as if she were seeing Hero for the first time. "Your husband was a soldier?"

"An engineer, but part of Napoleon's forces, and committed to social reform. He was primarily employed in assessing fortifications that had been damaged, with the intention of recommending repairs or demolition. He didn't live to see his idol come to his inglorious end." She said this so calmly that she felt a bit shocked; a year ago she could not have spoken so tranquilly of Fridhold. "He was injured in his work six years ago, and the fever that followed killed him."

"That must have been very upsetting for you, losing him in that way," said Hyacinthie in apparent indifference.

To her astonishment, Hero heard herself say, "It spared him the Russian Campaign."

Hyacinthie blinked. "Yes," she said slowly. "But he died, so why does the how of it matter?" She looked toward Ragoczy, to see if he was listening.

"Fraulein!" Hero exclaimed.

At this point Ragoczy intervened. "You know how hard it was when your parents died, Fraulein Sieffert. This was just such a loss for my friend and her children." He blotted the answer he had just completed very gently, taking care not to smear the edges of the note.

"You have children?" Hyacinthie asked.

"Three sons and a daughter. They are with my husband's father." She stopped herself from revealing anything more.

"Three sons and a daughter," marveled Hyacinthie. "Tell me about them."

"My oldest son is eleven, then twin boys who are nine, and my daughter, who is eight," said Hero.

"They must provide consolation for you," said Hyacinthie because it was expected of her, and because she sensed that Hero missed her family.

"When I see them," said Hero distantly. "Siegfried will soon be going off to school. He's the oldest."

Ragoczy folded the note and wrote *Graf von Ravensberg* in his neat hand on the envelope. "I thank you for serving as the messenger for your guardian, Fraulein Sieffert. If you will extend your goodness and take this to him on my behalf? Thank you." He reached for the sealing wax, and struck the hanging flint-and-steel to light the wick embedded in the wax.

Hyacinthie beamed at him. "It is my privilege." She could not keep the satisfaction out of her voice.

As the wick flared, Ragoczy turned the stick of wax, encouraging a small drop to fall onto the back of the envelope. "I hope your uncle is satisfied with his book now."

"He said the necessary corrections had been made," said Hyacinthie.

"Then I hope he will be gratified by the discussion it engenders when it is published," Ragoczy said, pressing his signet-ring into the wax and leaving an impression of the eclipse. He waved the envelope twice to be sure the wax was cool.

"And I hope you will have a pleasant journey back to Ravensberg," added Hero.

"It is a long journey to make," said Hyacinthie, rising to take the sealed envelope Ragoczy held out to her. "I don't know when I shall see Amsterdam again."

"Let us hope you may come here before too many years have passed," said Ragoczy. "It is a city that improves with revisiting, more so now that the Netherlands have become a proper country again."

"Will *you* come here again, Comte?" Hyacinthie asked so coquettishly that Ragoczy had to stifle a laugh as he exchanged a quick glance with Hero.

"I have business here, so it is very likely that I will," said Ragoczy. He bowed slightly to Hyacinthie. "Would you like one of my servants to accompany you back to your hotel?"

"It isn't far, and I want to purchase some muslin and lawn on my way. But thank you for your concern." She tilted her head and achieved a shy smile. She slipped the envelope into her silver-link reticule. "I will hand this to my uncle the instant I see him."

"You're most kind," said Ragoczy as he moved toward the open parlor door. "Convey my greetings to the Graf."

Hyacinthie was reluctant to leave, walking slowly and sighing once. "Thank you for the lemonade and biscuits."

Ragoczy bowed once more. "A pleasure, Fraulein."

Kuyskill appeared in the entry-hall as if conjured from the air. He guided Hyacinthie toward the door, opened it for her, and stood watching her open her parasol and descend to the street. Only then did he close the door and say to Ragoczy, "She is up to mischief, Comte."

"Not mischief, but she is after more than a note for her uncle," said Ragoczy. He was about to go back to the secretary when Kuyskill went on.

"Rogier is back from the docks and has an inventory for you. Shall I send him in?"

Ragoczy looked at Hero. "Will you excuse me a moment?"

"I will excuse you as long as you need," she replied with a wave of her hand. "I have to write to my children before we leave, and now is a good time to do it."

"Thank you," said Ragoczy, falling in behind Kuyskill.

"You should have sent a servant with that young woman. She shouldn't be out on the streets alone like that," said Kuyskill, making no apology for addressing his employer so critically.

"I do not disagree, but she refused escort, so what can I do?" Ragoczy countered. "Her guardian is careless with her; I cannot offend him by forcing my servant upon her."

Kuyskill nodded slowly. "Probably so," he allowed as he opened the door to Ragoczy's study where Rogier was waiting. "I still don't like to think of her, unaccompanied."

But Hyacinthie was not alone on her erratic course back to the hotel: Otto Gutesohnes was at her side, deferential and gallant all at once. He had donned a long duster-coat and threaded two lashes through the buttonhole to show off his occupation, and carried his wide-brimmed coachman's hat in his hand; he stayed by her side as she dawdled past shops and vendors' stalls.

"So you must tell me: how long have you driven for the Comte?" Hyacinthie asked as Gutesohnes escorted her over a narrow bridge; she spoke in German and she smiled provocatively as she asked.

"I haven't worked for him very long. I am his courier. His coachman broke his leg so I am taking his place until he is healed." He returned her smile.

"Courier? You carry messages for him?" She knew the answer but wanted to keep him talking.

"Messages, dispatches, books, whatever he asks," said Gutesohnes.

"That means you travel alone?"

"From time to time," he answered cautiously, not sure what she intended and not wanting to spoil such a promising flirtation.

"He must trust you, to send you on such missions."

"He has allowed me to prove myself," said Gutesohnes.

"How far have you gone for him?" She twirled her parasol.

"Oh, to Heidelberg and to Koln thus far, with stops along the way in both instances." He waited. "I may be sent to Praha in the fall."

"Would your travels, perhaps, bring you to Austria—to Salzburg, perhaps?" There was no mistaking her intention now. "My uncle is often preoccupied with his studies, and I might be able to slip away to the gamekeeper's cottage, if I knew I could meet you there."

He had not expected such a direct invitation, and so he walked on in silence for a short distance. Finally he said, "I would not want to compromise you in any way, Fraulein."

"No one would know," she said. "I can send you a note, telling you where the cottage is, and—you *do* read, don't you?"

"Yes," he said. "I'm no scholar, but I am not a dolt, either."

She beamed. "Then we can write to one another."

"But your guardian wouldn't approve, would he," said Gute-sohnes, halting as three dogs came trotting up to them, noses busy.

"That doesn't matter. I'll give you the direction for my governess; she will receive notes for me."

"And she'll tell your uncle," said Gutesohnes, ever more certain that this was too reckless. He coughed discreetly. "You shouldn't be involved in anything clandestine."

She slapped playfully at his arm. "You're much too discreet for that, aren't you?"

Gutesohnes shook his head. "I fear for you. It isn't fitting that you should engage in anything that would smirch your reputation, particularly not at your age, when the Graf is seeking to find you a husband."

"Smirch my reputation?" she mocked, thinking of all the nights she had passed with her uncle in her bed. "If no one knows," she said patiently, "it means nothing."

"But a rumor could ruin you," he cautioned her.

"I don't care," she announced.

"You should care," he said. "You can throw away all your happiness in the world in a foolish gesture." He knew this was true, but he was flattered that she would take such a chance on his behalf. "Save your acts of defiance for a man who is worthy of your hand."

Her laughter was high and harsh. "You don't know, do you?" She glared at him through a smile. "No, you don't know."

Startled at her change in demeanor, Gutesohnes hesitated. "Know what, Fraulein? I don't understand."

"No," she said, ignoring him. "You have no notion. None at all."

"Notion about what?" he pursued, confused and nonplussed.

"Nothing! You wouldn't understand in any case," she declared, and walked more quickly, forcing him to hurry after her along the street that bordered the canal until they reached the Majestic Hotel, where her uncle was preparing to depart. At last she slowed and was willing to look at him once more, this time with her seductive smile firmly in place. "You've done your duty. You can report back to the Comte now; tell him I thank him for his concern, and that I look forward to seeing him again," she said with an ill-concealed smirk as she went up the marble steps.

"But he didn't—" he objected, wanting to convince her that his company had been his idea, not an order from his employer; he received what might have been a blown kiss for his efforts.

Text of a letter written in Greek from Ismail al-Rachad in Antioch, to Saint-Germain Ragoczy, Comte Franciscus at Château Ragoczy near Lake Geneva, Yvoire, Switzerland; carried by private courier.

To the most highly regarded Comte Franciscus, the greetings of Ismail al-Rachad on this, the 2ⁿᵈ day of September, 1817, by the calendar of you Infidel dogs,

I have received the gold you were good enough to send to me not two days since, and I have spent a third of it already, may Allah be praised for magnanimity. The cargos of your three ships held in harbor will be released and the ships permitted to set sail by the 10ᵗʰ of this month, which would not have been possible without the money you have provided. It is truly as you observed in your letter: gold and license keep close company. The sum I have paid—which I will not demean by calling it a bribe—has made me keenly aware of how readily the local authorities may be persuaded through indulgence. This was not unknown to me before, but it has been demonstrated with such stark clarity that I can only marvel at how openly these men abuse their offices.

I am sorry to report that the Daystar *has had an outbreak of fever among her crew, and before she can sail, a dozen sailors must be replaced. Through the mercy of Allah the lives of most of these men has been spared: there is a good physician here, and he has said that the crew has contracted inflamed livers from poor water. The water-barrels are all going to be replaced and those men too ill to sail will be taken into the physician's care until they are dead or sufficiently recovered to return to the sea. I am working with Captain Irkul to find men to sail with the ship on or before the 10th.*

I am doing my utmost to secure a safe passage to Egypt for the de-Montalia woman. As she is of your blood, I am obligated to arrange such for her, but I must tell you that it is not very prudent to permit a young woman to travel alone in this part of the world. There are many dangers that threaten her, most of which I doubt she comprehends or is prepared to deal with. I trust you know what you are asking for her when you charge me with the duty of getting her the passage she seeks.

There has been an improvement in shipping of late, and I am glad to say that your ships are sailing with full holds. For the next year, if all goes well, we should recoup a good portion of the losses of the last two years, if Allah wills it. If this continues to be the case, I will finally send for my family and set them up in a suitable house. I may even take a third wife. In five years, I will purchase a ship of my own and if Allah favors my endeavors, I will have my own shipping company before I am thirty-five. The men of my family are long-lived, so I have a good expectation of seeing fifty years. A man can accomplish a great deal in fifty years.

I am grateful to you—dog of an Infidel though you are—for all the opportunities you have provided me, and I am certain that you will never have cause to regret the trust you have placed in me,

> *Your most devoted servant*
> *Ismail al-Rachad*
> *factor, Eclipse Trading Company*
> *Antioch*

2

Risky though it was on such a stretch of road, Gutesohnes whipped his team to a gallop, shouting encouragement to the horses as the coach lurched along the coach-route cut into the steepest side of the mountain above the River Orbe under a brassy sky that made the coachman squint as much as the rising dust. "Half a league, my comrades!" he yelled at the horses as he held the reins with straining hands in a frantic effort to retain what little control he had left; he tried not to listen for the hoofbeats of the horses of the highwaymen behind him.

"There are trees ahead," Ragoczy called out through the carriage's open window. "They may have confederates waiting there."

"I'll be alert," Gutesohnes shouted back. "Just two days from Yvoire. Two days! You'd think we'd be safe, so close to home."

"The men are desperate," said Ragoczy, half-emerging from the on-side window, one of his pistols in his hand. "Not that I will be able to hit anything, but it may back them off. You say there are five men?"

"Yes. I saw five," Gutesohnes cried out.

"We turn on-side shortly, do we not? And the road descends?"

"Less than half a league," said Gutesohnes, his voice going ragged.

"Very good," said Ragoczy, and sighted the barrel of his pistol to the rear of the coach; the vehicle swayed dangerously, but Ragoczy kept himself in place. "I will fire above their heads—let us see if that slows them down." His pistol had two barrels and both were charged. As the turn brought the road behind the coach into view again, he took what aim he could, then pulled one trigger, and almost immediately, the other. The knuckles of his hand on which the barrels rested burned through his glove, but he remained in position to see if he had done any damage to their pursuers. Unable to discern what had become of the group of cloaked-and-masked men, he slipped back into the coach, blowing on his knuckles to cool the welts; Hero was hanging onto the hand-straps and doing her best to maintain her composure.

"They warned us in Cossonay that there are bandits about," she said without accusing him in any way as she watched him put down his double-barreled pistol and take a smaller pistol from under the armrest. "This could have been avoided. We should have employed out-riders."

"So they did warn us, and we might well have avoided this, had we heeded them," Ragoczy agreed as he inspected the pistol before readying himself to shoot at the outlaws once again. "And we know now that out-riders would be helpful, so long as they assisted us and not them. I hope our second coach is more fortunate than we have been." He gestured toward the rear of their vehicle. "There have been times that such warnings were ploys to put travelers into the hands of brigands, who posed as out-riders."

She considered this unpleasant possibility. "Yes. That could happen."

"One must weigh the possibilities and make the best decisions under the circumstances."

"They can go faster than we can, can't they?" she asked, a slight tremor in her voice. "They'll overtake us."

"They can, but not safely. As we topped the last rise, one of their men was crowded to the edge of the road; he and his mount fell, and they are somewhere down the canyon. The highwaymen are now without their leader and his deputy: their horses are tiring rapidly." He did not add that soon it would be unsafe for the four gray Kladrubers pulling the coach to continue at this precipitous pace, and that they, too, were becoming exhausted; the team of fine Bohemian carriage horses had been his most extravagant purchase in Liège and it offended him that they should be put at risk.

"Yes. The servants—their coach should not be far behind us. Do you think they'll be set upon, as we have been? Isn't there some way to warn them?"

"The indication of a fall from the road ought to alert them that something is wrong," said Ragoczy. "I doubt these highwaymen will strike again at anyone today, not after that fall." He had great confidence in Rogier's ability to deal with whatever he encountered, but he kept that thought to himself.

Sighing, Hero clung more tightly to the hand-strap. "I hope you're right."

"They have lost a horse and I am assuming the rider was injured, too. Neither man nor horse will be easily brought up from the fall." He remembered many times when he had been forced to out-run pursuers: it was an experience he never got used to. "Can you charge my pistols for me?"

"I know how to," she said. "Where is your—"

"In the small leather box, in the other armrest, the one with the broad shoulder-strap. You can save me some time if you would tend to my pistols." He pulled himself half out the window and fired again, just as Gutesohnes applied the brake to help the horses slow down as the road began its sharp descent. Ragoczy swore an oath in a language only he understood, his hand trembling with the rattle of the carriage. His arm, jolted by the tightening of the brake, was off-aim, but that proved a lucky chance as the shot struck high in the chest of the lead horse of the five highwaymen. The horse staggered and went down, tumbling down the road, legs flailing, taking his rider and unseating, in addition to the stricken horse's rider, two of the men who tried—and failed—to get over their fallen companion.

Gutesohnes managed to pull his team in to an edgy trot, holding the Kladrubers in as he regained control of the coach and his team. "How many now, Comte?" he called back as the coach swung into a grove of trees and was slowed still more by their encroaching presence.

"They're falling back, and not a moment too soon," said Ragoczy loudly enough to be heard inside the coach and on the driving-box. "I'm sorry about the horses. They meant us no harm."

"No, that they did not," agreed Gutesohnes, tugging back on the reins to keep the team from breaking into a run.

Ragoczy slid back into the coach window, narrowly avoiding a collision with a massive tree-trunk growing at the edge of the road. "I think we're safe for now," he said to Hero as she handed him his recharged pistol.

"They aren't following us," she said uncertainly.

"No. And no one is emerging from the forest ahead of us." He stowed the pistol in the armrest along with his cartridge-box. "For now we seem to be safe. If there are no more problems, we will reach Lausanne tonight, and be back at Château Ragoczy by night-fall tomorrow." He gave her a reassuring smile. "I don't think any robbers are bold enough to venture as far as the lake."

She shook her head as she began to weep. "I'm . . . I'm sorry," she stammered.

"Why should you be?" he asked, holding out his hands to her.

"Because . . . because . . ." She sobbed openly.

"Because you are calm when things are dangerous and upset when the danger is past?" he suggested, having seen this kind of behavior on many previous occasions.

"Distraught," she admitted, still crying but also laughing. She pulled a small handkerchief from her reticule and dabbed at her eyes. "I'm . . . abashed."

"Abashed? There is no need," he said, moving onto her seat and putting his arm around her. "You are reliable beyond all reckoning. You have no cause to feel abashed."

She bristled at this. "What do you mean, I have no cause?"

"I understand you do feel abashed," he went on, "and it saddens me that you do not value yourself highly enough to see that you deserve your name, and that you have done better than almost anyone—man or woman—could hope to have done." He felt her relax under his arm, and he leaned over to kiss her forehead. "I hold you in high regard, whether you do or not."

She raised her face, her eyes red and still filling with tears. "You always know what to say to brighten my mood," she said, shaking her head slowly.

He kissed her cheek. "You make it sound as if I indulge you, which is not the case."

"So you say," she murmured while she crumpled her handkerchief and wiped her face with it. "Oh, what's the purpose of reassurance, but to help us forget our failings?"

"I would rather think it has to do with comfort, and the reiterance of pledges of devotion." He took her hand which did not contain her handkerchief and brought it to his lips. "I am grateful to you for charging my pistol," he went on evenly. "Yours is a very useful skill."

She laughed a little. "One you knew I possessed."

"No," he corrected gently, "one I *hoped* you possessed. With your travels, I thought it likely that you had been taught to shoot."

"Oh, yes," she said, more grimly but no longer weeping. "My father insisted."

"Very good," Ragoczy approved, and pulled her a little closer to him. "You have forgot nothing."

She straightened up. "I should hope not. He would have slapped me silly if I had failed to learn something so important."

He bit back the sharp remark that rose in his thoughts, and instead, he kissed her hand again. "I thank you for being ready to help in a difficult situation."

"It was that," she agreed, and gave a long, slow sigh as she settled against his shoulder. "I wish I didn't seem to unravel when difficult situations end."

"Better then than in the middle of them," he said, noticing the coach was going at a walk now, over more deeply rutted road, although it was no longer descending steeply. There were farmhouses in sight, and the first signs of a village ahead. He tapped on the ceiling of the coach to gain Gutesohnes' attention, then called out, "Why are we slowing down? Is the team worn out?"

"Nothing like that," answered Gutesohnes. "The team can go on to Lausanne if they aren't pushed again. No, Saint-Ivroc is less than a league ahead. You know Saint-Ivroc."

"Very small," Ragoczy recalled. "Maybe fifteen houses at most, and a market-square with a trough and a fountain."

"And a tavern for the marketers. No posting inn," Gutesohnes added. "Do you want to stop?"

"Why?" Ragoczy asked.

"To make a report?"

"To whom? For all we know, the highwaymen live here. In remote places like this, robbery is often the only way to make a living." Ragoczy considered for the better part of a minute, then said, "If the coach seems sound and the team is all right, give them a chance to drink at the village trough, and then we will continue on, at an easy pace."

"Very good," said Gutesohnes, and pulled the team down to a slower walk so that the coach rolled into the town as inconspicuously as possible.

"Would you like to step down?" Ragoczy asked Hero as he felt the coach finally stop moving.

"No, not really. Not here," she answered. "It is all so empty. Is it just that it's mid-day and they're all at dinner?"

"Perhaps. You need not alight if that is what you want," he said as he opened the door and let down the steps. Descending, he went to the front of the team and patted the neck of the off-side wheeler. "I am sorry that you had to do that."

"Better than being stolen by those roughians," said Gutesohnes as he climbed down from the driving-box. "And you wonder why I prefer being a courier."

"You might still be set upon by highwaymen," said Ragoczy as he reached up into the bottom of the driving-box for the wooden pail, which he took to the trough and filled for the wheeler nearest him; the leaders had sunk their noses into the water. He held the pail while the horse drank, then went and refilled it for the other wheeler. Looking about, he said, "The square is truly deserted just now."

"It's mid-day, or close enough, as you see. Most places are shut for the dinner hour. And many of the town's young men died in the recent wars, or so I have heard." Gutesohnes made a quick survey of the square. "There is one open door, I see."

"Where?"

Gutesohnes cocked his head toward the tavern that faced the market-square. "I'm going to get something to eat and drink."

"As suits you best," said Ragoczy, then added, "Will you bring a bottle of cider for my companion?" He offered the pail of water to the second wheeler, holding it while the gray gelding did his best to shove his nose through the bottom of the pail.

"Certainly," said Gutesohnes, already striding away toward the tavern.

Hero leaned out the window of the coach. "You are not going to join him, are you?"

"No, I am not," he said. "We should be traveling soon." He pulled a twig from the nearest horse's mane. "I want to reach Lausanne before sunset."

"You fear more highwaymen?" she asked, her voice trembling.

"Highwaymen? No." He put the empty pail back on the floor of the driving-box. "Nothing so obvious. I want a chance to inspect the coach thoroughly and make any repairs needed before we venture on."

"Do you think repairs will be necessary? This coach is so new, and we have not used it too harshly." She sounded worried.

"I think the axles should be inspected, and the wheel-rims. The harness may also have sustained damage and may need repair. And after the way we careened down the mountainside, I think the springs must need adjusting." He patted the rump of the wheeler and saw a cloud of dust rise from the gray coat. "And the horses will need to be groomed carefully. When we get them back to Château Ragoczy, they will have to be bathed."

"Well, if you *will* drive gray horses . . ." she said. "They show every speck of dust and grime."

"That they do," he said. "I'll want to clean my pistols and charge them again."

"Will you trust your team to your grooms?" she asked.

"If they were the liver sorrels, I would probably brush them down myself. But these Kladrubers are not so attached to their people as the liver sorrels are." He watched a cat with a mouse in its jaws sneak past the trough and into an alley between two closed buildings. "The horses will need three days of rest after such work as they have had."

"Will you bring the liver sorrels back from Liège any time soon?" Hero asked. "I do so like them."

"I may do. They'll be at Château Ragoczy before winter, that much I can assure you." He patted the shoulder of the on-side leader as he made his way around toward the door. He began to wonder how much longer Gutesohnes would take for a quick meal; they should be under way soon, he told himself as he checked the horses' mouths, hoping the escape from the highwaymen had not damaged them. He had examined the Kladruber's legs and feet by the time Gutesohnes sauntered back, a sly smile beginning to spread over his face, a bottle of cherry cider in his hand.

"The highwaymen we encountered live in the village up the hill, or so the locals claim. There are nine of them, seven of them were soldiers in Napoleon's army, and have found no way to earn a living but banditry." He handed the bottle to Ragoczy, then grabbed the rail and pulled himself up into the driving-box. "They claim they have tried to get the authorities to remove them from this region, that the bandits are all strangers in the region. The landlord of the tavern offered to buy them passage to America." He laughed—and the sound revealed that he was still shaken from their get-away—and occupied himself with pulling the reins into his hands. "Best get inside, or I may go without you, Comte." He winked broadly to indicate he was joking, not insubordinate.

"You've had a tankard or two of beer, I assume, and will be calmer shortly," said Ragoczy as he climbed up the steps, pulled them up, and closed the door. After he gave the cider to Hero, he tapped the ceiling of the coach to signal that he was ready to depart.

"Is he capable of driving safely?" Hero asked as Ragoczy settled across from her. She began to pry the wax-sealed lid from the bottle, using her pen-knife in her reticule to do it. Settling back against the squabs, she reached for a travel cup in the holder next to the hand-strap, and poured out about a third of the contents of the bottle.

"Oh, yes. This wildness is much more nerves than drink. He is still half-expecting the robbers to resume their chase, and to be forced to risk the team in out-running them." He felt the coach begin to move off at a decorous pace. "You see? There is no reason to worry: the horses will keep him honest. They came through the chase well enough, but the off-side wheeler has a cut on his leg that I suspect is from a bit of flying rock from the roadway. It will need dressing tonight, and perhaps again tomorrow night."

"When we will be back at your château," she said quietly.

"So I imagine we will be, if that one stretch of road is still holding its repairs," said Ragoczy as the coach moved on into the lovely early afternoon. Above them seraphic clouds drifted, serene as plainsong, impervious to the crags of rock and ice below, and too exalted to dally over the orchards and field farther down the flanks of the mountains. Orchards and vineyards hung with fruit and the fields were shaggy with grain or filled with grazing cattle, goats, and sheep. The worst of the summer heat had passed, and although the day was warm, it was not stifling.

"When do you expect to come to Lausanne?" Hero yawned, nearly dropping the travel cup as she attempted to block her open mouth with her hand. "I'm sorry. All the excitement is catching up with me."

"Do you want to rest?" he asked, reaching for the concealed lever that would transform the two seats into a bed.

"Yes, but in Lausanne," she said, laying her hand on his arm. "If the day starts to close in and we are still on the road, then I might change my mind, but not just now. Now I want to doze. I wish it could be like this when I travel to visit my children, but it will be rainy or snowing by the time I depart for Austria."

"At least you will finally spend time with your children," said

Ragoczy, aware that the Graf von Scharffensee had hoped to discourage Hero's visit by choosing the most inclement part of the year for it.

She smiled wistfully. "I know I have done the right thing, putting them in their grandfather's hands, but I cannot help but miss them." She drank nervously, clearing her throat between sips.

"Perhaps he will relent when he sees how much good your visit does them." He doubted that would be the case, but he was prepared to encourage her as much as possible.

"Do you think they'll be glad to see me—my children?" she asked, and very nearly held her breath as she waited for him to answer.

"I cannot see why they shouldn't," he answered. "You haven't been cruel to them."

"They might think so, I have been away so long." She bit her lower lip and poured out more cider.

"You children probably understand why, in their own way: children comprehend so much more than we assume they do." He stroked her hand. "Do not fear that you have been supplanted in their hearts by their grandfather. They must long for you, as all children long for their parents."

"Are you certain of that?" She had intended to snap at him, but this was a cry of hopelessness.

"Children may deny their longing, and they may claim to have forgotten it, but very few of them actually do," he said. "I've observed that for myself, down the centuries. Yours cannot be so different, can they."

"I try to anticipate a good reception, but I don't expect one." She looked out at the distant spire of a church. "What village is that, do you know?"

"I regret to say I do not," he answered, recognizing her desire to say nothing more about her coming visit to Scharffensee. "Are you hungry?" he asked. "We have cheese and water and wine still, and a few of those Viennese rolls left." He indicated the small door behind her head that held the food he mentioned.

"No. I will in a while, but just now I'm not ready to eat. The cider will suffice." She put the tips of her fingers together. "We are going along at a good speed, considering. I think your grays could trot forever. For now, I want to look out the window and see nothing but the mountains and the river and the sky."

"Very well," he told her, and kissed her gently before moving back in his seat, where he remained, silent and a bit preoccupied for nearly twenty minutes while she finished her cider and returned the cup to its holder.

"It saddens me to see the seasons change," she remarked as she handed the empty cider-bottle to him.

"Everything changes, soon or late," he said, and was still for another quarter hour. Then he began to speak again, as if continuing a conversation. "There was a time, many centuries ago, shortly after I first came to Egypt," said Ragoczy distantly, "when I often wondered, when I wakened from sleep, if I had died the True Death in my stupor but did not know it. I began to think that perhaps everything I did was the imagining of the dead, that I had not survived but would not admit I had not survived, and so repeated everything I had done in life, but only in my un-dead mind. It took a girl bitten by a rabid dog to jolt me out of that cocoon of delusion."

Hero looked up, mildly startled. "What?"

"It was a long time ago, of course, and I am certain that I was still recovering from the many decades I had spent as a demon in a Babylonian oubliette." He stared off at the mountains beyond the coach. "I had nothing but my own loneliness and the fear of the sacrifices I was regularly provided to sustain me. Being taken to Egypt was the first step in my awakening." He considered the past in silence.

"When did you arrive in Egypt?" She was intrigued and wary at once, not prepared to hear anything she disliked.

"A very long time ago. They took me to Memphis first."

"Who was Pharaoh?" she asked. "Do you remember? Do you recall anything from so long ago?"

"Many of those things would be better forgotten," he said bluntly. "Yet I recall so much of that time."

"Then you do remember?" She looked surprised at this admission. "Truly?"

He nodded slowly. "It was fifteen hundred years before the Christian calendar, and Pharaoh was Hatshepsut." He tried to think of something to say that would reassure Hero; he laughed once, softly. "Hatshepsut was a woman, very imposing and capable, as she had to be to be Pharaoh. She came aboard the ship on which I traveled and I was presented to her as a captive. I had never seen anyone like her."

"Did you love her?" Hero asked, then put her hand to her mouth, shamefaced. "I didn't mean that. It was spiteful of me to speak so."

"No. I did not love anyone then. At my best, I was indifferent." He leaned back as much as the seat of the coach would allow. "Not that a foreign slave would be allowed anywhere near Pharaoh without all her guards around her, and the priests. No, they had better uses for me than as an oddity to entertain Pharaoh: I was made a slave of the Temple of Imhotep, and assigned to care for the dying."

"How awful," said Hero with distaste, for she had seen field hospitals and knew what they were. "How did you manage?"

"Indifferently, at first, both in skill and in attitude. I cared only that the priests were satisfied with my work, nothing more." He felt the road begin to dip again, and said, "Lausanne is about two hours ahead, I think."

"If all goes well," she said.

"If all goes well," he agreed. "I doubt we'll have any trouble on this stretch of road. It is well-traveled once the crossroad is reached, in about half a league." He put his hands together, fingertips touching lightly. "And if there are no more difficulties, we should be at Château Ragoczy before dark tomorrow. We will depart early and travel as far as Saint-Gingolph before resting. If we arrive late in the day, we will not continue, but spend the night there. If we have made good speed, we will go on. The horses will suffer otherwise." He looked over at her. "I hope you will not be too disappointed if we have to wait an extra day to return."

"No. No, but I am weary of travel."

"As am I," he said, and fell to watching the sky and the lengthening shadows. "The Kladrubers are wearier still, and Gutesohnes along with them."

The coach passed the crossroad at Renens-en-Haut and continued on toward the lake. There were more houses now, and the promise of a town ahead—Renens—and the road to Lausanne. Gutesohnes pulled the team to a jog-trot and steadied them through increasing traffic. At one point he halted them completely to permit six mounted dragoons to go past them, then set the team moving again.

"I could see the other coach, about a league behind us, while we waited for the dragoons," Gutesohnes called down to Ragoczy.

"Very good. They've closed the gap. I am sure they made an easier passage through the mountains than we did." Ragoczy saw Hero shudder miserably; he softened his voice. "It is over. The highwaymen are gone. We need only concern ourselves with pickpockets and sneak-thieves."

"What a consoling thought," she said, too brightly.

"You understand the risks all travelers take in strange towns," he said, so levelly that she managed to gesture agreement without any sharp words. "It is wise to keep in mind that travelers' inns often cater to those who prey upon them as well as the travelers."

"Why should I fear, since I am with you?" Her banter fooled neither of them, for it was clear from her demeanor that the threat of being robbed frightened her.

"And you will stay in the private parlor I engage for your use. As soon as Rogier is with us, I will task him with ensuring you are not exposed to the unmannerly fellows who are bound to be in the taproom."

The coach lurched to a stop, and Gutesohnes called down, "Sorry. There are pigs loose on the road."

This simple announcement set Hero to giggling, the first indication of her release of tension. "Pigs."

"Probably being driven home from market," said Ragoczy calmly.

Her giggling continued. "I sound so . . . missish. I don't . . . You'd think I'd never traveled before."

"You are trying to reassure yourself," he said. "That escape this morning was very frightening."

"Even for you?" Her spurt of laughter made her look about in chagrin. "I don't mean anything . . . wrong."

The coach began to move again, and Gutesohnes called down, "Which inn?"

"Le Corbeau et Hibou," answered Ragoczy.

"I know the place," Gutesohnes assured him, adding, "The team is very tired."

"They have had a hard day," Ragoczy agreed.

Hero had brought her unmirthful laughter under control, and now she said, "You're very understanding, Comte. But I am appalled to think such a minor disruption could work such a change in me."

He took her hands in his own. "I know you have been about the world, and seen many things, but that does not mean that you are immune from fright. The chase this morning was fairly brief, but it well and truly rattled me. I expect it did much the same for you."

She took a long, slow breath. "Thank you for understanding."

"Le Corbeau et Hibou," called out Gutesohnes. "Right ahead."

Ragoczy lifted her hands and kissed them. "You might thank Gutesohnes, too. We were saved by his driving."

She nodded twice. "I will," she declared, and began to make small repairs to her appearance as the coach swung into the innyard and ostlers ran out to assist the coachman with the horses.

Text of a note from Professor Erich Teich at Heidelberg University, to Wallache Gerhard Winifrith Siefert, Graf von Ravensberg at Ravensberg, Austria; carried by academic courier.

To Graf von Ravensberg, the felicitations from Professor Erich Teich of Heidelberg, on this, the 18th day of September, 1817

My dear Graf,

I thank you for informing me of your forthcoming publication on the properties and character of blood. This will provide a much needed text that many of us have wanted to have to hand in our pursuits. By your innovative work, you may have provided a basic thesis from which all of us concerned with anatomical studies might clarify our thoughts and observations. I congratulate you on your accomplishment, and I look forward to reading your book as soon as it is made available. Now that I have returned to my university I can endorse your work freely. Many others will be equally pleased to learn of your efforts, which will doubtless inspire lively debate from Poland to England.

> Wishing you every success
> I am
>   Erich Teich
>   Professor of Anatomical Studies
>   Heidelberg

3

Hero crumpled the letter and let it drop from her nerveless fingers. She began to shake, her face now the color of whey. "Oh, God!" she cried and dropped to her knees on the entry-hall carpet, huddling over the paper as she began silently to weep.

Ragoczy, who had been seeing to the unloading of the two coaches, saw her fall and broke off his effort with a quick signal to Rogier. "What is it?" he asked as he went to her and went down on one knee beside her, his back to the open door to shield her from curious eyes. "Hero?"

"She's dead," Hero muttered, and thrust the letter into his hand. She did not sob but tears shone on her face.

"Who is dead?" he asked as he smoothed the sheet and began to read.

Hero shuddered heavily as she tried to speak, but failed.

Ragoczy perused the Graf's note, appalled at the lack of sympathy extended to the child's mother. "What a terrible loss for you," he said as he reached the end of it and reached to set it on a decorative urn near the stairs. "I know it's inadequate, but I am very sorry."

"Annamaria. Annamaria. Annamaria," she said as if repeating a prayer. "I should have gone to her. I should have insisted that the Graf let me see my children." She hugged herself and began to rock back and forth, still bent over her knees on the carpet.

"You had no way of knowing," said Ragoczy, aware this was useless and that Hero was in the thrall of her grief. He motioned to Rogier to keep away.

"I *should* have known. I'm her . . . I *was* her mother." Suddenly she let out a howl of anguish and fury that made the château ring. "God, God, God, what am I going to do? She's buried already. For weeks! I can't mourn her with her brothers." All the warmth had gone out of the bright afternoon; for Hero, everything had suddenly sunk into shadow, and that now held her as if in an invisible shroud. "If we'd pressed through yesterday, I would have learned of it sooner," she said dully.

"And been no more able then to change what has happened than you are now," said Ragoczy with such kindness that she was able to lash out at him. "Had you been here, you still could not have reached Scharffensee in time to—"

"Little you know about it! You, with your centuries and centuries! She didn't have even a decade. She was about to turn nine." She put her hands to her face and finally the sobs came. "*Not yet nine!*"

"Nine is very young," Ragoczy agreed, unable to think of anything more to say.

"She hadn't any chance. All she did was learn French." Her sobs deepened. "It is wrong!"

Ragoczy laid his hand on her back to steady her as her rocking increased. "Hero."

"Life is cruel!"

"Life is indifferent," said Ragoczy as consolingly as he could. "It is we who are cruel. Or kind."

Suddenly she rose up and lunged at him, but whether to attack him or fall into the haven of his arms, she herself could not tell. "You don't know anything about it! Nothing! It doesn't touch you. It touches me. Annamaria was *mine!*"

He held her close to him, letting her struggle against him, but supporting her. "You love her and will always miss her. Grieve for her, Hero."

"You are . . . you!" She shoved at him and almost pushed herself over. Reaching for the letter, she bundled it into her hand and glared at him. "She's gone. I have lost her."

Without moving, he said, "Sorrow is always private."

She wiped her face with the ends of her shawl. "And so it will be with me." She wobbled to her feet. "You will never be able to suffer as I do."

"No, I cannot; I have never had a child," he said. "But I know what it is to grieve." He took a step toward her; she motioned him away as if in panic. "What will you let me do for you, Hero?"

"I? Nothing. Nothing." She turned and ran for the stairs.

Ragoczy stood still, overwhelmed by the immensity of her sorrow, until he heard her door slam, and then, as if shocked to action, he climbed the stairs and knocked on her door. "Do you want—"

"Go away!" she ordered.

He hesitated, not willing to leave her in such agony. "You need not endure this alone, Hero."

"And why not?" she challenged, her voice thick with emotion. "We all bear our pain alone, don't we?"

"Not wholly alone," he said, thinking of T'en Chih-Yu, of Tulsi Kil, of Heugenet, of Xenya, of Orazia, of Acana Tupac, of Leocadia, of Demetrice, of Ignatia, then, most unhappily, of Csimenae. Each memory was a reproof to him, but he added, "You need not bear all your loss alone."

She took a long time to answer. "She missed her father so much. At least they may be together now." Again she was quiet. Then, "Go away, Comte. Go away."

He heard the clock in the parlor chime three, and he felt the day slip from him. Many memories crowded in, reminding him of times he had acted to ameliorate a friend's distress and times he had not; neither response had actually succeeded in alleviating the friend's misery. He chose not to intrude. "If you want me, for anything, you have only to ask. I will do whatever I can for you."

"Will you offer to restore her to life?" The accusation cut, as she intended. "You restored Rogier to life, so you say."

"No. That is beyond my skills," he said quietly.

"Then go away while I choose my mourning clothes."

"I'll return in an hour to learn how you are faring." He was about to turn away when her voice stopped him once more.

"And what will you do in the meantime?" she demanded, her voice rising. "Will you do your best to put this behind you? You have put so much behind you already."

"I will spend the time composing a letter to your father-in-law, urging him to permit you to visit as soon as possible, for the sake of your sons, and to do honor to your daughter," he said, and went away from the door before she said anything that might lessen his determination.

At the foot of the stairs, he found Rogier waiting for him. "I have told the staff, my master. Do you want the house draped in black?"

Ragoczy gave a little nod. "I am not a relative; full-mourning would be presumptuous. Half-mourning will serve. And a yew-wreath with gray bands on the door." He started toward his study, then stopped. "Will you have Gutesohnes come to me as soon as he has washed? I fear he must carry a message for me, leaving at first light tomorrow."

Rogier's ascetic features softened. "You are sending him to von Scharffensee, aren't you? You're going to intercede."

He answered in Russian. "That I am. Let us hope I prevail upon him to relent in his efforts to keep her from her sons."

In the same tongue, Rogier said, "It would seem his obduracy is fixed on keeping them apart."

"I believe that is true," said Ragoczy. "But circumstances are different now, and I must apply to him, for her sake, if not for her sons'."

"Do you think you will emerge with what you seek?" Rogier asked. "For her sake, I hope you will. At present, she will not deal with any disappointment well."

"I am going to cogitate on the problem," said Ragoczy in the Swiss version of French. "Do send Gutesohnes to me when—"

"—he has washed," Rogier finished for him. "That I will. He should not be long."

"Already in the bath-house?" Ragoczy surmised.

"In the largest tub."

"Then I will expect him directly."

"And Madame? Will you tell her what you've done?" There was a note of dubiety in his question.

"In an hour, I will see if she is willing to speak with me, and I will decide then what to say. She knows of my intentions." He looked at the fan-light over the door. "It was such a lovely day when we left Saint-Gingolph."

"The day is still lovely," said Rogier sadly.

"That it is," said Ragoczy, and entered his study. He stood just inside the door, thinking, unmoving. Then he walked to his secretaire keyhole desk, pulled down the writing-board, and drew up his chair, but once more, he faltered, lost in thought. When he finally sat down he had an idea that he thought might work. Taking a sheet of heavy, cream-laid paper out of its drawer, he selected a pen, fitted it with a trimmed quill, pulled out the inkwell, and began to write the first of two letters, choosing his words with great care for both. He had just completed sealing the second letter with wax and his sigil when Gutesohnes knocked on the door.

"Comte? You wanted to see me?"

"Yes, I do. Come in," he said, swinging his chair around to face his coachman, whose shock of dark hair was still damp from his bath. "I'm sure you know what has happened."

"Madame von Scharffensee's daughter? Yes. A great pity."

"I am asking the Graf if we might be permitted to visit. And I am sending a note to von Ravensberg to ask if we would be welcome at his Schloss." Seeing the surprise in Gutesohnes' face, he went on very smoothly, "If I have another reason to come into Austria, it will be more difficult for von Scharffensee to refuse my request on Madame von Scharffensee's behalf."

"The Graf is an ambitious man," said Gutesohnes. "Von Ravensberg, I mean."

"You are right in that: he is. I am counting on it to ensure our welcome. Their homes are roughly twenty leagues apart. You should be able to stop at Scharffensee, go on to Ravensberg, then return to Scharffensee and bring back the Graf's answer. Von Ravensberg will no doubt consent. It is von Scharffensee who may balk."

"Will he let me deliver your message? He could refuse to see me, couldn't he?" Gutesohnes asked.

"We must hope that he will accept the letter," said Ragoczy, the line of his mouth grim. He could see that Gutesohnes wanted to ask another question, and so told him, "Go ahead: what is on your mind?"

Gutesohnes coughed uncomfortably. "It's just that . . . Von Ravensberg's ward—Hyacinthie?—she was very flirtatious in Amsterdam. It may be awkward to see her again. That might turn von Ravensberg against my errand."

"That young woman flirts with everyone," said Ragoczy. "I doubt you have anything to fear from her, or from von Ravensberg on her account."

"I don't want to be accused of attempting to compromise a nobleman's ward," Gutesohnes persisted.

"I doubt that will happen. Her behavior must be known. Her guardian is surely aware that she is entertaining herself, and will put no store in it." Ragoczy realized that Gutesohnes was truly worried. "You may readily avoid her, if you feel it prudent. Keep to the servants' quarters and let the steward carry letters for you."

Gutesohnes was visibly relieved. "Very good. Very good." He gave a forced chuckle. "Rogier told me that I am to leave tomorrow at first light, but surely you mean the day after?"

"No," said Ragoczy cordially. "Rogier informed you rightly. You depart at dawn tomorrow."

"But—"

"You will have the opportunity to sup early and retire ahead of the household. If you are worried you will not sleep, I will provide you a draught for that. If you have trouble rising, I will have another draught to help you waken."

"Yes, Comte," said Gutesohnes.

"It is urgent for Madame von Scharffensee to visit her sons. That requires we make ready promptly, and have her traveling again as soon as may be." He reached into the corner where a tall wooden stand was filled with rolled maps. "So let us plan your route now." He rose and went to the bow-fronted sideboard where he unrolled the map and held it that way with two beautiful paper-weights of cobalt Venetian glass. Using an ivory letter-opener, Ragoczy pointed out the route he had in mind. "Remount at Saint-Gingolph: the stabler has my horses available. Turn south along the river. You should be able to make Martigny by nightfall; it is a hard ride but not impossible." He had made it himself, many, many years ago, under far worse conditions. "Go to Le Perroquet; Angelo will take care of you there. Continue east along the river to Brig. The road is harder and steeper from there, so spend the third night at Oberwald. Another two days should bring you to Chur, unless the weather worsens."

"Two or three days," said Gutesohnes. "The road is a hard one and travel can be very slow on it."

Ragoczy moved his finger along the map. "Ravensberg is near Salzburg, as you can see." He pointed to the place. "And Scharffensee is—" He put the tip of his letter-opener on the place.

"In that case, Comte, I think I had best turn south at Reichenau and not go as far as Chur. I will enter Tirol from Silvaplana and

Vinadi. I can travel faster; there is less traffic on that road, and I can take a day off my travels, and ensure I find inns that do not charge a fortune to sleep four to a bed."

"Then, shall we say eight days to Scharffensee?" Ragoczy suggested. "A night there and then two days to Ravensberg?"

"Ten days. That will keep me from exhausting the horses. If the roads were better—or safer—I would try for a shorter journey, but . . ." He turned over his hands to show he was helpless to remedy the problems.

"But." Ragoczy tapped Scharffensee again. "Shall I say two weeks? If you can accomplish your work sooner, that will be excellent, but two weeks should suffice to complete your mission. If you can accomplish the journey in less time, you will be rewarded for your efforts." He removed the paper-weights and began to roll the map once more. "Do you need this?"

"No; I have some from my previous employment. I used to spend my evenings memorizing distances." He frowned. "If the roads were in better repair, I could travel faster. But I don't want to risk the horse, not in those mountains."

"Certainly not." Ragoczy returned the rolled map to the stand in the corner, then picked up the two letters from his secretaire desk. "I would appreciate it if you would report to me on the state of the roads. If there is any part of the road where it would be dangerous for a coach, I will want to know about it."

"That I will," said Gutesohnes, taking the letters and slipping them inside his leather waistcoat. "I have a pocket for letters," he said.

"An excellent notion. Your travel-sack and your waistcoat only."

"A wallet for food and money—although I carry most money in my shoes." He patted the top of his boot.

Ragoczy laughed. "Many of us carry valuable things in our shoes." In his case, his soles were lined with his native earth that allowed him to walk about in daylight and to cross running water without agony. "See that Uchtred provides you with food and water for your first day. I will give you money for your expenses, tomorrow morning."

"When I leave at dawn," said Gutesohnes, sounding worn out.

"Which it is why you must sleep well tonight. You've had a hard few days, and you need to take care." Ragoczy started toward the study door. "Remember my offer—I do have tinctures that will help you sleep, and ones that will help you waken. You have only to ask."

"Did Hochvall take any of your preparations?" Gutesohnes asked suspiciously.

"Yes. In fact, he still does. It helps him to strengthen his leg as the bone knits."

"I saw him in the stable. He's looking better, but he's still using a crutch to get around. A coachman can't use a crutch."

"He will do so for at least a month more, I would reckon," said Ragoczy, who had not seen him since their return. "I will determine his progress later today, after you are ready for your mission."

Realizing he had over-stepped, Gutesohnes said at his most conciliatory, "I probably should have something to help me sleep. If you have a preparation that eases aching muscles, that would be useful as well."

"I have an ointment," said Ragoczy. "You shall have it after you eat."

Gutesohnes ducked his head. "Thank you, Comte."

"Given the task I have assigned you, it is the least I can do," said Ragoczy, holding the door for Gutesohnes.

Astonished at this unexpected courtesy, Gutesohnes almost bowed himself out of the room. He closed the door carefully, then hurried away down the corridor leading to the rear of the house, where he came upon Balduin and Uchtred; he informed them of his early departure.

"I have a duck on a spit even now," Uchtred told Gutesohnes. "It will be ready in a little over an hour. Turnips with butter and onions, new bread, butter, and cheese. I will rise early to make your food for the road."

"Half the château will rise to see me off, in fact?" Gutesohnes suggested sarcastically, but unable to conceal his satisfaction at the thought.

"Possibly," said Balduin, and went to pour each of them a large glass of beer from the pitcher of it taken from the barrel that Farold, the local brewer, had just delivered. "We will all wish you a safe and swift mission."

"Amen," said Uchtred.

While the three men were sitting down on kitchen stools to enjoy their drink, Ragoczy left his study and climbed the stairs. He made his way to Hero's door, knocked on it, and said, "Hero, are you all right?" Then he waited for an answer. When none was forthcoming, he said, a bit more loudly, "I am dispatching a letter to your father-in-law, proposing that I bring you to Scharffensee so that you and your sons may condole together. It will be on its way tomorrow morning."

There was a sound from inside the room, not quite a word, but it encouraged him.

"Gutesohnes is going to carry my request to the Graf." Again he waited, and again he heard something beyond the door. "He will probably be gone two weeks, but as soon as we have an answer, I will prepare to take you to them."

"Do you think he will permit the visit?" The question was not loud but there was great bitterness in her question. "Thank you for trying,"

"I cannot promise he will extend an invitation to you, but he is not likely to say no when it is I who will bear the responsibility of getting you to Scharffensee." He was about to go on when she interrupted.

"Of course. You are a titled gentleman of fortune," she said bitterly, "not a widow of limited means."

"If that will suffice to get you to your sons, then so be it," Ragoczy said.

There was a sharp intake of breath, and then the latch moved and the door opened. Hero, pale and shaken, stood blocking the way. "Whether you succeed or not, I *do* thank you for trying." She had a damp linen handkerchief in her hand and she pressed this to her eyes. "Please."

"What is it?" Ragoczy asked gently.

"I need time to myself." She said it in a rush, as if she expected to be chastised.

"As long as you like," he said, hearing the slight trembling in her voice.

"But perhaps tonight, you would come to me?"

He looked at her in some surprise. "If that is what you wish, I would be honored."

"Not to do anything," she went on. "Just so I will not sleep alone."

"That is doing something," he said, his dark eyes fixed on hers. "I would be honored," he repeated.

She held out her hand to him, her fingers cold; her nails had all been bitten and the edge of one was bleeding. "I don't deserve your kindness, Comte."

"Hero." He touched her cheek, so lightly that she barely felt the caress; there was a world of sympathy in her name.

"But extend yourself a bit more: have Wendela bring me a glass of wine and a bowl of broth in an hour," she said hurriedly, then stepped back and closed the door.

Ragoczy stood still, waiting in case she should open the door again, then, when he heard the clock strike four, he went back down to the ground floor, his attractive, irregular features set in lines of concern. He returned to his study and lit the oil-lamp on the low-boy, dispelling the first gloom of the coming evening. After pacing the room slowly, he sat down at his secretaire-desk, where he sat staring blankly at the windows.

"My master?" Rogier ventured from the door.

Ragoczy looked up as if startled. "What is it, old friend?"

"Hochvall is here." He coughed diplomatically. "I can arrange for him to return, if you would prefer?"

It took several seconds for Ragoczy to answer, but when he did, he rose from his chair. "No. There is no reason to do that." He started toward the door, paused to turn down the lamp, then went to Rogier. "Where is he?"

"In the servants' parlor. He has lost flesh while we were away." Rogier held the door for Ragoczy and closed it behind them.

"How is his demeanor?"

"Uncertain. I suspect he has found his recuperation difficult." Rogier opened the door that led into the servants' wing of the château. Located to the west of the kitchen, its lower floor had the parlor and dining room of the household servants, with two floors of bedrooms above, one for men and one for women. The parlor, with west-facing windows, was bright still, although the shadows of the mountains were spreading toward them. An oil-lamp had been lit and placed on the small chest on the far side of the room.

Ulf Hochvall was seated in one of the upholstered chairs, his crutch lying beside it. As Ragoczy came into the room, he struggled to his feet, hopping to keep his balance. "Comte."

"How do I see you, Hochvall? Are you improved? Is your leg healing?" Ragoczy studied him as he spoke: Rogier was right. The man had lost flesh, and his skin looked dry and slack.

"I am better but I am not yet strong," said Hochvall. "I have had a fever. Levien came from Yvoire to bleed me four times."

Ragoczy sighed, thinking of the many arguments he had had with Levien's physician on the subject of bleeding. "That may not have been entirely wise. Bleeding can sometimes increase a fever."

"It relieved mine," said Hochvall.

"Then you are one of the fortunate," said Ragoczy. "Your leg— how does it hold up?"

"It pains me if I use it much," Hochvall said with a motion of defiance.

"Not surprising, given the severity of the break." He stepped back. "Come toward me. Without the crutch." This last instruction made Hochvall stare. "Lean it against the chair and try taking a few steps toward me."

Reluctantly Hochvall did as he was told, making sure the crutch would not fall before he turned toward Ragoczy. "I do not walk very well," he said before he took his first few steps.

Ragoczy could see that the injured leg was twisted inward, and he frowned. "Did anyone rewrap your leg after I set it?"

Hochvall halted. "Yes," he admitted. "I know you said not to, but it was itching so ferociously that my woman insisted I scratch it. That was shortly after you departed. She and my son worked to rewrap it correctly."

"I am sure they did," said Ragoczy. "But they did not—" He stopped, knowing it was useless to say anything more.

"They did their best not to hurt me," said Hochvall in their defense.

"I am certain of that. But in not hurting you, they have harmed you," said Ragoczy with great patience. "When a bone is just starting to knit, it can easily be unseated from its alignment, which is what has happened here." He went and picked up Hochvall's crutch and handed it to him. "If you will practice walking without it, you will be stronger and will improve, but, I fear you will always limp." Ordinarily he would have tried to soften that blow, but with other demands weighing on him, he could not summon up the words.

"Limp?" Hochvall repeated, unbelieving. "But can I drive a coach with a limp?"

"I do not know yet," said Ragoczy. "In time you may recover enough to manage it," he said, all the while trying to decide which of the various tasks that needed doing could be assigned to Hochvall.

"I'm a coachman," Hochvall insisted, his eyes growing wet.

"I know Yvoire needs a good drayer," Ragoczy suggested. "If you start there, you can build yourself up again, regain your strength. I am willing to help you establish yourself."

"A *drayer*? Wagons and carts!" he exclaimed scornfully. "I am a *coachman! A coachman!*" He flung his crutch down, slewed around, took a half-step, stumbled, and fell.

As Ragoczy went to help Hochvall to his feet, he wondered how many other things would be broken that day.

Text of a letter from Reinhart Olivier Kreuzbach, attorney-at-law and factor, at Speicher near the Kyll River, Rhenish Prussia, to

Saint-Germain Ragoczy, Comte Franciscus at Château Ragoczy near Lake Geneva, Yvoire, Switzerland; carried by postal courier.

To the Honorable Comte Franciscus, Saint-Germain Ragoczy, my most cordial greeting on this, the 27th day of September, 1817,

Regarding the progress of restoration of your castle above Zemmer since you stopped to inspect it on your way to Amsterdam, there has been much activity. Most of the kitchen is now in good repair, and the storage cellars are once again clean, drained, and sound. For foodstuffs, wine, clothing, furniture, and other such items, the cellars will now provide reliable protection through the winter. There will be windows installed on the ground floor in the Great Hall, the withdrawing room, the morning parlor, and the sitting room, which should then be capable of coming through the winter relatively unscathed. The dining room and servants' quarters may also be finished shortly, if the rains hold off for another month.

I have taken your advice and retained Pasch Gruenerwald as supervisor of the rebuilding. He has chosen most of the workmen, hired a cook for them, and allocated places for their occupancy in the castle so that their own comfort is contingent upon their proper performance of the work they are paid to do. He reports that most of the men are more than willing, good-paying work being so hard to find, although he has had to dismiss two workers for pilfering goods and supplies. Most have been satisfactory.

The amount you have deposited to cover the expenses through the coming winter are more than adequate. I have assured the men that they need not fear they will not be paid the full amount agreed upon. The joiners and carpenters will arrive in the spring to continue the finishing of the interior. Your wishes are clearly expressed in the instructions you provided and I will keep current on the progress being made, so that you will not be disappointed at the standards upheld by these craftsmen.

I am still puzzled by your intention not to occupy the castle yourself, but to have Madame von Scharffensee and her children as your tenants. Surely that is a most extravagant gesture. Do you realize

what an expense it will be to maintain the castle and staff suitably
for them. I am aware that your fortune is vast and that you have
sufficient wherewithal to provide for Madame and her family, and
that you are not constrained by religion or politics from putting your
funds to this use. You say the castle is a small one, and I concur, but
I also know that it is much more than most widows with children
can hope for. Still, your business is your own, yet I would be failing
in my fiduciary responsibilities not to bring this to your attention.
Having done so, I will

Commend myself to your good service,
Reinhart Olivier Kreuzbach
Attorney-at-law and factor
Speicher, Rhenish Prussia

4

"Come on!" Hyacinthie called out to Rosalie as she ran up the hill,
her skirts lifted almost to her knees. Her high-waisted frock was a
bit faded and plain, but in this setting it lent her a charm that fancier
garments would not have. All along the flanks of the mountains, oak,
hawthorn, and larch were burnished with brilliant leaves that stood
out red and russet and gold against the stands of fir and pines;
above, the sky was the luminous blue of the fading year. Schloss von
Ravensberg was a league-and-a-half behind them, partially hidden
by the shoulder of the ridge they were climbing. The wind was brisk
up here, and the grasses sang with it.

Rosalie, who was six, was struggling to keep up, her pale features turning ruddy from her effort, her short legs churning. There
was a smudge of dirt on her cheek and a tear in her skirt, both tokens of a fall she had taken early in their climb, the first blight on
what had promised to be a welcome treat. The chance to get out of

the Schloss had been so tempting when Hyacinthie had made it, and was turning out to be just as unpleasant as life in the Schloss had proven to be. She was flattered to be singled out by her shining, older cousin, and determined to make the most of this opportunity. She scrambled, determination on her little face. "Slow down, Cousin Hyacinthie!"

But Hyacinthie laughed and kept going. There was a path leading into the woods not far away, and she was determined to get there. It was essential to her plan that Rosalie be completely beyond the Schloss' view before she led her off to the abandoned wellhouse. "You can't catch me," she cried out, just tauntingly enough to guarantee that the child would follow her.

Determined to show she could indeed keep up with Hyacinthie, Rosalie forced herself to keep going, though she was panting and getting tired. Soon she would be out-of-sorts and testy, but for now she was still game for their adventure. "Just go slower." She continued climbing, hot from effort and cold from the wind. Only her stubborn determination to prove herself to Hyacinthie kept her going.

"I've got something you'll like to see," Hyacinthie said, enticing the child. She had reached the narrow track that served as a road to the high pastures where shepherds took their flocks in summer.

"I'm coming," said the child, growing cross as she kept up her arduous climb.

"You're doing very well," Hyacinthie shouted to Rosalie. "It isn't much farther. Just the other side of this copse." The shelter of the trees was welcome, for now no one could see them. "There's a path here, an easy one."

Rosalie muttered but persevered. In a matter of five minutes she had reached the stand of trees where Hyacinthie waited, pacing up and down the trail. "Well. What is there to see?"

"It's this way," said Hyacinthie, holding out her hand for Rosalie's. "We should go through the trees. There's a well-house on the other side."

"A well-house?" Rosalie asked, interested in spite of herself.

"I'll show you," Hyacinthie promised, leading the way. The distance through the trees was short, and in thirty strides they were through the copse and at the edge of a high meadow, just now quite empty but for an old Tyrolean well-house that was a short way off. "There."

Rosalie looked where Hyacinthie was pointing, and stared. "It's pretty old." She hated to admit that she was disappointed in the place, not after all she had done to reach it.

"Built two hundred years ago, the shepherds say," Hyacinthie told her.

"So long," Rosalie exclaimed.

"It isn't used much anymore. The well isn't clean. That's why most people have forgot that this well-house is here." She started across the meadow toward it. "It's really a special place."

"Really?" said Rosalie, her mouth forming an O of fascination. "Why is it special?" she asked as she hurried after Hyacinthie.

"Because almost no one knows it's here," said Hyacinthie. "Just you, and me, and the shepherds."

Rosalie giggled. "This is our secret?"

"Yes," Hyacinthie said conspiratorially. "Our secret. Only between us." She was almost at the entrance. "Do you want to go in?"

"Oh, yes," said Rosalie, almost sighing with pleasure.

"We can sit on the old benches for a little while." Hyacinthie stretched languorously. "Rest a little before we start back. Maybe we can look into the old well. They say it's filled with treasure."

"We can," said Rosalie, feeling very grown-up.

"Then let me welcome you to your very own Schloss," said Hyacinthie playfully, opening the door, laughing at the moaning of the old hinges. "Ghosts," she whispered, and joined in Rosalie's renewed giggles.

The well-house was not large, and its interior was simple. There were benches along three of the walls, and there were two clerestory windows letting in light without revealing if anyone might be inside. This afternoon the illumination was soft, revealing the flaking paint on the carpentry-work on the walls, and the old well, a low circle of stones with a wooden lid over it.

"This is . . . really nice," said Rosalie, shivering in the chill of the interior.

"I should think so," said Hyacinthie, brushing off one of the benches and sitting down; she offered Rosalie an encouraging wink. "Go on. You'll find it's very pleasant. We're out of the wind, in our special, secret place."

"Special," said Rosalie as she wiped at the dust on another bench and got a splinter in her hand for her trouble. She let out a little shriek of dismay and tried to use her teeth to pull it out.

Hyacinthie got up and came to help her. "Here. Let me look at it," she said, settling down beside the child. "Oh, dear. You did get hurt, didn't you?" She pressed the splinter and paid no attention to Rosalie's whimper. "Hold still; I'll pull it out for you." Without waiting for the little girl to respond, she got hold of the end of the splinter with her fingertip and thumb and abruptly jerked it out of her palm.

"Ouch!" Rosalie protested, this time sucking on the injury while she tried not to cry.

"There. All gone. It will be better soon." Hyacinthie got up again and went back to the bench she had selected for her own use. "Tell me, Rosalie: are you happy to be here?"

Rosalie nodded several times, then took her hand out of her mouth and said, "This is a fine secret."

"No, not this place," Hyacinthie said, irritated at her inattention. "Then—?"

"Ravensberg. The Schloss." Hyacinthie realized she had been too rushed, and modified her question. "You and Hedda have been here a while. I was wondering how you liked living here."

'The Schloss is very . . . grand," said Rosalie, becoming wary.

"That it is," said Hyacinthie. "But do you *like* it? Are you happy here?"

"It's very nice," said Rosalie, watching Hyacinthie, trying to determine what she wanted to hear from her.

"Nothing troubles you?" This question was sharper than the last. The child's face went closed. "No."

Hyacinthie wanted to shake an answer out of her, but forced herself to smile. "You can tell me. This is our secret place. Nothing you tell me will ever be repeated. On my honor." She made the sign to ward off the Evil Eye.

Rosalie squirmed on her bench and rubbed at her eyes with her undamaged palm. "I'm not supposed to talk about it."

"Then there is something," said Hyacinthie.

"In a way," Rosalie said, trying to minimize the damage she had done.

"Tell me." She leaned forward, elbows on her knees. "I'll never betray you."

Betray seemed an awfully big word to Rosalie, and she wriggled in discomfort. "I shouldn't."

Hyacinthie made herself laugh. "Not to those outside the family, of course you shouldn't. But we're cousins"—she recalled how carefully her uncle had explained that she and the two girls were not related; she steeled herself to her task—"and we can talk about family things, you know."

"Uncle Wallache said that—"

"Uncle Wallache wants us to be careful. You know how he keeps secrets. So do I." She could see from Rosalie's expression that she had found the key. "He's told you to keep secrets for him, hasn't he?"

Rosalie nodded. "Ja."

"And he has said it would be very bad of you to talk about them, hasn't he?"

"Ja," the child said again, her chin quivering; she was becoming uncomfortable with Hyacinthie's persistence, especially since she was almost positive Uncle Wallache would not approve.

"But, don't you see, he meant other people: he didn't mean *me*." Hyacinthie flung her arms wide. "You know he didn't mean me."

Rosalie was confused now, and frightened. She had promised Uncle Wallache to keep their secret, but even more than keeping the secret, she wanted someone to know, to understand, and here was Hyacinthie, lovely and sweet as a spring dawn, offering her the chance she sought, and the assurance that it was all right. "I can talk to you," she decided aloud.

"Yes. Yes, my little pet, you can," said Hyacinthie with fervor and a shine in her eyes that Rosalie did not recognize. "This will be the secret of our secret place."

"Oh, yes," said Rosalie, relief visible on her face.

"And so you will feel less worried about your secret, I will tell you one of mine first." She beamed at Rosalie. "Would you like that?"

Rosalie nodded, too awed at this offer to speak.

Hyacinthie pretended to search her thoughts for a secret, all the while knowing how she would get Rosalie to confide in her. "You know Uncle Wallache's laboratory?"

"The big room where he spends his afternoons," said Rosalie proudly.

"Yes. Well. I know what he does there." She nodded twice to make her point.

"But we're not supposed to go—"

"I got into the room once, and watched." Hyacinthie beamed the same was Rosalie was beaming.

"Tell me," said Rosalie, full of anticipation.

"You know that men from the village sometimes come to help Uncle Wallache in his work?" She waited for Rosalie to nod. "Well, I saw them go into the laboratory, and there Uncle Wallache took his equipment and drew blood out of the man."

Rosalie made a face of disgust. "Why?"

"He believes blood has many secrets. He plans to show what some of them are." Hyacinthie thought of the many times she had heard von Ravensberg boast of his theories and his methods. "That is what his book is about."

"Blood?" Rosalie was shocked.

"Jawol. Blood."

Appalled, Rosalie sat very still. "That's . . . horrid." She liked the sound of the word, and she repeated it for the satisfaction it gave her. "Horrid."

"It is what he is doing." Hyacinthie could see she was losing the child's attention. "You mustn't let him know I told you, or I'll get in trouble."

"You?" The notion that Hyacinthie could be as vulnerable as she was shocked Rosalie.

"Of course," said Hyacinthie, as blithely as possible. "Uncle Wallache doesn't think females can understand his studies."

"Perhaps they can't," said Rosalie, because she was so baffled.

Rather than challenge her, Hyacinthie said, "I know another secret, one you and I can share between us: you mustn't tell anyone."

"I won't," Rosalie said somberly.

"Herr Schmidt—the Magistrate in Eichenbrucke?—he keeps a woman in Ravenstein. They have two children. I heard Herr Schmidt talking with Uncle Wallache about it, a year ago. He was laughing." Her smile was delicious.

"A Magistrate would do something like that?" Rosalie marveled.

Now that the child was absorbed in their game, Hyacinthie made the most of it. "And another secret: once I saw Herr Lowengard— you know, the mousy fellow who takes care of business matters for Uncle Wallache?—I saw him making water and there was a *wart* on his thing. A big one."

"A wart?" Rosalie was once again enthralled.

"Yes." She made this an expression of triumph.

"Does it hurt?"

"What?" The question was so unexpected that it threw Hyacinthie off her stride.

Rosalie repeated carefully, "Does it hurt?"

"The wart? I don't know; it might," said Hyacinthie. She stood up and moved to the covered well in the center of the well-house. Very casually she opened the wooden lid that had once sealed the well; time and rust had rendered the lock on the lid useless. With the lid shoved aside, Hyacinthie sat on the broad stone rim of the old well as she went on. "What do you think?"

"I think it might, too," said Rosalie after a brief moment of consideration. "Uncle Wallache's hurts me."

It took all her determination for Hyacinthie to conceal the stab of jealousy that went through her at this admission. How dare this child even mention Uncle Wallache's attentions! Now they came to the heart of it: this child had dared to supplant her in their uncle's desires! It was an unendurable insult, but she contained her wrath. Soon she would have her revenge, she told herself. She managed to keep her voice light. "I didn't like it much at first, either." That much was true, and she said it at her most engaging.

"You didn't . . ." Rosalie stared in amazement.

"When I was younger, of course," said Hyacinthie as if this were not galling to her. "A while ago."

"Before we came?"

"A little." She let Rosalie think that she and Hedda were responsible for her demotion, not her own developing body, more than four years ago.

"And he stopped?"

"A while ago," Hyacinthie repeated with a deliberate shrug. "He became bored, I suppose, as men will do."

"But you—How could he be bored with you?"

"Perhaps he expected something new?" It was a deliberate prodding.

"Me?" Rosalie was aghast. "Why me?"

"You're pretty, and you're . . . trusting, and you aren't ready to be married yet," Hyacinthie suggested, recalling all the things von Ravensberg had praised in her when he had first begun using her for his pleasure.

"Then you know . . ." She came to Hyacinthie's side, seeking the companionship of their shared experience. "He tells me it is what girls do to show their gratitude. He says that this is how girls make men care for them."

"Yes," said Hyacinthie.

"He said that this is what men want from girls."

"He's right." This admission angered her, but she concealed her ire.

"He told you the same thing?" Rosalie asked.

"He did," said Hyacinthie.

"Well." Rosalie considered what she had learned. "Then it isn't as much of a secret as he told me." There was the suggestion of a sob in the little girl's voice. "He said this was only between us, just the two of us."

"That's what he told me," said Hyacinthie, a sudden memory taking her back to when she was eight and her uncle had come to her bed. For the years he had lain with her, she had convinced herself she had engaged his heart, but once he abandoned her, she knew that what he had done was for himself, not for her. Only securing the true captivation of another man could remove her from her uncle's mastery of her—that, and returning pain for pain.

"He was *fibbing!*" Rosalie burst out, and started to cry.

"He was *lying!*" Hyacinthie rounded on her, and pushed her shoulders so that the little girl toppled backward into the well, her wail becoming a shriek as her falling body struck the stone walls of the well, and bounced off. Finally there was a murky splash, a whimper, a garbled shout that faded to choking coughs, then nothing. Standing beside the well, Hyacinthie waited until she was certain that all was silent, then she wrestled the lid back onto the well. Now that she had accomplished her purpose, Hyacinthie was sorry that it had ended so quickly. She had hoped for a little longer to make the child pay for what she had done. "No matter," she said aloud as she took stock of her appearance. There was a small tear on her dress where the lid had snagged the material, and several dusty smirches. She was fairly sure there was a little dirt on her face. All could be accounted for by claiming to have taken a fall while hiking. She also decided that the fall could account for Rosalie being missing: when Hyacinthie fell, Rosalie, who had caused it, ran off—Hyacinthie had supposed she had returned to the Schloss, but had been in no condition to ascertain that for herself. The explanation was a good one, she thought, and one that would leave her blameless. In order to make it more convincing, she made herself scrape her elbow on the wall of the well-house until it bled. Then, satisfied, she set out for the Schloss, not moving too quickly so that her claims of injury would be more readily believed. As she made her way along the narrow paths back down the mountain, she let herself recall every detail of her vanquishing Rosalie. By the time she entered the Schloss the shadows were lying around the place, cast by the higher peaks, and the staff was beginning to bustle, getting ready for supper. Hyacinthie made for her room and rang for Idune, the maid she and the girls shared, telling her as soon as she entered her room. "It is very annoying. I have damaged my dress. I took a fall on my walk with Rosalie. What a scamp she is."

Idune tisked as she came to help Hyacinthie out of the garment. "Thank goodness, Fraulein, that it is not one of your newer garments."

"I wouldn't wear them on a walk, especially not a walk with a child." As she said this, she could feel excitement fizzing through her: she had done it! She raised her arms and bent over to help Idune pull the dress off.

"Just so, Fraulein," said Idune, taking a moment to assess the worst of the damage. "I think you had best consign this dress to your donation-box. It isn't going to be mended adequately, no matter what we do." She held up the dress to the waning light from the window. "This is really too bad to be saved."

"Then don't bother." Hyacinthie went to her armoire and studied what she had ready. Finally she chose a dress of cotton-lawn in an amethyst shade with an embroidered corsage edged in lace. "I think this will do."

"A very nice dress," Idune approved. "And a shawl? The evenings are becoming chilly."

"The rose one," said Hyacinthie. "And violet scent. Violets are so fashionable just now." She lifted her arms and helped Idune to ease her arms into the fragile sleeves.

"That scratch on your elbow will need a poultice tonight," said the maid as she buttoned up the back of Hyacinthie's dress.

"Probably," said Hyacinthie with extreme disinterest.

"And Rosalie? Where is she?" Edeltrude asked as she adjusted the drape of Hyacinthie's skirt in the back.

"Um? What do you mean? She ran ahead after I fell." This was

Hyacinthie's moment of triumph, and she relished it. "Surely she is in her room."

"Not that I am aware of," said Idune. "But she may have returned while I was at my sewing."

"Very likely," said Hyacinthie with no indication of worry or rejoicing. "If you want to run along and help Rosalie and Hedda dress, I can fend for myself now. I'll change my shoes and fix my hair myself."

"Jawol, Fraulein," said Idune as she made for the door.

Hyacinthie was just finishing putting her hair up in a flattering knot when she heard the first calls of alarm. First Idune, then three other servants began to make their way through the Schloss calling for Rosalie. Humming a little song by Mozart to herself, Hyacinthie fastened a locket on a silver chain around her neck, draped her shawl over her arms, and prepared to descend for supper.

Text of a letter from Helmut Fredrich Lambert Ahrent Ritterslandt, Graf von Scharffensee at Scharffensee in Austria, to Saint-Germain Ragoczy, Comte Franciscus at Château Ragoczy, near Lake Geneva, Yvoire, Switzerland; carried by Otto Gutesohnes.

To the Comte Franciscus, Saint-Germain Ragoczy, the Graf von Scharffensee at Scharffensee sends his greetings on this, the 8th day of October, 1817, through the good offices of the Comte's messenger,

My dear Comte:

I have received your most unconventional offer to visit my home with my daughter-in-law, so that she may spend time with her sons. You state that you believe that all of them will grieve less for Annamaria if they are permitted to spend time together.

While I disagree with your concerns, I have no doubt that my daughter-in-law can be tedious about her children, and so I will welcome her for a three-day visit. Siegfried has returned to school and cannot be spared for her by the time you propose, but Bertram and Berend will be here. I will arrange for their tutors to spend only half-days with them while Madame von Scharffensee is with us.

You, however, I do not believe I can welcome to this Schloss, given your irregular relation with Madame von Scharffensee. You may well seem the usurper of their father's memory in their mother's life, and I will not subject the boys to such an insult. If you are willing to provide her transportation and escort in any case, then I will order a room prepared for her, and inform the twins that she will make a brief stay here, to see them.

The season of rain and snow shortly bearing in upon us, I would like to suggest that the visit be postponed, at least until late March, when the chance of being delayed due to snow in the passes is much reduced. I can almost pledge to have Siegfried here for part of the spring, which may suit my daughter-in-law's purpose better than coming here in autumn, when the journey will be harder and the way dreary.

I will await your answer with every assurance that I will live up to all the particulars included in this communication, and I depend upon you, as a gentleman, to honor what I have charged you to do. My daughter-in-law is no more feckless than most women, but I know better than to impose these conditions upon her directly, for she would balk at them in the full tempestuousness of her Italian nature, which neither you nor I can want. I therefore urge you to exercise what influence you have with her to restrain her impetuosity and bear herself with dignity in these sad times.

> *Until I have your answer*
> *I remain,*
> *Sincerely,*
> *Helmut Fredrich Lambert Ahrent Ritterslandt*
> *Graf von Scharffensee*

5

Augustus Kleinerhoff stood in the entry-way of Château Ragoczy, his hat in his hand, his double-caped cloak of oiled wool soggy and dripping. "I am very sorry, Comte, to have to call upon you in this way, but there has been trouble—serious trouble."

Ragoczy, very elegant in his heavy black-silk twill coat with swallow-tails, black embroidered dark-red satin waistcoat over a white-silk shirt and a conservative cravat, black-superfine unmentionables, and side-button shoes, regarded his visitor sympathetically. "Herr Kleinerhoff. Come in." He motioned toward the guest-parlor, signaling to Balduin to light the lamps. "The rain has turned the day dark, so we will need to provide some illumination."

Staring at Ragoczy's fine clothing, Kleinerhoff hesitated. "Do I interrupt? I apologize for coming unannounced, and if you—"

"You do not interrupt anything immediate," said Ragoczy. "My first engagement is late in the afternoon." He paused, then went on, making no mention of Reinhart Olivier Kreuzbach who had journeyed from Speicher and was presently at the best hotel—of three—in Yvoire. "I gather whatever brings you here must be important."

"Important? I fear that it is, which also makes it most unfortunate, which is because it is important, and I dislike being the bearer of bad tidings, yet so it must be," said Kleinerhoff, sounding a bit distracted. "I thought our differences in the village had been settled, that everyone was in accord, but I see now . . ." He followed Ragoczy down the short corridor to the parlor. "If the harvests had been only a little better, I think we could have avoided this."

"I take it this has something to do with the harvest or the stores I have provided," Ragoczy ventured, unflustered in spite of Herr Kleinerhoff's dismay. As he entered the parlor, he saw Balduin finish lighting the lamps.

"Both, I fear," said Kleinerhoff. He stood while Balduin relieved him of his dripping cloak; he turned abashed eyes on the puddle of water forming on the small Turkish carpet.

"I'll just take this to the kitchen, Comte," he said to Ragoczy. "We'll do what we can to dry it out."

"Very good, Balduin. And bring a large cup of hot buttered rum for Herr Kleinerhoff, if you would." He put his whole attention on Kleinerhoff as Balduin left the room. "And something to eat. He's had a long, wet walk to this château."

"Thank you, Comte," said Kleinerhoff, "but I do not deserve your good offices."

"This is hardly more than standard courtesy," said Ragoczy, and motioned his steward away; the purr of the rain on the windows filled the handsome chamber, reassuring in its steadiness. "So what has become of the harvest and the stores?"

"Become of them—a third of each has been stolen, or almost a third. More of the grain was taken than seed, but still—" Kleiner-hoff admitted miserably. "Yes, more grain than seed, which is better than if the seed were gone."

"A third," said Ragoczy, surprised by the large amount. "How did it happen?"

"I have . . . a report," Kleinerhoff ventured.

"Which I gather you do not entirely believe," said Ragoczy, watching Kleinerhoff's discomfort.

"No, not entirely."

"But you have not entirely convinced yourself that it is com-pletely mendacious," Ragoczy said, his past experiences reminding him of other, similar incidents.

"Not entirely," said Kleinerhoff.

Ragoczy nodded. "Well, give me the gist of this report, and you and I can decide what credence to attach to it."

"All right, Comte," said Kleinerhoff, and launched into the ac-count he had been provided. "This is what I have been told: It was late last night, after most of the villagers had retired for the night. A party of armed men came into the . . . the village hall and forced the guards to load up two gun-wagons with them. Did I say it was late at night? The report said the clock had struck midnight, but . . ." He kept himself from going on with some effort; he cleared his throat. "Herr Staub and Herr Quelle had the watch at that hour, and it is from them that I have this report: they said the men were armed with guns and swords, possibly soldiers from the recent wars. There are many such men about."

"That they are," said Ragoczy. "As travelers have cause to know." He thought a moment, then asked, "Did either guard notice anything else about the men? The kinds of horses they rode? What their clothes were like? their accents?"

Kleinerhoff shrugged. "They didn't mention either to me. They said it was late, all was dark, and the men were armed. They also said the rain was just starting, and that most of their trail, if they left one, would be washed away by now."

"How did the guards know the vehicles were gun-wagons?" He looked only curious, but he was concentrating on every nuance of Kleinerhoff's report.

"Herr Quelle spent some time in the army, a decade ago; he lost two fingers and was sent home. He was familiar with gun-wagons." Kleinerhoff sighed unhappily. "It has occurred to me, as it must do for you, that these two men may have more knowledge of the thievery than they have admitted."

"Yes," said Ragoczy gently. "It had."

"Well, that's hardly surprising," said Kleinerhoff. "They knew what to take, they knew where to come, and they were gone before anyone knew they had been there."

"It is the last that troubles me the most," said Ragoczy thoughtfully. "The place where the stores are kept might be learned by spending an hour or two in the tavern, given how the villagers talk, but this smacks of broader knowledge than what might be picked up in an afternoon. That they were prepared to take certain amounts is not astonishing, either, since the account says they had only two wagons. But how they left without raising any alarm—that concerns me, for it suggests that these men have spies in the village, or allies."

"Or both." Kleinerhoff went toward the window. "And how many others in our village are with them? Is it just this village, or are others involved? I have asked myself these questions since Herr Quelle came to my house last night."

Ragoczy sat down in one of the two grandfather's armchairs on either side of the fireplace. "How many men were involved, did either guard mention that?"

"Quelle said there were eight of them, and Staub said nine, when pressed. He claims there was one who stayed with the gun-wagons while his comrades came into the town hall to take their prizes." Kleinerhoff sighed deeply. "It is a terrible loss, no matter how many there were."

"It is," said Ragoczy. "But it is also most curious that such a group attracted no attention. Had a stranger come to your house, Behemoth would surely alert you. Surely one of the farmers would have provided a dog to the guards?"

Kleinerhoff made an impatient swipe of his hand. "I said we needed a dog to guard with the men, but Madame Bruell said that it would disturb the guests at the tavern, to have a dog barking all night."

"How often has she guests at the tavern?" Ragoczy inquired politely.

"Market days, some end up at the tavern all night," said Kleinerhoff. "But once the summer is gone, very few travelers stop here—not with Yvoire so near. I believe she has two men under her roof, one a tinker who comes twice a year, and another who is unfamiliar to Madame Bruell, and to some of the rest."

"So you have had only your neighbors and near-by farmers staying at the tavern on most occasions, and rarely in large numbers. This must trouble you: no one has mentioned noticing unfamiliar men about, aside from the single man?"

"No," said Kleinerhoff. "I have heard nothing of strangers, aside from him. With the rain, he is planning to stay on two days more."

"That makes all this the more perplexing," said Ragoczy. "If these armed men knew of the grain and seed, they must have been told about it, or have seen it for themselves, which leads to the inescapable conclusion that there was collusion in arranging the theft."

"I didn't want to think of it in that light," Kleinerhoff admitted dejectedly. "The village is depending on the grain and seed for next year."

"As head-man of Sacre-Sang, who can blame you for your apprehensions?" Ragoczy said, expecting no answer.

But Kleinerhoff punched his fist into his palm. "That is what is most distressing—that our village will suffer no matter who perpetrated the crime, or for what gain. Sacre-Sang may not be an important place, but it is our market and our home."

"Nine houses, a tavern, and a hall," said Ragoczy. "Enough to matter to many people; certainly all the farmers in the region depend upon your village for many things."

"Those in Yvoire think nothing of us," said Kleinerhoff. "But they eat our cheese and cabbages and apples, and our pigs and fowl."

"All the more reason to discover who stole the grain," Ragoczy said.

"Yes." Kleinerhoff glowered at the shutters. "It is a loss for all of us."

"But I wonder who benefits," Ragoczy mused.

"How do you mean?" Kleinerhoff asked, growing a bit pale at his own question.

Ragoczy answered in a level voice without a trace of rancor, "I mean that we are agreed that a local person had to be part of the robbery; therefore someone local must plan to profit from the theft, and profit handsomely, or why take the risk? Under the circumstances, it would be remiss not to consider that Herr Quelle and Herr Staub might be more closely connected to this crime than is apparent, or know who is."

"They wouldn't do such a dreadful thing," Kleinerhoff protested. "The donation you made helps them as well as all the rest of us."

"But not enough to try to keep the grain where it was," Ragoczy pointed out.

"Everyone agreed on the hall as the place the grain and seed would be safest."

"Someone may have had ulterior motives for supporting that decision." Ragoczy contemplated the middle distance. "In retrospect, the arrangement was designed to make theft easy."

"Armed men, Comte. You can't expect a pair of farmers to stand against armed men," Kleinerhoff pleaded. "They are not soldiers. They had a single pistol between them. I don't know if they had charged it or not."

"Odd, for night-guards not to be better armed," said Ragoczy, and indicated the roll-back frame-chair by the window. "Sit down, Herr Kleinerhoff. You look worn."

"I am. This has shocked me very much, Comte, very much." He dropped into the chair. "Very modern. Very handsome," he approved.

"More to the point, it is comfortable," said Ragoczy. "Take what ease you can. We may be here yet awhile." He pointed to the clock on the mantle. "I am at your disposal for the next three hours."

"Three hours!" It was more than he expected and he was taken aback. In order to gather his thoughts, Kleinerhoff glanced about the room and noticed that he had left muddy footprints on the beautiful scroll-and-rose carpet. "Comte. I am sorry. I apologize. I should have—"

"The mud can be cleaned, and in this weather, everyone will be tracking it," said Ragoczy gently.

"This is most distressing. Shall I go and remove my boots?" Kleinerhoff asked.

"There is no reason to do so, not now." Ragoczy took a firmer tone. "Remain where you are. Once the mud has dried, it will be taken care of." He turned his dark eyes on the head-man of Sacre-Sang. "You and I have more important matters to consider."

"Yes," he said slowly. "We do."

"So, if you will, turn your thoughts to who among your villagers would have good reason to take a risk so great as this one?"

"Great risk," scoffed Kleinerhoff. "You cannot think this was a risk at all, not with these robbers taking their booty without so much as a challenge to their theft."

"Exactly what we must assess," said Ragoczy patiently.

Kleinerhoff gave a dejected nod. "Just so."

Ragoczy settled back more contentedly, doing his best to help Kleinerhoff to stop fretting. "First, why do you suppose the robbers chose that time to make their raid—if it was a raid, and not a mutual plundering."

"I have been pondering that myself," said Kleinerhoff. "I have no answer."

"No doubt your questions increase, and will continue to do so until the problem is resolved," said Ragoczy, to encourage him to expound. "That is always a good beginning. When you have no questions, no answers are possible."

"I have many more now than I did three hours ago, and none of them provide me any comfort," he admitted, and was about to go on when there was a knock at the door, and Rogier entered bearing a tray with a large tankard filled with hot buttered rum; with it stood a selection of pastries stuffed with whipped cream, brandied custard, and ground nuts, and a wedge of sweet cheese. He set this down on the occasional table near Kleinerhoff, his manner abstinent but cordial.

"Thank you," Ragoczy said to Rogier. "Precisely the sort of array I had in mind."

"Will you want some of the pastries, Comte?" Kleinerhoff asked nervously. "Or the cheese?"

"No, thank you. I am going to dine later this evening. Do not let my reticence for indulgence interfere with your delectation: I hope you will enjoy what is offered." Ragoczy nodded to Rogier, who left them alone. "You are chilled, Herr Kleinerhoff, and who would wonder at it?"

"The rain has become heavy. At least there is no wind," said Kleinerhoff. "I hadn't expected it so early in October. It is only the second week, and it is damp as November." He picked up the tankard and lifted it ironically. "Another early winter."

"Not as cold as the last two," Ragoczy observed.

"No, not yet," Kleinerhoff said, and drank. As he lowered the tankard, he smiled for the first time. "Wonderful. Wonderful."

"I shall tell my cook that you approve," said Ragoczy politely. "Have a pastry and then let us discuss the robbery."

Obediently, Kleinerhoff took one of the little puffy cakes in his fingers, bent over the tray, and bit in. A powdering of sugar clung to his mustache as he chewed. When he was done he wiped his fingers on the kerchief he pulled from his pocket. "Superb. How pleasant for you to have such an accomplished cook."

"It is pleasant," said Ragoczy and offered no other comment.

Kleinerhoff had another drink of rum and leaned back in his chair. "The robbery. I have tried to consider every aspect of the crime, and I am still uncertain about it."

"In what way?" Ragoczy asked, knowing that now Kleinerhoff's tongue would be loosened.

"I have thought that perhaps Quelle and Staub made arrangements with the thieves, and they will profit from the crime by receiving a share of the plunder, a share they can use or sell, whichever suits their advantage. Or the thieves may be planning to sell all their loot and provide Quelle and Staub a share of their gain. But neither man is so poor that his suffering is not the same as everyone else's, and Emil Staub is my woman's cousin." He looked out the window again. "I have considered the very poorest farmers in the area, but none of them have the kind of equipment that these robbers had—"

"Were said to have had," Ragoczy corrected gently.

"Well, yes. None of them have wagons and only two have horses—draft ponies, actually, and everyone recognizes them." He rubbed the stubble on his chin. "I have other doubts about them. They could have provided information to such armed men as Quelle and Staub said took the sacks, perhaps in return for a share so that they could have more bountiful crops at the end of summer."

"That is a possibility," said Ragoczy, "but you do not seem to have convinced yourself."

"No; no, I haven't," Kleinerhoff said, and had another generous drink of the hot-buttered rum in an attempt to gather up his courage. "Herr Mouler, who has charge of the morning watch, suggested that you might have arranged the theft."

Ragoczy sat very still. "Did Herr Mouler say why he thought that?"

"He said you were the only man living near Sacre-Sang who had money enough to hire a company of armed men. He said that you had given the grain and seed as a means of achieving goodwill, and you had the sacks stolen so that you would not have to lose so much of your own stores." He drank again. "I am sorry, Comte. I told him he was wrong, but there are bound to be some in the village who will believe him because you are a foreigner."

"And an exile," said Ragoczy. "That is also generally known."

"It makes little difference to most of them: Napoleon left his share of exiles as his legacy, along with widows and orphans." Kleinerhoff drank again, and this time his smile was easier than before. "That makes little difference to the farmers here—you are a stranger, and they will always hold you in suspicion."

"Does that include you, Herr Kleinerhoff?" Ragoczy asked.

"I?" He laughed immoderately. "No. Of course not. Not now."

"So you did at one time—have doubts about me." Ragoczy saw Kleinerhoff nod unhappily. "You would have been remiss in your responsibilities had you been too quick to accept me: that would smack of influence and subornation."

"It is just the way of the Swiss," said Kleinerhoff apologetically.

"I can understand how some might be suspicious of me." He had almost forty centuries of such suspicions behind him. "I come from far-away, and although I am a man of means, I do not have a position in this country beyond the courtesy my title commands."

"You have conducted yourself very well, Comte," said Kleinerhoff. "You have concerned yourself with the welfare of the region, and you have been generous with those of us whose crops failed." He stopped to burp, then went on, "Not many know how much they owe to you—"

"And would not welcome the dreadful burden of gratitude," said Ragoczy, cutting off his encomia. "So it is just as well that they know no more than they do." He rose and went to tug the bell-rope. "A fire would be welcome, would it not."

Kleinerhoff nodded several times. "It is quite chilly in here."

"Then that must be amended," said Ragoczy, and when Balduin came to the door, asked for a fire to be lit and, in a much lower voice, requested a second tankard of hot-buttered rum for his guest.

"Shortly," said Balduin. "We are finishing up the preparations for Herr Kreuzbach's stay."

"Very good," Ragoczy approved, and gave his attention to Kleinerhoff once again.

"What do you want me to tell them, then?" Kleinerhoff asked.

"Nothing. You will not change their reservations, and if you are perceived to be protecting me you could endanger your own position." Ragoczy returned to his chair, but did not sit; instead he rested his arm on the mantle, one leg crossed over the other, the model of a modern gentleman.

Kleinerhoff blinked as he mulled this over. "I don't see why that would happen. I've been head-man for seventeen years: no one has ever questioned my judgment."

"How fortunate for you; I would not want to blot so sterling a record." He called "Come" as a knock on the door was heard in the room.

Steffel, the second footman, entered the room carrying a large basket filled with wood and kindling. "If I may, Comte?"

Ragoczy stepped away from the fireplace, saying, "By all means." He strolled over toward the window, stopping beside the maple bookcase.

"If you insist I remain silent, I will, but I think it would be better if more of the farmers in this region knew how much you have done for them." Kleinerhoff was becoming refractory as the strong drink continued to work on him.

"When the hard years have passed, perhaps," said Ragoczy as much to calm him as to concede anything.

"If some of the folk hereabouts are aiding bandits, knowing who their true benefactor is might persuade them not to aid outlaws," Kleinerhoff persisted.

"That would assume all farmers seek to have exactly the same thing, which I reckon is not the case." He put his hands together. "Whomelse do you consider likely to be involved?"

"Herr Feige has a son who may be with the robbers," said Kleinerhoff, looking embarrassed at such a revelation. "He fought in Poland and in Spain. They say he was wounded, and joined with other discharged soldiers to be outlaws, or so Herr Feige says. I haven't seen the lad since he was young." He yawned deeply. "I know that Heinrich Feige would do almost anything to aid and assist his boy."

"Is this common knowledge?" Ragoczy asked while Steffel laid the fire, taking care to place the kindling for best draw on the thick, short-cut branches.

"Most of Sacre-Sang knows it," said Kleinerhoff. "Sometimes we joke about it. Herr Dickicht has offered to pay Herr Feige in order to keep his lambs safe when driving them to market. No one takes him seriously. It is understood that the father is not in regular contact with his son."

"Are you sure of that?" Ragoczy asked.

"Naturally," said Kleinerhoff. "There have been officers of the justice courts looking for him for the last few years. Had they found anything of significance, I would be informed."

"Very well," said Ragoczy. "Is there anyone else you might entertain as a person of interest, as the English say?"

"Possibly Brigitte," said Kleinerhoff after brief reflection. "She knows more than almost anyone in Sacre-Sang does."

Although he had never met her, Ragoczy knew Brigitte by reputation: she was the town whore, and it was said that all gossip passed through her bed daily. "Do you think she might assist robbers?"

"Who knows what a loose woman will do?" Kleinerhoff turned his head sharply as Steffel struck a spark and blew on it to get the fire going. "Don't you repeat anything of what you hear, boy: you understand me?"

"Yes, Herr Kleinerhoff," said Steffel between gentle breaths on the spreading bit of fire.

"Be careful of servants," Kleinerhoff recommended as he slewed back to look at Ragoczy. "They know too much, all of them."

"In most households they certainly do," said Ragoczy.

The first little flames broke out in the kindling; Steffel stood up and ducked his head to Ragoczy. "I am finished, Comte."

"Thank you, Steffel. You may go." Ragoczy watched the young man leave the parlor; he regarded Kleinerhoff for a short while. "What are you planning to do to recover the grain and seed?"

"What can I do? We have no justice court here, and no magistrates' riders to hunt the robbers down. I had thought we might send observers to other markets, to see if any of the grain or seed is being sold there. But I fear that the robbers will not be foolish enough to keep the sacks you provided with the eclipse upon them. So I must assume such an effort would be futile."

"All these things are probably true," said Ragoczy, and was about to propose another approach when a knock at the door alerted him to the arrival of the second tankard of hot-buttered rum; eager to keep Kleinerhoff talking, Ragoczy went to admit Rogier so that he could resume his inquiry.

Text of a letter from Wallache Gerhard Winifrith Sieffert, Graf von Ravensberg at Ravensberg, near Salzburg, Austria, to Saint-Germain Ragoczy, Comte Franciscus at Château Ragoczy, near Lake Geneva, Yvoire, Switzerland, carried by private messenger and delivered ten days after dispatch.

To the most excellent Comte Franciscus, the greetings and regrets of WGW Sieffert, Graf von Ravensberg at Ravensberg on this, the 19th day of October, 1817,

My dear Comte,

I am most loathe to rescind my invitation to your proposed visit, but a tragedy has struck my household, and it has made receiving visitors not only malapropos, but potentially abashing to you should events take an even more drastic turn: one of my wards is missing. Rosalie, a charming child of six, as winsome and engaging as any child could wish to be, has vanished, and we all can do nothing but fear the worst. She is a beautiful child, trusting and vital, one who inspires affection in everyone. I have sponsored searchers to look for her, but they have found nothing although they have searched everywhere for her. Should any new information be provided as to her whereabouts it will be incumbent upon me to act quickly to return the child to her home here, and to lavish all attention upon her to make up for whatever ordeal she may have endured. Under such circumstances, I cannot engage to be entertaining guests, no matter how distinguished they may be. I trust you will understand my reluctance and will ascribe it to motives of concern for the child as well as the wish to receive you as a guest of your position and rank ought to be received. Postponement can ensure that will be the case, and for that reason, I urge you to accept this alternate arrangement.

Let me suggest that the spring may be a more satisfactory time for all concerned. The weather will be much better and the roads will be far more passable than they will be from now to April. I will then be announcing the engagement of my ward Hyacinthie, whom you met in Amsterdam, to Constanz Medoc of Trier, and between that and the publication of my book, we should have a most delightful time. Hyacinthie will also be more festive in her mood: just now she is filled with sorrow and has often declared it is her fault that Rosalie is missing, for she had taken the child on a walk and, because of a fall, was unable to accompany Rosalie back to this Schloss. Once she accepts that she may have been irresponsible in not insisting that the girl accompany her, but that the fate of Rosalie is in the hands of her abductors, she may begin to mend her heart. You will have a far better stay then than you will now, or for many weeks to come. The last thing I would wish for you—or for Hyacinthie—would be a visit marked by gloom and more disappointments. Come in the spring, I urge you, and be certain of a warm welcome.

I hope when I see you, the search for Rosalie will have a joyous outcome, but I will not permit myself to hope too much, lest all be dashed by the discovery that she has died. I refuse to consider that possibility, but it intrudes, no matter what I do to put it far from my thoughts, and Rosalie's older sister, Hedda, has been beside herself with grief, not allowing me to comfort her in the night when she cries piteously for her missing younger sister. It distresses me to be helpless to ameliorate her deep and all-consuming sorrow. You cannot imagine how it troubles me to be unable to offer the child the solace she so desperately needs, when, as her guardian, it is part of my duty to soothe all her misery away. I long to embrace her so that she and I may share the burden of Rosalie's loss, but Hedda is not yet willing to admit me into her confidences. Once she relents and allows me to provide sympathy combined with the care she requires, I have hope of her improvement. I speak of these things so that you will know my decision to change the time of our meeting is not the result of caprice, but rather my own deep regard for these girls as well as for you, yourself.

I will look forward to receiving your messenger again when winter is over, and in the meantime,

> *I am*
> *Most sincerely,*
> *Wallache Gerhard Winifrith Sieffert*
> *Graf von Ravensberg*

6

"I'm sorry, I'm sorry." Hero turned her tearful face toward Ragoczy. "Comte, I am so, so sorry." She clutched her pillow and held it close to her, the bedclothes in disruption around him. "I want to. Really . . . I wish I could . . . I shouldn't . . . I never intended . . ." The light from the lamp made wavering shadows on her face as if taking the chill from the room into its heart, muffling its illusion of warmth in flickering shadows.

He laid his finger lightly against her lips. "No, Hero, it is I who should apologize to you. It is too soon still."

"It isn't," she said, shaking her head in self-condemnation. "Or it shouldn't be. I shouldn't make you . . . You have been reasonable and patient and understanding. I couldn't ask for more kindness, not from anyone. I don't know why I should be this way, and to you, of all men." Had Fridhold lived, she would not have expected such sympathy from him as Ragoczy had given her. She touched his hand tentatively, then released it, as if even so little connection as this was unbearable.

"I am sorry that you have had to suffer your loss with so much worry." He thought of Ignatia, of Demetrice, of Acana Tupac, of Xenya, each with her own unquenchable grief, and he did his best to convey his concern. "You are trying to hold your sorrow at a distance while you wait to see your sons."

"I should be with them, no matter what my father-in-law permits; he could hardly turn me away if I should travel to Scharffensee. I should have insisted as soon as we returned from Amsterdam that we go there, but I didn't know the rains would come early, or—" A steely determination straightened her back and interrupted her weeping. "In the spring, I will not be put off: he will receive me whether he will or no. I will see my sons. It is my duty, and my right to be with my children." Then without warning a new bout of weeping came over her; she pummeled her fists into her pillow as if she wanted to strike her own body. "I don't know what's wrong with me."

"You are in mourning," said Ragoczy, making no effort to stop her.

"I *should* mourn. My daughter is dead," she exclaimed as she threw the pillow across the room. "She died without me to care for her."

"She did, and that is lamentable, but you could not have known she would die."

"Fridhold's father waited so long to tell me—too long. That is how the Graf has been since Fridhold died. He didn't want me to know about Annamaria. He doesn't want to tell me about any of them." She bit her lower lip.

"He is inclined to forget that you are part of your children's lives," said Ragoczy, striving to keep his remarks as neutral as possible, so that Hero would not feel she had to defend von Scharffensee for the sake of her children and her dead husband.

"Their lives and Annamaria's death," Hero interjected.

"He believes he knows best, as men of his station often do; it seems to me he is failing in his trust, largely because he deems that such a failure is impossible," Ragoczy remarked. "He fears you will influence your children—and he is correct: you will."

"My father-in-law doesn't care about them, not really. He thinks only to supervise them for my late husband." She began to weep in earnest, her expression filled with chagrin.

"He, too, lost a child," said Ragoczy.

"But Fridhold was grown, not eight years old." She trembled, her hands flexing, reaching for her arms.

"I doubt that matters," said Ragoczy.

"Whatever the case, it offered him no insight." She folded her arms, clutching at her upper arms with straining fingers. "If he has no compassion for me, well, that is his way. But he has none for my children, and that worries me."

"Understandably."

"He thinks of me as a rival," she said suddenly, "and he a jilted suitor. He blames me for the loss of Fridhold."

"So it would seem." Ragoczy was still appalled at the apparent unconcern von Scharffensee had shown toward Hero, and found this explanation as reasonable as any. "I wish I could ease your hurt."

"You mean you wish you could drink my blood, don't you?" she countered, and clapped both her hands over her mouth, turning stricken eyes upon him, offended by her own temerity.

"Yes," he said quietly and calmly. "I would like that; it would be nourishing and it would provide the intimacy for which we both long, if you are willing to allow me to touch you in more than your flesh."

"I shouldn't have said that," she whispered.

"Possibly not," he agreed without condemnation. "But there is truth in it."

She shook her head. "I didn't mean it, Comte. I didn't mean it."

"That may be, but you had to say something," he said as he took her hand in his, holding it palm up. "You said it to drive me away, for just now intimacy is more than you can bear."

"I . . . I suppose so," she confessed, her eyes welling with tears. "But I don't want that, not really."

A thousand years ago he might have pressed the advantage in that admission, but he had learned not to use that leverage: what it gained in the moment, it lost over time. He sat on her bed while she wrestled with her emotions, then, as she looked at him directly, he said, "But you aren't ready to make love yet, either; to you it feels like a betrayal of your child. You thought you were ready, and you miss my companionship, but now that you make the attempt, you see the loss is still too overwhelming, too raw."

She nodded twice. "You do understand."

"In my way."

Wishing to deflect his compelling gaze, she pushed back from him, and to add to her remoteness, she asked, "How is that? How can someone as old as you say you are understand?"

He recognized her ploy as an attempt to distract him, but answered her, his voice low and steady. "It is nearly four thousand years since I came into my vampiric life; I have spent most of that time saying good-bye, and every one of those losses left its mark on my soul. I may not understand your personal grief, but sorrow and I are old companions." He touched her arm. "I will not force myself on you; that would blight our closeness. When only our skins touch, there is little to bind us together."

"But skin is the best we have," she said morosely.

"It has not been so before," he said, as gently as he could, his dark, penetrating eyes on her. "I am willing to wait."

"Until I am old and wrinkled? Until I have grandchildren?" She clamped her jaws closed, as if to keep from speaking at all.

"If that is required," he said. "Time is more inexorable for you than for me."

"Because I am alive," she said. "Because every day brings me closer to the grave."

"And because you are alive, you age," he said, unflustered. "Age takes a toll on the passions as much as the body."

She glared at him, daring to meet his compassionate gaze and to ignore what he revealed in his eyes. "That is intended to cheer me?"

"No; I thought it would reassure you, so you will understand—"

"That you are patient?" she challenged. "Or is it easier to wait for a willing woman than have to search out another one?"

He remained where he was, still as water, seeing her tempestuous emotion worry at her. "You must not despair, Hero. You are not condemned to a lifetime of dejection and loneliness, much as you are convinced it is so now. Loss is always with us, but so is restoration."

"No? Can you be sure of that?" She pulled her night-rail more tightly around her. "You have never lost a child."

"I know you cherished hopes for your daughter, and all of them are left in shambles." He stared at the far wall. "It is going to be a freezing night tonight."

"And you, with your cool skin, will you keep me warm? Or is it I who should keep you warm?" As she heard herself speak, she was

almost overcome with mortification that she should be so unpardon-
ably caustic. She tried to think of something that would lessen the
excoriating impact of her remarks. "Comte, I apologize." That
seemed wholly inadequate; she tried again. "I don't know what's
come over me. I never intended . . ."

"But you do, you know: you intend to cut yourself off from all
pleasure and succor because you deem yourself to be undeserving
of either." He said this softly but he held her attention. "You want to
inflict pain on yourself."

She fixed her eyes on him as if mesmerized. "Why shouldn't I
bear the anguish? I deserve it."

"Do you think so?" He shook his head slowly. "No, Hero, you
need not flagellate yourself with whips or recriminations."

"You say that as if it were nothing but a change done as easily as
I might change my clothes."

"I think such changes are very hard." He gave her a moment to
speak; she remained silent. "But time will separate you from those
you miss more than distance. Each day memory slips them farther
away." His dark eyes were glowing, alive with the recollection of
those he had lost.

She studied him as if searching for any trace of duplicity. Finally
she clasped her hands in her lap and stared down at them. "Would
you like me to leave?"

"Leave? No, certainly not," he said, aware that her despair was
once again threatening to overcome her.

"Then what? You can't want to continue in this way, can you?"

"No, I would rather not have to carry on with so much unresolved heartbreak impinging upon us." He smoothed the revers of
his dressing-gown. "But I see no reason to cut our dealings short in
homage to your self-condemnation."

Her face went pale. "What do you mean?"

He rose from the bed and paced her bedchamber in a measured, deliberate tread. "If you believe you must immolate yourself
on the altar of family sorrow, you show neither your sorrow nor your
family much grace. I know you embrace your agony in order to keep

your daughter with you, made real by the pain of her death. You are convinced that if you set the agony aside, you will lose the memory of your daughter. But that approach, if continued, will turn the memory of her into something always painful, and she deserves better than that, as do you. Let her go, Hero, let her go; for you cannot keep her with you, and let all your thoughts of her be joyous ones, as they can be, in time, if you do not cling to her death." He stopped moving and gave his whole attention to her; his voice became more musical and his demeanor was filled with commiseration. "If I were uncaring, perhaps I would not be moved by your affliction; but we have a Blood Bond that will continue until the True Death claims one of us. It grieves me to see you add to your anguish in this way. What you endure is hard enough without increasing the wretchedness you want to put behind you."

"Is that what I am doing?" She had no part of softness in her question. "You have decided how I am to remember my own child?"

"No, I am telling you how I have learned to deal with centuries of losses."

She looked past him at a picture of a narrow stretch of river over which a broken stone bridge rising out of the current stretched unsuccessfully toward high banks; at present it appeared to be a reflection of her state of mind. "When spring comes, he will try to put me off again, my father-in-law. He will send my boys away, or tell me it is inconvenient to visit, or plan another journey for them to take."

"That he may, but it will not succeed." He sighed once. "You and I will yet visit Scharffensee, or whatever place he has taken your sons."

"You will do so much for me?" She sounded more tired than annoyed. "Why would you do this? I haven't done anything to merit your help."

"I do not bargain with those I love, particularly not about what you need." He went to put another small log on in the fireplace. "There is no reason to keep the room so icy. Let your body be warmed, by the fire if not by me. The frost on the windows warns you of a hard night."

"I should let it chill me; perhaps I will not be so distrait if I am cold enough." She leaned back against the satin-covered bolster, making a gesture of concession. "If you insist on heating the room, this is your château and I am your guest."

He watched as the log began to smoke as the low flames curled up around it. "I do not wish to impose upon you, but I would not want you to become ill."

"In imitation of my daughter?"

"It is one possibility, and one I have seen before." He touched his fingertips together.

"You mean I might sicken and die?" She laughed a bit wildly. "I would be with her and Fridhold then, wouldn't I? And my father-in-law would not have to deal with me."

"Possibly, but it would be a high price to pay for very little satisfaction." He drew up a chair to the side of her bed, and sat down, facing Hero across the silk of her comforter. "You may wish to make yourself free of the complications that have marked your life since your husband's death, but dying is not the way. You hope to be with your husband and daughter, but you forget your sons, who will need you as they grow older."

"They have their grandfather," she said.

"Who is what? sixty years old? How much longer will he live? And what will happen to your boys then? They have already lost their father and their sister. If they lose their mother as well, think of how abandoned they will be when their grandfather dies."

"He will provide for them."

"Money and lands, yes they are all very well, but that will not be what they seek most: context will be gone." He held Hero's gaze with his own. "It may be tempting to trust to the next world rather than this one, but—"

"How can you say that to me?" she demanded. "I have wanted to have my children with me, but my father-in-law has prevented it."

"Your father-in-law has laid down conditions he thinks are reasonable. You have to fulfill his conditions and he will have no cause to keep your children from you."

"The probate court awarded Fridhold's children to his father's care in lieu of Fridhold having made a Will, as they always do. He didn't know he would die so young, and the court upheld his father's claim without a hearing. How can I hope to gain the approval of the magistrates? The probate marshall makes that impossible." The way she asked made it clear that she had mulled over this question many times.

"You must have an acceptable residence, proper servants, and an income high enough to keep your children in a manner appropriate to their rank, or so the document you showed me stipulated. Have I erred in my summation?"

Hero shook her head. "Which my father-in-law knows is impossible. Were I in a position to live with my father, although he has some means, the court would not approve, nor would my father."

Ragoczy offered a one-sided smile. "That will change as soon as the castle above Zemmer is ready for its occupants. You said you liked it when we visited it on the Amsterdam trip. The Graf will not be able to object to your receiving your sons for a part of every year so long as you have land, a staff, and the income from the land to provide for your sons and yourself." He saw her take this in, astonishment mixed with dubiety as she grasped what he was telling her.

"You said I could live there, and my children, too," she said, picking her words with care. "I thought you intended to reside there, as well. That I would be your guest."

"No doubt I will visit, from time to time," he said. "But the castle should suit you and your sons most satisfactorily."

She blinked twice, not only in surprise but to keep from crying again. "You said nothing about making it mine."

"You will be my resident guardian of the estate, and as such you may live in it as your home for as long as it suits you."

"But it will be yours," she said, looking uncertain again.

"Yes. I will pay the staff and the maintenance, and I will deal with any taxes that may be imposed. You do not want to undertake such costs yourself, do you?" He saw understanding dawn in her eyes. "A widow owning an estate has little to protect her, but a widow managing an estate is not so vulnerable."

"I never thought about that," she said in a measured tone as she assessed what he had told her. "You're right, of course. No one should know that better than I."

"I will have Kreuzbach draw up a binding agreement that will satisfy any court that you have the security they demand for you to have at least partial domestic custody of your own children." He gave her time to sort this out. "They cannot expect you to have more than that to justify restoring your family to you."

"How do you propose to present this to the court?" She was becoming interested now, aware that he had the position and fortune to do exactly what he described.

"I thought I would present it to your father-in-law first," he said. "When we visit him."

"And he will deny you," she said with heavy conviction.

"Perhaps. But I can be persuasive. He will have to listen to me because we are of equal rank, if for no other reason."

Hero laughed harshly. "One nobleman to another, you mean."

Unfazed by her contempt, he said, "I can require his attention as you cannot." He moved closer to her, leaning forward in the chair.

She shook her head, then started to cry again. "I hate feeling so helpless," she exclaimed as she sobbed.

"That is why you may depend upon me. I know you are not helpless, just stymied." He would have liked to take her hand, but realized she would see the gesture as weakening her, so he only said, "You have not had an ally to turn to for many years."

"Are you trying to make up for that? Or are you trying to prove something to Madelaine de Montalia, and this is your opportunity to do so?" As soon as she said the name, she was sure she should not have, but she could not stop speaking. Letting go of her arms, she gathered her hands together. "I . . . Comte . . ."

"I have nothing to prove to Madelaine," he said softly. "Nor to you. You know what I am and how I live, and what I know because of it. Scratch and claw as you will, I know what you are because I know your blood, the truest part of your self. It will take more than harsh accusations to drive me away once we have touched."

She glowered at him. "Perhaps I have changed."

"Perhaps. Or perhaps some part of your character is newly come to light, but none of that can alter what I know of you." He made himself more comfortable. "You cannot reprove me with Madelaine's name, or that of anyone I have loved, not even your own." This, he knew, was not entirely accurate, for there was always Csimenae, who might still be hidden away in the fastness of the Pyrenees.

"Did you intend from the first that we should be lovers?" Her voice hardened.

"No, I did not," said Ragoczy. "Madelaine wrote to tell me that you had been treated badly by your family and needed an ally, something she could not do herself from the Ottoman Empire."

"So keeping me is a favor to her?" she asked, ending with a harsh laugh. "You indulge her through me."

"No; she sympathized with your predicament, as I know she told you before she proposed that she put me in contact with you." He set his concern aside and continued. "She provided our introduction. If she had not wanted us to meet, she chose a strange way to accomplish that goal."

"So she threw me to you?" Hero asked, aghast at herself for so callous a suggestion.

"No—and well you know it."

She wept more determinedly now, disgusted at all she had done and said since she summoned him to her chamber that evening. "Why am I behaving so . . . so shabbily?" she asked of the bolster.

"It is the way in which you come to terms with your grief," said Ragoczy. "You lash out."

"But at you? At Madelaine de Montalia?"

"You would lash out at Annamaria, if you could, for leaving you, as Fridhold left you," said Ragoczy, so kindly and with such empathy that she stopped weeping to stare at him. "I felt the same consuming anger for nearly five centuries, and I made myself the thing I most despised. Gradually Egypt changed that, but it was not easily done."

Hero used the corner of her sheet to wipe her eyes dry. "Madame de Montalia—I didn't slight her, not truly."

"Of course not," said Ragoczy, and got up from the chair. "You will want to rest, to recover yourself." He went to the side of the bed and bent to kiss her forehead. "Sleep well. We will talk more in a day or two—when you are ready."

She took hold of the revers of his dressing-gown. "I apologize, Comte. From the bottom of my heart."

"You need not," he said, making no attempt to disengage her hands. "Think of all you have said tonight as lancing a boil. Once you let out the poison, you will be able to heal."

"A boil!" She stiffened. "My grief is nothing like that."

"It will not be any longer," he assured her, laying his hand lightly on her shoulder. "But you might have let it become one. As it is, you are going to improve through the winter, and that will make your meeting with your father-in-law less arduous than it would have been otherwise."

"And I am expected to be grateful for your actions?" Hero demanded, then grabbed his hand. "I didn't mean that. I don't know why I'm behaving so dreadfully. I wish I knew what makes me—"

He lifted her hand, opened it, and kissed the palm. "You know why you struggle—you've told me. It is hard for you to take this on, and I know you will need time to come to terms with your emotions." His dark eyes rested on her amber-brown ones. "You are a capable and intelligent woman, Hero, but at present you are locked in self-condemnation."

She nodded, her face somber as she listened. "Comte—"

"I know you want to gather your sons around you and give yourself to them and to enshrining the memory of Annamaria, but that is unlikely to happen." He waited while she considered this, then went on. "You are a most resourceful woman, and able to shoulder burdens many another would not. But that does not mean you must mourn for all of your family, or believe you have failed if their grief is not equal to your own."

"That was never a question," she protested.

"No?" He stroked her hair. "Dear Hero, you have taken on the unhappiness and sorrow of others since you were a child. Did you not deal with all the arrangements when your mother died, so that your father could heal himself through work?"

She looked perplexed. "That was what was needed."

"You took it on," he said, and let her pull him down beside her on the bed. "You never asked for so much as a single hour for yourself, did you?"

"I didn't need an hour to myself," she said, her voice brittle.

"No; you needed days and weeks to restore your frame of mind," he said, continuing before she could argue the point. "Your father approved of what you did, and that, you decided, was all you required. But that was not true then any more than it is true now."

"Someone had to help my father. He had work that had to be done, and he was filled with sadness for my mother. They had been married sixteen years." Her sigh quivered.

"And you did well by her memory," said Ragoczy, "little though you may think so."

Hero leaned against his arm. "I could have done so much more," she whispered. "I should have done more—then and now."

"No one but you thinks the less of you for what you have done." He could not see her face, but the tension in her body revealed much to him.

"I haven't thanked you for putting the household into half-mourning. That was very kind of you." She moved so she could look directly at him. "Don't despise me for my weaknesses, Comte, I beg you."

"How could I despise you." He took her face in his hands. "I love you; you are willing to be loved, at least most of the time, and that banishes all contempt."

She moved toward the kiss he offered, and this time she did not feel that the pleasure that sparked within her was perfidious, aspersing her child's memory. There was solace in his hands and an-odyne in his presence: why had she not noticed before? Why had she refused him when he could provide consolation? In spite of all she had said, he had remained steadfast. She wrapped her arms around him, and indulged herself in his kisses. As she felt her unex-pected passion well, she broke away from him long enough to ask, "You will stay with me, won't you?" She very nearly held her breath waiting for his answer.

His promise was like the low strings on the guitar which he played so well, and his ardor all she could wish for. "As long as you like," he told her.

Text of a letter from Augustus Kleinerhoff in Sacre-Sang, to Egmond Talbot Lindenblatt, Magistrate, in Yvoire, Switzerland; dic-tated to the clerk of the court in Yvoire and carried by him from Sacre-Sang to Yvoire.

To the most excellent Magistrate, Egmond T. Lindenblatt, sitting in Yvoire, the greetings of head-man of Sacre-Sang, Augustus Kleiner-hoff, on this, the 20th day of November, 1817,

My dear Magistrate,

In regard to your inquiries concerning the various incursions ex-perienced in and around this village, it is my duty to report to you that we here have established a patrol made up of local men and their guard-dogs, the better to deal with the highwaymen and thieves who have taken to preying upon travelers and villagers alike. We have sentries in the village square every hour of the day and night, in groups of three men and a dog, so that if any miscreants are discovered, the alarm may be given without exposing the sentries to danger. This is just a first step, but it does initiate our determina-tion to end the reign of lawlessness that has marked our region for the last year.

With two hard winters behind us, we are beginning to hope for a bountiful spring and harvest this year, and therefore it is essential, in my opinion, that we prepare to defend our fields, our farms, our roads, and our markets from those who would plunder them. I have ordered that all farmers keep at least two guard-dogs on their properties, on long chains so that they will not run wild and damage crops and livestock themselves. Most of the farmers of Sacre-Sang are willing to try this in the hope that the worst depredations will be averted.

It is generally agreed that the culprits are a company of former soldiers who have turned to outlawry now that the army life is no longer possible for them. This is the most likely explanation for the problems we endure. Some believe that this company is in the pay of one or more of the major land-holders in the area, and they point from one noble to another. Baron d'Eaueternel is one who is mentioned in this regard because he supported Napoleon but escaped being punished for the support he provided, and Comte Franciscus because he is a foreigner. Neither man has been proven to have any association with these thieves, but the rumors continue.

I am persuaded that putting guards on the roads in small companies might lessen the amount of trouble the thieves can cause. We know from tales told by travelers that ours is not the only region so afflicted, and that the miscreants are often former soldiers. Perhaps, if there were a concerted effort throughout the country to apprehend these men and set them to some useful occupation, not only to provide them the means of earning a living within the law, but to require a level of restitution from those given a living, then much might be gained for all of us. We could even employ them as guards against other bandits.

I have been told that many former soldiers have gone to the New World, which has more than enough room for them, and ready employment. I would be willing to support a program that would send any captured outlaw to the Americas, with the provision that he not return to Europe for at least a decade. This solution would have the additional advantage of dispersing Napoleon's soldiers so that there can be no repeat of his Hundred Days if he ever returns to France. Without an army, he is just another fallen tyrant. How unfair that his men must suffer because of their loyalty to him, but that is the fate for those who fight on the losing side.

Thank you for providing your clerk to me, for he writes far more facilely than I do, and can turn my awkward scrawl into elegant and eloquent periods. If you require anything more of me, you have only to ask, and I will make every effort to accommodate you.

Yours to command,
Augustus Kleinerhoff
head-man of Sacre-Sang

7

"If I take two mules, I should be able to make the journey as handily as possible at this time of year," said Otto Gutesohnes as he paced around Ragoczy's study, ending up in front of the chair in which Ragoczy was seated, his fur hat in his hand, his muffler loosened and hanging around his neck. "The snows are not yet so deep that the roads are lost. Most of the damage done to the main roads last winter has been repaired, which will make for an easier passage."

"Take the two largest mules," said Ragoczy, "and if the passes are blocked, return here. I do not want you to endanger your life, and the mules, for my convenience: it is not convenient to lose dispatches, animals, and men." He cocked his head toward the windows. "It will rain in a day or two and that rain will soon be sleet, and then it will be snow."

"That means there will be ice at dawn, whether or not the skies are clear. If I leave an hour after sunrise tomorrow, I should have the best of light and warmth for my journey. Unless the wind rises, I should be able to travel ten leagues tomorrow, assuming the skies stay clear. I am not being overly optimistic; those mules are hardy beasts." He slapped at the front of his double-breasted travel-coat with its claw-hammer, knee-length tails. "I have enough warm clothes to keep me from freezing, no matter what the weather may do, and I will put full-body sheepskin saddle-pads on the mules. They will be able to stay warm."

"And once you arrive there, you will remain in Amsterdam until the end of winter if the weather requires it. Take no unnecessary risks," said Ragoczy firmly. "It will avail me little if you deliver the material entrusted to you and then are lost with news and books dispatched from van der Boom. Err on the side of circumspection, I beg you."

"As best I can," said Gutesohnes, for whom the thought of a month in Amsterdam was most appealing. "But if I start back and encounter hard weather on the way, do you want me to wait on the road at a posting inn or try to continue on?"

"I want you to remain alive, and if staying at a posting inn will accomplish that, then do it. You need not worry about making a lengthy stay—I will provide you with gold enough for such a necessity and a vial of my sovereign remedy, so that you need not succumb to illness, should you take a fever from other travelers." He had been making this concoction from moldy bread for centuries and found it truly effective against fever and infection.

"I do not plan to become ill, but then, few men do. Yet travelers often bring diseases with them; I have seen it in my journeys. Very well, I will take your vial, and any other preparation you advise. If you have an ointment for sores on the mules' legs, that would be useful, too. You know what cold can do to mules and horses." He shoved his big, square hands deep in his pockets. "It is fitting that you and I agree so that no disappointment is possible."

"An admirable goal," said Ragoczy with sardonic amusement.

"You make mock of me, Comte, but I am serious," said Gutesohnes, still inwardly amazed at how liberal Ragoczy was in allowing his staff to express their opinions. "I know you have expectations, and I know it is my work to fulfill them, therefore the greater my understanding of what you want, the likelier you are to be satisfied when I have completed my mission."

"I realize that, and I meant nothing to your discredit: I was thinking of some men I have known in the past." He did not mention that his past stretched back nearly four millennia, and that not all the men he recalled were as punctilious as Gutesohnes. "Some of them were not inclined to fret about disappointments."

"More fools they," said Gutesohnes. "I know that most men in my position would rather be prepared for . . . for any eventuality." His slight pause and too-easy smile made his remark seem glib.

Ragoczy wondered what Gutesohnes had actually been planning to say, but decided not to pursue the matter for now. "There are two small chests for van der Boom; they contain books and a pair of manuscripts with my translations into German and French. He is expecting them for the publishing program, and although I have made fair copies of all, having to deliver them a second time would delay publication by several months; your circumspection will be welcome for the sake of the works you carry." He saw anxiety in Gutesohnes' eyes, and went on in a more urbane manner. "If you want to remain in Amsterdam through the New Year, no matter what the weather, by all means do so; you will deserve time to recuperate from your travels. But while you are there, I urge you to inquire regularly about road conditions so that you may plan your return. I estimate now that, unless you are delayed by a storm, you should be in Amsterdam two or three days before Christmas. You may stay at my house there—I will give you an authorization that you may present to Kuyskill. Make the most of your opportunity, so that you will not leave with regret. As long as you are prepared to deal with bad weather, I believe you should have an uneventful journey. There are posting inns in Amsterdam which should have the most recent information on the weather, and the roads. Be wary of heavy rains; they can be more dangerous than snow."

"That I will," promised Gutesohnes. "I dislike mucking through mud more than I dislike wading through snow."

Ragoczy smiled faintly. "Neither makes for easy travel."

"I suppose not," said Gutesohnes, then added a request he feared might be refused out of hand. "May I take a small keg of brandy with me—to keep off the chill at the end of the day?"

"Certainly," said Ragoczy. "I will ask Balduin to select one from the cellar." He rose from his chair and went to the bell-pull. "Is there anything else you want?"

"Grain-mash for the mules, with oil." He nodded emphatically. "In cold weather, they'll need it."

"So they will. You may have as much as you think is wise to carry." He considered for more than a minute while Gutesohnes resumed his pacing. "I will see you have a wheel of cheese and a bag of raisins as well."

"The cheese will be most welcome, but I am not especially fond of raisins," Gutesohnes said.

"The mules are," Ragoczy said.

"That they are," said Gutesohnes, surprised that Ragoczy knew such things. "Very well."

"And a sack of nuts, for you," said Ragoczy. "In case you should hunger and not be able to reach an inn or a tavern for a meal."

Gutesohnes bowed a bit. "Danke, Comte."

"I know what it is to travel hungry, and I prefer to avoid it," said Ragoczy. "You will want one or two summer sausages, as well." He tugged the bell-pull twice, alerting Balduin to come, but not just yet.

"Very generous, Comte," said Gutesohnes.

"More practical than generous," said Ragoczy. "If you need help packing your case, tell Rogier, and he will assist you. He has a genius for such things." In the seventeen hundred years Rogier had been with him, the manservant had honed his packing skills beyond anything Ragoczy had seen before or since. "You may find his help instructive whether he assists you or not."

"I am able to fend for myself," said Gutesohnes, stung by the implication that he did not have such basic skills.

"Very well," said Ragoczy. "But I have found his help invaluable over the years." He let it go at that, trusting that good sense would prevail over stubborn pride.

"I will keep that in mind," said Gutesohnes, aware that he ought to accept the Comte's offer as a matter of respect.

Ragoczy went back to his chair. "You'll want a brace of pistols, too, I think."

"With the highwaymen about, it would be best," said Gutesohnes.

"Pistols it shall be. Inform Balduin of all your needs, and he will have them ready for you tonight. He should appear shortly. I will have the cases and chests for van der Boom loaded and closed in an hour; they will be taken to the stable to be put on the pack-saddle at first light. There will also be letters of instruction to you and to van der Boom ready to go into your dispatch-case."

"I will carry it on my person for all my travels. No one shall take it from me while I live," Gutesohnes assured him.

"It need not come to that," said Ragoczy. "But keep them with you unless your situation merits making a trade. I would rather have you alive to travel another time than thrown into a ditch as food for foxes."

"Put it that way and I understand you."

"Excellent," Ragoczy approved as a rap sounded on the door. "Balduin, you may enter."

The steward came into the study, a canvas apron tied around his waist over his knee-pants and high stockings; he had hung up his jacket and instead had a knitted jacket over his white-linen shirt. "What may I do for you, Comte?"

"You may gather together the items Gutesohnes shall specify. Then you may devote an hour to readying such necessities as he may require when he departs shortly after the next dawn. He will want sufficient amounts for a month on the road." He rose. "I am going to prepare the things he is to carry for me."

"If that is what you want," said Balduin with a nod to Gutesohnes to indicate his willingness to help.

"Meet me in this room in an hour and all should be ready." Ragoczy went to the door and let himself out of the study before Balduin could hold the door for him. He climbed the steps to his laboratory on the top floor, his energetic step alerting Rogier to his arrival.

"My master," he said in Imperial Latin as Ragoczy came through the door.

"I believe most of Gutesohnes' questions have been answered," said Ragoczy. "I need to prepare a small case for him."

"The sovereign remedy, bandages, astringent lotion of witch hazel, anodyne solutions of camomile and of powdered rose-hips for skin and internal doses, an ointment of olive-oil and angelica root for chapping and hives, a lotion of camphor against coughs, clarified wool-fat with willow-bark for abrasions, tincture of willow-bark and pansy for sore joints and heads, a poultice for drawing infections, a tisane of feverfew, and a tincture of milk-thistle to relieve the guts and muscles." He held out a large leather wallet suitable for being worn on a belt. "I have also put in a list of uses and cautions."

"Thank you, old friend," Ragoczy said in the same tongue, putting his hand on the wallet. "I should have known you would anticipate the needs of the journey."

"This is a reasonable precaution, especially in winter." Rogier gestured his accord as he went on, "The two cases of manuscripts and books are packed but I haven't yet closed them and locked them."

"You have left me with nothing to do but carry the lot downstairs," said Ragoczy, amusement flickering in the depths of his dark eyes.

"The lessons of experience," said Rogier.

"Indeed," said Ragoczy, his attractive, irregular features revealing only irony, not the dismay that much of his experience had produced.

"Have you decided which of the horses—"

"He prefers mules," said Ragoczy.

"Sensible fellow," Rogier observed.

"I think Vertrauen and Fest," said Ragoczy thoughtfully. "They are the largest of the mules and old enough to know what they are about; just the thing for a journey in bad weather. Vertrauen was sired by one of those large, shaggy, Belgian donkeys, and deserves his name." He had a brief recollection of Caesar, the donkey who had traveled with him after the Black Death struck, almost five hundred years ago; Caesar had been of that breed, a reliable and stalwart companion for almost thirteen years, and had ended his days in the stable at Olivia's Senza Pari.

Rogier considered. "Either Fest or Dorner. Dorner is less contrarious than Fest."

"Perhaps I should let Gutesohnes decide which of those two he prefers," said Ragoczy. "Is the athanor cool yet?"

"In an hour or so it will be." Rogier did not smile, but an amused light came into his eyes. "The molds are all Spanish and English, as I recall."

"Mostly guineas," said Ragoczy. "There are over a hundred of them, and twenty reales dorado. See that Gutesohnes has twenty-five guineas and five reales, if you would."

"That's a substantial sum," said Rogier, aware that it was more than twice the annual salary of the members of the household staff.

"He may have unexpected expenses," said Ragoczy. "He may need money for persuasion. He may have to buy another mule."

"He may make himself the target of highwaymen, as well. A solitary traveler with money is favored prey for those jackals."

"That is a danger, assuming it is discovered that he carries such a sum. As a messenger, the expectations are that he would not have so much with him," Ragoczy remarked. "Which is why most of the gold will be concealed. I will prepare him a purse with silver and copper and brass—he will not need to be obvious in the amount he carries."

"That is prudent, but where do you plan to hide so much gold?" He looked at the wallet. "Not in there, certainly."

"No, not more than three gold coins behind the ointment jar. There is a small pocket that will have room enough for three guineas. There are other places that can be used, such as the pockets in the lining of his fox-fur coat." Ragoczy gave a little sigh. "A pity he has no need for one of those double-walled water-barrels we used when we went to Delhi; he could carry a fortune without being detected."

"As you did then; you arrived in that city with a fortune in jewels, all hidden in the walls of your water-barrels; fortunately water is heavy, so the weight was not worthy of attention," said Rogier. "That would not avail Gutesohnes now. Still, whatever the case, if you are convinced he needs to have that money, then he shall have it, and welcome." For a second or two he said nothing, then added, "You can always make more."

"So I can," said Ragoczy.

"Unless the thieves hear that you have a fortune hidden in this château, and then there could be trouble. The local farmers would not come to your aid if the château were attacked, foreigner that you are." Rogier went to the nearest window and tapped on the glass to indicate the shutter beyond. "These can only fend off so much."

"I would like to think they would not be necessary," said Ragoczy, sounding suddenly tired. "But you have the right of it. I suppose I should bring in more weapons from the storehouse for the staff."

"You did provide Madame von Scharffensee an armed guard as well as Ulf Hochvall to drive her, and they are only going to Yvoire." Rogier gave Ragoczy a sharp look. "You know there is danger as well as I do."

"They will only be gone one night," said Ragoczy, worried in spite of his sensible precautions. "With winter coming, this may be the last time until March that she can go to purchase needlework supplies and order clothing from the seamstress."

"She is not the only person from these outlying places who is doing the same," said Rogier.

"Which may or may not be to her advantage," said Ragoczy.

"At least the weather is reasonably clear," said Rogier. "In a week, it may no longer be the case. The nights are getting much colder."

"It is likely that there will be more and heavier rain soon, as well," Ragoczy added.

"So Madame von Scharffensee will be back tomorrow—in the afternoon, I would guess."

"Hochvall said that they would be here by about three if the weather remains clear; if it rains, they will be later." Ragoczy glanced toward the windows. "I hope I have not waited too long to send Gutesohnes to van der Boom. Last year at this time there was snow on the ground, and more coming every day. I thought two days ago that the weather would hold for a week, but I no longer expect . . ."

"You think the weather change will bring winter in full strength," Rogier said, nodding. "It could be, and after the last two hard winters, another week may render the roads unviable once the rains begin in earnest. Most of them aren't fully repaired yet."

"I hope that Gutesohnes will be beyond the highest passes by then. At ten leagues a day, he should reach Dôle or even Dijon."

"He is going on the French route?" Rogier was mildly surprised.

"He will be out of the mountains sooner; that should speed him along. There is no compelling reason to take the German roads. Three years ago it would have been reckless to go through France, but no longer." He drew a folded map from his inner coat-pocket and opened it, pointing out the journey as he explained, "Here at Langres he will take the Meuse road to Sedan, where he will take the toll-road to Liège. From there, he may choose one of three roads to take him to Amsterdam."

"One of three," said Rogier. "And one will surely be open and in good repair."

"So I assume," said Ragoczy.

"There may be other difficulties."

"You mean bridges destroyed or flooded out, or roads undermined by water or cold, or devastated villages? Most of those sorts of things have been identified, and their dangers are known. You saw for yourself during our journey to Amsterdam how much is needed to be done, and what progress has been made. We passed through areas that were hotly disputed during Napoleon's brief return to power, and saw how much destruction was wrought because of him."

"That wasn't what I meant: there are more highwaymen in France than in Germany," Rogier warned.

"There are more defeated soldiers in France," said Ragoczy. "We can hope that they will not bother a messenger traveling alone."

Rogier needed several seconds to speak, and when he did, he directed his faded-blue eyes at the map, not Ragoczy. "You have fewer remounts at the posting inn along the French route."

"I believe Gutesohnes will not want to ride coach-horses to Amsterdam; the mules should be able to cover the distance if they are allowed a day to rest when they need it." Ragoczy shrugged. "Do you remember those Ju'an-Ju'an ponies? I would like to have a string of them now."

"Incredibly tough, and with remarkable endurance." Rogier waited a bit, and when he realized that Ragoczy would not say anything more, he changed the subject and spoke in French. "I should shave you tonight."

Ragoczy rubbed his chin, testing the stubble. "Yes, I suppose you should. What hour would suit you?"

"While the staff is at supper," Rogier suggested.

"In my chambers, then, while the staff dines."

"I will present myself with basin and razor," said Rogier, and gave Ragoczy a slight, sardonic bow.

"I have managed on my own, you know," said Ragoczy in much the same tone.

"Often and often. But without a reflection, your results are not always—"

"Neat?" Ragoczy suggested, and chuckled. "No, they are not— which increases my gratitude to you, old friend."

Rogier found such praise awkward, so he considered his next question carefully. "Have you answered the Magistrate yet?"

"You mean about granting the court officers permission to search this house? I have not decided yet, one way or the other."

"But you will inform them shortly, won't you?"

"It would seem I must," Ragoczy said, and sighed. "They have heard the gossip, of course, that the highwaymen work for me and their robbery is the source of my wealth. It could make for difficulties if the Magistrate will not believe I have maintained good stores of grain and seed; he may think that I have what was taken from the village, although why I should donate the sacks and then steal them back perplexes me. I have no sense of what reason they might attribute to such actions." He slapped the table with the flat of his hands. "It means I must ask Kleinerhoff to speak for me. He knows the truth of this."

"Do you think he will? speak for you?" Rogier ventured.

"The very question I have been asking myself. He has said that he will support me, but such pledges are easily given and more easily forgotten." Turning away from the table he went to secure the shutters, using the lever-pull so as not to have to raise the window. "The wind is rising."

"So it is," said Rogier, trying not to be put off by the crooning moan it made.

Although he knew that Ragoczy wanted to avert any more talk about the Magistrate's request, at least for the present, still he could not keep from observing, "Kleinerhoff knows how much you have done for Sacre-Sang. He will make a statement to the court, out of obligation if nothing else."

"I trust so," said Ragoczy, going to the next window to pull the shutters closed. "The accusations have not been made formally, and so it will not reflect badly on the head-man to speak for me. Once the complaints are official—" He opened his hands.

"Then why not encourage the search? It isn't as if the Inquisition were asking you for information."

"Something to be thankful for," said Ragoczy drily. "But this is not a time to bog down in accusations and counter-charges. If I can deflect the court's suspicions, so much the better. Whoever leads the outlaws—if such a man exists—I doubt if he is local, for everyone is under scrutiny just now."

"Do you think it is envy that makes these men accuse you?" Rogier asked.

"I think that may be part of it. And I am troubled by such

thoughts, for it could turn the people of Sacre-Sang against us." He sighed and went to close another shutter.

"You expect something of the sort to happen," said Rogier.

"I would be foolish not to," said Ragoczy as he worked the lever. "If you would light the lamps?"

"Of course," said Rogier, and set about this mundane task, all the while fretting; he had been through too many scrapes with Ragoczy over the centuries to be sanguine now. "What preparations have you in mind?"

"None as yet. I want to determine what I must do to cause the least disruption here." He closed the last shutter, confining the room to a shadowy twilight relieved only where Rogier had lit the lamps.

"You mean in Sacre-Sang, or in this household?" Rogier challenged.

"Both, if possible," said Ragoczy. "Information travels so rapidly now that the fewer inquiries we endure, the fewer questions will follow us."

"Does that mean you plan to leave Château Ragoczy soon?" Rogier kept his voice level.

"In spring; I will escort Hero to Ravensberg and Scharffensee," said Ragoczy as if he had not understood Rogier's intent.

"And then?" Rogier persisted.

"Then we must address the circumstances that confront us." Ragoczy's smile was faint and the light in his dark eyes was ironic. "But do not fret, old friend. We shall not be cast adrift on the world again: not this time." He began to gather together the cases to be entrusted to Gutesohnes. "Come. Help me carry these down to the study. The household will notice if they see me carry all this on my own."

Rogier sighed. "At least you aren't taking needless risks," he said, and went to retrieve the wallet of medicaments to add to the cases as Ragoczy picked them up and started toward the door.

Text of a letter from Madelaine de Montalia at the Grand European Hotel in Constantinople, to Saint-Germain Ragoczy, Comte Franciscus at Château Ragoczy near Lake Geneva, Yvoire, Switzerland;

carried by commercial courier and delivered two months after being written, during the time Ragoczy was absent from his château.

To my very dear Saint-Germain, on this, the 24th of December, 1817,
the birthday felicitations of your Madelaine, still in Constantinople,
who misses you as intensely as she misses her native earth and the
comfort of home,

I am entrusting this to a mercantile courier recommended by
your local factor at Eclipse Trading Company, who assures me that
it will be carried safely to Genoa and from there to Lake Geneva, all
without difficulty or delay beyond those of weather. No doubt the
man is being optimistic, but I cannot help but take advantage of this
opportunity to write to you, and to inform you of recent develop-
ments, and to let you know that you are never gone from my
thoughts or my dreams.

These have been a most peculiar few months, more than the last
full year has been. My planned journey to Antioch was postponed
until this coming spring, and so I have kept myself occupied by vis-
iting the few churches remaining in this city and examining the
manuscripts they have among their treasures. In some instances,
what I have found is treasure beyond price, and I am grateful for the
opportunity to inspect the ancient manuscripts. It has been most in-
structive, for I have happened upon a significant number of surpris-
ing texts, including an ancient collection of gospels that are no
longer part of the Bible; a few of them would undoubtedly be con-
sidered heretical. I spent the greater part of two months attempting
to translate the most ancient of these, and I confess, I could not do
them such justice as you would do; still I discovered many things of
interest about the earliest Christians that I believe most present ad-
herents to the faith would find unacceptable. Nonetheless, my cu-
riosity is piqued and I am more determined than ever to get to
Egypt.

About a month ago, we had a series of earthquakes in this city.
They were none of them severe, but a young American staying at the
Grand European Hotel, where most western foreigners stay, became

*agitated by the shaking. I finally made bold to ask why he was trou-
bled, and he told me that he came from Saint Louis, a small city on
the Mississippi River, and that shortly before he went to Boston to
university, that part of the world was gripped by a series of earthquakes, each more destructive than the last. He said the river flowed
backward and geysers of sand-and-steam erupted from sudden
cracks in the earth. The worst shaking came in the winter of 1812,
and caused much destruction and loss of life. He said that the Indians in the region warned that the ground was restless and that great
upheavals happened when the First Ancestor was displeased. Most
settlers paid little attention to these stories, thinking them only fables,
but now they listen to the legends of the Indians in the hope of
avoiding another such calamity. I find my curiosity about America
growing, almost to equal my curiosity about Egypt. The advantage
of being one of your blood is that I will in all probability have the
opportunity to explore both places.*

*You would probably remind me that I can afford to be patient,
and I know that is true in terms of years, but I dislike being made to
wait for no good reason but that the presence of a woman is not easily accommodated by Moslems. They are even more restrictive of
their women than are Europeans. I fear I will have to lay out a small
fortune in bribes if I am to reach Egypt in the next ten months,
which is my intention. Hero's father has advised me to ally myself
with an approved expedition as a means of gaining access to travel
permits. He himself cannot offer such to me, as he is bound for the
ruins of Palmyra, and will be away for at least four years. I have
some experience of that kind of exploration, and I fully comprehend
Hero's reluctance to travel with her father.*

*I have been granted permission to visit a monastery some ten
leagues from this city where truly ancient manuscripts are said to be
stored, and, weather permitting, I will leave in three days to go
there. I anticipate being away for three to four weeks, and should return here, to this hotel, in a month. I will have a guide with me, a
monk who is originally from Bulgaria, called Barlaam, who has
sworn to the Metropolitan to guard me for the glory of their faith,*

*and on the condition that I make full reports to him on all I found
when I return. He has offered to do what he can to find me passage
to Egypt, so I will be as accommodating as I prudently can be.*

*With congratulations on another year in your vast quantity of
them, and my heartfelt love*
        Always,
                Madelaine

8

Swags and wreaths of evergreens festooned the main parlor of
Château Ragoczy, and small candles stood above brass candlesticks,
their light joined with the glass-chimneyed oil-lamps to lend the
room a refulgent glow, so suitable for a dark day after Christmas.
Most of the staff had been given this day off along with Christmas
itself; all were provided with geese and suckling pigs for a fine
meal—the first year since the hard winter of 1816 that such generosity was possible. With the household staff gone, Ragoczy and
Rogier were the only ones in the house left to wait upon Hero and to
serve her the duck in dried cherries, cream, and brandy, and Christmas bread she had requested, and which were beginning to fill the
château with wonderful odors as they cooked.

"We dine in half an hour," Ragoczy announced as he came into
the parlor where Hero was engaged in complicated bargello-work,
her basket of yarns at her feet, her back to the unshuttered window
to make the most of the light; the fire-screen was angled to send
more of the warmth from the burning logs in her direction. She was
in a simple high-waisted woollen frock of burnt-sienna, and had a
shawl of coral angora-wool around her shoulders which she flicked
back from her needle-work to avoid catching its fringe in the pattern
on the canvas.

"We?" she asked playfully.

"You dine in half an hour," he dutifully corrected himself. "I will do so somewhat later."

"I do hope so," she said, looking up from her open-weave canvas. "Is it three already?"

"That it is," he said, and came across the room to her, his dark eyes fixed on her bright-brown ones. "I see you're making progress."

"I want to have these hangings done by the time the Zemmer castle is restored." She frowned as she inspected one line of scarlet wool. "I hope I have enough of this to finish the pattern. I'll never be able to find a match for it again. Red and green are never quite the same from batch to batch, no matter what the dyers say."

"You could always lighten or darken the pattern as it moves up the hanging," suggested Ragoczy. "Go from intense tones to lighter ones, or from these bright colors to more muted ones."

She considered this, then smiled. "A very good notion. I think it would make for fine results."

"Any work you undertake will have fine results," he said. "I am deeply appreciative of your present—six point-edge silk cravats. I thank you."

"You mustn't do that anymore," she said quickly. "You have done so already. And if you thank me again, then I must thank you for the tourmaline-and-diamond ring you presented to me as a Christmas gift, and the diamond-drop earrings." She secured her needle in the canvas and waved away his protestations.

"They suit you," he said. "I hope you will wear them when we travel to Scharffensee."

"I will, of course."

"And your other jewelry, as well," Ragoczy went on. "The pieces your mother left you, in particular. Your Baroque pearls are especially fine."

"So that my father-in-law will see I am not entirely without means?" She smiled sadly. "They would be likely to confirm his opinion that I am wholly dependent upon you."

"He would be mistaken," said Ragoczy.

"Would he? You house and keep me. That makes me . . ." She waggled her needle to finish her thought.

"It makes you what any other widow in your position would be, in the world as it is. If that displeases your father-in-law, he may arrange to house and keep you appropriately himself, for the sake of your children and to honor your husband's memory." He said it lightly enough but there was a spark in his enigmatic gaze that surprised her, and rather than pursue this fruitless discussion, she shifted the subject.

"He believes that should be my father's concern, or my sons', if they were old enough and in possession of their inheritance," she said, her mouth turning down.

"If your father's manner of living appealed to you, I might agree, but you already know what it is to venture about the world investigating ruins. If you wanted such a life—"

"As Madame de Montalia does," she interjected.

"Yes; as Madelaine does," he agreed smoothly, "that would be another thing. But you wish to live quietly with your family, and your father is in no position to provide that."

"Going to distant ruins is better than eating roots and moss, as so many did here, two winters ago. I wonder if Graf von Scharf-fensee thinks of that ever." She found herself troubled that such ruminations should intrude on what was supposed to be a quiet, cheerful day.

"It may be why he determined to have his grandchildren with him: he might assume he is better prepared to protect them from hardship." Ragoczy looked past her into the pale afternoon. "He lost his son, and he may fear he will lose his grandchildren, too."

"So you have suggested before," she snapped. "And he has lost my daughter for his pains." She put her hand to her eyes. "Oh, dear. I was hoping not to succumb to Christmas melancholy."

Ragoczy came closer, stopping next to her and touching her shoulder with gentle hands. "Your father-in-law cannot share his grief with you, and that is his misfortune; he has more to contend with than Christmas melancholy. Denied grief is a ravening wolf, one that devours all other emotions. You and he could provide much comfort to each other, if he would permit it."

"Are you preparing me for my journey?" She lifted her head sharply. "Do you think he will decide to welcome me because my daughter is dead? that he will let me mourn Annamaria and Fridhold with him?" Their conversation was becoming too perturbing; she again changed its direction. "I could not help but wonder: have you ever resented your birthday, being so near Christmas?"

His gentle laughter was filled with the full weight of his memories. "You forget that Christmas is a recent festival for me. No, I do not resent it; why should I? The Winter Solstice marked me as a pledge to our gods as tradition has marked the dark of the year for Jesus."

"Tradition?" She looked up at him.

"It was almost four centuries after Jesus died that his followers settled on the dark of the year for his birth—most heros from such parts of the world as he came from are traditionally born then. I have the advantage that it is truly my time of birth. My gods would not have accepted me to become one of them if that were not the case." He could see that Hero had gone waxen.

"Why would such an important thing be . . . be altered?" She prepared to rise. "Isn't it better to keep the time accurate?"

"No, not when his birth becomes a metaphor." He could read confusion in her expression. "And because the legend *is* important to those who are Christians, his early followers wanted to believe Jesus was as much or more of a hero than any predecessor, such as Mithras, who was also born of a pure mother at the Winter Solstice, according to legend. They made them both heros by their time of birth—the promise of light returning to the world." He held out his hand to her and gathered her into his arms. "Do not fret, dear Hero. When I consider such things, I prefer to think of my birth as being part of Saturnalia, not Christmas, in any case. But I keep the Solstice festival of the people and the times of those around me."

Hero shook her head. "My father told me all about Saturnalia. I don't think anyone should aspire to such excesses."

He pulled on one curl of bright-brown hair from under the prim lace of her widow's cap. "Festivities change, over time," he pointed out. "When I was still breathing, I marked these days by giving gifts to those who had served me well, not receiving gifts from them. In my heart I still hold that custom. Gifts presented to me were offered at Mid-Summer, when my father made a progress through his lands, and I went with him, at least until our enemies penetrated our mountains. We were given swords and jewels and food and wine at first, and then men to fight the men from Anatolia. I think I must have been seventeen the last time we made such a progress. It was a long time ago." It had been almost four thousand years since he had made that journey.

"It is difficult to imagine you seventeen," Hero said. "Do you ever long for those days? The happy ones, not the battles."

"Not for many centuries," he said.

Again she read something in his look that disquieted her, so she asked, "Have you ever been to Palmyra?"

"Yes; the pearl of the Syrian desert. Your father will find a challenge there." He kissed her forehead. "It was a very important city, a long time ago. It was large and prosperous, with thick walls and handsome markets, particularly their camel-market and horse-market. For many decades they had a guild for guides, and a guild for fountain-makers. There were even gardens with rare plants and tame deer. The travelers' inns were rarely empty for many decades." The Year of Yellow Snow had taken a toll on Palmyra, as it had on so much of the world, and the rising conflicts among the Persians and Syrians had turned its trading fortunes to ashes. "Most of the city is empty and in ruins, and has been for a long time. But there are some small villages near it. Your father will be able to live in a house, not a tent."

"Madame de Montalia told me that you had been over almost all the world, and that you knew more than anyone—" She broke off and went on in another voice. "Well, I suppose you would, wouldn't you?"

"My nature does not incline me to be a hermit in a cave," he said, releasing her and taking a step back.

She caught his hand to keep him near her. "I'm sorry. That was badly said. I didn't mean anything like that."

"I did not suppose you did," said Ragoczy, interlacing his fingers with hers. "This is proving to be a difficult day for you—more than yesterday."

"It's just that . . . Christmas, you know. Now that the day itself is past, the melancholy is . . . hard to ignore. It is a reminder of . . . I've been thinking of my family, and I cannot help but feel very alone." She cleared her throat, lowering her eyes in order not to meet his steady gaze. "Oh, not because of you. You have made the holiday as lovely as . . . I didn't want to burden you with all this."

"I am not burdened," he assured her. "It is small wonder that you should feel as you do."

She lifted her head. "Don't think that I am not obliged to you for doing so much to make the holiday . . . Last year, things were still too hard for much of a celebration, so this year, the change is more apparent."

"I need no explanation," said Ragoczy. "I have no requirements of you but that you do those things that please you."

"You will please me later, after dinner." She smiled suddenly, her eyes shining, determined to salvage the celebratory spirit of the day.

"That will be my pleasure," he promised her, offering her the crook of his arm. "It is nearly time for your meal."

"Rogier will not join me?" she asked.

"He has had his duck already," said Ragoczy, and did not mention that the duck had been raw when Rogier had eaten it.

"And I don't suppose that a servant would eat with me in any case," she added, a little disappointed.

"Rogier is not always such a stickler: he and I have shared meals in many places over the years," said Ragoczy, recalling the fowl and small animals he had hunted and taken blood from before turning the carcasses over to Rogier for the meat. "But here, he likes to preserve the niceties."

She slipped her hand into the bend of his elbow. "Then I will dine in a solitary state. So be it."

He led her toward the door, bowed her through it, and accompanied her to the dining room, where beneath a fully lit crystal-and-brass candelabra, Rogier had laid out a handsome place-setting of silver and porcelain on brass chargers, with linen napery and crystal glasses. "If you would?" He indicated the high-backed chair at the head of the table. "I am told you will begin with a new bread, hunter's soup, and a Bordeaux. Rogier has opened the wine and decanted it, and there is a white to follow." He indicated the crystal decanter on the side-board.

"You do not drink it, nor does he, and I cannot consume more than four glasses through the meal, or perhaps I should say, it wouldn't be wise for me to do so. Are you sure you want to open more than one bottle? What will you do with what's left over?" On impulse she removed her widow's cap and set it on the stool near her chair, revealing the neat, braided coronet of braids on the crown of her head.

"Add it to the soup for the staff tomorrow, as we usually do with open wine; there is a white to come, and then the Bordeaux again; that is the best I can offer just now," said Ragoczy easily. "We will do the same with the Champagne that Rogier has put on the kitchen porch to cool."

"Bordeaux, a white, *and* Champagne," Hero marveled. "They must have been laid down at least ten years ago."

"At least," Ragoczy agreed as he held the chair for her.

"How very elegant," she said, surveying the silver and linen arrayed on either side of the charger. She was about to speak again when there was a rap on the door connecting to the kitchen and an instant later Rogier came in bearing a platter with the first course set out upon it.

"I hope you will find this to your satisfaction, Madame," said Rogier as he placed the tureen in front of her, removing the arched lid with a flourish; he reached for her soup-plate and ladled in a generous amount; steam redolent of venison, boar, and mushrooms twined into the air.

"Thank you, Rogier; I am sure I will," said Hero, accepting the basket of bread still warm and fragrant from the oven.

"The next course will be ready in ten to fifteen minutes," Rogier informed her. "Not that I want to rush you."

"It hardly seems fair that I should be so lavishly served and you are left to tend the kitchen by yourself," she said as he started for the door.

Rogier paused in the doorway. "I enjoy cooking; it is something I do not often have to do, but I like to keep up my skills. This is a welcome opportunity for me." With that, he was gone.

"Your Bordeaux," said Ragoczy as he brought the decanter to the table and poured out a third of a glass into a pear-shaped crystal glass.

"The color is fine," said Hero, as much because it was expected of her as it was a sign of her expertise.

"So I understand," said Ragoczy and pulled up a chair to her right, turned its back to the table and straddled it.

She took the small loaf of bread and broke it in half, as good manners required, then pulled off a smaller section and dipped it into the soup for a moment. "The aroma is heavenly," she said before taking a bite of the bread.

"The soup is a bit more substantial than is usual for an opening course, and may be a bit overwhelming for the next course," said Ragoczy, "but it is readily prepared and will keep for three days."

"A hearty soup in winter is most welcome. This is excellent." She broke off more bread and again dipped it in the soup.

"I am told that Rogier cooks very well, but you may wish to tell him yourself," said Ragoczy, and watched her eat. When Rogier brought the trout with butter and hazelnuts, he opened a bottle of Lacryma Christi, pouring out the wine into a tulip-shaped, tall-stemmed glass.

"Thank you for this superb dinner. And for this delightful wine." Hero tasted it and drank it more quickly than she had intended, feeling the magic of the wine percolate through her veins. "I haven't had any of this in years. It was Fridhold's favorite."

Ragoczy started to add some more to her glass. "Then remember him with it."

She put her hand over the top of the glass, indicating she had had sufficient. "I don't want to overindulge. I would be ashamed of myself for doing so. On such a night as this, it would be an easy thing to cushion my sadness with wine."

"Then set the glass aside for now, and drink more when you like," said Ragoczy.

"I would, but I don't want to waste anything so valuable as these bottles must be," she said, confusion coming over her in a rush even as the tantalizing tastes and textures of the meal continued to work on her.

"I took all the wines for this evening from my cellar, so there is no reason to worry about the price—it was paid well before Waterloo. Well before Marengo, in the case of the Bordeaux."

"Still," she said, a bit vaguely.

"As you wish," he said, rising and placing the white wine bottle on the side-board. "If you change your mind . . ."

"I doubt I will."

He bowed to her and returned to his seat, and spent the next two hours waiting on her in a remarkably casual yet elegant way as the night gathered in around them and the fire crackled. Finally, when Rogier had brought the Champagne, he selected a tall, narrow glass for the sparkling wine and said, "There is brandied cream in pastry, if you would like it?"

She thought about her answer, then said, "Perhaps a little. I know it will not keep, and you cannot put it into tomorrow's soup."

"Your point is taken," said Ragoczy, and went to tug the bell-pull to summon Rogier. "A small serving, then."

"Yes, a small serving would be very welcome." After all the wonderful food she had been provided, she felt wondrously replete, sleek with pleasure, and content. She looked at the single charger remaining in front of her, and the two small spoons left; all the other silverware had been removed through the five courses of the dinner. Both her wineglasses remained, the red with a little of the Bordeaux staining the bottom of the bowl, the white empty; both bottles of wine stood on the side-board, the red more than half-full, the white slightly less than half-full. "I can't remember dining this well since Fridhold died. Nor having such wines, or three kinds of bread."

"Think of it as a thanksgiving for better harvests and the end of famine," said Ragoczy, bringing her glass of Champagne to her.

"Like the baskets of food you sent home with your servants?" she inquired as Rogier came into the dining room.

"Something similar, yes," said Ragoczy, and added to Rogier, "A small serving of the brandied cream, if you would."

"Of course," said Rogier. "With vanilla sauce?"

Hero smiled. "Yes, please, if you would." She took the Champagne and lifted the glass in a toast. "Thank you for all you have done for me through the year, and through the hard winters past." The day before there had been roast boar and hot spiced wine offered to those neighbors who came to the château. At the time Hero had thought that was a lavish gesture, but her meal this evening surpassed what she had had on Christmas in excellence and variety. Every part of her body was filled with satisfaction; a delicious lassitude was creeping over her, softening her demeanor.

Rogier's ascetic smile was as genuine as it was rare. "It is a pleasure, Madame von Scharffensee, to be able to serve you." He gave a crisp little bow, then turned and left the room.

"I can never thank you enough, Comte," she said as soon as they were alone. She was trying to think of an appropriate compliment when he cut into her cogitation.

"Then please do not make the attempt—I am not interested in gratitude," he said, his mellifluous voice as kindly and warm as the heat from the hearth.

She took a drink of the Champagne, aware that the wine—as well as the luxurious evening—was starting to go to her head; she put the glass down and said, "I will wait for the brandied cream."

Ragoczy held out his hand to her as he once again resumed his place on her right. "Do not fret, Hero."

"I'm not fretting . . ." She shook her head. "But I was about to: you're right on that account."

He lifted her hand and kissed it. "You need not fear that you must pay for every joy with greater pain," he said.

"I . . . try not to think . . ." She hastily had another sip of Champagne. "I don't know what I should say."

A knock on the kitchen door announced the arrival of the brandied cream with a small pitcher of vanilla sauce.

By the time Hero had finished her dessert, she was all but purring; the meal had been superb, much better than what she had had the year before, when food was still in terribly short supply; to have more than enough to eat, and of exceptional quality, was a true delight. She rose from her place and watched as Ragoczy expertly removed a puddle of wax from beneath the candlestick on the sideboard. "Is it time to retire?"

"I thought you might like to bathe with me first," he said calmly. "I've ordered the bath-house heated; there are robes for us both; that is, if you care to join me."

She was mildly surprised. "Bathe? With you?—tonight?"

"Why not?" he asked. "Only Rogier will know, and he will not gossip."

"I . . ." she said, and then reconsidered. "Why not? I think it would be a fitting end to this evening," she said, and in a surge of boldness she could only attribute to the wine, held out her hand to him and lead the way toward the side-entrance that faced the bath-house.

As they reached the side-door, Ragoczy took two old-fashioned winter cloaks down from pegs and offered one to her as he donned the other. "It is cold out, and snow is coming."

Hero pulled on the cloak and reached for the door-latch. "Rogier will let us back in, won't he?"

"I believe so," said Ragoczy, sounding amused.

"Then avanti," she declared, flinging the door open and stepping out into the night; a thin, cold wind sliced at them as they made their way across the side courtyard toward the looming bulk of the bath-house that was marked by a faint halo of steam. She moved carefully along the icy path, not wanting to fall; holding his hand steadied her as her kid-shoes slithered on the slick paving stones.

"I'll open the door for you," Ragoczy offered. "It is fairly heavy."

She laughed and let him move ahead of her, relinquishing his hand. Stopping still, she noticed the glow in the high windows of the bath-house. "There are lanterns lit. You planned this from the start."

"Of course," he said, pulling the door open and holding it against the insinuations of the wind. "You know where the dressing room is."

"On the right," she said as the door closed behind her. The vestibule was smaller than she thought it had been in the past, and that surprised her.

"You may undress in private, or you may allow me to assist you," he said as he removed her cloak and whisked it onto a coat-tree near the door.

She hesitated, not wanting to be too daring on Christmas. "I would like that," she said hesitantly.

"Very good." He removed his own cloak and drew her toward him, taking the time to kiss her thoroughly, to allow the kiss to develop all its complexity before moving back far enough for her to slip by him into one of the two dressing rooms.

"How warm it is," she said as she swung the shawl off her shoulders and folded it twice before setting it on the top of the small chest-of-drawers.

"There are towels in the bottom drawer," Ragoczy told her as he reached to unfasten the first of the seventeen buttons down the back of her dress.

"I'll remember," she said, standing still so that he could undo the buttons.

He kissed the nape of her neck as he finished his task. "I'll help you out of it."

This time her hesitation was even more brief. "It's best if I bend over and you pull it straight off from the shoulders," she said. "I'll get the buttons at my wrists." She set herself to do it.

"When you're ready," he said.

She shook her hands. "Step back and let me bend over," she said, keeping her back straight as she swung down from her hips.

"You are ready?"

"Go ahead," she said, and straightened her arms to make removal easier. She felt a gentle tug, and then she was standing in her under-clothes, a sprink of gooseflesh rising on her arms and shoulders.

He hung her dress on a peg and said, as he kissed her exposed shoulder, "If you turn around, I will attend to your corset."

Stifling a giggle, she did as he asked, all the while reveling in the delightful insouciance of the night so far, and the promise of greater transports to come. As the laces down her back were loosened, it felt as if the whole of her melancholy had been whisked away. "You will be bathing with me?"

"As soon as I undress," he said as he slipped the corset over her head, leaving her wearing only silk stockings, shoes, and under-drawers.

"Well, hurry. I am getting chilly." She laughed, to show this was nothing more than a slight distraction.

He removed his swallow-tail coat, and then his black-embroidered deep-red waistcoat. "I should warn you that I have scars."

"Who does not?" she asked, hugging herself as she sat down to remove her shoes and stockings.

He was unbuttoning his shirt and loosening his sunburst cravat. "Mine are . . . somewhat severe." He had taken care not to let her see him in full light, but now he could not avoid revealing his exten-sive abdominal scars.

"So you've said," she reminded him as she put her rolled stock-ings in her shoes and tucked them under the bench. "I've been in field hospitals. I've seen some terrible wounds." Admitting this made her a bit queasy, which she attributed to the rich food and wine.

He took off his shirt, hung it up, and unfastened his unmention-ables, stepping out of them as he dropped them to his ankles, where they puddled around his thick-soled black boots. Then he opened the chest-of-drawers and pulled out two large Turkish towels and handed one to her. "Wrap this around you; you will be warmer." He managed to keep his back to her.

She took it and swung it over her shoulders. "It is very nice," she said; the smell of damp fir was everywhere, and she sneezed once, as quietly as possible.

"Why not go on into the bath?" he suggested, holding the inner door open for her. "You know the way and the lanterns are burning."

"Will you join me?"

"In a moment," he said, and took her in his arms for another complex kiss, one that evoked longing and need in her.

"Do not be long," she said a little breathlessly as she broke away from him. "I find I am growing hungry for other nourishment." She touched his broad, deep chest before pulling the inner door open.

Left alone, he removed his boots and stockings, then wrapped his towel around his waist, securing it with an expert tuck. Satisfied that the room was secure, he followed her into the bath itself, and found her standing in the large tub up to her hips in hot water, her towel spread on the broad lip of the bath. He came up to the three steps leading down into the tub, and dropped his towel, noticing that she looked away from him as she caught sight of the swath of scar that ran from the base of his ribs to his pubis. Dismissing his failed hopes, he stepped down into the water beside Hero.

She wrapped her arms around him, letting the water buoy her up. "And to think I was near despairing," she whispered before pressing her mouth to his. "You banish despair."

His hands slid up her back and down her flanks, slowly, persuasively, suiting his touch to her response, growing more passionate as she felt desire coalesce within her, turning sensuality to something more intensely physical, a convergence of sensations that shook her; she had never before felt such extraordinary pleasure, or to have it triggered in so many ways. From the curve of her neck to the muscles of her calves, her body tingled, adding new arousal as Ragoczy continued to draw out her fervor. Dizzy with far more than wine, and exultant with the delirious freedom her body was approaching, she lay back against the lip of the bath and opened all her flesh to him. Gradually he sought out the core of her excitation, penetrating her with knowing fingers until she sighed and murmured, "Not yet."

"As you wish," he said, and slowed his ministrations so that she could relish every nuance of tantalization that would bring her to ecstasy.

"I want to feel all you can do," she said softly. "I want to find how much you can inspire in me." She lifted one leg and wrapped it around his thigh, then she steadied herself and leaned back so that he could caress her breasts. "This is . . ." She could not think of a word that would describe the ardor, the sensitivity, the stimulation that permeated her body and soul. "Everything." With that, she pulled him down into the water, so only their heads were above the surface; the warm water enveloped her, augmenting his embrace, and she succumbed to the culmination that had been building deep in her body; in a quiet part of her exultant mind, she was relieved that his scars had not blighted her fulfillment.

Text of an invitation from Wallache Gerhard Winifrith Sieffert von Ravensberg at Ravensberg in Austria, to Saint-Germain Ragoczy, Comte Franciscus at Château Ragoczy near Lake Geneva, Yvoire, Switzerland; carried by hired messenger and delivered twenty-three days after it was written.

On this, the 29th of December, 1817, Wallache Gerhard Winifrith Sieffert, Graf von Ravensberg requests the honor of the company of Saint-Germain Ragoczy, Comte Franciscus, on the 29th of March, 1818, and five days thereafter, at Ravensberg, to celebrate the betrothal of his ward and niece Hyacinthie Theresa Katerina Sieffert to Constanz Charles Medoc, scholar of Trier.

The Graf extends the hospitality of Ravensberg to the Comte and his guest, two body servants, and two coachman for the length of his stay. Line stalls for up to ten horses is available for your use. The Graf requests the courtesy of a response.

9

Augustus Kleinerhoff looked truly abashed. He stood in the entry-hall of Château Ragoczy, his heavy cloak flung open, his thick boots shedding ice shards on the carpet, his face so hang-dog that his greeting was more ominous than mannerly. "God grant I see you well; the brewer's son has a fever, and we fear it may be typhus: there was so much of it about a year-and-a-half ago, we cannot but worry for him. I am here to speak with the Comte," he said to Balduin.

"Would you like him to treat the boy?" Balduin asked.

"No. At least not now. Perhaps, if he does not improve—" He spoke a little louder. "An escort from Yvoire will be joining me shortly, with an order from the Magistrate, and the Magistrate him-self." He coughed, showing equal amounts of embarrassment and officiousness.

Balduin considered his response, affecting a lack of apprehen-sion. "The Comte is busy at present. If I may ask you to wait in the reception room, I will send a footman up to inform him you are here."

"Tell him it's urgent," Kleinerhoff insisted as he shed his cloak and handed it to Balduin. "I have been sent ahead to inform him of a summons from the Magistrate of Yvoire. He is taking advantage of the good weather to begin his inquiries into the robbers who have caused so much trouble in the region, and he has decided to begin here, where it is believed the criminals have protection from—that is yet to be determined." He cleared his throat. "There have been rumors that he says he could not ignore, for the events of the last year would seem to link the robbers to some form of help in this region." He could not conceal his pride at this honor of announcing the arrival of the Magistrate even as he felt ashamed to do anything against Ragoczy's excellent reputation; this would be likely to compromise the Comte's good opinion no matter what the results.

"The good weather should last another day or two," said Balduin, shutting out the brilliant January sunshine as he shut the door.

"Yes. This winter has been much kinder than the previous two, at least so far." This attempt at banter failed. "The road is fairly passable just now."

"I see," said Balduin, indicating the way to the reception room. "I'll have some hot spiced wine brought to you, and a bite to eat, as well."

Kleinerhoff was more confused by this kind offer, but he strove to maintain a proper demeanor. "Danke. Ja, danke. It is most kind of you." He swung around toward the corridor, nervousness making him clumsy; he nearly knocked over a cloak-tree, which he snagged and steadied. "Magistrate Lindenblatt will be here within the hour. You must have preparations to make."

"Very good. I will have the Comte so informed," said Balduin, watching while Kleinerhoff let himself into the reception room; satisfied that Sacre-Sang's head-man was properly bestowed, he went off to the kitchen, where he found Rogier with Uchtred, making the last efforts to quarter a lamb. He hung the cloak on a drying rod near the open hearth, and said, "Kleinerhoff is here. He needs to see the Count."

Uchtred paused in his cutting free the shanks. "Does he intend to stay to eat?" then added to the young man building up the fire beneath the spit, "Soak this in red wine."

"No, but he should be given hot wine and something—bread and cheese, or sausage. He has come from Yvoire and he must be cold and tired." Balduin paused thoughtfully. "The Magistrate from Yvoire is apparently going to be arriving within the hour. If you could prepare a collation for him and his guard? I'd guess there will be four or five of them in all. I'll build up the fire in the parlor. Where are the footmen?"

Rogier set aside his knife and rinsed his hands, wiping them dry on a length of soft cotton. "One isn't needed: I'll go tell the Comte of all this. Do you know what his purpose is for coming?"

"He's making an inquiry about the robbers, starting with this household," said Balduin. "According to Kleinerhoff."

Rogier took this in with no visible signs of dismay. "Just so. I'll attend to the Comte at once."

"Very good," said Balduin. "By the way, where are the others?"

Uchtred glanced about nervously. "I sent them out to gather eggs and mushrooms, and to bring in a couple of rabbits from the hutch in the barn. Everyone wanted a chance to go outside; we've all been cooped up for well over a week, and this is the first decent day since the sky cleared. Steffel is cleaning out the ashes in the bake-house oven. Hochvall is supervising the farrier in the stable and organizing a mucking and rebedding for the stalls; Clement has put the grooms to cleaning harness and tack. Fraulein Wendela and Frau Anezka are in the side-yard, airing the blankets. Peder is repairing the leak in the stable's cistern. The weather won't hold, and I thought—along with the rest of the staff—that we should make the most of it."

Balduin, who had been preparing the annual household inventory, said, "It is wise to make the most of these opportunities—they are so few."

"No doubt," said Rogier as he took off the butcher's apron he was wearing and reached for his coat. "If you will take refreshments to Herr Kleinerhoff?"

"I will," said Balduin, and went to take down a silver tray, and a smaller painted ironstone one. "The silver for Magistrate Lindenblatt. I'll set with porcelain and silver for him, of course."

"Of course," said Uchtred, and began to put the sectioned lamb into a large metal container. "I will attend to this directly. I have brandied fruit that I can serve with honey-rolls, along with monk's-head cheese; I'll serve that to the head-man as well, with pickled onions. I'll work out a center-dish for the Magistrate shortly." This last was more thinking aloud than announced purpose.

Rogier went up the backstairs and hastened to Ragoczy's laboratory. He stopped outside the main door to the laboratory and waited to compose himself, then he knocked. "My master?"

"Come in, Rogier," said Ragoczy, pulling himself away from the mounted magnifying glass and the notes he was making in the opened journal beside it.

"Kleinerhoff has come. It seems that you are to expect a visit from Magistrate Lindenblatt."

"Magistrate Lindenblatt? Why should the Magistrate of Yvoire be coming here?" Ragoczy held up his hand. "I know what it must be; someone has accused me of supporting the robber-bands in the mountains around Sacre-Sang."

"Are you certain?" Rogier asked.

"At this time of year, what else could it be? There have been hints and speculation about the robbers' connection to me for months. My taxes are current, my land is maintained, and my staff has been paid, so there can be no complaint on those accounts. Therefore I assume he is beginning an inquiry with a foreigner of position so that other landholders will assist him more readily."

"Kleinerhoff said it is an inquiry about the robbers, according to Balduin. There are no particulars that I am aware of."

"Just the rumors that have filled the region, and the disinclination of officials to impose upon one of their own." Ragoczy shook his head. "How petulant that sounds. I apologize, old friend."

"You have good reason to be wary of officials, although Magistrate Lindenblatt isn't Telemachus Batsho."

"All forgotten gods be thanked," said Ragoczy. "Nor is he Filipo Quandt."

"Who was Swiss, like the Magistrate: more to thank your forgotten gods for." Rogier paused.

"We must hope that Lindenblatt is not of Quandt's inclinations," said Ragoczy. "It would be very useful to have Gutesohnes return before the next storm. He will be needed shortly. As capable as Rand may learn to be, he is not ready to carry messages any distance, especially not in storms." The fifteen-year-old had been hired the previous November to carry messages to Yvoire and to posting inns less than half a day's ride from Sacre-Sang.

"Truly; he is too young, as well." Rogier agreed, then asked, "Speaking of those absent, Madame von Scharffensee is—?"

"Out," said Ragoczy. "She's gone to the horse-pasture to sketch. She said she would be back by four."

"When the light fades," said Rogier. "Is anyone with her?"

"Fraulein Serilde is with her. They will not dawdle once the sun sinks below the peaks, and with the wind increasing." Ragoczy glanced toward the shining windows. "I should change my coat since the Magistrate is coming. He will expect suitable regard for his presence." He thought for several silent seconds, "And I should probably write a note to Kreuzbach; I may need an advocate before this is over."

"Will you want to dispatch a messenger to him?" Rogier asked.

"Not just yet, and not with the weather about to change." He indicated the shining sky outside his unshuttered windows. "You can see how it is moving those thin ribbons of clouds."

"You're certain of that?" Rogier asked, squinting at the windows and the vista beyond. "Thin clouds are common enough in winter."

"As much as I am of anything so ephemeral as weather. The wind has shifted to the north-east and the ice on the pond is thicker. This sunshine is just an intermission between storms." Ragoczy reached over and closed his journal. "I will change, see Kleinerhoff, and then go on to my study. You will find a note to Kreuzbach in my secretary-desk; if you decide to send it—"

Rogier nodded. "If you need his advice, I will find someone to carry it to Speicher, someone reputable."

"I need not have asked, old friend." He stopped at the door and rocked back on his heel. "We would do well to go carefully. Tell the staff to be helpful to the Magistrate, and to take care to answer any questions he may put to them."

"If that is what you want," said Rogier.

"It is what is needed," said Ragoczy as he opened the door. "I heard wolves last night."

"As bad as last year?" Rogier asked.

"No, nor as bad as the year before. But they are proof that spring is still some weeks away. All the livestock must be in folds and pens tonight." He rubbed his chin. "The shave is still good enough. I have another four or five days left before the next one."

"That's so," said Rogier.

"I take it you have ordered refreshments?"

"And left Uchtred attending to their preparation."

"Thank you, old friend. I will be in my study in twenty minutes or so." He went out the door and started down the hall toward the stairs, pausing only when he heard a door on the floor below being quietly closed; it sounded as if it might be the library or the music room. Who, he asked himself, was still in the house and might be on this floor? And what would anyone be doing in the library or the music room? Almost at once he chided himself for being too ready to see enemies in the woodwork: this was not China or Peru or Delhi or Russia, and although he was a foreigner, he was not without position in the region. He continued down to his private apartments and let himself in to his outer chamber where his elegant armoire stood along with three commodore chests and a handsome marquetry chiffonier. Lacking a reflection, he paid no attention to the fine pier mirror of Venetian glass that stood next to the closet; pulling off his coat, he left it over the largest chest and went to the armoire to select one of more formal cut: he settled on a new, double-breasted claw-tail coat of black Florentine wool, the revers finished in black-silk twill. This he pulled on and began to check the folds of his silken cravat; nothing felt obviously awry, so he buttoned his coat, tugged at the hem of his waistcoat, and left the room to go down to discover what Herr Kleinerhoff had to tell him, taking the servants' stairs so that he could see what the state of preparation was in the kitchen before seeking out his visitor.

Rogier was back in the kitchen when Ragoczy walked into it; he perused Ragoczy's change of clothing and very nearly smiled. "The Magistrate will be impressed. Just elegant enough to remind him you are of higher degree than he."

"So long as he is willing to listen to me, then all should be well," said Ragoczy. "Uchtred is—"

"In the creamery. The butter should be churned by now, and he is also getting cream to whip."

"The Magistrate should enjoy that," said Ragoczy. "And where is Herr Kleinerhoff?"

"In the reception room. I have just taken a tray to him."

"Excellent," said Ragoczy, then added, "Perhaps it might be prudent to warn the household of our impending visit? They might be alarmed if they stumble upon the Magistrate and his escort unprepared."

"I'll attend to it," said Rogier, nodding to Uchtred as he came back into the kitchen with two large wooden containers in his hands. "He is going to make an omelette for the Magistrate, and offer the brandied fruit with this morning's bread. Brandy and wine, of course."

Uchtred set down the cream and new butter. "I should be ready to crack the eggs in half an hour."

"That should suffice, but delay your omelette until the Magistrate is safely through the door," said Ragoczy, and continued on through the kitchen toward the front of the château. He tapped once on the reception room door and stepped inside to find Herr Kleinerhoff biting into a curl of monk's-head cheese. "How good to see you again, head-man. I understand you come with tidings."

"Comte," Kleinerhoff sputtered as he struggled to get his mouth around the frill of cheese, his eyes boggling. Belatedly he shoved himself to his feet. "I . . . Comte, I . . . you must excuse—" Tall and bulky as he was, his size made little impression on Ragoczy.

"You may sit down and finish your morsel," said Ragoczy, indicating the tray atop the whatnot near the Dutch room-stove.

Kleinerhoff sank into his chair and muttered his thanks around the cheese. He reached for one of the pickled onions to help moisten the cheese so he could swallow it.

"I surmise you have come in advance of the Magistrate for some purpose other than to warn us? If the Magistrate intends to catch us unaware, this is not the way to accomplish his end." Ragoczy drew up one of the two other chairs in the room and sat down.

"He does not suspect you, Comte, although some of the land-holders in the vicinity do." He stared at Ragoczy, not daring to take anything more to eat; his second swallow cleared his mouth.

"That is something, at least," said Ragoczy.

"Yet we all agree that they have remained somewhere in the local mountains since their thefts continue." Kleinerhoff waved his hand to address all the region beyond the château. "They would not be remaining here if they didn't have some assurance of security, or so the Magistrate believes, which makes it likely that they have help from someone. Therefore an inquiry must be made."

"Very sensible," said Ragoczy. "Certainly the landowners in the region have reason to worry. Merchants, as well, have been discommoded by the highwaymen."

"Truly." Kleinerhoff rocked from foot to foot. "It is very trouble-some, knowing that these robbers are near at hand, but still we are unable to put a stop to what they do. Four days ago they took six sacks of oats and two sheep from Didier Foutinz in Saint-Ange, four leagues from here. Despite our best efforts, they remain at large, which raises doubts in the minds of many. I, as head-man in Sacre-Sang, know how much trouble these men have caused."

"You must hear all the complaints, and sooner than most," said Ragoczy, then indicated the chair Kleinerhoff had vacated. "Please. Sit down."

"Didier Foutinz himself came to tell me. Saint-Ange is a very small village. Most of us think little of it."

"The folk are therefore tempting targets for crime. Tell me what you have discovered about the robbers."

Kleinerhoff sat, but looked distressed. "The Magistrate in-structed me to reveal as little as possible. But if there is something you would like to impart to me, I will be sure the Magistrate hears of it, so that he may allow for that in his examination."

"I think it may be best if I wait for the Magistrate, to learn what it is he is trying to find out," said Ragoczy. "Very well, then: enjoy your refreshments and excuse me until the Magistrate arrives." He inclined his head politely, turned, and left Herr Kleinerhoff alone in the reception room. It was a short distance to his study, and he covered it quickly, going to his secretary-desk. Drawing a sheet of paper from its drawer, he selected a nib and used the pen-knife to trim it before he sat down to write to Kreuzbach. When that was complete, he took a second sheet of paper and prepared some instructions for Rogier. He was just setting his seal on the envelope when the sound of horses at the front of the château alerted him to the arrival of the Magistrate and his escort. He closed the front of the secretary-desk, then adjusted his cuffs as he heard Balduin open the front door. Rising to his feet he went to greet his guests.

Magistrate Lindenblatt was a tall, angular man approaching fifty, dressed in a long fur cloak and carrying a leather portfolio; he was followed by four soldiers, each armed with two pistols and a breech-loading Brevetee rifle and carrying ammunition boxes. Because Lindenblatt was somewhat short-sighted, he used a pince-nez to look about him. He removed his cloak, revealing a conservative coat and waistcoat of boiled Prussian-blue wool, and dark-gray unmentionables. The ride had left him in slight disarray, and he attempted to remedy this as he pulled off his gloves. "Comte Franciscus," he said, bowing just enough to be polite; he had met the Comte briefly on a number of occasions but had never had reason to exchange more than the most perfunctory greetings. "I take it Herr Kleinerhoff is here before me."

"He is, Herr Magistrate Lindenblatt." Ragoczy copied the bow.

"This is my escort." He indicated the soldiers. "I take it you have a room where they may rest and get warm?"

"Balduin will show them the way," and Ragoczy added, "The staff reception room, I think. It is not in use just now."

"I will attend to it," said Balduin as he finished hanging the Magistrate's cloak in the small closet near the door; such an important guest deserved more than a humble peg for his cloak.

"Thank you." Ragoczy indicated the direction to the parlor. "Magistrate—after you?"

Lindenblatt was used to a certain deference, but not from men of the Comte's rank, and so he hesitated before starting down the corridor, Ragoczy half a step behind him. "You do understand, Comte, that I would prefer not to have to do this, but with the talk all over the region, an effort must be made."

"I am certainly aware that this is a difficult time for Yvoire and the local villages," said Ragoczy, entering the parlor with the Magistrate.

"That it is." Lindenblatt stood in the center of the parlor, taking in its fine proportions and beautiful appointments. "Very nice, Comte. Very nice indeed."

"Thank you," said Ragoczy. "If you will have a seat? The settee is reckoned to be quite comfortable."

Lindenblatt moved behind the low table and sat down. "Most comfortable."

Ragoczy pulled up a Turkish chair upholstered in silk-and-leather, and gave the Magistrate his full attention. "What am I to do to assist you?"

When Lindenblatt spoke, it was to ask, "How large is this château?"

"Nineteen rooms, in the house itself. There is also a bakery and creamery, a barn, a stable, a bath-house, and a small gate-house, which is much in need of repair." He touched his palms together and added, "I employ a staff of eleven men, three boys, and four women."

"So your declarations say," Lindenblatt stated. "Your banker also informs me that you have a considerable amount on deposit, although he will not tell me how much."

"Of course," said Ragoczy.

"Of course," Lindenblatt echoed. "Which is what makes my purpose so very awkward. That a man in your situation should be thought capable of countenancing such amerciable activities is distressing." The admission was a difficult one, and he looked away from his host to the three framed paintings at right angles to the fireplace. "Do you collect art, Comte?"

"In a small way." He nodded to the mosaic icon next to the chimney, showing Saint Ephraem holding his book open to be read. "That is probably my most unusual piece. I found it in Constantinople." He did not add that the year had been 1448.

"Very interesting." He fidgeted and then forced himself to be still.

Taking the direction of their discussion into his own managing, Ragoczy said, "Perhaps you would like to tell me why you have come? With so much snow on the road, you have some urgency, and Herr Kleinerhoff has informed me of the general nature of your concerns, which I share. You need not soften the blow for me: I appreciate concision." His manner remained comfortably polite but there was something in his steady gaze that impressed Lindenblatt.

"I very much regret the circumstances that—" He stopped, visibly gathered his thoughts, and continued. "Due to suspicions about you and the robbers who have infested the region, I am about to assign two of my escorts to you in this house until such time as the robbers are brought before me in court, or you are exonerated of all suspicions. You are not to go beyond your property without at least one of the men accompanying you, and you are not to leave the region without permission of my court." He scowled at the table in front of him. "Any dealings you have with the robbers will be discovered and noted."

Wholly unflustered, Ragoczy framed his question carefully. "I have an attorney-at-law in Speicher; may I instruct him to prepare a brief to submit to you on my behalf?"

"It is somewhat irregular, but it is acceptable to me. If it comes to trial, you will need to find a Swiss advocate." Linbenblatt sat a little straighter and spoke more quickly as he went on. "Any correspondence with the attorney must be read by the guards. They are literate and have had some experience in dealing with covert exchanges."

"I will be expected to house and feed these guards?" Ragoczy asked urbanely.

"For the time they are here, yes. The court might refund a portion of the costs you incur on their behalf, assuming you are found blameless." The Magistrate gave a little sigh. "It is a demand that troubles me, and if your innocence is established, it will be considered an imposition, but the court cannot be seen to accommodate crime."

"Certainly not," said Ragoczy. "I'll instruct my manservant to keep track of the costs the men incur."

"Our efforts to root out the criminals will begin in earnest as soon as the snow melts enough to allow easy passage on the major roads. It is impossible to conduct a proper search at this time of year, but this is also the time the robbers must be receiving the most help from whomever is aiding them, and therefore, we must be on guard, to prevent the robbers' allies from providing food and supplies for the winter. We will be dispatching patrols to all the villages in the region: Sacre-Sang, Saint-Brede, Le Roche, Halle, Saint-Ange, Mervelle, Niecte, and Lederin, to make inquiries."

"Is anyone else in this region being asked to take in guards and confine his activities?" Ragoczy inquired.

"Not yet," said the Magistrate, clearly unhappy with this revelation. "I regret the necessity, but we must take action."

"Certainly you must, and promptly." Ragoczy held up one hand to stop any more explanations; he lost none of his cordial demeanor. "Then I should perhaps mention that I have planned to travel in March, assuming the matter of the outlaws is not settled by then. I am bidden to Austria, to the seats of Graf von Scharf-fensee and Graf von Ravensberg. The times are set and it would be very awkward to renege on either engagement."

"It may be necessary to ask you to disappoint the earlier commitment. My guards would have no authority outside of Switzerland, and if you absent yourself before the matter of the robbers is settled, at least in regard to you yourself, it may be seen as flight."

"I will instruct my attorney to address that in his brief." He stopped as Balduin knocked on the door; regarding Lindenblatt he asked, "Are you placing me under arrest?"

"No, but I am giving you an Order of Detention, on the terms I have already described." His eyes flicked toward the door. "Do your servants gossip?"

"I have always assumed so," said Ragoczy, rising to answer the door.

"Then you may want to warn them that they may be questioned by the guards." This last was offered as a kind of truce. "I hope they will not have to appear in court."

"And I, as well," said Ragoczy as he went to admit his steward to the parlor. "I have ordered a light repast for you, Magistrate Lindenblatt. I hope you will enjoy it." He stood aside to allow Balduin to bring the well-laden silver tray to the low table in front of the settee. "If there is anything more you would want, you have only to tell me."

"This is most gracious of you, Comte," said Lindenblatt as Balduin bowed and withdrew, pausing in his departure to quietly inform Ragoczy that Madame von Scharffensee had returned and was in the music room.

"Tell her I will join her in a little while," said Ragoczy, then returned to the Turkish chair, drew up the ottoman, and prepared to answer all questions Magistrate Egmond Talbot Lindenblatt might put to him.

Text of a letter from Reinhart Olivier Kreuzbach, attorney-at-law and factor, at Speicher near the Kyll River, Rhenish Prussia, to Saint-Germain Ragoczy, Comte Franciscus at Château Ragoczy near Lake Geneva, Yvoire, Switzerland; carried by professional courier and delivered twelve days after it was written.

To Saint-Germain Ragoczy, Comte Franciscus, the greetings of Reinhart Olivier Kreuzbach in Speicher, on this, the 20th day of January, 1818,

My dear Comte,

I have in hand your request for a brief to be prepared regarding your situation. First, let me tell you how shocked I am that a man of such probity as you possess should ever be regarded as a supporter of desperate criminals. Second, I assure you that I will attend to this with all due haste, and see that all information I can ethically release is provided to the Magistrate Lindenblatt in an amicus curiae presentation as speedily as may be. In addition, I will present assurances of your determination not to become a fugitive, and will attempt to have the soldiers removed from your château. I will, as you suggest, provide records of your trading company activities in order to demonstrate your own losses to robbers as well as providing some notion of the extent of your resources.

Because of the severity of this accusation, I have taken the liberty of contacting Gunther Jaccobus Schreiner of Bern, to ask if he would be willing to represent you in your appearances, if any are required, before the Magistrates' Court. I gave my letter to the courier this morning and will not receive an answer, I would reckon, until the second week in February, barring any more severe storms. I am sure Herr Schreiner will be not only able but willing to act on your behalf. He has such credentials as must be acceptable to the Magistrates of Yvoire.

I am pleased to tell you that the road to your castle above Zemmer is almost finished in its resurfacing. By summer the place should be quite habitable, and I hope I will have the honor of calling on you there before the year is out. I am informed that work on the roof will resume as soon as the weather permits, that the stable is complete, that the creamery is restored and the bakery will be so in another month. Work on the bath-house will begin as soon as the trunks of earth you have stipulated be used in the foundation actually arrive. I have your plans in hand and will deliver them promptly to the workers as soon as the ground may be dug up.

Regarding your travels, I am confident that I can secure time away for you, although it may not be possible to gain you the five to six weeks you requested. My bona fides should make some accommodation possible, and so I believe that you may plan on at least three weeks for your journey to Austria. You may be required to supply a bond, but that, I assume, will not be a hardship for you.

In the continuing pledge of my dedication to your interests, I am,

Most sincerely at your service,
Reinhart Olivier Kreuzbach
Attorney-at-law and factor
Speicher, Rhenish Prussia

PART III

HYACINTHIE THERESA KATERINA SIEFFERT VON RAVENSBERG

*T*ext of a letter from Saint-Germain Ragoczy, Comte Franciscus, at Château Ragoczy near Lake Geneva, Yvoire, Switzerland, to Helmust Fredrich Lambert Ahrent Ritterslandt, Graf von Scharffensee; carried by coachman Otto Gutesohnes and Hero Ioacasta Ariadne Corvosaggio von Scharffensee.

To Helmut Fredrich, Graf von Scharffensee, the greetings of Saint-Germain, Comte Franciscus, on this, the 17th day of February, 1818.

My dear Graf,

I am devastated to be unable to join you and your grandchildren for the occasion of the visit of your daughter-in-law. It is unfortunate that I should at this time be detained by pressing legal matters which demand an expeditious response. I ask that you excuse me, and I trust that you will understand my predicament and not judge me too harshly for circumstances that are beyond my control. I am confident you will receive her respectfully for her children's sake.

Your daughter-in-law has with her not only the coachman, but her maid and an escort of two armed men whose purpose it is to protect her from any harm that may threaten her. They will all bring her to Ravensberg, where I will once again meet her at the conclusion of her visit with you. She is carrying a small box of uncut gems that are my present to you, as well as a pair of etchings from the last century showing two perspectives of Salzburg, which is her gift to her children. She herself brings a case of brandy for you.

I hope that this finds you well; may this year bring you good health, good harvests, the good-will of our neighbors, and content-ment for all who dwell under your roof,

> *Most sincerely,*
> *Saint-Germain Ragoczy*
> *Comte Franciscus*
> *(his sigil, the eclipse)*

1

"Nutzen is falling asleep," Rogier said to Ragoczy as he came into the laboratory shortly after midnight; most of the household had retired three hours ago, and it was not surprising that Romolo Nutzen was inclined to join them, though he had vowed to Magistrate Lindenblatt that he would watch Ragoczy from sunset to sunrise.

"At the top of the stair, or the foot?" Ragoczy asked, not taking his eyes off of the alembic before him. "And Ilel?" He was fairly certain that the daytime guard, Hermann Ilel, was not up.

"He retired with the rest," said Rogier. "I think he is growing accustomed to life in this household. His curiosity is diminishing. Nutzen, whose name must be ironic, is at the foot of the stairs on the second floor, between the guest rooms, your own quarters, and mine."

"It has been most inconvenient, having those two determined to find us at a disadvantage." He moved back on his stool and looked over at Rogier. "At least Hero is bound for Scharffensee. She was more troubled by the Magistrate's guards than I am. She said they were intrusive. It made her uncomfortable when I spent time alone with her, knowing we might be observed."

"Do you think we will have to accommodate them much longer?" Rogier asked.

"I hope not." Ragoczy adjusted the little flame under the almebic. "This should finish distilling in an hour or so."

"Will you remain here, or are you going to retire?"

"I thought I might go to the library and look at what van der Boom has sent."

"The new chest that came yesterday, or the chest that Gutesohnes brought?" Rogier cocked his head toward the dying fire. "Shall I build that back up?"

"No reason to," said Ragoczy a bit distractedly as he studied the alembic and finally adjusted the flame again. "Have you sent off the household accounts to the Magisrate yet?"

"No, not yet. I have to ask Uchtred for his kitchen records—how much of the food came from local farms and how much from your property. And how much from your trading resources."

"The fruits we had from Italy last summer, for example?" said Ragoczy. "Yes. They will want to know if our supplies exceed our uses, and if they do, what we do with the dispensables."

"They will also want to verify our purchases and costs," said Ragoczy, feeling very tired. "If I had some proof regarding the robbers, I would gladly provide all I know to the Magistrate, but, alas, I do not have any dependable information, not that would demonstrate that the rumors are nothing more than malice and worry."

"Do you have suspicion as to whom the culprit might be?" Rogier looked toward the door and continued in the language of Persia fifteen hundred years ago.

"Nothing that is defensible, or legally convincing; I am not fully convinced of it myself," said Ragoczy, also in the Persian tongue. "I would like to find a clue that would direct the Magistrate's inquiry toward those who might bear some responsibility in this situation; it would probably require more guards posted in private homes, but it might stop the outlaws."

"Would you actually make such an accusation toward anyone in the region?" Rogier asked.

"If I had verifiable evidence, I would," said Ragoczy. "This atmosphere of misgiving is becoming hard to bear."

"Then you do think they are being helped," said Rogier.

"I do. At first I doubted it, but no longer." He went to his chair by the fireplace and turned it to face the other chair in the laboratory. "Consider what has happened. Two merchants have lost their goods to highwaymen in the last month—this, in spite of the added patrols of Magistrates' soldiers assigned to those routes kept open in winter. These are men who have braved the elements to deliver their merchandise to market ahead of many others, when the roads are dangerous because of the weather; many of the most frequented roads are not safe for any traveler. Yet they were stopped by the robbers, who had good information on these merchants, and were prepared to attack them in the most precarious parts of the snow-clogged roads. That might be luck once, but twice? I cannot believe that the robbers keep men posted on two different roads all through the winter on the chance they might happen upon a prize." He shook his head. "So I must conclude that they were told of the merchants, what they carried, and what roads they traveled."

"It is a curious coincidence," said Rogier.

Ragoczy made a sound between a laugh and a snort. "Curious indeed. You and I have faced greater dangers over much longer time and have rarely had to deal with highwaymen sent specifically to ambush us. In more than nineteen centuries that has happened— what?—three times? The Baghdad road was the worst."

"Not that we haven't been ambushed in the ordinary way occasionally," said Rogier.

"Alas," Ragoczy agreed wryly.

The two were silent, then Rogier said, "I take it you are planning to go out tonight."

"For an hour or two, perhaps," said Ragoczy. "To walk the northwest end of the grounds, and to observe the road. I may go as far as the horse-pasture. I would rather we not lose any more sheep."

"Some claim you have given them to the robbers," said Rogier, his face set in disapproving lines.

"It is easier to think that than to admit the thefts are actual crimes."

"Will you be looking for the robbers, or will you be taking care of other needs?" Rogier kept his voice low.

"Tonight I will search for robbers. I am not overcome with hunger, not yet, and it is a three-hour walk to Sacre-Sang just now, which would make it likely that the guards would realize I was out of the château; I will need an excuse to go there openly, and tend to finding nourishment before I return. Hero has only been gone three days. In two or three days I should probably find a sleeping woman to visit as a dream, but not tonight." He started toward the door. "If you need me, you will find me in the library, at least for an hour. After that, I will leave as I have left on other occasions—through the music-room window. I will be back well before dawn."

"Do you think you might actually rest then?" Rogier asked as he prepared to secure the door behind them; Ragoczy, he knew, slept little, but on those rare occasions he did, he fell into a stupor that immobilized him for a minimum of three or four hours at a stretch.

"I may," said Ragoczy, and made for the stairs, his crisp footfalls muffled by the carpet. Rogier let this pass. "I will go to my quarters shortly. I will not retire for a while."

Speaking a bit more loudly, Ragoczy said, "Until morning, then," he said in French. He pointed to the foot of the flight of the stairs, where Romolo Nutzen was propped against the wall, his eyes closed.

"Yes. Until morning," Rogier repeated, adding to Nutzen, "If you would like some coffee, I would be pleased to make it for you. You seem a bit drowsy."

Nutzen shook himself and moved out of the way of Ragoczy and Rogier. "Coffee would be helpful," he said, his face coloring brightly. He yawned suddenly and reddened more deeply.

"If you will attend to that, old friend," Ragoczy said. "I will thank you and bid you good-night." He nodded and went along to the library, closing the door as soon as he entered. He turned up the low-burning oil-lamp by the door and went to light two others, for although his dark-seeing eyes could manage very well in such dimness, reading required a bit more light.

One chest of books—the larger one, carried by Gutesohnes— had been set on the floor, the smaller, delivered yesterday, had been placed on the reading-table. Ragoczy chose the chest on the floor, lifted it almost effortlessly to the reading-table, then unbuckled the broad leather straps holding it closed. Inside were thirty books, six months of Eclipse Press publications, each wrapped in heavy paper, with the title of the book contained printed on the paper. There was also a broadsheet announcing the Eclipse Press titles for the next eight months. Setting this list aside, Ragoczy began to remove the books from the chest, unwrapping each and folding the paper before examining the volume inside. The first was *Hallowed Halls: a history of English public buildings* by E. J. E. Mayfield-Jeffries, its text augmented with engravings by Harmon Dene. Ragoczy skimmed the first fifty pages, then carried the book to its place on the shelf. Next was *Raison d'Etre: pensée et romans,* in which Professeur Durand Oiepied struggled to reconcile the illogical elements of storytelling with rationality. Third was *Blutwissen,* W. G. W. Sieffert, Graf von Ravensberg's work on the nature of blood. In an hour Ragoczy had unwrapped and shelved nine of the books; only the concern for the contents of his alembic on the floor above pulled him away from this task as the clock over the mantle struck one.

This time Nutzen was awake, a deep cup of coffee half-finished on the third stair. "Comte," he said.

"Guard," Ragoczy acknowledged. "Is the coffee to your liking?"

"For the most part, yes," said Nutzen. "I like a bit more cream, but your man doesn't know that."

"You must inform him," said Ragoczy, preparing to move by him. "I have to attend to something above-stairs."

Nutzen scooped the cup out of the way and stepped aside. "Are you going to be long?"

"Probably not," said Ragoczy.

"I should stand outside the door, shouldn't I?" he asked as if suddenly aware of the backstairs that led to the top floor of the château.

"If you would prefer to do so, by all means," said Ragoczy, keeping all testiness out of his answer.

"The backstairs are uncarpeted," said Nutzen.

"You would hear me if I should descend them." Ragoczy waited, knowing pressing Nutzen would only serve to incline him to accompany him. "But you have your duty to do; you might as well come with me."

After several seconds of mulling, Nutzen said, "I see no need to do that." He almost smiled. "If you are longer than half an hour, I will have to come up to you."

"I will keep that in mind," said Ragoczy, and went up to attend to the alembic and the opalescent liquid that had been distilled from its contents. By the time he came down the stairs, Nutzen had finished his coffee.

"Twenty-three minutes," he said to Ragoczy. "Are you off to bed?"

"No; I am going to the music room. When I cannot sleep, I sometimes find that caring for the instruments I have collected is a worthwhile and soothing exercise that quiets the mind. I will probably nap on the couch there." He nodded to the guard as he went on down the corridor and let himself into the music-room, opposite his library. As soon as he had the door closed, he pulled off his coat and flung it over the back of the handsome couch, then gathered together four cushions and piled them on the couch in the approximate shape of a man sleeping, after which he arranged his coat on top of it, and angled the couch so that it could not be fully seen from the door, in case Nutzen should take it into his head to check on him. That done, he opened two cases of viols and lutes, removed a chittarone from one of them and set it out on the top of the closed forte-piano. For more than a quarter-hour he played the chittarone in a desultory way, pausing frequently to adjust its tuning-pegs and drone-strings. At the end of that time, he put the chittarone back on the top of the forte-piano; he had other things to do now.

The bottom drawer in a cabinet containing scores, music paper, replacement strings, horse-hair and rosin for bows had two woodworker's smocks and a heavy, black-silk Hungarian dolman; Ragoczy removed this traditional tunic and put it on over his white-silk shirt, fastening the frogs carefully. From a pocket in the dolman skirt he withdrew black riding-gloves, which he donned before closing the drawer and going toward the main window at the end of the room. He drew back the thick velvet draperies and levered open the shutter of the end window, then opened it and stepped through into the blowing night. Standing on the roof of the dining room, he closed the window and shutter, making sure he could reach the small niche in the shutter that would allow him to open it from the outside.

There was a skittish wind blowing, not hard, but aleatorially;
Ragoczy was relieved not to have to deal with a blustery, snowy
night. Certain he could return to the music-room without great difficulty, he made his way along the roof to the edge and let himself
down along the trellis that in summer sported climbing roses but
now could boast only thorns and brittle whips and twigs. Ragoczy
climbed down, taking great care not to snag his clothes on the
thorns, and to be careful of his gloves. As he reached the ground, he
stopped in the angle of the wall with the extension of the dining
room and took stock of his surroundings. Finally, satisfied that none
of the staff was up, he carefully made his way toward the side of the
house away from the barn and the stable; there was no reason to
alarm the animals.

Trudging toward the front of the château, Ragoczy was careful
to scuffle a confusion of his footprints in the snow, so that it would
not be easy to determine if a man or a marten had come this way;
there was so little wind tonight, and no snow falling, that any tracks
would be clear come morning. He reached the approach drive and
kept to the edge of it, going down to the gate to the estate. During
the day it was kept open, but at sunset it was closed and the lock put
in place. He inspected both the lock and the gate itself, searching
for some sign of trespass. Nothing seemed out-of-place, but he took
the time to tug a fallen branch near the edge of the road by the old
gatehouse, the last remnant of the old Medieval villa Ragoczy's
château had replaced. He reminded himself that this coming summer he would have to have this taken down and a proper gate-house
built. But that was for later; a wailing from high up the slope reminded him that wolves were still about.

From the gate he made his way along the old stone fence in a
northeasterly direction, skirting the brambles that encroached and
would need to be pruned back in the spring. He reached the stile
that gave access to the shortcut to the outer fields; there was a
mound of undisturbed snow on each step. Farther on, he came
upon a dead rat that was more than half-eaten. He left it where it
was, not wanting to deprive any animal of a winter meal. The land,

which had been rising, now dropped down into a declivity when Ragoczy noticed that there was a new break in the old stone wall, and a large disturbance of snow, almost as if a wild boar had wallowed in it.

Charily he approached the opening in the wall, studying the break but finding nothing that suggested men had made it. There had been rumors of bears in the region, and Ragoczy knew from long experience that they were much more dangerous than wolves. The thicket on the far side of the wall also showed signs of a large animal having waded through it not long ago. Satisfied, Ragoczy climbed back up the slope and continued along the wall, stopping when he heard a rustling in the undergrowth and saw a shadowy creature come bustling out of a den and disappear into the brambles beyond. Too small for a badger, too low to the ground for a fox, he thought: a weasel or a ferret, startled by something up ahead. Ragoczy crouched down in the brush, watching and listening. A whispered warning from beyond the wall caught Ragoczy's full attention; he kept utterly still as he saw three men clamber over the rough stones. Two of them held hunting rifles, the third carried a large basket and a bull's-eye lanthorn.

"Where are the sheep?" were the first words Ragoczy could make out.

"They must be in the pen next to the barn," said one of the other two. "For winter."

". . . have your knife?"

"Both of them."

"Are there any guards?" This man slurred his words as if he had had too much to drink or his face was very cold.

"The grooms have quarters above the tack-room. They're supposed to keep a watch on the livestock."

". . . better be quick." Slurred speech again.

"What about dogs?" followed by an answer Ragoczy could not hear.

"This way." And one of them led the way past the horse-pasture and down the hill toward the barn.

Ragoczy remained where he was. He could follow the men, he could go to the stable and wake the grooms, but both would lead to the necessity of explaining what he was doing out of his house without a guard in attendance. If he returned to the music-room, the thieves might be gone by the time he climbed the trellis. He stared at the three men as they plodded away toward the barn, and he made up his mind: he would get to the barn ahead of them and cause the animals to become agitated. That would bring the grooms down from their quarters and he could slip away while the thieves tried to escape. Although the snow slowed him, Ragoczy could run much faster than living men; he kept to the shrubbery and other cover as he rushed toward the barn, striving to be silent as he went; confronting the three men directly could only bring problems, so he did his utmost to remain undetected. As he neared the barn, Ragoczy took a chance and rushed across the courtyard that served both the barn and the stable beyond, relying on the dark to cloak him against the snow.

Easing the barn-door open enough to allow him to slip through into the interior, Ragoczy moved down the main aisle toward the poultry-coops and rabbit hutches at the back. When he was about halfway from the door to the coops, he felt along the wall for something to rattle; he found a milk-can next to a pail, and knocked them together. The noise they made was not loud but it roused the animals—pigs, goats, sheep, and cattle all began to clamor as they milled in their various enclosures; almost at once the chickens and ducks joined in; a mule, upset by the cacophony, brayed in the stable.

Satisfied with his efforts, Ragoczy moved toward the side-door, planning to leave before he could be seen. He had got out the door and was in the process of closing it when he heard a shout from above the courtyard, and turned.

"You men! Stop!" shouted one of the grooms.

Ragoczy, hurrying toward the side of the château, saw a light come on in the servants' quarters, and picked up speed as he heard the confusion behind him increase. A few strides short of the protecting wall, a loud whistle from the would-be thieves halted him; an instant later a knife thudded into his right shoulder nicking the shoulder-blade as its thin blade sank deep into his flesh. Had he been a living man, the wound would have incapacitated him; as it was he staggered, then forced himself to hurry on as he felt blood spread down his back. Now the climb up the trellis seemed to be a tremendous undertaking, and one at which he could not afford to falter. His shoulder was beginning to ache in the deep, grinding way that meant damage. Using his left arm—his uninjured arm—he started up the trellis, doing his best to make little noise and to keep from being raked by thorns.

Four servants in night-robes came bustling out into the snow, two of them carrying cudgels. Staggering across the roof of the dining room, Ragoczy could see the men milling in the spill of light from the door. The noise increased in volume and confusion, and Ragoczy began to fear that Nutzen would be coming to wake him. He reached the window and found the finger-niche to pull the shutter open. The pain was eating into him as he worked the window open and hauled himself into the music-room. He could hear knocking on the door, and so called out, "Yes?"

"Comte," said Nutzen loudly. "Thieves."

"Is that what the fuss is about?" he asked, hoping his weak voice would be attributed to his being wakened.

"Balduin has ordered all the servants to help in the search."

"A fine notion," said Ragoczy, wincing as he touched the hilt of the knife in his shoulder.

"Do you want to join the search?" Nutzen asked.

"Would the Magistrate approve?" Ragoczy reached over to his back and worked the knife out of the wound, setting it on one of the open shelves, then struggled out of his ruined dolman before going to claim his coat, pulling it on as Nutzen opened the door.

"If I were to stay with you," said Nutzen at his most stalwart.

"But it is night, and from what little I could see from the window, there is much confusion below." He could not stand upright without increasing his agony, so he sank into the nearest chair. "Your pardon. I was deep asleep when the excitement began and I am still caught up in sleep."

"Shall I summon your manservant?" Nutzen asked.

"It is not necessary," said Ragoczy, wishing Rogier would come of his own accord.

"As a Magistrates' guard, I should help to apprehend the criminals," said Nutzen. "But my assignment is to guard you."

"I would imagine that Ilel will aid in capturing the thieves."

Nutzen looked woeful at this thought. "I suppose so," he lamented.

"You will be able to show that you remained at your post," said Ragoczy, wishing Nutzen would leave before the blood soaked through his coat and into the upholstery of the chair.

"And I can state that you stayed in your music-room," said Nutzen, trying to make the best of a bad situation. "I will attest to it."

Two loud cries from the front of the château rose above the din.

"Thank you. But you may need to help in an arrest." He made himself remain still as another jolt of pain shot through him.

This was more than Nutzen could endure. "I will send your manservant up to you, and swear him to be accountable for your whereabouts. As soon as I return, he will prepare an account for me of all you have done."

"If that is what you want," said Ragoczy; outside a howl of fury nearly silenced the grooms and servants. "They must need your help."

"I'll go." Nutzen nodded, stepped back, slammed the door, and took off down the hallway in long, heavy strides.

Ragoczy sank back against the padded back of the chair, his face sharply delineated by the affliction of his wound. He shuddered and closed his eyes, concentrating on ascertaining the extent of his injury. If his heart had been beating, he would by now have lost a great deal of blood. As it was, he had bled a fair amount, but not enough to throw his body into a dangerous chill, or to drain him of all strength. But he knew he would require Rogier's help if he were to keep this laceration a secret. "As secret it must be," he muttered.

Ten minutes brought Rogier to the music-room, his dressing-gown secured over his pale-gray shirt and dark-blue unmentionables. He let himself in, announcing, "Two men have been detained." Then his face went ashen. "My master—"

"I encountered a . . . problem." Ragoczy stopped. "Two men? I saw three."

"One is a local day-worker, a fellow called Jiac Relout, the other is a distant relative of one of the important men in the region, I don't know which one. He said his name is Serge Fabron." He approached Ragoczy carefully, changing from French to Persian. "What happened, my master?"

"Do we know who the third man is?"

"We don't know," said Rogier, turning pale. "You're wounded."

"A cut." He tried to chuckle to show how minor it was, and failed.

"When did this happen?" Rogier demanded.

"Less than half an hour ago," said Ragoczy.

"Who did it?" Rogier's voice roughened with concern.

"I wish I knew." Ragoczy sagged back against the chair. "This will have to be reupholstered."

"Never mind the chair—let me have a look at the injury," said Rogier, reaching out to claim Ragoczy's coat.

"No," said Ragoczy. "Not yet. No one can know about this. There would be too many questions if it became known that I was wounded while I was outside the château."

Rogier considered this briefly. "It could be very difficult," he agreed, then offered his arm. "I'll help you down to your apartments. In case anyone should be watching."

"If you would walk with me, that will suffice." He got slowly to his feet and turned around. "How much blood?"

"Not much, if one isn't looking for it," said Rogier. "But the coat is—"

"Beyond saving? So I fear. I can tell it is becoming sodden with blood." Ragoczy said as he tried not to become vertiginous as he came around to face Rogier. "I'll need a basin of water and some rags. Bring your razor and say you are going to shave me; I want no significance assigned to you tending me. You might tell them you will also cut my hair. With the house in an uproar, I have no hope of sleeping so I might as well be groomed; if you will tell them that, old friend."

Rogier gave a grim smile. "I'll ask Uchtred to put together a light meal—something with hot chocolate, as a treat. That will take their mind from any activities I perform, and with hot chocolate to soothe them, they will sleep soon enough."

"Thank you," said Ragoczy, and took a hesitant step toward the door. "I take consolation in Hero's absence. This is not an experience I would want her to share." As he pulled the door open, he staggered, and Rogier came to his side.

"It is better than scorpions on Cyprus," said Rogier as he assisted Ragoczy through the door and closed it again.

"Or crosses in Mexico," said Ragoczy as he teetered toward his room at the other end of the corridor.

There was a rush of noise within the château. "Balduin and the rest have returned," said Rogier.

"Get me to my quarters, and quickly." Ragoczy's voice was strong enough to make this a command, but his pale-olive complexion was blanched.

"You may rely upon me," said Rogier, unobviously assisting Ragoczy.

Ragoczy sagged against his armoire as Rogier got him into his room. "For which I am more grateful than you will ever know," he said in his native language before he collapsed.

Text of a letter from Professore Attilio Aurelio Augusto Corvosaggio in Antioch, to his daughter, Hero Iocasta Ariadne Corvosaggio von Scharffensee, in care of Saint-Germain Ragoczy, Comte Franciscus at Château Ragoczy near Lake Geneva, Yvoire, Switzerland; carried by academic courier and delivered eleven weeks after it was sent.

To my daughter Hero, the affectionate greetings of her father on this 17th day of February, 1818,

My dear girl;

In four days we set off for Palmyra. Our expedition is at last ready, thanks in large part to Madelaine de Montalia, who has generously provided us with funds for supplies that have proven to be more expensive than anything we anticipated. I am sure you remember her; she sends you her cordial regards, and asks me to inform you that she is still trying to get to Egypt.

I have used the delay most effectively, spending a great many hours with travelers who have passed by the ancient city and have made a number of recommendations about what might be retrieved from it even now.

I still believe that I will be gone for two years at least, and for that reason, I have appointed my cousin Andrea San Otherio to handle my affairs, for as an advocate, he will be in a position to protect my assets and my reputation. Should any misfortune befall me, he will attend to it, so that no unpleasant duties will fall to you. I have provided as much of an inheritance for your sons as I am able to spare from the sums I must provide to my wife. You and she have had your differences, but you will allow that I am obliged to set aside the bulk of my earnings for her maintenance. Any questions you might have for me should be addressed to him in Bologna.

Let me urge you again to consider employment at a well-reputed girls' school. There is no disgrace in earning a living from teaching, and you cannot expect your Comte to support you forever. Distressing as it may be, you must admit that your current arrangement cannot continue indefinitely, and it is appropriate for me to remind you of this as I bid you farewell for a considerable time. Teaching is an honorable profession for a woman, and one at which you should excel. If your father-in-law dislikes such a solution to your present awkward situation, then let him remedy it in the name of his dead son, or resign himself to the necessity you having to earn a living. I apologize for putting this so bluntly, but you are a well-educated woman, and your knowledge can be as marketable an asset as a pretty face and pleasing manner.

I must hand this to the courier in ten minutes, so I will close with

*every assurance of my paternal love, and my request that you pray
for this expedition, for our safety and our discoveries.*

*With my affectionate devotion,
Your Father, Attilio Corvosaggio
presently departing from Antioch*

2

"But what am I to tell Magistrate Lindenblatt? He thought you were
taking your guards with you," Balduin protested as he watched
Ragoczy load the last of his cases onto his older traveling coach,
stowing them on the shelf behind his seat and buckle them in place.

"Given the events of the other night, the guards are needed
here, as the Magistrate and I have agreed. He has known of my engagement, and he has agreed that it is satisfactory that I go, so long
as I employ his coachman. Because of what Relout has told them,
there is good reason now to suppose that the robbers are getting no
help from me, or anyone here, and that allows Lindenblatt a degree
of tolerance in my regard, no matter what the rumors say."

"But without a guard, some in the region will say you are flee-
ing," Balduin said with unaccustomed fervor.

Ragoczy came out of the coach. "The Magistrate knows better.
He expects us back in five weeks, weather permitting. If we are
gone more than six weeks, we will have to send a message of explanation, if it is not on account of weather. He will know about bad
weather." He gestured to Guion Charget, the Magistrate's coachman, who was checking the harness on the four red-roan Ardennais
cold-bloods. "Hochvall is in no condition to take this journey, and so
the arrangement is suitable; I would have to hire a coachman if the
Magistrate had not provided his." He got out of the coach and began to walk around it, making sure it was ready to leave; the dim,

early morning light and a little fog rising a hands-breadth above the slush made the coach look as if it were floating in the air.

"And you're taking just the one coach?" Balduin frowned, searching for factors that might require a delayed departure. "Didn't Herr Einlass inform you that he had another coach available?"

"He did, but I have already got two coaches on the road with Hero, which means three of them will return, and a dozen horses. I have only one more coach and one more four-horse team in the stable, and I would not like to have to risk all my coach-horses for travel with winter still upon us. You may have some need of a coach during our absence. This way you will have a vehicle and a team to pull it." Ragoczy had donned a black-wool great-coat cut in the Hungarian fashion, its broad collar concealing the stiffness in his shoulder; his clothes beneath were also Hungarian in style. "You have my instructions, authorizations, and my proposed route of travel. Rogier and I, Hildebrand, and Herr Charget should be sufficient to make this journey."

"Dietbold could also be spared. With you away, it isn't always easy to keep the footmen occupied."

"Hildebrand will be sufficient," said Ragoczy, checking the straps on the boot of the coach. "If Dietbold becomes bored, he can always be put to polishing furniture."

Balduin sighed, his breath fogging before his face. "If only I could convince you that there are good reasons to remain here another week at least."

"There may be excellent reasons, but the invitation is specific, and we are expected at Ravensberg by the twenty-ninth of March, and that gives us just fourteen days to get there," said Ragoczy. "You will discover I have addressed most of your concerns in my instructions: very little is different than when we went to Amsterdam last summer."

"But the roads were open in summer," Balduin protested. "The days were longer."

"And we were set upon by highwaymen," Ragoczy added helpfully.

Balduin glanced up at the pale clouds smeared across the sky. "There could be snow again tonight."

"But probably not until tomorrow or the next day," said Ragoczy, "and with luck, we should be at least fifteen leagues along the road."

"A pity you don't know Charget better," said Balduin, making a last effort.

"Yes," agreed Ragoczy. "But the Magistrate vouches for him: who am I to question his judgment." He continued around to the side of the coach and opened the door. "Two fur rugs, a basket of brandy and cheese." These would be for Charget and Hildebrand, but there was no reason Balduin should know that. "A box of books. Trunks in the boot, and the presents for our host and for his niece, as a betrothal gift. We are expected at the Old Wagon in Saint-Gingolph tonight, and so we must leave shortly. It is nine leagues to Saint-Gingolph and not all the road is completely cleared of snow."

As if to add urgency to Ragoczy's remarks, Rogier, dressed for their journey, came out of the side-door, bearing a leather-bound chest in his arms. "Your medicaments," he explained as he prepared to climb into the coach with it.

"Very good," said Ragoczy, opening the door and letting down the steps. "We should be back in five weeks to accommodate Lindenblatt. If there is a delay, word will be sent. Do not fret, Balduin. The time will pass more quickly if you do not fret."

Rogier took his place on the seat facing backward. "Hildebrand is finishing his cream-roll; he will be out within five minutes."

"Is his traveling-case stowed?" Ragoczy asked.

"It is," said Rogier, sketching a salute toward Balduin as Ragoczy climbed in beside him, flipped up the steps and shut the door.

"I shall make written records for every day you are gone, a full record of everything. You and the Magistrate may examine it upon your return." Balduin regarded the coach balefully.

"I thank you for that, and I wish you a pleasant end of winter. Let us hope the last of the snow falls in March, not April, or May." Ragoczy gave a slight inclination of his head.

Balduin returned the nod more deeply, conceding defeat. "May you travel swiftly and safely to your destination, and return without incident." He stepped back and watched as Charget, wrapped in his coachman's cloak and swathed to the eyes in mufflers, his broad-brimmed fur-lined hat crammed down on his head, came to the side of the coach and climbed up to the box at the very moment Hildebrand burst out of the château, tugging on his hat as he ran for the footman's perch at the back of the coach; he hauled himself up as Charget whistled to the team, starting them toward the gate.

The Ardennais carriage-horses were fresh and they moved out at a jog-trot, making their way down the drive steadily, their harness jingling in the crisp morning air, the sound of their hooves on the frozen road steady and firm. As they approached the gate, Jervois, who had run down from the château, hurried to open it, waving his excitement as the horses slowed for him. The gates swung back and the coach went on through, the wheels leaving deep grooves in the thin mantle of snow; Jervois stood in the opening, waving until the bend in the road carried the coach out of sight and along the road to Yvoire.

"In the summer, we could take the short-cut through Sorbeny to Montriond."

Rogier looked out the window of the coach at the high peaks. "But now they are all filled up with snow, and perilous. It would take days to get there, if we could manage it at all. The horses would be worn out, and the coach would probably need new wheels." He threw one of the fur rugs over his lap and knees, holding one out to Ragoczy, which he declined with a single gesture. "Do you think, when the Allies withdraw from France, that they will return this region to the French, or do you think the Swiss will keep it?"

"That will depend on how the withdrawal goes," Ragoczy said, taking note of the places the road needed repair. "If there is no hostility, then I assume that in time the French will want to reclaim a good portion of it."

"That may be why so many German-Swiss have been encouraged to move into this region," said Rogier.

"It may," said Ragoczy.

Rogier accepted this as an invitation to silence; he slipped his arm through the strap hanging from the ceiling and prepared to nap as the coach howled along to Yvoire, stopping only briefly at the Town Hall to hand over a bond to Magistrate Lindenblatt's secretary against Ragoczy's return from Austria, assurance of the Comte's swift return. A receipt was prepared and notarized, and then the coach was on its way again, going east along the shore of Lake Geneva toward the village of Saint-Gingolph.

The next day brought them to Riddes a little after dark; it took determined persuasion accompanied by a gold coin to arrange matters with the hotelier: despite their late arrival Ragoczy and his servants were allowed to stop for the night at the Stag and Ram, the most luxurious of the three posting inns in the town.

"We will need to go a shorter distance tomorrow," said Rogier as he took care of Ragoczy's personal cases. "In this weather, the towns will close their gates at sunset."

"Yes; they will," said Ragoczy. "And the horses are getting tired."

"Then a day of rest here might be good for all of us. Charget and Hildebrand are showing signs of inner chill," Rogier observed.

"The weather is changing, and not for the better," Ragoczy said. "By tomorrow there will be snow again."

Rogier unrolled a thin mattress atop the hostelry's bed; it was filled with a thin layer of Ragoczy's native earth. "Do you think it will last long?"

"The storm? a day; perhaps two," said Ragoczy. "I think we had better plan to remain here tomorrow if it's snowing. I have no wish to be caught on the road in a snowfall. This is not a good stretch of road on which to be stranded: there are too many avalanches."

"No, not a good place," said Rogier. "They would not find us until May."

Ragoczy reached for the small portfolio that held his maps. "We will need to determine which of the passes are open and then decide which road is best."

Rogier saw that Ragoczy held his right arm close to his body, favoring it. "How is your shoulder?"

"A little sore," Ragoczy admitted. "If only vampires healed as quickly as the living."

"But you don't," said Rogier in a blend of sympathy and exasperation.

"Nor do ghouls," said Ragoczy with a faint smile.

"I'm not the one who had a knife in my shoulder," said Rogier directly. "You do not often reveal when you hurt, so it would seem you are most uncomfortable."

"It is the long hours sitting still," Ragoczy said.

"So a day of light activity is welcome," Rogier suggested.

"For all of us. The horses could use a thorough grooming—I will attend to that tomorrow. We must also purchase more food for the coach so that Charget and Hildebrand will have something to eat on the road."

They discussed various exigencies of travel for more than an hour, then Ragoczy retired for the night. In the morning he waited until his coachman and footman had breakfasted, then descended to the main floor of the inn. After paying for their second night and the meals they would need, Ragoczy went off to the stable to take care of the Ardennais team, brushing the mud from the long, black feathering around their hooves and retying the neat, braided knots in their black manes. The whole task took over two hours, and by the time Ragoczy went back to his room, Rogier had returned from shopping with sausages, beer, cheese, and a crock of preserved quinces.

"I'll arrange for fresh bread in the morning, and a pippin of butter," Rogier announced as he stowed the comestibles in the hamper.

"The horses will be ready for the next leg of the journey. Their shoes are holding, their legs are in good shape. Their travel-coats are clean, their harness is cleaned and oiled. I've paid for extra grain for them tonight." Ragoczy swung his arm to exercise his shoulder. "It will be another month at least before I have my strength back."

"And six months before it stops hurting," said Rogier wisely.

"Very likely," said Ragoczy.

The next morning they left Riddes at the back end of a storm that was now raging eastward. The road was three inches deep in snow—not so deep that the old berms on either side of it were lost in drifts, but sufficient to make for slow-going. By nightfall they had covered under eight leagues, arriving at Unterleuk as the two church-bells of the town tolled the Angelus. The next day they covered nine leagues, and the day after, ten. News of an avalanche held them at Chur for a day while Ragoczy and Charget decided which road to take into Austria, and as soon as word was brought that the avalanche had been cleared enough for traffic to move past it, they resumed their travels, arriving at Ravensberg thirteen days after they left Château Ragoczy. The sun was producing a watery shine through a film of clouds and the wind had died down, promising better weather ahead.

"Very good time, considering all the factors; we have a day to spare," said Ragoczy as he climbed out of the coach in the Ravensberg courtyard shortly before three in the afternoon; he handed two gold coins to Charget and one to Hildebrand, saying to the young footman, "Come to my room later and I will give you an ointment for the chapping on your face. It will stop the peeling."

"Danke, Comte," said Hildebrand through stiff lips.

Charget unwound his heaviest muffler and doffed his hat, watching as the grooms hurried out from the stable. "Be sure you check the on-side wheeler. His hock is a little stiff, I fear."

"I have a poultice for that," Ragoczy told his borrowed coach-man.

"A good thing," said Charget. "He'll need it."

"That's Grenadier," said Hildebrand. "His harness-partner is Hussar."

"And the leaders are Dragoon and Fusilier," said Ragoczy, moving aside so that Rogier could bring out a few of their cases and baskets.

Three footmen were approaching from the Schloss, one dragging a low wagon for baggage. They came up to the coach and began to unload it while the grooms unhooked the team and led them away to the stable.

"I'll come to check them shortly," called out Charget to the grooms.

"They'll be ready," one of the grooms called back.

Behind the footmen came the steward, very dignified in his most formal daytime clothing. He offered Ragoczy a bow. "On behalf of the Graf von Ravensberg, you are most welcome here."

"Thank you," said Ragoczy, knowing it was expected.

"Five other guests are here before you. If you will accompany me, the servants and your man will see to the disposal of your bags." It was rude to stare directly at a noble guest, so the steward directed his gaze over Ragoczy's left shoulder. "They are assembled in the billiard-room."

"It will be my honor to meet them," said Ragoczy. "But I will need twenty minutes to change clothes. I would not want to expose von Ravensberg and his guests to all the grime of the road."

The steward bowed. "As you wish. You will be taken to your room at once; I shall inform the guests that you will join them directly."

"That will be much appreciated," said Ragoczy, and signaled to Rogier. "I will meet you in the room."

"Very shortly," Rogier said as Ragoczy followed the steward into Ravensberg.

The Schloss was in the grand tradition of a century ago, and the current Graf had done his utmost to make the Schloss as splendid as he could. Ragoczy stood in the entry-hall that was flanked by two curving staircases that served to frame the great corridor leading into the Great Hall. Two suits of armor stood on either side of the staircases, and an elaborate chandelier in brass and crystal hung from the high ceiling; only four candles were lit at present, and small puddles of wax on the marble floor revealed that this was a customary courtesy.

"The servants' stairs are in the back, and there is another interior staircase, as well." The steward pointed to the gallery where the stairs met. "Edelfonsus will take you to your room." He clapped his hands, and a young man in household livery came hurrying. "Comte Franciscus has arrived and wishes to change his clothes. He will be in the Rose Room, if you will take him there?"

Before Edelfonsus could speak, a burst of giggles came from the Great Hall, and Hyacinthie rushed forward. She was arrayed in a fashionable dress of fine-spun wool the color of lilacs, with a high neck decorated with a narrow lace ruff; from a neatly tied black ribbon on the corsage of her dress depended a small portrait of a young child. As she came up to Ragoczy she held out her hand and curtsied. "Welcome to Ravensberg, Comte. It is such a pleasure to see you again."

"Fraulein," said the steward, making it as much a reprimand as a servant could.

"Oh, I met the Comte in Amsterdam. I need not stand on ceremony with him, since he's not a stranger. Need I?" This last was directly to Ragoczy.

Ragoczy kissed her hand. "It is a pleasure to see you, Fraulein, and to wish you happy."

Aware that the servants were watching, Hyacinthie made a charming pout. "To give up my life to another so soon," she said, and cast a mischievous glance at Ragoczy. "Mutze disapproves of me, don't you, Mutze?"

"It is not for me to say, Fraulein," the steward answered stiffly.

"But you don't approve of this reception, not while Rosalie is still missing. You think we should have postponed the celebration, and so do I. But my uncle is determined." She waggled her fingers at Edelfonsus. "Well, come on. Lead the way. I won't go farther than the gallery."

"I think it better that Edelfonsus take me up," said Ragoczy. "I undoubtedly need a clean shirt and another pair of boots. I should improve my appearance altogether."

Disappointed but unwilling to relinquish him, Hyacinthie said, "At least you came alone. That's something."

"Hardly alone: Rogier is with me, and a coachman and a footman as well." He nodded to her as he began to ascend the stairs.

"Not that. Your friend isn't with you." The smile Hyacinthie offered was dazzling although her eyes remained cold.

"Ah. She is with her children at Scharffensee and will join me here in a few days," said Ragoczy.

Hyacinthie resisted the urge to stamp her foot. "So soon?" She turned away.

"I expect so," said Ragoczy, stopping so Edelfonsus could pass him and lead the way to the Rose Room.

"Will her children be with her?" She could not keep the anger completely out of her question, but the smile remained firmly affixed to her mouth.

"No, I think not," said Ragoczy, wondering what the servants would make of their conversation.

"That's something," Hyacinthie murmured, and swung back around to look at Ragoczy. "You may decide to enjoy yourself while you're here, Comte, without waiting for Madame."

"I expect your uncle will entertain us all," Ragoczy said at his most neutral as he reached the gallery. "I shall return directly."

Hyacinthie curtsied. "I'll be waiting."

Ragoczy said nothing more as Edelfonsus guided him down the main corridor to another hallway, where he pointed to the three doors away from the tall, narrow windows.

"The second room is yours. The room beyond is for your manservant. One of us will take you to the Graf when you have readied yourself."

"That is very good of you," said Ragoczy, handing the young man a silver coin. "Will my manservant be up soon?"

"Five more minutes," said Edelfonsus. "He is coming by the side-stairs—they're the nearest."

"Are other rooms in this corridor occupied?" Ragoczy asked, looking toward the third door.

"That is for your . . . companion. Upon her arrival." Edelfonusus blushed and took a step back.

"Danke," said Ragoczy, and went to the center door, trying the latch carefully before letting himself into the bedchamber allotted to him: it was a room of good size, with a neat fireplace taking up one corner. The bed was large with elaborate hangings in the color that gave the room its name, with a broad stool beside it to help him climb up into it. The carpet had a pattern of roses worked into it, the same shade as the hangings. Elaborate sconces with oil-lamps flanked the bed, and on the opposite wall there were two more sconces on either side of a tall mirror. The walls were paneled in oak but for the north-facing wall, which included a window-seat and three mullioned windows that provided the room with a fair amount of light. Ragoczy walked over to the windows, removing his Hungarian great-coat, and looked out into the small garden beneath, and the rising hillside to the east, all the while wondering what to do about the mirror, for he cast no reflection in it.

A tap at the door warned him that Rogier had arrived with his bags; he draped his great-coat over the end of the bench and sat down in the embrasure of the window-seat, calling out, "Enter."

Rogier, in the company of two footmen, came into the chamber, took swift stock of it, then directed the servants to put the bags down away from the mirror. He gave each man a silver coin, saying, "You have done good service. I will attend to my own cases a little later; right now my master needs my assistance to dress for the evening."

The two footmen hurried out of the room, afraid to be curious.

Once the door was closed, Ragoczy rose and came over to Rogier. "I trust you can do something about—" He gestured to the mirror. "Not that it is not very fine: it is. But I would rather not look at it; it is too disconcerting."

"I have a sheet I can put over it." Like all proper manservants, he carried changes of bed-linens when traveling, since many hostelries were not inclined to use the best bed-linens for their guests.

"If you are asked about it, what will you say?" Ragoczy unbuttoned his coat and began to remove it.

"Probably that you may misconstrue the reflection in this unfamiliar place and might damage the mirror. Since it is unquestionably valuable, I have taken this precaution." His smile glinted and vanished.

"Excellent," said Ragoczy, putting his coat on the bed and unfastening his cuffs. "I should change these, too. If you will get out a clean collar and cuffs, and the ruby cufflinks?"

Rogier had been unbuckling the straps on the largest trunk. "It shouldn't take me long to find them. They're in the middle drawer."

Ragoczy tossed his cuffs on top of his coat. "The waistcoat seems all right."

"For this evening, I should think so. I assume you want the black evening coat with the swallow-tail and the black-silk cravat?" Rogier asked as he pulled out the items in question. "And the dark-gray unmentionables."

"Yes; and the Italian evening pumps." He unfastened his cravat and it, too, was added to the clothes on the bed. As he reached for the discreetly frilled cuffs Rogier handed him, Ragoczy remarked as he put them, "Hyacinthie greeted me."

"So I understand," said Rogier. "The servants are abuzz about it."

"I will keep that in mind," Ragoczy said, and took the silver cufflinks Rogier held out to him.

By the time he left the Rose Room, some twenty minutes later, Ragoczy was elegantly arrayed for the evening. His appearance was all that could be wanted in good company in any city in Europe. Even his magnificent ruby stick-pin in his lapel was restrained and in excellent taste. His only other jewelry was his signet-ring marked with his eclipse device.

True to her word, Hyacinthie was waiting for him at the foot of the two curving stairways. "One would never think you had been in a coach for days on end," she said in girlish approval. "In Amsterdam, you were always turned out perfectly."

"Thank you, Fraulein. That is very generous of you." He spoke quietly, aware that servants were watching.

Impulsively she reached out and took his arm. "Oh, I wish I were in Amsterdam again. Winter here is so dreary."

"Winter in Amsterdam can be fairly wretched," he said, "with storms pounding in off the North Sea."

"But Amsterdam is exciting," she protested winsomely. "It's full of people, and things to do. Not like this place."

"Then you must be looking forward to your marriage," said Ragoczy as she escorted him into the billiard room. "Trier is an interesting place."

"But to be married in order to achieve it," she said as if this was the first time the thought had crossed her mind. "It is a hard bargain we women must make." She smiled widely, in case she had offended him. "You brought another coachman."

"Gutesohnes is driving Madame von Scharffensee. He will bring her here." He slipped his arm out of her grasp as they neared the billiard room and the sound of conversation reached his ears.

The slight was a small one, Hyacinthie thought as she fell a step behind him; he should not have pulled away from her. It was a little thing, but she decided he would pay for it, and pay a high price. I will not be disregarded, she said to herself, and followed Ragoczy into the billiard room where the guests were waiting to be introduced to the distinguished newcomer.

Text of a letter from Egmond Talbot Lindenblatt, Magistrate, of Yvoire, Swiss France, to Reinhart Olivier Kreuzbach, attorney at law, at Speicher, Rhenish Prussia; carried by messenger and delivered eleven days after it was written.

To the respected advocate R. O. Kreuzbach of Speicher, Rhenish Prussia, the greetings of the Magistrate E. T. Lindenblatt of Yvoire, Lake Geneva, Swiss France, as we are now designated on this, the 1st day of April, 1818

My dear advocate,

Pursuant to the matters regarding your client, Comte Franciscus of the Château Ragoczy of this town, it is my duty to inform you, during the absence of the Comte, of the following developments in respect to the robbers of this region, to wit: that the two men captured at Château Ragoczy while in the apparent act of robbing the estate, both have been identified. One is Jiac Relout, a day-laborer from Sacre-Sang, the other is Paulot Desarmes from Halle; his occupation is not known. Each has said that the third man with them was Loys Begen, another day-laborer from Sacre-Sang, who has not yet been apprehended. Both declare that they know nothing of the fourth man a few of the servants claim to have seen: I am inclined to think that the man is a product of confusion not observation.

I have obtained sworn statements from each that they do not know whom the robbers deal with, that they were acting on their own, and that they chose Ragoczy because his generosity suggested he had goods and livestock to spare. Both swear that it was Paulot Desarmes who made arrangements with the robbers so that they would not fear for their lives, for it has been the practice of the robbers to kill any known to be preying on the same travelers and estates that they consider to be within their domain. That is the word they are purported to use: domain. These thieves are haughty men, and as ruthless as the barons of old. Relout and Desarmes have requested the protection of the courts until the robbers are apprehended; they say they will not survive if they are released from custody before the robbers are caught.

At this point I would like to keep the guards at Château Ragoczy, not because I still have suspicions, but as an attempt to draw out those who help the robbers. I am convinced that if I can lull these men into a state of submission, I can turn that to the advantage of the court. With the Comte in Austria, I can see no reason to change my arrangements, and unless you wish to protest my ploy, I will continue it, at least until such time as the Comte himself returns to advise me of his wishes. With this joint administration beginning, I feel it is to the benefit of everyone in the region to resolve this matter as quickly as possible; therefor I would be very much obliged if you, on behalf of the Comte, will indulge this subterfuge so that the worst criminals may be brought to justice at last, and a danger to all of us finally ended.

*I look forward to your response and thank you for all assistance
you can render in these difficult circumstances.*

Most sincerely,
Egmond Talbot Lindenblatt
Magistrate, Yvoire, Lake Geneva
Swiss France

3

A small group of musicians had assembled in the Great Hall at
Ravensberg and were setting up their instruments and music
stands on the low platform at the far end of the room. Von Ravensberg stood in the archway between the dining room and the Great
Hall, watching the men jockey their chairs and stands into position
while three servants wrestled a log into the cavernous fireplace,
placing it atop a nest of kindling; beside him Ragoczy took stock of
the excitement around them, noting how the whole of the Schloss
thrummed with activity in anticipation of this culmination of four
days' festivities.

"Seven guests still haven't arrived," von Ravensberg said unhappily.

"They may still do so. It is five hours until your banquet and
eight hours until the ball." Ragoczy watched one angular fellow
with a flute try to place his sheet music on the stand without tipping
it off the edge of the platform. "This being the apogee of your
celebration of your ward's betrothal, allowance must be made. You
have thirty-five guests in the Schloss already, not an inconsiderable
number, considering everything."

"I know Hyacinthie was hoping for more, but I told her she cannot expect to assemble a hundred suitable guests here at Ravensberg: there isn't room enough, and unlike the cities, we must keep

ourselves to those of suitable rank and importance, whose numbers are not so great as those that might be found even in Salzburg." Von Ravensberg offered a reminiscent smile. "She was such a lovely, biddable child, so sweet; always looking for ways to please me. But now she is a demanding young woman, eager to work her will on men."

"I am sure you have done the best you can in arranging the ball," said Ragoczy out of courtesy.

"Actually, Herr Lowengard, my man-of-business, has managed all of this, in terms of invitations and such—engaging the musicians, hiring extra servants and such. He is a reliable man who understands how things must function in this world; I leave most of the workaday matters to him."

"No doubt you approved the guest list," said Ragoczy, his irony all but undetectable.

"That I did. All but four of those invited pledged to be here, at least for the banquet and ball," said von Ravensberg. "Your companion, Madame von Scharffensee, got here three days ago, in good time, and coming a considerable distance. I am concerned that others have not been so punctilious."

"Madame von Scharffensee was fortunate; she arrived shortly before the rain." Ragoczy motioned toward the windows, where drops shone in the sporadic mid-day sunshine. "The roads may be too muddy for travel."

"Possibly," said von Ravensberg, unconvinced. "If this ball is not a success, it may blight the occasion for Hyacinthie. I would not want her to be disappointed." He turned away, and when he spoke again his tone had changed. "I have prevailed upon six of my guests to allow me to draw their blood, to continue the work described in my book. Would you consider adding to their number?"

Ragoczy hesitated. "I am not of Austrian or German blood," he said at last.

"You said you were of Hungarian ancestry," said von Ravensberg.

"Yes; of an ancient Carpathian House," Ragoczy said, revealing none of the consternation he felt. "We were strong in the eastern mountains well before the Saxons came." He might have added the Romans, but decided not to.

"I see," said von Ravensberg. "Well, then, would you want to watch my procedure?" He attempted a smile. "I am glad that you appreciate my restricted population for study. I am grateful to you for your candor in that regard. Research can be so easily distorted by failures to observe the proper parameters. Many another might have made an effort to conceal his antecedents in order to be included in my efforts."

"That is one of the reasons I thought it best to mention this to you," said Ragoczy. He glanced toward the windows again. "Your staff is still waiting for today's arrivals, are they not?"

"I have ordered those who can to watch the approach and to make every effort to admit the late-comers to the Schloss. I want the gates to stay open until we have sat down to our banquet." Von Ravensberg's attention was commanded by the leader of the musicians. "Yes, Maestro. What is it?"

The musician stood up, his violin and bow in hand. "Is there a keyboard instrument in the Schloss, Graf?" he asked. "When we made arrangements for this ball, your man of business said there would be one available."

"There is a clavier in the music-room on the floor above. Do you require it for this evening or for practice now?"

"If you could arrange to bring it down and have it tuned . . ." The musician managed to look disquieted while doing his utmost to conduct himself properly.

"I will deal with the clavier while the guests are resting," said Ragoczy. "And I will tune it."

The lead musician favored him with a thoughtful look. "You have some knowledge of the instrument, perhaps?"

"I do," said Ragoczy. "I collect instruments, and can play some of them tolerably well."

"Um," said the musician, not wanting to offend any of the Graf's guests.

"If you would like, I might play some dance melodies while you and your companions have your twenty minutes to eat," Ragoczy offered, and saw von Ravensberg stare in astonishment. "It would allow those who wish to continue dancing to do so." He did not add that it would account for his absence at the midnight supper. "I know the works of Mozart and Rossini, and Schubert as well. I will not abash you, or our host."

Saying nothing to Ragoczy's offer, von Ravensberg raised his voice. "Do not trouble yourself, Comte; I'll order the servants to bring the clavier down. It may take an hour or so." He gave a hard, disapproving look at the servants who had finished at the fireplace and were now lowering the first of three large chandeliers in order to put new candles in place. "Be careful there."

"Yes, Graf," said the senior of the three, and added some orders in an undervoice to his comrades.

Von Ravensberg touched Ragoczy's sleeve. "The days have got away from us, I fear. I was hoping we might have an opportunity to discuss my book before you depart. Are you willing?"

"Certainly," said Ragoczy, trying to discern von Ravensberg's reason for this invitation.

"Then you may want to acquaint yourself with my preferred methods. I am going to prepare my laboratory. If you would like to join me there in half an hour?"

"Half an hour it is," said Ragoczy, who was curious about the methods von Ravensberg employed. "On the upper floor of the new wing?"

"Exactly," said the Graf as he walked out of the Great Hall without so much as a last look around.

Ragoczy would have liked to talk with the musicians but knew this was an inconvenient time, and so went up to the Rose Room, where he discovered Rogier in front of a standing tray busily cutting up some collops of raw veal and setting them on a plate.

"My master," he said, continuing with the last preparations for his meal. "I have Herr Schillnagel's man in my room, and I did not want to explain to him about my appetite; he might be taken aback."

"Herr Schillnagel arrived this morning with his sister? The tall man with the wide mustache?" Of the eight guests who had come since early morning, Ragoczy had yet to be introduced to six of them.

"That is the man. All body-servants are sharing rooms for tonight. I thought it best to eat in here, where Neuntefeld cannot see me." He kept on, wielding the knife expertly. "The meat is very fresh."

"As I can see. It looks quite delicious," said Ragoczy.

"You would never eat this," Rogier chuckled.

"Just because I do not eat does not mean I cannot appreciate good cuts of meat, or fresh vegetables, for that matter." Ragoczy stretched, still favoring his right shoulder. "I am bidden to our host's laboratory to see him draw blood."

"Do you want to see it?"

"I cannot decide, but it is likely that my curiosity will prevail, and I will observe him." He walked down the room and came back. "I have seen enough anatomy classes to have banished any thrill in watching more, but I cannot help but be inquisitive—how he goes about his study, and how he arrives at his conclusions. I am a bit surprised that he waited until this occasion to ask me. Or perhaps he was making up his mind if he should even make such an offer; he must be convinced that I will not abuse his hospitality by claiming his study for my own."

Rogier smiled sternly. "If he knew of your—"

"I am thankful he does not," Ragoczy said, cutting Rogier short as he stopped near the fireplace. "His book is not very specific about his methods, for fear of others . . . shall we say, purloining? . . . them for their own uses." He sat down in the high-backed easy-chair that was tantalizingly close.

"He's not worried that you'll purloin them?" Rogier asked.

"Apparently not. He is aware that I am involved with Eclipse Press. I assume he wants to establish the authenticity of his techniques, or something of the sort." He shifted forward in the chair, elbows on knees. "Is Hero about?"

"I haven't seen her." Rogier had rarely known Ragoczy to be so restive when there was so little apparent cause for him to be.

"For how long?" Ragoczy inquired; aside from one frantically rapturous night together after her arrival, she had made a point of staying away from him so as not to compromise either of them in the eyes of von Ravensberg's guests.

Rogier considered. "About an hour and a half ago. She was on her way down from her room."

"How was she?" Ragoczy asked.

"She said she had a headache, but it wasn't sufficient to keep her in her bed," Rogier said, watching Ragoczy while he went on, "She breakfasted with the other ladies about two hours ago in the morning room, and said that she was going with them all on a tour of the old wing, since the carriage-ride through the country wouldn't be pleasant in the rain. I understand there are some interesting features in the old wing." Satisfied with his labors, Rogier took his plate and went to the window-seat to dine.

"I see," said Ragoczy, a frown deepening between his brows.

"I think she is still tired from her journey," said Rogier.

"It has been a hard time for her," Ragoczy conceded.

"She said she would take a rest before dressing for the ball," Rogier added helpfully. "When the tour is over. Hyacinthie is eager to show them as much as possible."

"Hyacinthie is giving the tour?" Ragoczy put his fingertips together. "Not the steward or Herr Lowengard?"

"Hyacinthie: enthusiastically. She knows the Schloss better than anyone, from what Madame von Scharffensee described. The staff said she has explored every building on the whole of the estate." Rogier shook his head. "If you like, I will check on Madame von Scharffensee when she returns for her nap."

"If you would; thank you," said Ragoczy, dismissing the unfamiliar twinge of apprehension that went through him. "I believe most of the guests are planning to rest this afternoon."

"So they can dance until after midnight; the banquet and midnight supper should give them strength for the evening," said Rogier. "This is quite a grand occasion for Ravensberg, I gather. The staff tells me that the Graf rarely entertains, and not on this scale.

Fortelle, the senior footman, has been in service here for eighteen years and can't remember another occasion like this one. They're all a bit overwhelmed."

"And with one of his two new wards still missing, I would imagine some of the staff would feel this is an inappropriate celebration, one that ought to have been postponed; the house is not officially in mourning, but it is far from being filled with delight," said Ragoczy as he shoved himself out of the easy-chair.

"A few do think that; Fortelle thinks they should all be in half-mourning until Rosalie's fate is known," said Rogier. "Two or three of them express worry about the remaining child—Hedda. They say she is very down-cast and silent. Hardly surprising: losing her parents and her sister all in the same year—" He set his fork down and opened his hand to show his emotion.

"Von Ravensberg says he wants to ease her grief," Ragoczy mused, a distant concentration in his gaze. "I believe it is generally understood that Hyacinthie resents his attention to the children."

"She is hardly more than a child herself, and about to marry a man not of her choosing. It is hardly surprising that she might feel put-upon," said Rogier.

Ragoczy shook his head slowly. "There is something more."

"How do you mean?" Rogier asked.

"It is little more than a sensation, like a cold breeze on the neck." He came toward the window-seat. "The rain seems to be clearing."

"The roads will still be muddy," said Rogier. When Ragoczy remained silent, he went on, "Werther, the under-cook, says that Hedda has been weeping every night, and that Hyacinthie becomes angry because of it." He ate more of his veal. "What do you make of the bridegroom?"

"I would not have thought him a good mate for Hyacinthie," said Ragoczy. "But my opinion has not been sought."

Rogier shook his head. "She has her sights set higher."

Ragoczy understood the implication, and said, "Oh, no. I am not what she longs for, no matter what her hopes may be. She would be appalled if she knew anything of my true nature."

"You think so? Her maid, Idune, says that since you have come, Hyacinthie talks of no one else. Most of the staff find her infatuation diverting." He forked another small wedge of veal. "I only mention this so that you can take care. That young woman is determined to get what she wants."

"This is her betrothal celebration. I doubt she would be so lax as to embarrass her uncle and her fiancé at this moment." As he spoke, Ragoczy held up his hand. "Now that I am warned, I do understand the problem, and I will be on guard. I will have no hint of impropriety in my dealing with her."

"I trust your discretion," said Rogier, and finished his veal.

"You know me too well, old friend," said Ragoczy as he came back from the windows.

"Keep what I've told you in mind, my master. That child is inclined to follow her own desires. All the servants say so." Rogier carried his plate back to the tray, then went to the traveling chest to pull out Ragoczy's formal clothes for the evening, and to find something appropriate for him to wear for the rest of the day.

Before seeking out von Ravenberg's laboratory, Ragoczy donned a smock of black Egyptian linen to protect his clothes. With the help of a footman, Ragoczy quickly made his way to the staircase that led to it; he knocked on the door and waited to be admitted.

"Come in, Comte. Come in and be welcome. You know Baron Weidekraft, of course." He pointed out the well-dressed stocky man seated on the chaise longue. "He is to be the first today."

"Comte," said Weidekraft.

"Baron," he responded.

Von Ravensberg held out his syringe, turning it in his hand so that the glass tube caught the light. "This is the instrument I shall use. As you can tell, the glass body will allow me to gauge how much blood I have taken, so as not to drain you too much, Baron." He managed a single, uneasy laugh. "With such a night as we have ahead of us, you will want to have all your stamina, won't you?"

Baron Weidekraft had removed his coat and the cuff on his right sleeve and was in the process of rolling it up. "You said above the elbow?"

"If you would," said von Ravensberg. He turned to Ragoczy. "I believe the vein in the bend of the elbow gives much the best results."

"You may be right," said Ragoczy, trying to gauge the amount of blood von Ravensberg might want.

As if anticipating Ragoczy's question, von Ravensberg said, "I will use the blood the Baron provides to perform a number of tests. The most important is running a current of electricity through the blood. There is much to be learned from that procedure; my work is a beginning, but there is so much more to accomplish. I believe it may be possible, in time, to use electricity to reanimate those newly dead. Others have had some interesting results from similar experiments on the bodies of the recently deceased that—"

"Graf," said Baron Weidekraft. "If you don't mind?"

Von Ravensberg looked askance. "I am sorry, my dear Baron. I did not mean to offend you in any way." He took an iodine swab and rubbed it on the bend in Baron Weidekraft's elbow. "To promote healing," he explained, then brought the syringe around so that its hollow needle was directly aimed at the vein. "If you will close your fist? I will not have to poke so hard if you will tighten your hand."

Baron Weidekraft obliged, watching the needle as it neared the vein. He let out a yelp as von Ravensberg slid the point into his skin and set it in the vein. Almost at once, blood welled in the syringe; von Ravensberg withdrew the small plunger, increasing the flow of the blood. The Baron turned pale as he saw the syringe filling steadily. "What are you doing, Graf?"

"Taking the sample," said von Ravensberg with a kind of dreamy excitement. "This will be a wonderful contribution. I can see the quality of your blood already. My tests will only confirm what I am certain I observe." He had taken enough to fill a soup-ladle and showed no inclination to stop. "If you feel light-headed, lie back and close your eyes. I will shortly be done."

Ragoczy could see that there would be a large bruise in the crook of the Baron's arm, but did not mention this. "How much more will you need?"

"Not much. Do you see this line on the syringe?" He moved his finger so that Ragoczy could make out the precise black line. "I used to take somewhat less, but then I would often run out of the sample before I had run all my tests, which was most inconvenient. This provides ample for my purposes."

"My physician bled me but two weeks since," said Weidekraft.

"A sound practice," von Ravensberg approved. "More men should do so. There would be less epidemic disease if all men were bled regularly."

Ragoczy knew he was expected to agree, but could not, so he said, "Many patients cannot tolerate frequent blood-letting."

"The weak ones," said von Ravensberg in dismissal; he was satisfied with the amount of blood in the syringe at last. He looked down at Weidekraft. "I am almost done. I have made this as quick as possible, Baron."

"Danke," said Weidekraft, sounding a little tired.

"I will withdraw the needle. I want you to put your handkerchief to the puncture to stop any secondary bleeding. In a moment I will send you on your way." He removed the needle from the Baron's arm and held the contents up to the light. "Such a dark color. Very deep and rich." He nudged Ragoczy with his elbow. "What do you think? Do you know anything about blood, Comte?"

"I have some knowledge of it, yes," said Ragoczy, keeping to himself the opinion that Baron Weidekraft might be in danger of developing a spasm of the lungs.

"Then let me show you what I am doing to unlock its secrets," he said, moving off toward his work-bench. As an afterthought, he said over his shoulder. "Sit up slowly, Baron. When your dizziness fades, you may go, with my thanks."

Baron Weidekraft mumbled something, but levered himself upright on the chaise and sat for a time as if lost in thought; he hardly listened to his host's eager explanation to Ragoczy while he hurried about his work-bench. After a few minutes he checked his handker-chief and rolled down his sleeve but did not bother to retrieve his cuff. Finally he was able to rise and toddle to the door, letting him-self out without disturbing von Ravensberg.

Ragoczy had watched the Baron depart out of the tail of his eye, and thought that the man would surely need to rest before the eve-ning's festivities. He interrupted von Ravensberg apologetically. "My dear Graf, I am most gratified to see your extensive tests you per-form in your studies. I am deeply impressed. But let me recom-mend that you test no more subjects today, or you will have guests unable to enjoy your banquet and ball later."

It took von Ravensberg almost ten seconds to realize what Ragoczy was saying to him. "I take your point. You are right, Comte: as you and I are of approximately equal rank, I take no offense in this interjection. Yes, you are right—I have been letting my disci-pline supercede my obligations as a host." He looked at the small glass tube of blood with the electrical connections attached to both ends. "I will complete this before the blood starts to coagulate, and then I will tend to the gala we will enjoy tonight."

"Then I ask you to excuse me now," Ragoczy said with a slight bow. "I have learned much, and I will devote some cogitation to your techniques." He started toward the door only to be halted by von Ravensberg's comment. "I am glad your good friend Madame von Scharffensee is with you now. My niece can be such a fool."

Text of a letter from Klasse van der Boom in Amsterdam, to Saint-Germain Ragoczy, Comte Franciscus at Château Ragoczy near Lake Geneva, Yvoire, Swiss France; carried by private courier and deliv-ered twenty-one days after being written.

To the most excellent Comte Franciscus, the greetings of Klasse van der Boom in Amsterdam on this, the 3rd day of April, 1818

My dear Comte,

I have sent a request to Professor Olav Pedersen of the University of Uppsala, requesting that he prepare for Eclipse Press a history of

*the reign of Charles XIII, whose death in February must have a great
impact on all of northern Europe, particularly since his successor
was at one time Napoleon's general. Jean Baptiste Bernadotte may be
recognized as Swedish for the sake of the Crown, but he is still a
Frenchman, for all that. As soon as I have an answer from Professor
Pedersen, I will inform you of his decision. It would be a real accomplishment to have such a publication available in the next eighteen
months. I know that is an unrealistic dream—the book has yet to be
written and we cannot drop all other projects for this one—but I believe that such a history will be eagerly sought, and not only by universities, but by learned men, politicians, and others. I apologize for
acting without consulting you on so ambitious a project, but I am
convinced that in this case time is of the essence. I hope you will
agree with me, and will not withhold the necessary funds for this
book.*

*I am also in receipt of a most intriguing manuscript by a Harold
Woodham, a Canadian who has been traveling in America along the
frontier west of the Mississippi River for three years and has made
his journals of that time into a book of great interest. The actual
grammar and spelling are not good, or so James Pomeroy tells me,
but such things can be fixed, and I have turned that task over to
Pomeroy. I have found, as you suggested I would, that Pomeroy is a
most useful addition to our staff here: his skills in his own English
language as well as his abilities as a translator in Greek, Russian,
and Czech have proven their worth many times over. As soon as his
year of probation is complete, I would recommend his engagement
without hesitation. In fact, we will be hard-put to fulfill our publishing schedule for 1819 without him. The work that Woodham has
submitted, in Pomeroy's capable hands, will undoubtedly be improved.* Lives and Customs among the Peoples of the American
Plains *has references to native groups about whom little or nothing
has been published before—or certainly not in Europe.*

*Another interesting manuscript I have received and about which
I am undecided is from Padre Diego Reyes, a Jesuit serving at Santa
Maria en Cielo in Zaragoza, called* A History of the Inquisition in

Spain. *Since that body is still nominally functioning, publishing the work could be construed as an assault on the Church itself, and that could be to our disadvantage. The manuscript is of a reasonable and pious tone, more inclined to support the Inquisition in all but its most flagrant excesses, but it does discuss a few of the questionable practices of the past, actions that cast the Inquisition in a more questionable light than the Church has endorsed. While I am convinced that the book has merit, I am not persuaded that it is a good project for Eclipse Press. Would you be offended if I suggested to the Padre that he submit it to another publisher, perhaps Neu Geschichte in Lubeck? It is far more along their lines than ours, and I do think it is worthy of publication. If you do not object, I will return the manuscript with a letter that Padre Reyes can use when sending the manuscripts to other publishers, Neu Geschichte in particular.*

I am in the process of compiling our schedule for the second half of next year. As soon as I have completed it, I will dispatch it to you with all haste, and I will be glad of your comments on any aspect of the schedule you wish to make. Our sales continue to increase, not as rapidly as I would like, but steadily, and the numbers of copies ordered also increases. If our fortunes continue to improve, in another two years we will be able to expand our program once again, and undertake to reach a much wider readership than is presently the case.

In anticipation of that happy day, I am

> *At your service,*
> *Klasse van der Boom*
> *printer and publisher*
> *Eclipse Press*
> *Amsterdam*

4

Hero pulled off her pelisse, her head throbbing, tossed the garment on the single chair in her room, then sat on the bed, unbuttoned her shoes, and lay back with her eyes closed, hoping a short sleep would stop the ache; she could not face an evening of eating and dancing with her skull feeling as if it had been caught in a vise; her eyes felt as if they had been blackened and her tongue seemed too large for her mouth. Ever since breakfast with Hyacinthie and the ladies, she had been feeling a bit unwell, as if something she had eaten was not quite wholesome. She knew she had to rid herself of the pain and the irritating dazzle in her eyes. She was wondering if she should rub her temples with violet-water, or call Ragoczy to ask him for something from his case of medicaments, when there was a knock at the door. "Yes?" she called. "Who's there?"

"Rogier, Madame," came the answer.

She sat up. "Oh. Come in, Rogier," she said, feeling her hair to be sure the knot was properly in place, and thinking it was awkward not to have her maid in the room as well. "Is anything the matter?"

The door opened and Rogier entered, leaving the door ajar to prevent any semblance of the clandestine. "My master asked me to see how you are."

"I have a headache," she admitted, but could not bring herself to say anything that might cause Ragoczy to worry when he learned of it. "A rest should make it go away in an hour or so."

"Would some tincture of willow-bark help, do you think?" Rogier ventured; he saw she was pale and her face showed signs of strain. "I have that and tincture of pansy as well, or something stronger, if you wish."

She shook her head. "I think I will manage with a little sleep."

"It is likely to be a long evening," Rogier persisted. "You might do better to treat your discomfort now, so that you will not have to leave the festivities early." He saw her hesitate. "I could bring them to you, and you can use them as you see fit."

This suggestion appealed to her. "That would be most welcome, Rogier; thank you."

"If there is anything else you require?"

"No; the two tinctures should be more than enough. I know the Comte doesn't provide laudanum for the headache—or much else other than open wounds to be stitched closed." She pinched the bridge of her nose, making a face as she did. "If you will see I'm not disturbed until three?"

"Of course, Madame," said Rogier, and withdrew to the Rose Room to get the two glass bottles of tincture and a ewer of cold water from the rain-pail outside the window. He brought these in to Hero, setting them on the night-stand next to the bed. "Here you are, Madame. I noticed that your room-ewer was not here, and so I took the liberty of bringing this to you as well."

Hero looked at the bottles and the ewer. "This should be sufficient. If I need anything more, I shall call you. At three I should send for Serilde to help me with preparing for the evening." She had brought a lovely garment: a bias-cut, dark–spruce green, vine-pattern jacquard formal gown with a slight train and prim neckline, a reminder that she was in mourning for her daughter, but not so forbidding as black or dull-purple would be; it was preferable to her other formal gown in dark-amber silk, suitable for private feasts at Scharffensee but too festive for this occasion. The green was preferable in every way. To accompany it, she had a magnificent necklace of diamonds and emeralds, with matching emerald ear-drops, gifts from Ragoczy, that would do much to lend her grandeur in this select company. She trusted Serilde would have the garment ready by the time she rose from her nap. With this in mind, she mixed small amounts of the tinctures in her bedside glass and added water. The taste was not too unpleasant; she reminded herself that this could help her to recover. Once again she leaned back, adjusted the pillows to ease her head, then made up her mind to fall asleep: twenty minutes later, she drifted into a light slumber, and thirty minutes later was solidly asleep.

Shortly after three, Serilde knocked on Hero's door, then went in, walking as softly as she could. She found Hero still sleeping, looking a bit pale but otherwise well. Deciding to give Hero a little more rest, Serilde took out the ball-gown Hero would wear and hung it on the dressing-rack next to the armoire, then selected the dancing slippers and silk stockings before hanging up the pelisse Hero had taken off two hours before. A glance at the clock on the night-stand reminded her that it was time for Hero to be up; she went to the bedside and gently said, "Madame von Scharffensee? Madame von Scharffensee?"

Hero opened her eyes slowly, winced, then looked around. "Serilde. What time is it?"

"Fifteen minutes past three, Madame. You asked to be wakened." Serilde smiled a little. "You will be expected downstairs at five."

"Five. Yes. I remember. Hyacinthie and Constanz." She stretched as she sat up. "Then I suppose I had better dress."

"Yes, Madame."

She saw the gown, and smiled approvingly. "I see you have anticipated me."

"You told me what you wanted for this evening yesterday." Serilde kept her eyes on the gown, not Hero.

"I thank you for being so thorough." She thought of the many times she had been traveling with her father, when she rarely had the help of a well-trained servant. "I do appreciate your efforts."

"How are you feeling, Madame?" Serilde asked, thinking back to the warning Rogier had delivered an hour ago.

"A little dull, but generally better," she said.

"Rogier said you had the headache." She said it matter-of-factly, in case the information were incorrect.

"I did, but it is gone now." This was almost accurate: a little remnant of pain was stuck behind her eyes, but was not enough to complain of; she would have another glass of water with tinctures before she went down to the ball and she was sure she would be ready to face the evening.

"Should I ask the Comte to—"

"No, that won't be necessary; I'm quite restored," said Hero, already feeling perplexed by the headache, for she rarely got them. Perhaps the exigencies of travel had tired her more than she realized. "You already have my ball-gown out." She did her best to smile as she got to her feet. "I'll want my lightest silk underwear, and the most flexible body-band I own."

"Will you want a shawl?" Serilde asked.

"It would probably be best. I think the lovely black one, the one my father sent me from Ankara. It's so light-weight."

"That it is," said Serilde, remembering that the shawl was in the second trunk. "I'll get it directly. After I have laid out your other things. I take it you want the long silk under-tunic?"

"Yes, if you would. The silk is preferable to the cotton." She turned as Serilde approached her so that she could unfasten the sixteen covered buttons down the back of her walking-dress. "You may rest in this room after you have your dinner and your free hour. I don't expect you to wait up for me: I can wake you when I come up."

"You anticipate a long evening," said Serilde, who knew the Schloss servants were predicting the festivities would go on past two in the morning.

"It's likely. Nothing as late as city parties can run, but well past midnight." She was not enthused at the prospect. "I'll need your help, but I don't expect you to stay awake."

"That is kind of you, Madame," said Serilde. "I will be glad to obey."

"Thank you," said Hero, striving to summon up a sense of gaiety for the evening; turning toward the mirror on the middle panel of the armoire, she said, "What are we going to do with my hair tonight, Serilde?"

"I was thinking something simple; with your jewels and the pattern on your gown, a braided coronet will set off the rest and still frame your face. It is also more fitting to your circumstances." She came to Hero's side and touched her bright-brown hair. "Since you say you will not dance—"

"I'm in mourning for Annamaria. Dancing would be disrespectful," said Hero.

"And the Comte does not dance," said Serilde cannily. "Still, you're right. It is bad enough that the Graf has ignored his missing ward for this occasion—you need not follow his example."

"I don't intend to slight him," said Hero, noticing as she swallowed that her head was still a bit sore and her muscles were strained because of it.

"No one would think you would, but you can't help but demonstrate his lack of regard for the missing child." She sighed. "These matters are never easy, are they, Madame?"

"Not in my experience," said Hero.

"It is a fortunate thing that we shall be leaving the day after tomorrow." Serilde spoke as if of nothing more than a change in the weather, but there was much more hidden in her remark than was readily apparent—Serilde was homesick and weary of being away from Sacre-Sang.

"As you say," Hero agreed.

Serilda returned to her present concerns. "Shall I set out the violet scent, or would you prefer the tuberose?"

Hero thought, and said, "Violet, I think."

Serilde opened one of the drawers in the chest and extracted a glass bottle with an elaborate stopper. "Here you are."

"Put it on the dresser, if you would, and then help me out of this frock." She was unbuttoning the cuffs; she bent at the hips to allow Serilde to remove her walking-dress, leaving her standing in a chemise and petticoat over her body-band. She untied the petticoat and stepped out of it, then tugged off her chemise, leaving her in nothing more than a body-band, garters, and under-drawers. She motioned to the laces up the back of the body-band and said, "I should probably wear a bosom-lifter as well."

"I packed the body-band that has a bosom-lifter attached," Serilde reminded her. "It is silk and lightweight."

"That's just what I need," said Hero,

Serilde finished loosening the lacings; with a practiced sweep she removed the undergarment and put it on the end of the bed. "I'll fetch the new body-band."

"Thank you," said Hero, feeling the chill of the room, and wishing that the Schloss was as warm as Château Ragoczy. "Are all the rooms in this place drafty?"

"Every room I have been in is," said Serilde, bringing Hero the body-band with bosom-lifter. She held this over Hero's head so Hero could slip her arms through it, and settle it in place on her torso, then set to tightening the lacings. "How much, Madame?"

"Not too much. There is a banquet tonight, and a supper at midnight. I don't want to burst my stays." She felt no hunger at the mention of food, and was mildly puzzled, since she had not dined at mid-day.

"As you wish, Madame," said Serilde as she did her best to adjust the body-band as Hero wanted.

The long silken under-tunic was selected from her drawer of lingerie; Hero applied a little of the violet perfume between her breasts and then readied herself for the jacquard ball-dress. Serilda slipped the gown over her head and carefully pulled it down into place, taking time to puff the tops of the sleeves and then to straighten the under-arm seam from shoulder to wrist before she busied herself fastening the twenty-two buttons down the back of the gown. When she was finished, she brought out the necklace and ear-drops, handing them to Hero.

"If you will make sure the latch is secure?" Hero asked when she had put on the necklace.

"Certainly," said Serilde, inspecting the complex closing. "It looks tight."

"Thank you. I'll put on my ear-drops after you have dressed my hair."

"Do you want wool-fat for your hair, Madame?" asked Serilde.

"No; I think you've given it sufficient. It is shiny." She pulled the pins out of her hair, loosening the easy knot that was now seriously askew. "I have four pins with diamonds in them. I think I should wear them. If the coronet is to be held in place with pins, surely these would do?"

"As soon as I have brushed your hair, I'll get them, Madame."

"Thank you," said Hero and gave herself over to her maid's expert ministrations.

It lacked fifteen minutes of the hour of five when Ragoczy tapped on Hero's door and was admitted by Serilde; he was very grand in a formal evening suite of black pumps, black-wool unmentionables, a waistcoat of damask black-and-red, a shirt of white-silk and a cravat of black, and a formal coat with swallow-tail cut from black, dull-finish satin. His ruby stick-pin shone on his broad lapel, and his device—the heraldic eclipse: a disk surmounted by raised, displayed wings—hung on a red riband around his neck.

"Oh, very good," Hero exclaimed as she caught sight of him. "You will take von Ravensberg's breath away."

"It is not my intention to do so," said Ragoczy even as he offered her a small, graceful bow. "You are a vision tonight, Madame."

She smiled and played with the hang of her shawl. "Between us, the others will be utterly out-shown."

He offered her his elbow. "Not that it is wise to be too conspicuous."

"I quite agree," she said, slipping her lace-mittened hand through his elbow. "And yet it is tempting."

"As soon as you are ready?" He offered her his arm, and smiled at her as she laid her hand on it. "As we go down, tell me how you found your sons."

She went to the door with him, saying, "I fear the visit with my boys wasn't all I had hoped."

He opened the door and stepped out into the corridor, allowing her to emerge from the room before he closed the door. "Why was that?"

"I'm afraid they are becoming like their grandfather. I had no notion how much he disapproved of me." Her attempt at a smile ended badly. "I knew he felt I was a poor match for his son, but it's much worse than that."

He stopped walking and took her hand from his arm to kiss it. "You would be a fine match for any man of good character, and any rank."

She stared at him. "Tell von Scharffensee that, would you?"

"If it will ease you, I will: my Word on it," he vowed.

From the staircase landing, Hyacinthie watched Ragoczy and Hero, her eyes narrowing. She scowled as she saw Ragoczy kiss Hero gently on the mouth, then use his silken handkerchief to wipe her eyes. With a furious titter, she turned and rushed down the stairs.

"Are you ready to go down? Would you prefer to wait?" Ragoczy asked Hero as he refolded his handkerchief.

"I suppose I'm ready." She once again placed her hand on his arm. "We might as well do this, since we're here."

Ragoczy escorted her to the steep marble staircase and led her down, taking care that she did not trip on her train when it tried to slither under her feet. As he reached down and adjusted the fabric, he noticed a flicker of worry in her eyes. "Is something wrong?"

She had neglected to take a second dose of the tinctures, but decided to say nothing of it. "It is the train. I have forgotten how to walk down stairs without becoming entangled."

"That is why I am here," said Ragoczy, and nodded to Herr Zeidergung and his wife, who were starting down the stairs behind them.

"Good evening, Comte, Madame," said Herr Zeidergung to Ragoczy.

"And to you and Frau Zeidergung." Ragoczy continued to guide Hero down the stairs while taking care to keep her train from getting underfoot again.

The Reception Room was decorated with garlands of vines and a vast bow above the fireplace mantle. Four servants were on hand to pour various libations and to pass plates of herb-flavored cheese to the guests. Two long settees were at angles to the fireplace, providing warmth and ease to those preferring not to stand before the banquet was ready. The consort of musicians, from their place in the ballroom, were tuning up, making ready for a long night of playing; the sound of their instruments carried into the Reception Room, and added to the hum of conversation.

Von Ravensberg arrived with his silent and down-cast ward Hedda. Both were dressed formally but in restrained style, in token of their ongoing sorrow for Hedda's missing sister. The Graf made a point of keeping the child with him and speaking to her frequently, his hand on her shoulder.

"I don't know that this is an appropriate gathering for that girl," Hero observed to Ragoczy as she watched von Ravensberg present Hedda with a glass of watered wine.

"I would tend to agree with you," said Ragoczy. "But I wonder why you say so."

"The company has no children. The nearest one to a child other than Hedda is Hyacinthie, and that makes matters quite awkward for her, for she has no one to share her thoughts with." Hero accepted a glass of straw-colored wine, tasting it once before setting the glass on the sideboard next to them.

"It does not please you?" Ragoczy asked.

"It's not that," she said. "This is going to be a long evening and I have no wish to over-indulge."

"I understand your reticence." Ragoczy nodded to Professor Engelhaus, whose book on infectious diseases would shortly be submitted to Eclipse Press in Amsterdam.

As the Professor approach, Hero excused herself, saying, "I will find you before I go in to dine."

"Enjoy the company," Ragoczy said, and gave his attention to Professor Engelhaus and his theories on pernicious and laudable diseases.

The musicians in the ballroom began to play pleasant airs that would not intrude on any conversation; most of the guests hardly noticed them.

Half an hour later, Hyacinthie arrived in the Reception Room; her ball-gown was a lovely shade of lilac and set off her betrothal gift from her fiancé: a necklace of amethysts and pearls. She was smiling a bit too brightly, and her laughter was a shade too loud, but she made her way through the guests to Medoc's side, and took his arm in a proprietary way before finding her uncle. She frowned briefly at Hedda, then called for a glass of wine. When the gong rang for the banquet, Ragoczy found Hero talking with Hedda, and offered her his escort into the banquet-hall.

"I think Hedda and I will go in together," said Hero. "It will be less obvious that you are not eating."

"Everyone here knows that I have a tiresome condition that makes it necessary for me to take nourishment in private," said Ragoczy, a smile at the back of his eyes.

"That they do," she agreed at once. "But tonight such a lack would be particularly noticeable."

"All right," said Ragoczy, bowing over her hand. "I relinquish you to her." He looked at Hedda, seeing the first sign of animation he had seen in the child since his arrival at Ravensberg. "Good appetite to you both."

Hedda stared at him. "Papa used to tell me that," she said as if unaware of what she said.

"Mine still does," said Hero, and took Hedda's hand.

"Your Papa is still alive?" Hedda marveled.

"I hope so," said Hero, and went through the arch into the banquet-hall; the last of von Ravensberg's guests followed after them.

Ragoczy watched them go, then went to the ballroom and sat down at the clavier while the hired musicians set their instruments down and trudged off to the servants' hall for their dinner. Ragoczy spent the next hour playing works by Scarlatti, father and son; he remembered the father with real affection, recalling the opera he had composed for Giorgianna in Roma over two centuries earlier. His fingers found their way through the tunes of the opera with ease, and he let his mind wander until he saw Hyacinthie approaching him, a half-empty glass of Champagne in her hand. He stopped playing and waited for the young woman.

"Very pretty," Hyacinthie said without any suggestion of enthusiasm.

"You are too kind," Ragoczy replied, and began to play again in a desultory manner.

"Why aren't you in the banquet-hall with the rest of us?" She set the glass down on the clavier's music stand.

"You know I dine in private," he said calmly, and continued playing.

"It's strange of you," she told him bluntly. "You would do better to join us. I want you to—"

"I regret that I must disappoint you, Hyacinthie. Console yourself that there are thirty people who wish you well here tonight."

"Them!" She flung up her hand in disgust. "They are here to please my uncle, not me. Not even he cares—"

"I'm sorry it seems so to you," Ragoczy told her, not wanting to encourage her outburst.

She took his response to heart and changed her manner. "I wanted to thank you for the gift you brought me," she said.

"I am glad you like it," Ragoczy said, now playing a little Haydn.

"Who wouldn't like a jeweled clock? It is better than endless plates and bowls. As if I were going to spend my life in the kitchen!" She leaned on the opened lid of the clavier. "It is by far the richest gift anyone has given me."

"Your uncle is giving you five days of celebrations," Ragoczy pointed out.

"That's different."

"Why do you think so?" Ragoczy asked.

"I think so because he is sending me away. You've seen the man he wants me to marry. He's old and bald and he is a stick, just a *stick*."

Ragoczy studied her intently, his enigmatic gaze making her uneasy. "If you feel so displeased, why did you accept the arrangement?"

"Whomelse am I to marry? My uncle wants to be rid of me, and he knows Medoc is eager for a wife." She stifled a sob. "If I do not marry Medoc, what will my uncle expect me to—" She stopped and lowered her voice. "If you wanted to take me away, I would go with you. You needn't marry me. But I know you would do well by me. Madame von Scharffensee says so: you do well by her."

"Fraulein, you must not talk so to me. It is not fitting. If you are so unhappy, speak to your uncle now, tonight, and discontinue the engagement. The longer you wait, the harder it will be to end." He was unexcited by her agitation, and deliberately kept his voice soft and level so they would not be overheard.

"He doesn't care about what I want," she said in a furious whisper. "He has Hedda now, and that's all he cares about. That and the blood. At least Rosalie is gone." She caught her lower lip in her teeth and stared at him. "I know how to please a man. That's one thing Uncle Wallache taught me. You would not be disappointed."

"But you might be," said Ragoczy, comprehension taking hold of him in a gelid fist. He thought of Hedda's silence and felt a cold dread for the child, and a vitriolic despair for this young woman.

"How could I be disappointed? You are rich and kind." She narrowed her eyes. "I can make you want me."

Ragoczy did not respond to the challenge, saying only, "I am older than Medoc, you know."

"It doesn't matter. You're not like him."

"No, I am not," said Ragoczy, and considered his next step very carefully. "You must know that what you propose is impossible."

"Because of Madame von Scharffensee?" she demanded, nodding several times to herself.

"No; because you are too young, and I am . . . what I am." It was less than the truth, but a genuine concern to Ragoczy. He did his best to lessen her disappointment.

"You mean an exile." Hyacinthie clenched her hands. "I don't care."

"You would, in time," he said kindly. "But you can extricate yourself from the engagement and your uncle; you need not require me to bargain you out of your predicament. I will be willing to help you find a suitable post—"

"Be a tutor like Frau Schale? Is that what you think I want?"

"I think you want to free yourself from—"

She did not allow him to finish. "You would make me a *servant*?" Her eyes blazed with fury. "A *servant*?"

"I was thinking the mistress of your own school," he said gently.

"But a servant, nonetheless." She raised her hand and slapped him before she turned on her heel and hurried away, calling back over her shoulder. "How dare you? I thought you would *help* me!"

Ragoczy watched her go, a cold dismay coming over him. As he resumed another Scarlatti air, he decided it was a very good thing he and Hero would be leaving shortly.

Text of a letter from an anonymous informant in Saint-Ange to Egmond Talbot Lindenblatt, Magistrate, Yvoire, Swiss France; left at the municipal hall in Yvoire.

On the night of April 5ᵗʰ, 1818,
*   Magistrate Lindenblatt,*
*   I believe it is my duty to inform you that I have observed a num-*
ber of cloaked and masked men leave the Bradnauer farm and pro-
ceed along the village lane to the road leading to Sacre-Sang. I
counted at least nine men, all mounted, all carrying pistols in saddle-
holsters. The hour was after midnight but before the clock struck
one. I was on guard at the fountain in the market-square. I am not
ashamed to say I hid from the men and resolved to follow them, for
the night being very dark, I doubted they would ride faster than a
walk; they would not risk their horses for no reason. It was ap-
proaching two when they reached their destination.
*   Keeping close behind them, I continued to trail them until they*
reached the edge of Sacre-Sang, where I observed them enter a
house near the village church by its kitchen door, leaving their
horses tied behind the barn. Shortly after, a single man arrived on
foot. He, too, was cloaked and masked, and so I cannot say beyond
all doubt who he was; he carried a sack over his shoulder containing
I know not what, but I can say he must be from the area of Sacre-
Sang, for I heard no horse before he arrived, therefore I assume he
walked, and with such a burden, I doubt he would travel far.

The guard in the village paid him no notice, which convinces me more than all the rest that the man is from the immediate vicinity. It is most sad to think that the suppositions are true and that the aid for the outlaws of this region comes from a man or men who lives here. I wish I had been able to discover who the local man is, so that he might be called before you for an explanation of his activities. As it is, I can say only that the man seemed tall, but that may be because of the sack, and that he remained with the masked men for two hours, and when he left, he was no longer carrying the sack he had brought to their meeting, but I had to slip around the house to the church so that none of the men could see me, which gave me only an instant in which to observe the local man.

I realize that it would be improper and useless for me to make a formal accusation on this small amount of information, but I will continue to keep watch, and it may be that I will have another opportunity to observe these robbers again, and learn more about them. If I should do, I will inform you at once, as I do now, through the good offices of Pere Stechnadel of Saint-Ange, who has taken down my account and prepared it for you.

*Believe me
Your friend*

5

Hero's left eye was too swollen to open, and her brow was crusted with her own blood, but she struggled to memorize her surroundings in the hope that she would be able to report them to the authorities: it allowed her to believe she would not die here. She was tied to an old wooden frame that might once have housed the gears from the water-wheel; it leaned against the wall so that she was more upright than supine, but she could not stand, so the bonds forced all of her weight onto her wrists and ankles. The knots were tight enough to hold her firmly, so tight that after an hour, sensation was deadened in her hands and feet. The area where she was confined was small, dark, and dank. Broken beams lay at odd angles to the floor; many had lichen and mosses growing on them. Only one fair-sized window high up the wall provided any hint of the day outside, and it was fading as the steep little valley fell into afternoon shadow. The smell was dank, slightly woody and slightly moldy. The constant guggle of water provided the kind of sound the ocean could—steady, loud enough to intrude, but not so loud as to overcome. A pair of glass-chimneyed candles sat on the upended barrel near the door, their length half-gone, their glass chimneys already faintly clouded with soot: Hero reckoned she had been dazed for the better part of an hour, and that, in turn, worried her.

Light, rapid steps traipsed up the steep, rickety stairs from the floor below, and a moment later Hyacinthie, her dress torn, her walking shoes mired, her hair disheveled, all but bounced into Hero's improvised cell. "Awake at last," she enthused. "Well, Madame, and how did you enjoy your nap? You were unconscious for more than half an hour." Her eyes were bright as splintered glass and her voice was almost a shriek.

". . . m . . . not 'njoy." She was appalled at how stiff her lips were, and how much it hurt to try to move them. She tried to remember how she had got here, and had a dim impression of leaving the Schloss with Hyacinthie, following her along a maze of woodland lanes, and then . . .

"I'm sorry to hear that, as I'm sorry I had to hit you with my walking-staff, but there was no other way," said Hyacinthie in a singsong parody of good manners. "I suppose you don't know how long it took me to drag you up here, since you were unconscious. It took quite a while to tie you up, too. I ought to leave you alone to rest, but I couldn't, not before I reassured myself that you were comfortable." She approached Hero watchfully, alert to any sign that her bonds were untied. "Still caught fast. But the spider was a woman, Arachne, wasn't she? in the Greek myths?—I think so. Frau

Schale gives me so many things to remember, as if any of them are important." She picked up a long, thin knife from where she had left it. "Let me see. Veins near the skin are blue. My uncle says the blood bears all our secrets, and I still don't know yours. I should have more blood to study, as he does." She came to Hero's side and with a playful flick of her wrist, cut off Hero's left ear-lobe, dismissing Hero's shocked cry with a furious titter. "You cannot say you'll miss it, Madame. And there is blood now. My uncle does not study female blood, but I think it means as much as males', don't you?"

Hero wanted to shout at her, to demand to be released, but all she could manage was a muffled sort of roar. Tears of vexation and anger filled her eyes, making her left eye hurt even more as the tears pressed against the swollen tissues. She felt the blood run down her neck, the only thing warm in the chilly room.

"Your blood is your heritage, so my uncle claims, and by studying the blood, heritage can be determined. He intends to show that every race, every nation, has its own blood, and that identifies those who share blood." She whisked the knife along Hero's cheek. "How bright it is, like a fire in winter."

All Hero could manage was a muffled scream of outrage.

"You are so helpless," said Hyacinthie.

"Sto'!" Hero wralled.

"What a foolish woman you are, Madame." Hyacinthie put her hands on her hips, mimicking the manner of a parent to a recalcitrant child. "You cling to the Comte because no one else will have you, and you cannot see that it is pity, not affection, that keeps him with you. Better to let him go so he can have someone who will adore him and serve him. You are too old to pleasure him. He will want someone younger. Your death will show your devotion to him better than your life."

". . . don' . . . know," Hero managed with a terse, single burst of laughter. "The Com' . . . He's old."

"He is a grown man, who knows the world and will take me everywhere; he will not lock me away in a draughty house with no one for company, no friends but his to call upon us, never take me to balls or buy me pretty things," Hyacinthie said as if daring Hero to contradict her. "If Herr Medoc is acceptable to Uncle Wallache, the Comte must be much more so."

"He's . . . old," Hero repeated.

This time Hyacinthie did not respond to the jibe. "I know he will want me as he has never wanted you, as soon as you are gone from his life." She wiped the knife on her ruined skirt. "I wonder how long it will take him to forget you?"

"Ne . . . ver," Hero forced herself to say, doing everything she could to enunciate in spite of her split lips and loose teeth.

"At least his memories will not require him to see you as you are now, all cut and bruised and bleeding. He would be revolted, disgusted. If you had the misfortune to survive, you would be hideous to look upon, all scared and battered." Hyacinthie giggled. "What a tragedy that would be."

Hero felt tears again, and the same revulsion she had experienced when she had glimpsed Ragoczy's scars; she was ashamed of her weakness. The last thing she wanted to do was reveal any sign of dismay to this freakish young woman, or to admit any of her accusation could be right. She did her utmost to speak clearly. "What now?" The effort the question demanded of her was enormous and it left her feeling depleted. She tried to move her fingers and toes but could not.

"Now I arrange to gather your blood. I have a glass jar for it. I need to study it, don't you see?" Her laughter was short and terrible. "Then you will vanish—just vanish."

"Why . . . mus' I?" Hero muttered.

Hyacinthie was not listening. "Originally I planned to burn this place down, but I realized it would attract attention, and you might be rescued before you died, so I reconsidered. A fire was too obvious. Vanishing has advantages. Perhaps your body will wash up down-stream, but if I wedge it under the log-jamb a little way down-stream, it may be a while before you're found, and by then you'll be nothing but bones. No one will know they're yours. You will be only a memory, and even that won't last very long, you being a stranger in the area." She scampered over to the window. "I won't move you until dark, and that gives you another three hours. Don't worry," she said glancing flirtatiously over her shoulder. "I've thought it all through. They won't find you here."

"'s this . . . what . . . you did . . . t' the—" Hero struggled to speak; she hoped to keep Hyacinthie talking while she tried to think of a way to escape. Her father had taught her, on their travels, always to think, never to panic: now his lessons would pay off.

"Rosalie, you mean?" She came back to Hero's side. "Rosalie vanished, too. Uncle Wallache thinks it was Gypsies who took her."

"You . . . don'?" Hero was feeling quite sick; she tasted bile at the back of her tongue.

"No. I know what happened." Hyacinthie did a quick, dancelike turn. "She fell down an old well."

Any hope that Hero had that she might be able to appeal to Hyacinthie's compassion faded to nothing. "When?"

"At the end of summer, I think it was, or a little later." Hyacinthie shrugged. "I don't think she's still alive, if you're wondering about it." She came up to Hero and lightly ran the point of the knife along Hero's jaw, leaving a bloody path behind. "I haven't broken your nose yet—that's for later. My uncle Wallache told me it hurts horribly, worse than breaking a leg." She went back to the window. "And it's worse than being poked by his thing in all the places he— He used to say he'd break mine—my nose—if I didn't let him do—" She stopped abruptly. "I was a child then. I needed to be taught. I needed to show my gratitude." she said dutifully.

Hero blinked her right eye, trying to decide what Hyacinthie meant. She was appalled at what the young woman seemed to be saying, but her behavior was so peculiar, she might misunderstand her intentions. "When?" she asked again.

"I was much younger then, and there was only me to cater to his needs. He told me I was the center of his home." She smirked, but the smirk faded. "He stopped with me after my courses began. He said it would be dangerous to continue and so I did not receive him again. He ignored me after that." Her voice rose. *"Ignored me!"* She slashed at Hero's arm and paid no attention to her screams. "Once he had Rosalie and Hedda, he couldn't wait to be rid of me. Of *me*! What could I do?" Her knife sliced at Hero's skirt, nicking her shin. "He gave me to that old man! *ME!*"

Hero flinched and clamped her jaws shut, not wanting to give Hyacinthie the pleasure of hearing her shriek. *Much more of this,* she thought distinctly, *and I will pass out again.* A dizziness was forming at the back of her skull so that every motion made her a bit queasy. She was very frightened, but in a distant sense, as if she were watching herself rather than having the experience. This could not last, and she knew it, but she determined to make the most of it as long as it continued.

Hyacinthie lit another candle and placed it near Hero. "So I can see you better. You've only got the one eye open." She stared toward the window, her face dreamy. "They say bears used to come here, that they tore down the door. Bears or not, the door is gone. I might be able to get people to believe that bears ate you."

This boded ill for Hero; she looked toward the window, blinking to clear the scum of tears and the last bit of blood from her eye. "Wha . . . are you go'n' to do?" she struggled to ask.

She put the jar on the floor under Hero. "I need some more of your blood, so I will take it, to see how much it changes while you lie here." Hyacinthie wiped the knife again, her eyes glittering as she contemplated her task. "Now, Madame, where should I begin? Not the throat: the throat's too fast. The leg might be good. Behind the knee, perhaps, or in the groin. Uncle Wallache says there are many large vessels in the legs." She cocked her head, thinking. "I don't know how quickly I want you to die. I'd better decide that first, don't you think?"

"Tha' wou' . . . be wise," said Hero, knowing Hyacinthie was completely unaware of her sarcasm. She tried to speak more clearly. "Unwise."

"What? Killing you?" Hyacinthie all but sprung onto her toes. "But it *is*. It is very wise. You cannot be allowed to have him, not any longer. I need him, and I can make him want me." She raked the point of her knife along Hero's left sleeve, all the way from her shoulder to her fingers, leaving a long furrow opening the length of her arm. "You have had him long enough. I will have him now."

Hero felt her weight shift a little, and realized that Hyacinthie had cut one of the ropes holding her to the gear-housing. She tried to pull on the rope, but the long cut was bleeding and it hurt to move. She took a deep breath and tried again.

"Soon the deer will come down to the stream to drink," Hyacinthie crooned. "The shepherds will bring in their flocks, and the cows will go home for milking." She swung around to glare at Hero. "So you mustn't think that you're going to be rescued if you hear steps along the path. No one knows where we are. No one cares."

"How . . . can you . . . be . . ." Hero asked; what little vision she had was starting to blur, from tears or loss of blood she could not tell.

"I know because I planned it to be this way. I have left nothing to chance," Hyacinthie declared. "I worked it all out. I'm much cleverer than Uncle Wallache thinks I am. I am not a stupid woman, no matter what he believes. He should have kept me with him. I could help him. I can help the Comte."

"How?" Steeling herself, Hero dragged on the cut rope, and this time she felt the fibers give way, and pain shot into her hand.

"I know how to study. I know how to do the observations my uncle does. I have kept journals of my own, private ones. I have recorded all that has transpired at Ravensberg since I came. This will show how useful I am, to Uncle Wallache and the Count. I know the Comte is interested in all this because his publishing house produced Uncle Wallache's book. Uncle Wallache says—" She saw that Hero had freed her hand, and that it was now dangling at her side, bleeding steadily. "You want to hurry death along, is that it?"

"No. I . . . wan' . . . ou'," Hero said, trying to get her arm to work. She could feel only weakness and pain in her loose hand, and that frightened her more than Hyacinthie's knife.

"In a while," said Hyacinthie at her most soothing. "You needn't rush. We still have plenty of time."

Hero summoned up every bit of strength she could and jerked against her remaining bonds; the ropes did not give, but the gear-housing jolted against the wall and a board from the wall behind her fell with an abrupt bang that was loud as a thunder-clap in the enclosed space.

"Enough of that!" Hyacinthie screeched, and threw herself atop Hero, her knife raised and ready. She made an effort to stab down, but the gear-housing moaned and the upper brace sagged.

Another board fell, and then came the sound of heavy footsteps from below, and men shouting from somewhere nearby.

"No! It's not time!" Hyacinthie swung off Hero and rushed to the top of the precarious stairs, her face set in a ferocious smile; Hero forced herself to listen intently, to remain as still as she could, until she knew who had come into the mill. "They must go away."

"Fraulein Hyacinthie! Madame von Scharffensee! Are you here?" The voice was Herr Medoc's. "Call out if you can hear us."

Hero heard this and wanted to shout aloud, but she could only make a muffled cry, and wondered if she could be heard at all.

"There are stairs. Be careful going up them," said a voice Hyacinthie did not recognize. "Some of the treads are loose, or rotten."

"Thanks," said Medoc, ascending.

Hyacinthie took a position where Medoc would not see her at first; she crouched low, and as his head appeared in the stairwell opening, she launched herself at him, snarling as she raised her arm to shove her knife down through his shoulder deep into his chest, leaning down hard to drive the point as far into his lung as possible. Blood spread down his jacket and he coughed wetly. Hyacinthie withdrew the knife and was rewarded with a spurting fountain that struck her face and upper body; she plunged the knife in again, this time into the base of his neck. He jerked, blood sprayed from his mouth, and he made a clumsy attempt to dislodge her from his back. She hung on as he staggered, knees collapsing and sending him face forward onto the sagging treads, where he lay, bleeding and spasming as life left him, and Hyacinthie rose, knife still in hand, face and shoulders encaramined, to confront Heller Wegbruden, who had picked up a large plank to serve as a shield against her. The metallic odor of fresh blood intensified, along with the stink of relaxed bowels.

"Hyacinthie!" Otto Gutesohnes shouted from the open doorway below. "Hyacinthie! Don't!"

"I'll kill you!" she shouted at the men coming into the mill. She struck out with her foot, hit the plank, and sent Wegbruden back down the stairs, not quite falling, but stumbling enough to impact the pillar at the foot of the stairs.

"Stay where you are!" Gutesohnes told her. "I'll come get you."

"No!" She looked around wildly. "Go away! All of you!"

Gutesohnes spoke for all of them. "I can't do that, Hyacinthie. I have to carry Herr Medoc back to the Schloss."

She screamed and kicked at Medoc's corpse, then made her way up the stairs again, only to find Ragoczy, his clothes marred by moss and splinters, in the act of freeing Hero from the gear-housing. "You!" She hesitated, baffled by his presence: none of this was what she had planned. "How did you get here?"

"I climbed the outside of the mill," he said calmly as he continued to work on Hero's bonds. It had been a hard climb and his shoulder was sore from the effort.

"How could you? It's steep." Hyacinthie regarded him suspiciously.

"It was not an easy task," he said, and bent to free her ankles, saying to Hero, "Do not try to stand. I'll hold you."

"You won't," said Hyacinthie, her fury returning. "You can't."

"But I can," he said, keeping his voice steady. "If I do not help her, and soon, she will die from her wounds."

"Yes! She will!" Hyacinthie said with renewed purpose. "She should die." She ran at Ragoczy, knocking him away from Hero and stabbed his arm near his half-healed wound. He gasped and she was on him, gouging at his face. "You can die with her!"

Ragoczy fought off the cold ache that was spreading through his arm and shoulder; he seized her wrist in a powerful grip, then pushed her off him and wrapped his arms around her, confining her in an unbreakable grasp. "Gutesohnes!" he shouted. "Come up! Now! Bring the rope." Blood from her face and clothes added to the ruin of his shirt and coat.

Hyacinthie struggled and twisted in Ragoczy's effective restraint. She kicked and poked at his leg with her knife, cursing him comprehensively in terms that would have astonished her uncle to hear.

"I will not let go, no matter what you call me or where you cut me," he said levelly. "You have done damage enough, Fraulein: you will do no more."

"Goat-fucking scum," she yowled, trying again to break his hold, to no avail. "I wounded you, you toad-turd!"

"Yes. You did wound me," he said with almost no emotion; she continued to squirm, and he said, "You will not get away, you know."

Gutesohnes swore as he did his best not to step on Medoc's body. "There's a lot of blood," he warned as he emerged in the upper room; he was pale and distressed by what he saw. "Mein Gott," he exclaimed as he caught sight of Ragoczy and Hyacinthie, and Hero, sagging against the gear-housing.

"Fraulein Hyacinthie needs to be subdued before—"

"You shall not *touch* me, you son of a syphilitic Turk," she spat at Gutesohnes.

"—we can carry her back to the Schloss." He increased the tightness of his clench as she poked her knife into his hip.

"Don't! *Do not! DO NOT!*" She flung her head back and wailed in fury.

"I am afraid I must, Fraulein," said Gutesohnes, appalled.

"I will *kill* you!" Hyacinthie crowed.

"You had best get the knife from her," Ragoczy recommended. "She will use it if she can."

As if to prove this, Hyacinthie thrust her knife into his thigh. "Bleed! Why don't you bleed?"

Gutesohnes approached hesitantly; he did not know how to confine Hyacinthie without offending her sensibilities, and although he knew it was a foolish reluctance, he found it difficult to overcome a life-time of habit. In the hope of calming her, he spoke to her as he would a startled horse, on one note, unhurrriedly. "I am going to take your knife, Fraulein Hyacinthie. Don't do anything reckless, will you."

For an answer she screamed and tried to lunge at him; Ragoczy held her fast.

"Comte, I don't know what—"

"Start with the knife, and then get your rope around her feet and work your way up," Ragoczy said.

"All right," Gutesohnes said in a tone that was far from convinced this would work. He took a step closer and saw the knife-blade flicker as she tried to keep him at bay.

"Carefully," Ragoczy warned him. "She will not hesitate to hurt you."

Hyacinthie growled something nasty and stabbed Ragoczy again.

Hero, who had been observing all this as if from a distance, now gathered up as much determination as she could, and in spite of the muzziness obscuring her thoughts, she fell forward, grabbing for the knife. She felt a cut open in the web between her thumb and finger, but she held on grimly and finally jerked the knife out of Hyacinthie's hand before crumpling onto the floor.

Gutesohnes moved in quickly and worked rapidly to tie Hyacinthie securely, in spite of her taunts and spitting. Panting with his last effort, he regarded her, aghast. "What has happened to her?"

Ragoczy shook his head. "I do not know. But whatever it is, it is deep and long-coming." He thought back to others he had known whose sudden lapses into madness had terrified and bewildered all who saw them.

"Can anything be done?" Gutesohnes asked while Ragoczy knelt beside Hero. "For Fraulein Hyacinthie?"

"For now, we can return her to the Schloss." He touched Hero's neck gently, reassuring himself that her pulse still beat there. "Will you bring up the sack of medicaments from below? I must clean and bind these wounds before I can move Madame." He did not add that her blood loss had already put her in danger.

"What of Fraulein Hyacinthie?" Gutesohnes asked, eyeing her wrestling with her bonds.

"I rely upon you and Wegbruden to carry her. I doubt she will walk on her own accord." Ragoczy motioned to Gutesohnes to move quickly.

Hyacinthie yelled obscenities.

"I'll be back in a minute or two. Then we'll get Medoc off the—" With that, he picked his way down the stairs, again taking care not to touch the body, and to step around the treads made sick and sticky with blood.

"Vile! You're all *vile!*" Hyacinthie's wriggling over-balanced her and she fell to the floor, cursing more emphatically. "You have shit in your veins, or you would bleed," she said, glaring at Ragoczy. "You are unnatural."

"Some would say so." Ragoczy glanced toward her to be sure her bonds were firm, then spoke to Hero. "As soon as Gutesohnes returns, I am going to bandage your arm and your face. We must staunch your bleeding first, so I'll put rolled lint to help stopper the wound, and I'll give you some of the sovereign remedy I have so that you will not have to endure the fever of infection for very long. I'll use a salve to treat your wounds, one that will lessen the hurt and encourage proper healing."

Hyacinthie laughed furiously. "He'll do all that for you, and more, but you will still be scarred." Her laughter rose, then stopped as abruptly as it had begun.

Hero opened her eye and focused on his face. "Will I?" she asked. "Be scarred?"

Much as he wanted to tell her something else, Ragoczy could not lie, although he softened the blow as much as he could. "Very likely."

"Oh." It was the answer she dreaded, and she turned her face aside so she would not have to endure the compassion she saw in his unwavering gaze.

Text of a letter from Oskar Cavelle of Halle, to the Egmond Talbot Lindenblatt, Magistrate, Yvoire, Swiss France; carried by private messenger on foot and delivered two days after it was written.

The greetings of Oskar Cavelle of Halle to the Magistrate Linden-blatt of Yvoire, on this, the 6th day of April, 1818.

On my oath and as God may see the truth of what I say, pledged before the priest of Saint-Piere-le-Moine, who is also serving as scribe, that these are the things I have witnessed:

Eight days since I ventured up to the shepherds' station above Boege, in order to prepare and stock it for the summer when the shepherds remain out with their flocks; as the head of the wool-workers in Halle, it is my duty to attend to the shepherds' stations throughout our area, and to resupply these stations as such is re-quired. The station of which I speak now is among the largest of the five we have: there is a spring there, so water is plentiful, and the shepherds' station has been maintained there for many, many gener-ations. When I reached the station, I saw at once that it had been oc-cupied most of the winter. There were no foodstuffs left in the station-hut, the pens had horse-dung in them, and the bedding had been removed from the sleeping-racks inside the station-hut. I also discovered a leather bag of gun-powder, which I am sending with this account to make my account more credible.

In examining the rest of the shepherds' station, I came upon parings from horses' hooves in the largest pen. I would have thought the wolves would have eaten them all, as they do, but there were some that were untouched, and three horse-shoe nails as well. There were signs of horses' chewing on the wooden fence enclosing the pen. There was also a small amount of rotted hay in the manger that clearly had not been there all winter. These various factors have led me to believe that there were outlaws in the station through part of the winter, which worries me, for they may return here again, this time not only to take supplies, but to steal sheep, or to hold the shep-herds for ransom. It also means that they are likely still in the area and may be planning to strike out at our farmholds and markets as the summer comes on. That is the most disturbing possibility of all, for then everyone in the region will suffer, not just the shepherds and those of us who work with wool.

Among the items I have found around the shepherds' station, and they were few, was a beer-stein bearing the mark of the tavern in Sacre-Sang, which I am convinced indicates that these men are likely the men who stole from their stores. It may be coincidence, or it may have been left there by one of the shepherds, not the outlaws, but it could be a significant discovery, and so I bring it to your attention.

Perhaps if the Magistrates' Guards could be sent to scour the high valleys the criminals might be discovered and detained before they can work any more mischief, or perhaps the men of the region may be granted the right to detain any suspicious men to bring to the attention of the Magistrates' Court. Whatever you decide, I am prepared to do my part in bringing an end to the robbers' reign of lawlessness.

If you wish to learn more from me, send me word and allow me four days to reach Yvoire; I cannot leave my work without arranging for someone to serve in my place while I am gone. With that single reservation, I am

> Yours to command
> Oskar Cavelle
> (his mark)
> woolworker of Halle
> Swiss France

6

"I hope," said Ragoczy, doing his best to present an unperturbed demeanor, "that Madame von Scharffensee will be well enough to travel in two or three days; her fever is much diminished and her appetite is returning. If she continues to improve, we will be gone shortly. I regret, Graf, that we have had to trespass on your hospitality in this way." He spoke with sincerity; he did not like being at

Ravensberg and wanted to be gone from the Schloss at the first opportunity: he knew Hero shared his aversion to the place.

"You have reason to want to be gone," said von Ravensberg in punctiliously.

"As you must want us gone." Ragoczy had been busy in the library for most of the morning, and was a bit surprised to see von Ravensberg here. It was four days since the confrontation in the old mill and only the second time Ragoczy had encountered von Ravensberg since Medoc's funeral, two days before. During those intervening days, the Schloss had been filled with a growing tension that was made more oppressive by the occasional screams issuing from the room to which Hyacinthie had been confined; they echoed eerily through the Schloss as if she were already a ghost haunting it.

"I realize it is a great inconvenience for us both, for you to be kept here while your companion recovers from her wounds, at least to the point that her healing begins and it is safe for her to travel." He coughed once and fingered the revers of his Turkish dressing-gown. "You must feel it keenly, for there is certain to be pressing business awaiting your return to Yvoire."

"You must feel this keenly, as well, and will be glad to have us gone. Your prospects for coming months cannot be happy ones for you," said Ragoczy, puzzled by von Ravensberg's behavior; with the hurried departure of all the guests but Ragoczy and Hero, the Graf had cut himself off from most of the household, emerging from his laboratory for meals and little else; his appearance in the library was unanticipated, leaving Ragoczy to wonder what von Ravensberg hoped to accomplish.

Outside the window a light morning shower was giving way to gloriously blue skies and a day as clean-swept as the floor of the Great Hall. Snow remained on the high slopes, but the freshets and streams were active and full, evidence that most of it would be gone in a month. The scent of cherry and apple blossoms filled the air, carried through the open windows on a flirting breeze.

"What cannot be changed must be endured," said von Ravensberg. "Things have been thrust upon me that I must—" He stopped. "Not that I would wish you to leave while your companion is making her first recovery from—but your presence creates an awkwardness." His tone implied that he wanted to be rid of that awkwardness.

"I apologize for any discommodation our presence may cause you; I wish we were able to leave at once: believe this. Nothing would be more welcome to me than to relieve you of some of the burdens we have inadvertently imposed. In a day or two we will at least remove to Ravenstein, to the posting inn. Of course I will provide the wages for your staff whose service you have lost in our maintenance, and money for the hay and oats my horses consume," Ragoczy said, putting the book he had been reading aside.

Von Ravensberg's face was expressionless. "All things considered, giving you the shelter of my roof is the least I could do, being that my niece is the cause for your remaining at Ravensberg. No recompense is necessary. It would be crass of me to accept your generosity." He went to an easy chair near the fireplace, stood beside it but did not sit down. "I wanted to inform you that I have received notification that the Magistrate will be here this afternoon, with his clerk, to make an official determination in regard to how Constanz Medoc died. Before any judgment can be rendered, the Magistrate will decide if there can or should be a trial. I wonder if you would like to address him directly, given the severity of the attack you sustained? Or would you prefer to say nothing about it, for Madame von Scharffensee's sake."

Ragoczy did not answer at once, and when he did, it was with conviction. "I think it may be prudent to give my report. The event was a confusing one; Magistrate Schmidt will have many accounts to compare. The more information he has, the more apt he is to arrive at the truth."

"Certainly; if that is what you want," said von Ravensberg as if this were a final disgrace; he refused to look at Ragoczy. "You are completely within your rights to do so, and any embarrassment you sustain is not likely to follow you as far as Swiss France. The Magistrate will be grateful for your testimony." He sighed, still unwilling to look directly at Ragoczy. "An exile, like yourself, does not have to uphold the same decorum that those of us established in a place have to preserve."

Ragoczy did not respond to von Ravensberg's deprecation. "You have much to stomach at present." He regarded the Graf in studious sympathy. "Your patience is wearing thin: hardly surprising, with so much unresolved."

"I have my burdens; you have yours. I am cognizant of your scruples, and I can hardly blame you for—You endured much at my . . . niece's hands, you and Madame von Scharffensee. I cannot tell you how chagrined I am by how she has behaved." He waved one hand in dismissal. "Enough of this most calamitous reflection. What's done cannot be undone. I will do as much as I can to guard our name; I gave Medoc a fine burial, so we cannot be said to have slighted him, and I have arranged to pay my ward's dowry to Medoc's brother, as a tribute to his memory." He assumed an unctuous air, and went on as if this were the sole purpose of their conversation. "You may like to come to my laboratory; I am subjecting the latest sample of blood I have to an electrical current. Surely this must interest you."

"Ordinarily it probably would, but just now, I think not," said Ragoczy, more for good manners than genuine emotion.

"As you wish. If you change your mind, I will be pleased to demonstrate my process to you. I am sure you will find it fascinating." He inclined his head and turned to leave the room.

Ragoczy's question stopped him. "Have you thought of what will become of her? Of Fraulein Hyacinthie?"

Von Ravensberg shot an infuriated glance at him, but gave no other outward sign of displeasure. "I assume they'll execute her. The privilege of my rank does not extend to her, and she must answer for her deeds without me to shield her. The law cannot be seen to condone murder. She has killed her fiancé and attempted to kill Madame von Scharffensee and you."

"She is not sane," said Ragoczy in the manner of someone commenting on the weather. "The court will make allowances for that."

"Why should the court do so?" Von Ravensberg was on guard now, for all that he tried to seem confident.

"If not her state of mind, her age should have some effect on the degree of responsibility she is assigned." He thought back to Rome, where sentences were often reduced for those under the age of twenty-one. "There is legal precedence for such judgment."

"The mercy of a quick death and then a memory soon forgotten would be the most she should hope for, not a lingering hell in an asylum, or a life of confinement in a prison, the object of the most vile attention and humiliation." Von Ravensberg came a few steps back into the room. "You have no wish to see her free, do you?"

"No, but I doubt her death will negate her deeds," Ragoczy said.

"It will answer Medoc's family," said von Ravensberg, "and help to restore the honor of this House."

A distant shriek shuddered through the marble halls of the Schloss.

"Do you think so." Ragoczy said, making no mention of the cry they had both heard and wondering if von Ravensberg would mention it. "Why is that?"

Von Ravensberg did not say anything about the sound; he shook his head. "You cannot understand. It is not in your blood. You have no grasp of our nimiety in the eyes of the public—"

"I know that riches and possessions are often envied by those in less advantageous circumstances," Ragoczy interjected.

"Then you know the resentment we suffer on that account. Despite your wealth, as an exile, you are unable to comprehend the manner in which we will have to ameliorate—"

"Because I do not see that making a sacrifice of an insane child will rehabilitate your family name? Given her history, no, Graf, I do not understand; I am baffled by your posture in regard to her," Ragoczy kept his temper in check, asking in his most reasonable tone, "How can you be indifferent to her plight?"

"This from you? How many times did she stab you?" Von Ravensberg folded his arms. "I was told it was eleven times."

The actual count was twenty-three times, and every wound she inflicted still ached. "Something along those lines," he answered in as unflustered a voice as he could. "She was raving when she did it."

"You find that an excuse?" von Ravensberg asked. "I would have thought you, of all people, would hold her accountable for her actions."

"Because she stabbed me?" Ragoczy shook his head. "She is not the first who has, and she will not be the last." Over the centuries he had received many dire wounds, but the only one that had left a mark on him was the scars that crossed his abdomen, tokens of the evisceration that had killed him almost four thousand years ago; since his death no injury, no matter how hideous, had left a lasting scar.

Von Ravensberg nodded twice. "That is what I meant. Her attack on you—a man of rank equal to mine—cannot be allowed to go unpunished. I am surprised that you are not demanding retribution more vehemently than I. She concealed her acts, which shows that they were purposeful, not impulsive, as true madness is known to be. That you had to seek her out and withstand her attempts on your life . . . And that is not all: she has maimed your companion. Madame von Scharffensee will walk with a limp and her face will never recover from the marks she made on it; you've said so yourself."

"That is more difficult to pardon, but I doubt that Madame von Scharffensee will be restored because Hyacinthie is dead."

"A philosophy of weakness and concession!" von Ravensberg declared. "You will not find such pap in the veins of Austrians."

"I doubt you will find character in the blood at all," said Ragoczy, his reserve becoming more marked.

"Blood is blood; it carries the national vigor, and the heritage of every man alive. Even you cannot deny that. One day I shall demonstrate it beyond cavil, no matter how little you may think it possible.

What is borne in blood is the measure of the man," von Ravensberg said.

"No, Graf: what is borne in blood is the incarnation of the soul," Ragoczy responded quietly.

"Soul?" von Ravensberg scoffed. "You know very little about it: I have devoted my life to its study."

"I know it is the sum total of the uniqueness of the person who possesses it. Nothing is more personal, more essential, to any living human."

"That is what I seek to demonstrate: blood is our heritage, a thing to be measured and certain, not some foolish romantic notion of the supernatural," von Ravensberg said emphatically. "Every nation has its character that is given at birth. Austrians and Germans are the descendants of the Franks. More than the French, we bear the heritage of Charlemagne."

Ragoczy recalled the very tall, big-shouldered, strong-willed leader of the Franks from a thousand years before, and the men he gathered around him. "They were ambitious barbarians—as were almost all peoples in Europe then."

"You tell me my niece is a barbarian because she is Austrian? Barbarian! Hardly. Not that any man of education would believe that of Charlemagne: he was the founder of our civilization, a great man of vision." Von Ravensberg tapped his toe impatiently, his eyes snapping with annoyance.

Ragoczy refused to be distracted by von Ravensberg's self-congratulatory claim. "I tell you that Hyacinthie is Hyacinthie and no one else; her blood is unique to her, far beyond being Austrian. Heritage she may have, as do all people, but she is inimitable, as is everyone else." He paused, thinking that he would never want to taste her blood no matter how great his need, then continued, "Whatever inclined her to such fury did not come from her blood, it came from what life has imposed upon her."

"That inclines you to defend my niece?" Von Ravensberg's countenance was filled with incredulity.

"It is certainly part of it," Ragoczy said.

"She has done so much to you," von Ravensberg said in astonishment as he regarded Ragoczy with an expression that combined shame with contempt. "Yet you would not execute her."

"And you would." Ragoczy turned the full weight of his dark, enigmatic eyes on von Ravensberg.

The Graf did his best not to flinch. "I have been taught that if we, the leaders, abuse the law, bend it to our fancy and make it lax, we cannot be surprised when our lessers do the same. It for us to set the example, to endorse the actions of the courts, and to support the Magistrates in their duties. You bewilder me. Comte: you say you are of an ancient House, and yet you would spare her life."

"Hyacinthie is mad. I cannot hold her responsible when she cannot be held capable of distinguishing the nature of her acts."

"One of those humanists, are you? a follower of Rousseau and the rest of those foolish idealists? Do you glorify the common man and the state of nature?" von Ravensberg asked, as if finally satisfied to know what prompted Ragoczy's stance. "A man of your rank should have more sense. Those so-called reformers are our enemies. You aid them, but they would destroy you."

Ragoczy did not respond to the rebuke. "I have said it already: she is your niece, and you must share some responsibility for her actions. You did not see her at the mill, or felt the strength her anger gave her. She learned her fury somewhere. You have guided her steps: where she has gone you have sent her."

"I?" He gave Ragoczy an incredulous stare. "How can you make such a claim? You say her blood is singular in character, and so must she be."

Two high, yowling wails reverberated through the Schloss, another reminder that Hyacinthie was still within the walls.

"I say all of the human species has the capacity to do violence, and the capacity for compassion. Like you, I have studied the human condition for many, many years, and I have seen everything that humanity can do." He disliked this kind of intellectual fencing, but he was seeking answers, and was prepared to continue until he had them.

"So you do fancy yourself a philosopher." Von Ravensberg did not make any effort to hide his contempt.

"Nothing so presumptuous," said Ragoczy. "But I have some little understanding of the nature of blood: it is blood that shapes much of what becomes of anyone but it is only a potential: life imposes upon us all; how the impositions are met is found in the blood, unless the exigencies of life go beyond the capacity of blood." He thought of Acanna Tupac, of Leocadia, and Csimenae, all driven by events beyond the limits of their character into desperate acts. "You have been responsible for Hyacinthie as a youngster, and so her upbringing, her education, and her training have been in your hands. You have molded her character to suit your own purposes, as many guardians do. She has been under your protection for most of her life, and yet it seems that you had no notion of the state of her mind. You—a man of science, who prides himself on his observations— you had no apprehension that your ward, your niece, was in such desperate straits that she succumbed to madness. I cannot help but wonder why this should be so."

"I assumed she was . . . excited at the thought of her coming marriage. It is a great thing to be promised in marriage, especially for an orphan like her, who has only the portion I grant her to bring to the union. Many girls experience some trepidation when contemplating nuptials." Von Ravensberg started toward the door again. "It is what I thought when she seemed a bit . . . flighty."

"Marriage was the only cause of her mercurial frame of mind?" Ragoczy asked; he tapped the book on the table at his side. "Her journals suggest otherwise."

"Her journals?" Von Ravensberg went white about the mouth. "What journals?"

"Did you not know she kept them?" Ragoczy offered him a mirthless smile. "Another thing it appears you do not know about Fraulein Hyacinthie."

Von Ravensberg gave a fussy tug to the sash of his dressing-gown. "What journals do you mean?"

"The ones Frau Schale had Fraulein Hyacinthie keep since she became your ward's governess. I came across them in one of the lower shelves, behind an atlas of Europe." Ragoczy picked up the volume and riffled its pages. "This one is for 1811. It is most illuminating."

"Why should you call it that?" Von Ravensberg shrugged, but his stance was more tense than it had been. "The ravings of a child approaching insanity. Nothing in her journals can be believed by sensible men."

"You say that, yet you do not know what they contain," Ragoczy observed.

"I know she must have written of incidents that led to her madness, or revealed its presence. They can have no bearing on reality. Any competent man of learning will know this, and take it into account if he should read any of her writings."

Ragoczy picked up the journal. "But the records must be presented, you know; there are witnesses to her allegations."

Von Ravensberg gave a derisive hoot. "Witnesses? I'm sure!"

"They are identified in the journals." Ragoczy leveled his gaze at von Ravensberg again.

"Who? Who would speak against—"

"Against you? It is you she condemns, as I suppose you must have guessed. Why should she not speak against you, when it appears you have forgot your duty to her and used her most dreadfully?" Ragoczy asked. "You shall discover this has bearing on her case when the Magistrate hears my account of Medoc's death."

"You would do this, in my own house?"

"Others will second me. Your niece is not as alone as you assume she is, and there are those who know what she has endured at your hands. I have no wish to expose anyone to your displeasure, and I assure you that insofar as it is possible, I will limit my revelations to the Magistrate and no one else. You cannot be charged, in any case. The law protects you." He rose and went to a stack of leather-bound books set out on the trestle table under the south window.

"I will bring an action for slander against you if any hint of my niece's demented fantasies is bruited about." Von Ravensberg was shocked and outraged, but he conducted himself as a man of rank must. "My niece lies."

"You say that when I have not yet told you what she describes," Ragoczy mused aloud. "You deny something you purport not to know: I find that a curious posture for an innocent man." He ran his finger along the spines of the journals. "I have read all but the last two journals, and what they contain . . ."

"—is lies! How many times must I tell you." Von Ravensberg clapped his hands to punctuate his outburst.

"Why do you say that, when you say you do not know what the journals contain? Why do you persist in denying her reports?" Ragoczy laid his small hand on the journals. "I have taken the liberty of copying out some of the more significant passages—in case any of these journals should be damaged or lost." His voice was bland but his dark eyes burned.

"What are you telling me?" Von Ravensberg took three hasty steps toward Ragoczy. "Do you say I would destroy the ravings of my niece?"

"You could be tempted," said Ragoczy. "Few men want to have their private transgressions, and the wickedness of their families, revealed."

"Do you accuse me of this?" von Ravensberg demanded, all signs of politesse gone. "You, who have eaten my food and accepted my hospitality now reward me with this calumny?"

"I am concerned about what I have read," said Ragoczy.

"You believe what you have read? How can you?"

"I do not disbelieve it," said Ragoczy. "This troubles me, which is why I have undertaken to discover the truth of her claims."

"What temerity!" Von Ravensberg was rigid with rage.

"I believe I owe a full report to the Magistrate," said Ragoczy.

"And you admit this to my face, yet remain on my estate? You insult me and my House, here, within my Schloss?" Von Ravensberg's face was flushing, and his mouth was square with anger. "What manner of man are you, that you would treat me with such disrespect?"

"If you insist, I can remove to the nearest posting inn, as I have proposed to do," Ragoczy suggested, "but that might draw more attention to you, Graf, at a time you say you want as little notoriety as possible."

"You are insolent." He turned on his heel. "No better than a peasant."

Ragoczy chuckled. "Dueling is against the law, even for men of our rank. I will not be provoked, nor will you; you will not put yourself at legal risk." He touched the journals again. "I only wish you could be held accountable for what you have done, but the law spares you that."

Von Ravensberg made a visible effort to bring his temper under control. "If your companion were not still in danger, I would have my servants expel you from the Schloss. As it is, I want nothing more to do with you. You exist for me as a tolerated thief, and only for two days more at most. Then whether your companion is ready to travel or not, you must depart." He strode to the door. "I will withdraw my book from Eclipse Press, of course, and you can pay me for those sales of which you have deprived me." Satisfied that he had preserved his dignity, von Ravensberg slammed out of the room, leaving Ragoczy alone.

Half-an-hour later, Rogier found Ragoczy still in the library, the stack of journals on the table next to his chair. "I am sorry to disturb you, my master, but Gutesohnes has asked me to inquire if it is true that the Magistrate is coming this afternoon." His unfailingly correct manner removed any hint of his opinion of the request.

"I have been informed that he is," said Ragoczy.

"Then Gutesohnes says he would like the opportunity to speak with the Magisrate. He wants to give his account of Medoc's death." Nothing in his demeanor revealed his opinion of this intent, but Ragoczy had known him since the reign of Vespasianus, and could interpret Rogier's silences.

"Tell him to present himself to me in an hour and I will arrange it." He studied Rogier's face. "What is it, old friend?" he asked in Byzantine Greek.

Rogier answered in the same tongue. "Madame von Scharffensee is fretting. Serilde has told me that she has twice tried to remove the bandages on her face, and she doesn't want to have any more syrup of poppies rubbed on her mouth where her teeth are broken. She got the bandages off her hand."

"Ah." Ragoczy reached for the journals. "If you will carry these to the Rose Room, I will visit Hero and do what I can to reassure her."

Rogier gathered up the journals. "Where would you like me to put these?"

The shriek this time was long and ululating; neither man spoke until it had faded.

"So long as you keep them with you, within sight, you may put them where you choose," said Ragoczy. "I will present them to the Magistrate later today."

"They have bearing on the case?" Rogier asked, although he felt certain they did.

"I must hope they do," said Ragoczy as he left the library with Rogier, his thoughts already on Hero and what he would say to her, knowing the truth would provide her no comfort.

Text of a decision handed down by Magistrate Schmidt of Eichenbrucke, and entered into the records of the court there.

From the Magistrates' Court of Eichenbruke, under the seal of this office on the 9ᵗʰ day of April, 1818

Having reviewed the case of the violent death of Herr Constanz Medoc of Trier, killed at Ravensberg Schloss on the 4ᵗʰ of this month, I hereby give my findings:

That Herr Medoc was killed by his fiancée, Fraulein Hyacinthie Theresa Katerina Sieffert von Ravensberg while of unsound mind,

That Madame Hero Iocasta Ariadne Corvosaggio von Scharf-fensee was kidnapped and violently assaulted by said Fraulein von Ravensberg, suffering many disfiguring wounds as a result,

That Saint-Germain Ragoczy, Comte Franciscus, was also injured in the attempt to detain Fraulein von Ravensberg,

That the groundsman Heller Wegbruden suffered a sprained

ankle and bruised arms from his efforts to detain Fraulein von Ravensberg.

Therefore I hold that Fraulein Hyacinthie Theresa Katerina Sieffert von Ravensberg is responsible for the death and the injuries stipulated above, and for which the most severe penalty possible is death.

In mitigation, I have received evidence and testimony that indicates:

That Fraulein von Ravensberg, ward of Wallache Gerhard Winifrith Sieffert, Graf von Ravensberg, has been subjected to the lascivious attentions of her guardian and uncle, from the age eight until she was fourteen. These incidents are recorded in the journals of Fraulein Hyacinthie von Ravensberg, and are corroborated by testimony from Frau Jakobine Schale, who has served as governess and tutor to Fraulein Hyacinthie von Ravensberg since the Fraulein was first taken into care by her guardian, and Idune Ulme, the maid who has served Fraulein von Ravensberg for six years, and the girl Hedda for one.

That these repeated forced seductions worked upon Fraulein von Ravensberg's mind until she was incapable of discerning right behavior from wrong. This is supported by accounts given under oath by Comte Franciscus, his coachman, Otto Gutesohnes, who participated in the capture of Fraulein von Ravensberg, and Arndt Lowengard, Graf von Ravensberg's man-of-business, who has observed Fraulein von Ravensberg for as long as Frau Schale has, and who has made notes in his diary of instances of unacceptable conduct by Fraulein von Ravensberg.

That due to this disruption of her moral development and distortion of her thought processes, Fraulein von Ravensberg is not culpable for the crimes she has committed to the degree an unimpaired adult would be, for which reason, I am declaring that she is not sufficiently responsible to be put to death, but shall instead be confined to the asylum at Adlerfirst for the rest of her natural life.

That although Graf von Ravensberg cannot be prosecuted for any act he committed with his ward and niece, for none of what he has done can be regarded as treasonous, nevertheless, his conduct is of so abhorrent a nature that I order his present ward, Hedda, aged eight years, be removed from his guardianship and placed with the Sisters of the Annunciation at the orphans' home here in Eichenbrucke until an acceptable and appropriate family be found to take her in. As difficult as such a separation may be, I am persuaded that it is preferable to leaving her in the care of Graf von Ravensberg. I am indebted to the Comte Franciscus, who has donated 200 German marks to her care, and who has pledged to provide her a dowry when she decides to wed.

In conclusion, I recommend that the personal records of Arndt Lowengard be copied and entered into this record along with the transcriptions of the accounts of those already stipulated.

As to Graf von Ravensberg's insistence that his ward be hanged for her crimes, I recommend that such ravings be disallowed, in recognition of the role his behavior has played in this most tragic event.

> *Submitted by*
> *Radbert Bonifac Schmidt*
> *Magistrate of Eichenbrucke*
> *Austria*
> *(seal of the court)*

7

Summer was waning, but the day was quite warm this first week in September, and the air was heavy with the scents of the first harvest. From the open windows of the Château Ragoczy it was easy to see the field-hands at their work, and to hear the activity in the kitchen yard and around the barn. The bake-house was cooling after its early morning use, and firewood was being loaded into the bath-house in preparation for the evening's bathing.

Walking a bit unsteadily, Hero had descended from her room, handsomely dressed in an elegant walking-ensemble of a dark-teal-green more suited to Vienna or Paris than Château Ragoczy. She wore a dashing hat that held the heavy veil that covered her face and throat. "I am so excited," she said to Ragoczy as she entered the smaller of the two withdrawing rooms. "I must thank you again, Comte. I never thought you would actually be able to arrange this for me. I still don't quite believe it's happening. I am most deeply obligated to you."

Her formality saddened him, but he knew he could do nothing to change her withdrawal from him, that attempting to restore their intimacy would now lead only to greater alienation. "It is my honor, Hero." He came across the room and kissed her gloved hands, retaining them in his own for as long as she was willing to permit it.

"You have always been generous, and kind, always so kind, and I am aware of it, and I thank you . . ." She was becoming flustered at her own effusion.

"Hero, Hero," he said gently. "There is no need for you to thank me; if you must, a single merci will suffice."

But Hero had to finish. "I know you have reservations about this, about my taking the child in, but there is no reason you should be worried. I have had several months to think it out, and I am satisfied that neither Hedda nor I will suffer because of this." She stared directly at his cravat. "I promise you, I do not expect this child to be a substitute for Annamaria. I do know they are not the same. But Hedda and I should be able to find some comfort in each other." She slipped her hands out of his and looked toward the window. "What time did the messenger say the coach should arrive?"

"He estimated it would be here before noon; Gutesohnes was planning for a departure after Mass," Ragoczy replied. "You have two hours at least."

"I wonder if I should have gone to Eichenbrucke and accompanied her back here?" She started to pace, trying her best to limp as little as possible. "We could have had leagues and leagues together, and several evenings in good posting inns. She and I would be friends by now. Will she think the less of me for not going to get her?"

"I believe it is better that she travel with Oberin Josepha; Hedda knows her, and it will ease her fears, and the fears of the nuns. Think how it must seem to her, to be thrust into a new household about which she knows nothing, in a place she has never been. Such changes frighten grown men, and she is a nine-year-old girl. Hedda has already been deprived of her family twice, and she will not embrace a third one too quickly; give her the opportunity to bridge the gap with a familiar companion," Ragoczy said, not wanting to remind Hero that she was not yet ready to make such a long journey; the move to the newly restored castle at Obenzemmer would be difficult enough.

"The poor child must be terrified." Hero sat down suddenly. "That's what worries me: that she will be too frightened to—" She would not let herself go on.

Ragoczy considered his words before he spoke. "She would be most unusual if she had no fear, or lacked optimism for this new direction her life has taken. Since her parents died, she has had much to endure."

Hero swallowed to stop her tears. "I want to make her happy, if I can. She ought to be happy."

Ragoczy went to her side and lightly touched her shoulder. "I know you would like to spare her any more misery, and to provide her with everything she has missed, but it will take time. All changes in her life for the last three years have been for the worse. Do not expect her to be too jubilant, Hero; she is likely to be reserved: you are kind-hearted enough to respect that. She has been through so much—"

"Something I can understand," Hero interposed. "She and I have had so many losses. It will give us a bond."

"I hope you will find that it is a satisfactory one."

"As soon as we can set up at Obenzemmer, I think we should be able to make our lives together, on our terms." She looked up at

Ragoczy through her veil. "Do you think Hyacinthie really killed her sister Rosalie?"

"I think Hyacinthie believes she did," said Ragoczy carefully.

"But did she?" Hero persisted.

"It does seem possible," he said with great regret, remembering Csimenae again, and Srau.

"Do you suppose Hedda knows?" Before he could answer she went on, "Surely no one would tell her such a dreadful thing."

"She most certainly knows, whether she has been deliberately told or not. Servants gossip, children reveal secrets, nuns whisper: she will have heard several versions by now, I should assume, and she will have chosen one of the versions to believe. Whichever version that may be, it will be the one she expects to hear from you." He felt her move back from him; he removed his hand. "She will likely ask you what you know."

"But how can I tell her that Hyacinthie claims she killed Rosalie? It would be too cruel."

"She will have heard worse by now, Hero; if you make light of her knowledge, you will find she will feel slighted." He touched her shoulder again. "If you tell her what you know, she will respect you, dreadful though your information is."

"I couldn't tell her anything so heinous," said Hero. "Hyacinthie's demeanor alone would be too painful to describe. It is all too painful for any child." She stared at her hands as if she could see through the gloves. "I hope she will not ask to see my face, or not until she is used to me."

He dropped down on his knee beside her, speaking earnestly, "Let me advise you not to dissemble. Any modification of the truth may be held against you. Children have a sense about prevarication, no matter how well-intentioned. The child will not trust you if you offer her any mendacity."

"How will she know?" Hero asked. "I could soften what I have learned—make it less dreadful. I wouldn't have to lie."

Ragoczy waited several seconds, then said, "I know very little about children, except that they are often quite absolute. The few I have known have taken a strict view of the adults around them. If you fail this child now, she may well think that you are like all the others she has known, and she will not trust you." He held out his hand to her, but she did not take it.

"I will find a way to make that up to her," said Hero in a burst of purpose. "She and I will have a lot of time to help her put such misfortunes behind her."

"I hope you will succeed," he said, rising.

"Do you think I can't?" she challenged.

"If I thought that, I would never have arranged for you to adopt Hedda," he said matter-of-factly.

Emboldened, Hero asked, "About that: why do you do it, Comte?"

"Help you adopt Hedda?"

"All of it." She hesitated, then plunged on. "Why did you try to fix my face? Why did you bother to search for me at Ravensberg? Your shoulder still pained you, but you didn't hesitate, or so I was told by Serilde. Why did you plead for mercy for Hyacinthie, after all she has done?"

The ticking of the grandmother clock seemed suddenly loud as he composed his answer. "If you had the wealth, and the time—especially the time—that I have, would you not do the same? Time is the operative notion here: had I died the True Death when I was executed, I would be nothing more than a very minor Bronze Age prince, hardened by battle, conquered by invaders, forgotten to history, no more brutal than my kith and kin, and no less so. Time has changed that."

"How could you call yourself brutal? You are the most cultured, educated, capable man I have ever met," she protested.

"That is what I meant by time. Nearly four thousand years of undead living has taught me to value life in all its brevity, and all that comes with life." He knew this was insufficient, so he added, "Vampires are often loathed, when we are believed in at all, and for some of us, this brings a terrible bitterness, corrosive to their undying lives and destroying all chance at retaining humanity." He looked away from her, down his long memories. "I have some experience of bitterness, centuries ago, and I know how it venomous it is." His smile was swift and sad. "Compassion is preferable to vitriol. Both can be painful, but compassion builds bridges and bitterness destroys them. Even the loneliness is preferable to rancor. Where there is deprecation and contempt, there can be no intimacy, and for me intimacy is the heart of vitality, and the substance of life; without it my life would be utterly desolate; I could survive, but as a tiger survives, or a jackal. So if I love you—and I do love you; I love you and I know you—then it is my privilege to do what I can to offer you any fulfillment I can, to ease your burdens and lessen your pain." It was more than he intended to say, and he realized he may well have said too much.

She inhaled to speak, then let the air out slowly, not quite sighing, but measuring her response. "Then, if you are willing to ease my burden, I will do the same for Hedda, and do all I can to ensure she has a decent life from now on." Behind her veil, her eyes were very bright.

"I have no doubt of that," he said, and sensed that she was near weeping. "Let me ring for Balduin and have some chocolate brought in for you."

As if recalled to herself, Hero said, "Oh, yes, please. If Uchtred wouldn't mind. I know he is planning a special dinner."

"It is mid-morning and his meats will be turning on the dinner spits in an hour. He can make chocolate for you while he supervises his new assistant. You will not impose upon him." He tugged on the bell-pull by the mantle, and waited until Balduin knocked on the door. "Madame would like a cup of chocolate. And I hope the little pastries will be ready for the child's arrival?"

"So Uchtred tells me," said Balduin. "I should mention there is a coach approaching from the gate—not one of yours."

Ragoczy was a bit nonplussed. "Do you know whose it is?"

"I will in five minutes," said Balduin.

"Then you had best warn Uchtred that there will be guests—bread, cheese, apples, and beer should suffice to offer them." Ragoczy glanced over at Hero. "Do you want to greet the visitors?"

She shook her head and touched her veil. "No."

"Then if you will excuse me? I will be back with you before Hedda's coach arrives." He hoped this would be the case; he opened the door.

"Go on," she said, waving him away.

Balduin was filled with activity, all but bouncing on his toes. "This is a most important day, isn't it, Comte?"

"It is," said Ragoczy. "Go off to the kitchen to inform Uchtred of Madame's order, and mine for my guest. Tell him some dispatch is needed, for the girl is expected before mid-day, and with any luck, the visitors will be gone by then. I will go out to greet them." He walked quickly to the front door and went out onto the broad step; a light breeze fingered his fashionably trimmed hair and plucked at his star-burst cravat, but no slight disorder in his clothing could lessen his air of urbane elegance, or so he hoped, having no reflection with which to reassure himself. As he stared down the drive, he thought, How inconvenient it is to have Rogier in Obenzemmer, supervising the installation of the staff there, but this could not be changed. He heard the rumble of the coach and the steady hoof-beats from the pair pulling it, and tried to guess who was coming.

The panel of the coach bore the device of the Magistrates of Yvoire, and Charget was driving; as the pair were drawn up in front of the entrance to the château, Ragoczy saw that Magistrate Lindenblatt was its sole passenger. "Comte," he called out as he opened the door and let down the steps.

"Magistrate," said Ragoczy, stepping down to shake his hand and to offer a sketched salute to Charget on the box. "Welcome, Magistrate. To what do I owe the honor of your visit?"

"I have some news—good news," said Lindenblatt, his visage a mask of worry. "I trust it is good news."

"Thus your present delight?" Ragoczy asked, indicating the

open door. "Well, whatever your errand, come in and take a little refreshment." As they entered the château, Ragoczy saw Dietbold hovering, and said, "The Magistrate and I will be in my study. Please bring a refreshment tray for him."

"Merci, grand merci," said Lindenblatt, a bit out of breath. "I have had a very busy morning, and it isn't over yet."

"What has happened?" Ragoczy asked as he ushered Lindenblatt into his study.

"It is a little . . . a little difficult . . ." He waited until the study door was closed, then said, "We have discovered who it is who has been aiding the highway robbers." As if this announcement had deprived him of his energy, he sat down abruptly.

"And have you ascertained that your information is accurate?"

"Lamentably, we have," said Lindenblatt. "The source is unimpeachable."

"That is a welcome development, after so many months of depredation; I am curious to learn why it should also be lamentable," said Ragoczy. "I know the region will be relieved to know their harvests and stores will stay their own through this year, and that travelers will not be set upon." His enthusiasm was expressed mildly, for he could see that Lindenblatt was still distressed.

"Yes, yes. Of course. But it will be . . ." His words trailed off. He gathered his resolve and began again. "We have evidence and proof—very credible proof—that the man who has been a second leader to the robbers is well-reputed in the region, not the sort you would expect to be helping criminals: Augustus Kleinerhoff." His head dropped as if he had been struck a blow.

Ragoczy stood very still. "Kleinerhoff? The head-man of Sacre-Sang? Are you sure?" If this were true, Ragoczy wondered how he could have been so mistaken in the man.

"Sadly, yes I am." He put his sugar-loaf hat on his knee. "I will explicate how I come to know this in a moment."

"The second leader, you say?"

"Yes." There was a brief silence while Lindenblatt gathered his thoughts. "He has an assistant of a kind, as well."

"If your information and your proof is correct and trustworthy," Ragoczy appended. "Are you certain it is accurate?"

"Unfortunately, it is." Lindenblatt nodded, looking even more uncomfortable. "I must ask you to discuss this with no one, to say nothing until the court publishes its findings on the matter, which will be tomorrow afternoon at the earliest. As the case has bearing on you, and as I have need of access to one of your staff, I am going to take you into my confidence. Do I have your pledge of confidentiality?"

"You have my Word," said Ragoczy. "I am willing to remain silent for as long as required."

"Thank goodness you are willing." Lindenblatt took a large handkerchief from his pocket and wiped his face. "I am still much troubled by all we have learned."

"You will have a difficult time in the region if what you say is true. It is one thing to mete out justice to the robbers, but quite another to persecute local men." Ragoczy had a short, unpleasant recollection of the trouble at Padova, at Cuzco, and of Jui Ah at Mao-T'ou fortress.

"I am aware of that; I would be more elated if some other had been revealed as the miscreant." Lindenblatt steadied himself and added, "What is most distressing is that the leader of the band of robbers is Kleinerhoff's nephew, from Halle. He was a Captain of cavalry under Napoleon, and has suffered because of his loyalty. He gathered a group of former soldiers around him, and some men of dubious probity, and they became the heart of his band, with the aid of Kleinerhoff and his assistant." Now that he had revealed so much, he seemed about to collapse from exhaustion.

"As sad as all this is, why do you want to see someone on my staff?' Ragoczy said with unfailing courtesy.

"Because it seems one of your household has acted as a . . . as a connection between the robbers and Herr Kleinerhoff." He stuffed his handkerchief back into his pocket. "I regret to inform you of this, but the investigation has shown that this is true. I have seen the sworn testimony, and I have reviewed the evidence. It explains why some thought you were part of the outlaws." His cheeks grew ruddy, and he was about to continue his oblique apology when the knock on the door interrupted him.

"I have ordered refreshments for you," said Ragoczy. "I hope you will not refuse them."

"No, I won't; I am parched and famished," said the Magistrate. "I would like to think you will not hold my duty against me."

"Whom do you seek here?" Ragoczy asked as he went to open the door.

Hildegard brought a tray into the room and carried it to the occasional table next to Lindenblatt's chair. "Magistrate," he said as he set it down.

Lindenblatt nodded and said to Ragoczy. "You know, in my father's day, no servant would address any of us directly. They spoke only when spoken to, and would not look at their betters."

"This way is much more practical," said Ragoczy. "The change is for the good."

"I hope so," said Lindenblatt, and poured himself a large glass of beer from the stoneware pitcher Hildegard had brought.

"I'll ring for you when the Magistrate is through, thank you," said Ragoczy, dismissing Hildegard.

"Comte," said Hildegard, and left the room, closing the door firmly behind him.

Ragoczy watched while Lindenblatt took a long drink of beer, then asked again, "Whom do you seek here?"

Lindenblatt set down the glass. "I regret to say that our information shows it is your second coachman."

"You mean Marcel Lustig? He has worked for me only two months."

"No, no, not Lustig. Ulf Hochvall." He spoke the name as if confessing to a great wrong.

"Hochvall?" Ragoczy looked shocked. "Are you sure?"

"I wish I were not." Lindenblatt took a second long draught of the beer and reached for a wedge of cheese.

"He has not been in my employ since the end of April." Ragoczy paused to consider how to go on. "I have helped him set up in a drayage business in Sacre-Sang; Kleinerhoff aided me in making the arrangements; being the head-man of Sacre-Sang, he was in a position to hurry things along." He gave a single, ironic laugh. "This is not what Hochvall wanted, but he was resigned to it: since his leg was broken, Hochvall has not been able to handle a coach-and-four. Both of us hoped his leg would mend completely, but since it did not, I have sought to provide him a living of some sort. He was disappointed not to be able to continue as a coachman."

"If that is the case, he has repaid your generosity most shabbily," said Lindenblatt, swallowing his cheese with the help of a sip of beer. "He has been passing information to Kleinerhoff for the last three years. He has occasionally sheltered the robbers in your coach-barn. It was he who sought to turn suspicion on you."

"That is . . ." He left the rest unsaid.

"The mark of an unworthy man," said Lindenblatt. "I will have to order him charged; I had hoped to do so while I was here, but if he is in Sacre-Sang, then I must shortly go there." He took another wedge of cheese and bit into it, chewing vigorously.

"The villagers are bound to know you are coming. The harvesters will announce you as sure as fanfares." Ragoczy tapped the secretary-desk. "If they support Herr Kleinerhoff, then you may find it difficult to arrest anyone."

"Just this morning most of the band of robbers was captured by the Magistrates' guard. All of them have been offered the opportunity to receive a reduced sentence if each of them will give a sworn statement to the court in regard to all their activities. That is proceeding as we speak. I have seen what the guards seized, which includes two registers of loot and booty. I had no idea of how extensive their activities have been."

"And you are certain that Kleinerhoff and Hochvall are implicated?" Ragoczy asked sadly.

"I have proof in three forms, including several letters from Kleinerhoff that were seized during the arrests of the robbers, describing where and when the band could strike for best results. He mentions Hochvall in a dozen notes, describing how trustworthy he is, and approving his knowledge of roads and lanes in the region. Kleinerhoff's hand has been recognized by my clerk, who knows it very well." He finished his glass of beer. "I am dismayed to have to inform you of all this, but better that you hear it now, from me, than from someone else with incorrect information."

"True," said Ragoczy. "I am grateful to you for tending to something so distasteful in such a prompt manner." He lifted his head, hearing another coach approaching. He turned to Lindenblatt. 'If you will excuse me?"

"Another visitor?" Lindenblatt asked nothing more as he took his hat from his knee and replaced it on his head. "I will not be long here; there is much yet to do." He rose to his feet. "If you will do me the service of coming into Yvoire tomorrow for the first court procedure, I would very much appreciate it."

"Yes, of course," said Ragoczy. "At what hour?"

"At nine I will begin. If you would, bring with you all correspondence you have had with Herr Kleinerhoff, and any records you have of your dealings with Hochvall. If you arrive half-an-hour early, I will brief you on what is to come. Magistrate Fulminus will be handling the actual charging of the outlaws, but I am still primary administrator of the case." He looked back at the tray. "I wish I had had more time to enjoy your hospitality. But there is much to do."

Ragoczy held the door for him. "I will be in Yvoire at eight tomorrow morning, and will be at your disposal."

"Merci, Comte," said Lindenblatt and sighed. "Now that we are Swiss France again, we must speak in French. When we become Swiss again, we will probably revert to German, or possibly Italian."

Ragoczy expressed no opinion, but nodded seriously and indicated the front door where Balduin was waiting. "Until tomorrow, Magistrate. I thank you for doing me the courtesy of making this call."

Outside, the second coach was nearing the turn into the paved courtyard; grooms were coming from the stable to take it in hand.

"Preferable to a summons, isn't it?" Lindenblatt said, then started down the broad, shallow steps toward his coach.

"Balduin, if you will inform Madame von Scharffensee that—" Ragoczy began, only to hear footsteps behind him.

"Is this Hedda?" Hero breathed from just behind his shoulder. "Is that her coach?"

"I assume so; Gutesohnes is driving," said Ragoczy, stepping aside so that Hero could see the four Kladrubers come to a halt behind the Magistrates' coach.

"Oh. Oh, dear," said Hero as a sudden stab of panic went through her. "I hope I have done the right thing, that she and I will—What if this doesn't work out?"

"That is the gamble we all take whenever we extend ourselves," said Ragoczy with such kindness that Hero gasped. "What matters is that you are willing to try."

"You're right: I mustn't lose sight of that," she decided aloud. "Shall I go out to her?"

"You may want to wait until she is out of the coach, so you may take your cue from her." As Magistrate Lindenblatt's coach pulled forward to turn around, the second coach came up to the edge of the steps.

"We traveled quickly," Gutesohnes called from the driving-box. "The horses have earned their oats today. They kept up a steady trot for three leagues." He set the brake and prepared to get down.

Balduin stepped forward, opened the door and let down the steps, then moved aside to allow the passengers to get out while Gabriel, the new footman, got off the rear of the coach and unbuckled the boot-cover.

First out was Oberin Josepha; the Mother Superior was impressive in her dark-gray-and-white habit, although her starched headdress was a bit wilted. She bowed rather than curtsied. "Comte Franciscus, it is good to see you again," she said in German.

"And you, Oberin." He bowed slightly to her. "I trust you had a good journey?"

"Oh, yes," said Oberin Josepha. "Your coach is quite luxurious." She swung around, her habit shielding the descent of the second passenger. "Come along, child. We have reached the home of the Comte. You remember him, and Madame von Scharffensee."

A small figure in a dull-pink frock emerged from the coach, climbing down the steps backward, and taking refuge in the ample folds of the Oberin's habit, large, chary blue eyes peering around the nun.

"Oh, welcome, welcome, Hedda," said Hero. "Please come in. Both of you."

"She is a little shy," said Oberin Josepha. "Come, child. Make your curtsy. The lady is going to take care of you from now on. Show her how much you appreciate her care." She covered her annoyance with a suggestion of amusement. "This isn't a game, Hedda."

Hedda hung back.

"Until tomorrow," called out Magistrate Lindenblatt as his coach started down the drive, picking up speed.

Ragoczy held up his hand in farewell, thinking that he should probably decide which of his records to take with him in the morning. He held out his hand to Hero. "Let the nun bring her to you. It will be less upsetting that way."

"I want to hug her, but I suppose she will need time for that." Hero sighed once. "I don't care how long it takes: I want her to be glad to be with me."

"That is an impulse I understand well," he said and fell in beside her, offering the steadiness of his arm as she came down the steps.

"Hedda," said Hero. "I am here to welcome you."

The child took firm hold of the Oberin's skirts.

Gutesohnes alighted at last and slapped his duster, laughing at the clouds that arose from the canvas. "Take the team to the stable and walk them for twenty minutes, then turn them out in the big paddock," he ordered the grooms. "I will come to see to their grooming in an hour."

"When you have finished with the horses," Ragoczy said, raising his voice to be heard, "then come to my study. You and I have matters to discuss."

Gutesohnes ducked his head to show compliance. "After dinner, if you will permit."

"Certainly," said Ragoczy, glad of the reprieve, however brief. Before nightfall, he would have to send word to the stable to have a horse saddled for him at six in the morning., but that could wait; now he had a much more pleasant task—to walk out toward the carriage with Hero to greet the diffident child in the drab frock and simple straw bonnet, who stood at the side of the travel-rumpled Mother Superior, and do all that he could to make both of them feel welcome at Château Ragoczy.

Text of a letter from Madelaine de Montalia in Athens to Saint-Germain Ragoczy, Comte Franciscus at Château Ragoczy, near Lake Geneva, Yvoire, Swiss France; carried by commercial messenger and delivered thirty-two days after it was written.

To Saint-Germain Ragoczy, my favorite Comte, the greetings of your Madelaine on this, the 19th day of November, 1818,

My dearest Comte,

I discover I must thank you yet again. I have today received confirmation that I will be able to sail on the Evening Star *from Athens to Alexandria as soon as the winter storms have passed. I have sent word ahead to the Imperial Hotel, reserving the suites you mentioned, and providing the copy of your assurances for the manager. I will carry your authorization to draw on your accounts there, although I hope I will not need to encroach on your generosity. As deeply as I long to travel upriver on the Nile, I will be content to remain in Alexandria until appropriate arrangements may be made. Simply being in Alexandria will bring me many steps closer to the Egyptian monuments I seek. I know I would not be going there had you not intervened.*

For that reason, I ask you to permit me to find an expedition bound up the Nile on my own. If I linger in Alexandria for too many years, I may change my mind and appeal to you to aid me in my search, but for the time being, I think it behooves me to do all that

*I may to find an expedition planning to do the sort of work I am in-
terested in undertaking. I am learning to be patient, so I do not insist
on an immediate opportunity, but I would rather set out sooner than
later. I have money enough to purchase my passage and then some,
which should suffice to persuade any antiquarian of my usefulness.*

*Here in Athens there is much excitement over the success of the
Serbian Obrenovics leading the recent uprising against the Ottoman
Turks, as well as his supplanting of the Karageorgevics. While many
applaud Milos Obrenovic's audacity, others are outraged at his murder of Kara George. The feud developing between the families prom-
ises to spread out through the Balkans, and may lessen what remains
of the Turkish hold on the region. Everyone in Athens has an opinion on the matter and will discuss it at the slightest opportunity.
There are many here in Athens who believe the Ottoman Empire
must collapse, and that the sooner that happens, the better it will be
for everyone, including the Turks. While I do not agree completely, I
am fairly certain that the Ottoman Empire cannot continue on as it
has been for much longer. If the Serbs can separate themselves and
their territory from the Ottomans, so can many of their client countries, including Greece.*

*No, I have no wish to become part of any insurgency; escaping
the Terror was enough to convince me that revolutions are as likely
to destroy the supporters as the opposition. I would much prefer to
be allowed to do my work in peace. Yet I listen and I know what I am
seeing: this reminds me of Paris before the Bastille was stormed and
those six unfortunates were rescued. I can feel it in the air, which is
one of the reasons I am glad to be leaving this place in three months
or so. I will be traveling with Missus Neva Colchester, who is a very
respectable widow of thirty-eight summers, going to Egypt to be a
governess to the children of Sir Beresford Rollo, the diplomat. If my
reputation is to be protected, I am sure she is more capable of preserving it than almost anyone I have met. I understand her husband
was an officer in the British Army, killed in the Peninuslar Campaigns against Napoleon. She has said he left her with a small legacy
and a house north of London which she cannot afford to occupy*

alone, and no one in her family who wishes to share it with her. So rather than sink into genteel poverty, she has decided to put her education to good use. Her work in Egypt is supposed to last for five years with the possibility of extension if she proves satisfactory.

I tell you this so you will not think I have lost all regard for the good opinion of others. I have not and I will not flout customs out of vexation or botheration. But I find I am chafing at the limitations that are so much imposed in this part of the world. I have always assumed I could find a way to accommodate expectations, but in this part of the world, I will not go about swathed in a kind of tent, looking out at the world through a small screen in front of my eyes. As shocking as many of the Greeks and Turks think it, I will continue as I have done from my first journey to Asia Minor: I will dress and conduct myself as a European scholar. And I will make a point of going to church, to show I respect religion. It is fortunate that the tales of vampires being unable to tolerate religious places is untrue, or I would find my sojourn here much more difficult.

Saint-Germain, I do miss you. I miss you as I miss my heartbeat or the hunger for food. Every day I think of you, and I wish we could spend more time together. I comprehend your reservations about such an attempt, and in the rational part of my mind, I share those reservations. But when it is late and the moon is low in the western sky, I cannot help but regret that it must be so. For no matter whom I choose to love, nothing will ever supplant my love for you: I will always be reminded of you, of your gentleness as passionate as any work of van Beethoven or von Weber. All that I am I am because of you. Nothing will ever change that, nor would I want it changed. From now until the True Death, you will be first in my heart, as dear to me as the life you have given me, and my soul.

Eternally,
Madelaine

EPILOGUE

*T*ext of a letter from Hero Iocasta Ariadne Corvosaggio von Scharffensee at Obenzemmer to Saint-Germain Ragoczy, Comte Franciscus in Iraklion on Crete; carried by commercial courier and delivered forty-nine days after it was written.

To the most excellent Comte Franciscus, Hero von Scharffensee sends her fondest greetings on this, the 7th day of May, 1823,

My dear Ragoczy,

Your attorney and factor, Reinhart Kreuzbach in Speicher, informs me that you are still traveling, so I have asked him to arrange for a courier to bring this to you wherever you may be. I would just as soon continue to keep Gutesohnes here, so Kreuzbach will engage a commercial courier to bring this to you.

It hardly seems credible that two years have passed since I last saw you, but so it is, and I am sorry that more was not possible. I am so grateful to you for bringing the sad news about my father to me directly rather than entrusting it to Gutesohnes or some other hired servant. I have finally found an official to help me to arrange a Christian—albeit Orthodox—burial for him and his companions, which his executor is unwilling or unable to do. I thank you for the introduction to your Turkish factor, who has proven most reliable in these negotiations, and willing to do all that the Ottomans require to bring this sad episode to a conclusion. I suspect that this smoothing of obstacles is your doing, too, and I add that to my reasons for gratitude.

I am troubled by the news in Europe. Just when I see a glimmer of hope, there is an uprising, or a plot, or an assassination. The last three years have been tumultuous ones, what with a new King of England, a new heir in France, a revolution in Spain, an attempted revolt in Naples, a war of Independence in Greece, Bolivar and de

San Martin victorious in South America, Mexico casting off the
Spanish yoke, West Africa and Haiti up in arms, Brazil emancipat-
ing itself from Portugal. The recitation alone is exhausting; the actu-
ality is undoubtedly dangerous. Even the mad rush to Egypt, thanks
to Champollion's work on the Rosetta Stone, is tiring to contemplate.

On a lighter note, I have hired a second tutor for Hedda, who is
now fourteen, and beginning to show promise. She has an ear for languages and so I have expanded her instruction to include Dutch,
Czech, Greek, and Spanish in addition to the French, German, Italian, and English she already knows. I would like to enroll her in some
advanced school in two or three years. I know the Università of
Padova has graduated women from time to time, and I seek your advice if this might be worth pursuing for Hedda. She is reluctant to
leave Obenzemmer, and has said she would like to remain here doing
her own studies, but I hope against hope that perhaps she will decide
to broaden her horizons and seek a wider world for herself, for as
awkward as life may be for educated women, it is preferable, I think,
to do as much as one can to improve the state of other women than to
accept the strictures of society and remain dependent creatures.

I have, as you may imagine, been reading the work of Mary
Wollstonecraft. I agree with her wholeheartedly, and were I less
hideous to look upon, I would do more to help vindicate her stance
by teaching young women more than needlework and how to address members of the peerage. I have also read her daughter's book
Frankenstein: or the Modern Prometheus. As innovative as the
novel was, I prefer the mother's work to the daughter's, although for
Hedda, it is the opposite. In fact, Hedda has proposed that she may
turn her hand to fiction one day. She declares she would like to write
a roman-à-clef about her childhood and all that she experienced in
the time she was with the Graf von Ravensberg. I am of two minds
for such a project, for I fear raking through such coals could ignite
more fires than creative ones. But she has said that she remembers
her ordeal every day, and hopes that writing may provide an exorcism of sorts for her. She has already stated an aversion to marriage,
which is an imprudent position for such a young woman as she is to

take. If you were here, I would implore you to talk with her, but as you are gone, I have asked Herr Kreuzbach to discuss the advantages and disadvantages inherent in such a manner of life. He has been instructed not to discuss any aspect of marriage, for that would surely turn her against anything he says.

Pasch Gruenerwald has become head-man in Zemmer, and has instituted a regular patrol in the region. Every week we are visited by a courier who makes a report to Zemmer, and if aid is needed, or trouble suspected, there is quick action for a response. This has made market-days far more pleasant than they have been in the past, for they are guarded, and where needed, Zemmer's guards provide escorts for those bringing livestock or produce to market. We have had good harvests the past two years, and that has supplemented your most magnanimous provisions for us. Now that the journey to and from Zemmer is protected, the field-hands are much more willing to trudge the two leagues to work here, and so we have enlarged our plantation. In time we may be able to become fully self-supporting.

Thank you for your invitation to visit Château Ragoczy at any time. I may do so in the fall; Hedda and I will be traveling in the summer—since you and I never got to Roma to attend the opera, I have arranged that Hedda and I will do so. My twins have been asked to join us, but I anticipate they will decline the invitation. For such travel, I have the veil studded with diamonds you gave me when we moved here, and that should serve me very well. If you should be in Roma then, it would be a delight to see you again. That is for later, of course, and only if fortune should allow our paths to cross. Until that time

My fondest love,
Hero von Scharffensee

P. S. We have received word that Wallache von Ravensberg is dead, killed while hunting when his own gun misfired. Hedda is sure it was suicide.